Praise for *River of Ink*

'Potent, beautiful and wholl
of a reluctant revolutionary
chapter. A wonderful, memc
Orange Prize-winning author

'A highly accomplished debut. ... moments of grace and beauty to pure horror in this enthralling novel' Mahesh Rao, author of *The Smoke is Rising*

'Cooper vividly reconstructs a long-buried society and creates in Asanka – a coward reluctantly forced into acts of courage – a likeable, multifaceted narrator' *Sunday Times*

'Cooper endows his work with persuasive historical accuracy and detail, but the "juice" of his own work is the intensely poetic quality of his prose' *Independent*

'An author with a rare skill for deploying heavy research with a light touch, for revelling in the seductive possibilities of style without losing sight of narrative drive, and for making profound points while also delivering first-rate entertainment. Cooper's own pen is certainly a formidable weapon and it will be exciting to see him wield it again in years to come' *Asian Review*

'Polonnaruwa is resurrected with its alleyways, gardens, palaces and teeming inhabitants . . . Yet the research is displayed with a light, effective touch, never holding up the action. This intricate, interlayered tale harks back to a time when the written word held unstoppable power and prestige' *Financial Times*

'Cooper's *River of Ink* is an exquisite offering whose words sing in the blood. This is a tale of ancient Sri Lanka, a tale of conquest ... *k Review*

A NOTE ON THE AUTHOR

PAUL M.M. COOPER was born in south London and grew up in Cardiff, Wales. He was educated at the University of Warwick and UEA, and after graduating he left for Sri Lanka to work as an English teacher, where he took time to explore the ruins both ancient and modern. He has written for magazines, websites and also worked as an archivist, editor and journalist.

@PaulMMCooper
paulmmcooper.com

RIVER OF INK

PAUL M.M. COOPER

BLOOMSBURY

LONDON • OXFORD • NEW YORK • NEW DELHI • SYDNEY

Bloomsbury Paperbacks
An imprint of Bloomsbury Publishing Plc

50 Bedford Square
London
WC1B 3DP
UK

1385 Broadway
New York
NY 10018
USA

www.bloomsbury.com

BLOOMSBURY and the Diana logo are trademarks of Bloomsbury Publishing Plc

First published in Great Britain 2016
This paperback edition first published in 2017

Map by Emily Faccini

British Library Cataloguing-in-Publication Data
A catalogue record for this book is available from the British Library.

ISBN: HB: 978-1-4088-6218-6
TPB: 978-1-4088-6222-3
PB: 978-1-4088-6229-2
ePub: 978-1-4088-6223-0

2 4 6 8 10 9 7 5 3 1

Typeset by Integra Software Services Pvt. Ltd.
Printed and bound in Great Britain by CPI Group (UK) Ltd, Croydon CR0 4YY

To Sarah, who was worth it all

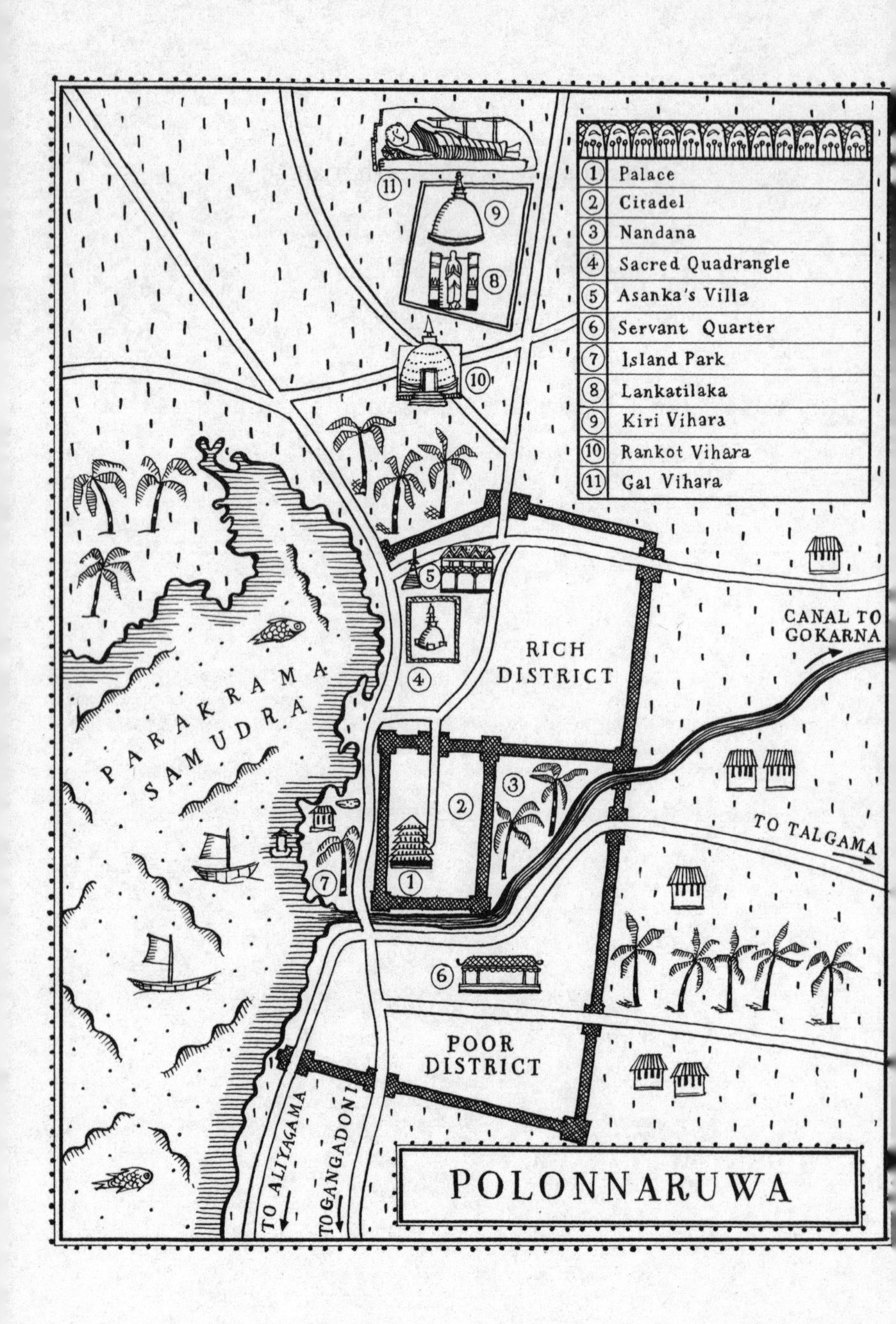

1 Palace
2 Citadel
3 Nandana
4 Sacred Quadrangle
5 Asanka's Villa
6 Servant Quarter
7 Island Park
8 Lankatilaka
9 Kiri Vihara
10 Rankot Vihara
11 Gal Vihara
RICH DISTRICT
POOR DISTRICT
PARAKRAMA SAMUDRA
CANAL TO GOKARNA
TO TALGAMA
TO ALIYAGAMA
TO GANGADONI
POLONNARUWA

රට වටකර වැට බැන්දත් කට වටකර වැට බදින්න බැහැ

Rata watakara weta bendat, kata watakara
weta bandinna beh

'You can build a fence around the country, but you can't build a fence around the mouth'

– Sinhala proverb

'. . . and there landed a man who held to a false creed, whose heart rejoiced in bad statesmanship, who was a fire in the forest of good . . . who was a sun that closed the night lotuses of wisdom, a moon that closed the day lotuses of peace, a man by the name of Magha, an unjust king sprung from the Kalinga line'

– *The Chulavamsa, the Chronicles of Sri Lanka*
Chapter LXXX – The Sixteen Kings

Book I

Smoke

Chapter One

Do you remember the mynah birds that used to live in the courtyard outside your room? On the day the city fell, they were all twittering louder than I'd ever heard them, and flying from tree to tree in a flock. The noise was tremendous. While I watched them through the lattice, I was thinking about what would happen if the King had cords tied to each of their tails, how it wouldn't be long before the net they wove would wrap up the sky and black out the sun. There was a man out there too, a Muslim man, sitting beneath a shade tree with lamps lined up on a blanket, singing in a slow, cracked voice. 'Little lamps, buy your little clay lamps for the long, dark nights.'

You must remember this. You were sitting right there beside me, your back straight and your forehead furrowed, murmuring the letters to yourself as you cut them.

'Ma–ha–ra.'

You were a quick learner, and by then I didn't have to guide your hand. I did sometimes, though, because its back was smooth and freckled and cool to the touch. I would glance at your moving lips, too, and the winding interlaced ribbons of hair that rolled down your back. That hair – I still dream of that hair sometimes. When I do, it melds with my dreams of rivers, so I am floating in it, then drowning. It was hot, and I was losing control of myself, sitting so close, so I tried to watch the mynah birds instead.

'You've been looking out there for so long,' you said. 'What's so interesting?'

'Just the birds,' I said. 'Have you ever seen so many flocking inside the city?'

You didn't answer. I listened to the noise they were making and the sound of your stylus slicing paper, a scratching like the insects that burrow through the palace woodwork at night.

A girl of your position should never have been writing; a man of my position should never have been teaching you. We both knew these things, and so fear was our constant third classmate. Sometimes, maybe once or twice a week, we would hear footsteps outside the door of your room, or the sound of raised voices in the servant quarter outside, and we would hush each other. One of us would be overcome by panic, and then the other would always follow. We would fumble to pack everything away – the charcoal, stylus, oil, paper – cramming it into my bag, shovelling it under the table. Then the footsteps would pass, or the voices would start arguing about the price of a cupful of millet, and we would catch sight of each other, hearts pounding, hands dirtied with charcoal dust and oil, and breathe out.

But when the bells began to ring on that day, it was different. You didn't stop writing. You barely moved, and I'll always remember that. Even the birds outside faltered in the air, swung around and weaved back to their branches, as though they knew the difference between the bronze bells in the temples and the heavy iron ones on the walls. Those short, yelping peals.

Soon the bells were joined by shouting in the distance, and the sound of hooves in a nearby street, but it didn't immediately occur to me what was going on. In the courtyard, the Muslim man stopped his singing. He wrapped up his lamps. Before long, some common people ran out of a door and down the street with their children, then I could see the King's soldiers out on the main road. It was then I knew. Kalinga Magha, the man they were calling 'the demon king', had arrived.

'Watch the curl on your lha,' I told you, and heard my voice high and reedy, like a boy's. I coughed, and touched your hand as though to guide you through the letter's tail. Your skin was cold. I could feel you shaking. I was going to say something else, though I didn't know what, when a boy in red-brown servant's clothes ran into the courtyard outside and began shouting my name.

'Asanka!' he shouted. He sounded scared. 'Master Asanka!'

You ducked your head a little, though it was impossible for anyone to see in through the lattice.

'Who is it?' you hissed.

'I don't know,' I said. 'He looks panicked, though.'

'Maybe he's one of the King's new messengers.'

'Maybe. I should probably—'

'Will you come back?'

I stood up, and you stayed where you were, looking up at me.

'Yes, of course. You know I will. What about you? Will you still be here when I do?'

'I'll be right here,' you said, and after holding me for a long moment in your gaze, you turned back to your writing.

'Pi–ri–tha.'

Right then, right at that moment, I could have changed everything: grabbed your wrist, told you to pack your bags. But I was never the kind to take sharp turns in life, any more than the water in a river decides one day to flow over the hills. That was the time to escape, and I let it slip away.

I pulled aside the curtain, squinting in the daylight, and the boy shouting in the courtyard caught sight of me with relief. He scuffed the dust with his heel.

'Master Asanka! The King wants to see you,' he said, his eyes wide with fear, a bead of spittle on the corner of one lip.

'What's so urgent?' I said, but before I'd finished saying it, the boy turned and began to run back in the direction of the King's Highway. 'Where are you going?' I called after him.

'His Majesty said that once I'd told you, I could leave!' the boy shouted back. 'He said there are already too many ghosts here!'

The boy disappeared around the corner before I could answer, and I felt fear lurch inside me. King Parakrama hadn't been himself recently, not since the army had come back beaten or since the monks had taken the Buddha's tooth from the city to hide it from the invader among the high passes of Mount Kotthumala. I looked up at the lattice of your room, where I knew you were looking back. The Muslim man had begun to pray beneath the shade tree, but he looked up at me for a second, as if to say, 'Well, the King's orders are the King's orders', which they most definitely are. I turned and made my way up to the palace.

As I write this, I realise that I am a man with more regrets than scars.

The King's Highway was full of people flooding towards the south gates with their belongings piled on to carts or loaded on their backs. There were soldiers with spears and dirty cloths, too, and men on horses and all kinds of holy men among the crowd. I had to push through the whole unclean mass to cross the road, and none of the peasants paid any attention to my fine robes or ruby earrings as they pushed and ran and shouted past me. They were all babbling like fools, and the words that were passing between them were: 'Kalinga Magha. Kalinga Magha. Magha from Kalinga is coming.'

I looked to the north, and saw columns of smoke rising above the walls, a haze of red dust darkening the sky. The citadel wall bristled with spears beneath its canopies. And the palace, *aiyo*, it was so beautiful back then. On my way up to the royal quarters, I saw maybe a dozen or more breathless messengers taking the steps three at a time. I didn't need to knock when I got to the top: the guards at the King's chambers nodded at me and pushed the door open.

When I stepped inside, I found King Parakrama standing at the balcony with his back to me, the city stretched out before him. He was trembling. In the distance, past the white domes of the temples and the clutter of clay and leaf rooftops and the snaking outer walls, the largest army I have ever seen was gathering in the rice fields.

I could hear them now: the rumble of fifty-thousand footfalls, the conches, throbbing drums and voices, the spears bashed on shields, the trumpeting of many elephants. All of it like the sound of a high waterfall after rain. Sweat rivered the King's back, and his shoulder blades were almost touching.

'Asanka,' he said, and combed a hand through his hair. 'When you were a child, did you ever think that you might live for ever? Not for ever, maybe, but do you know what I mean?'

When the King asked me this kind of question I had learnt to agree, then to keep quiet and let him speak.

'Yes, Your Majesty,' I said. 'I'm sure I can remember the feeling.'

It was a lie, though. Since my father died when I was six, I have always been aware of my own death, lurking some day in the future. The King grunted.

The throne room wasn't usually so hot. That day there were no servants operating the fan, or carrying water. I felt a blind, liquid fear filling every corner of my body. I watched the army massing outside the gates like the shadow of an enormous cloud, and knew without doubt that the walls would be overrun, the guard would fall, and the city would burn. Every moment I wasted in the palace was another moment closer to our deaths. The itch went right down to my fingertips. I had to get back to you. We had to escape.

'Great lord, I apologise, but I need to return to my apprentice as soon as possible,' I said, trying to keep the fear from my voice. 'He's the – the son of someone important, you understand, and I've left him waiting there with no guidance at all—'

'Asanka,' the King said, choking a little. His back was still turned to me. 'When a king – there's something – there's something I have to tell you.'

But he didn't get to finish. There was the sound of running feet outside, the doors were pushed open, and two generals burst into the room with heaving chests. I could rarely tell the generals apart, all thick-bearded and dressed for war even during festivals, but they knew who I was. They both glanced at me and I felt as detested as a stray dog.

'Great King, my radiant lord,' the taller began, 'we had no idea – the heretic from the mainland – he marched nearly two *yojanas* overnight. Nothing – nothing is ready!'

The King said nothing. He didn't turn from the balcony. The generals took it in turns to ream through a list of all the weak points in the defences, every gate unbarricaded, every division that had fled south or been wiped out, the dry wells, the soured rice, the number of horses, the number of elephants. With every item, I felt a cavern yawn a little wider inside me. The King's legs were shaking now, and as I watched another bead of sweat slide down his back, a mantra began in my head.

I've led a good life, I told myself. *I've never hurt anyone. Let him dismiss me soon, Lord Buddha. Let him dismiss me soon.*

'My King,' one of the generals said, 'we don't have the rations. One month rice, one millet. Four months, if you close up the citadel and let the farmers go hungry. After that, it's bark and jasmine buds, even for the swordsmen. And the rains will end soon. You know the way this goes, my lord – and once the elephants start to weep, the mahouts will have to butcher them. For the meat, Your Highness.'

'I saw a calf weeping just yesterday, My King,' the other said. 'All of them are already thin and yellow-eyed. Ellu the trainer thinks the hunger will make them fiercer, if it comes to fighting, but weaker too.'

'And tougher as meat. You should see the monsters the Kalinga brought with him. Juice streaming from their temples, people are saying. Tusks like bargepoles. He'll take from the villages: food, water, whatever he needs. Magha can outlast us, my lord.'

'We beg you, Your Highness, great lord of the three lands. We live to carry out your orders. But what should we do?'

Nothing. I moved to let the breeze pass over my skin, let it cool the beads of sweat that were crawling out of my armpits and down my ribs. I watched the dust and smoke of the enemy army furrowing the sky, marking time. Then, without turning, the King spoke.

'There's nothing we can do,' he said. 'What kind of king would I be, to watch my people starve? How would they remember me?' The silence was as thick as earth. 'Pamu, Tharupiyam, how would they remember me?'

'I don't know, great King,' they each said.

'Asanka?'

'I don't know, my lord. Please, my lord, I have to—'

He raised his hand. Oil dripped in the lamps, and from outside the far-off sound of a child crying drifted up to us.

'Open the gates,' the King said. 'Open them and leave them open. We can only pray that this boy from Kalinga, this Magha, has mercy somewhere in his heart.'

'Great King!' one of the generals almost shouted, forgetting himself. 'They'll burn everything. The schools, the temples.'

But the King finally turned around then, and we all saw that his eyes were full of tears.

'All I want is to make love with my wife for the last time,' he said. 'These are your king's orders. Tharupiyam: send for the Queen. Pamu: tell the men to throw down their arms and open the gates. Then do what you will.'

My heart was beating as if trying to climb up my throat. I watched the generals' faces, the muscles twitching in their jaws. I wanted them to tell the King that he was mad, that they would never open the gates to a savage from the mainland who had spent half the rainy season pillaging our holy sites. But, after a moment, one of them stood to leave with his head bowed. Then the other stood, and they backed out of the room, neither of them meeting the King's eyes. Once they shut the door, I felt desperately alone in the silence.

King Parakrama turned to me. 'In the end it's all we can ask, Asanka, to die in a woman's arms. Get out of here, forget your apprentice, and be with your wife while you can.'

'Thank you, Your Majesty,' I said, hoping he wouldn't see the guilt in my face. I gave a hurried bow, but before I could turn away, King Parakrama rushed forward, right across the room in great strides. He took me by the shoulders as though to kiss me.

'Asanka!' he whispered in a voice glazed with tears. 'You're the most enlightened man I've ever met. The beauty of your similes has overjoyed my every step. Tomorrow you'll write your poetry in heaven.'

It's strange: after three years of service this was the first time that the King had ever touched me. I saw my own embarrassed surprise in the glassy curve of his pupils, and had to gather together my words like dropped apples.

'Thank you, Your Majesty,' I said, and his eyes became full of simple fears. I remember thinking, in that moment with his face a handbreadth from my own: *all my life I've done nothing but imitate my betters.*

Nobody knows what happens after death, even the most well-read philosophers. As I left the throne room, it wasn't the peace of nirvana that calmed me, not the silence of peace, or the weary duty of rebirth, but the thought of heaven the way the mainlanders and Tamils describe it. A terraced mountain watered by many rivers, with women and men cooling in the shade of pavilions and flowering trees. The golden city of Indra, with gardens and floating palaces cut from crystal. All of it so different from the world around me, which was dusty and cruel and nothing at all like a story.

I lifted my sarong to hurry down the palace's many steps. If I were a good man, which I am not, I might have gone back to my villa, with its climbing flowers and shaded courtyard. I might have dismissed the servants, comforted my wife and prayed in our shrine until the enemy came for us. I think my life would be a very different thing if I were such a person.

Instead, I hurried back to your room in the servant quarter, to tell you that we had to escape the city.

On my way back, I saw Her Majesty Queen Dayani in the palace forecourt, attended by ladies, walking to the arms of her husband. Her face was hard. The face of a girl, I often thought, though I wasn't much older. I often spoke with the Queen during my time at court, but that day when she walked past me and only bowed, I knew to my depths that everyone in Polonnaruwa would be dead by sunrise. I felt the city close around me like a tomb.

The streets were empty now. Even the King's Highway was almost deserted, and the sound of the gathering army was growing louder. There was blue smoke in the air from some abandoned clay oven, and I passed many shops and houses broken into by looters, picked through by the red monkeys, littered with unswept fruit skins and alive with flies. On street corners, the shells of gamblers were left scattered on their tables. For calm, I made a list of splendid things.

Water drunk when you've woken in the night.
The glass beads rich women wear in their hair.
A basketwork litter hurtling down the street at speed.

I remember how, on my way back, I passed a militia band, all white cloths and bamboo spears. They were using slaves to haul a spiked woodwork wound with thorn scrub up to the Mahatita Gate. They hadn't got the order yet. I wanted to shout out to the warriors that the King had surrendered, that they were lashing the labourers for nothing, but an old black-and-pink-dappled elephant was dragging a felled tree behind them. Leaves scattered everywhere between the cobbles, and the sound of the mahout's hammer thudding at the beast's skull made me want to scream.

My hatred of elephants . . . it may seem ridiculous to you, but at the time it was one of the strongest fears in my heart. That day I remembered what Ellu the trainer had told the generals, and I tried to catch the rage of hunger behind the monster's black eyes before I darted down a side street. What a shameful secret. Because of this encounter, my chest was heaving even before I passed through the canal district, and the enemy host began to chant all together: '*Va! Va!*' or something like that. A dread throbbing sound.

I broke into a run, skidding in gutter clay, knocking over piles of oyster shells, and taking short cuts through alleys I would never dare to enter on a normal day. Every door and window was closed. By the time I got back to the servant quarter, there was no one around, no Muslim man with the lamps, no smoke of fires, no voices. Even the mynah birds had flown off to wherever they go when they're not ruining people's lessons with their twittering. I saw only one person on my way back to your room: a wine-tapper I recognised from the baths, hunched over in the corner, whimpering and trying to bury something in the earth with his hands. I walked up the steps, and called in through the curtain.

'Sarasi? Sarasi, are you in there?' No answer. 'Sarasi?'

My heart was sinking into my stomach. How could I be so stupid? I drew the curtain aside, and stepped inside to find your cushion empty. The room was still in darkness with only the light from the lattice spilling into the shadow, illuminating that small corner by the window. I knew it then: you had tricked me, you had pretended to love me so I would teach you to write, and now you were gone. I had been the world's greatest fool. I went over to the desk where a single leaf of paper was left, a short poem scratched into it. It was the story of a pair of lovers who die unmarried and spend the rest of their new lives trying to find each other.

'I told you I'd be right here,' you said from behind me. I spun around. I could just about make out your shape, kneeling in the shadow at the back of the room. 'You thought I'd gone, didn't you?'

'I – no, I—'

'It's all right, Asanka. I didn't think you were coming back either. I wrote a poem while I waited, but it's all wrong.'

Steel flashed in your hand.

'What are you doing over there?'

You brought your face out of the shadows, and I raised my hand to my mouth. You were holding a blade. You had sliced off the sleek ribbons of black hair in your plait, and hacked at what remained so that your scalp showed in patches through the remaining tufts. You looked like a beggar. I felt a knot in my throat.

'Your hair! Your hair – *anay*, Sarasi, why did you do that?'

'You know why,' you said, and dropped the knife on to your mattress with a thud, throwing your long braid on top of it like a killed snake. 'Oh, but you've never been in a siege before, have you? You've never seen what happens.'

I shook my head glumly, and knelt down to stroke the limp braid.

'The King's going to surrender, isn't he?' you said.

'How – how could you know that?'

'A king who's going to fight doesn't summon his poet.'

I stared into the darkness around you. 'He wanted to say goodbye.'

You shrugged, and went to where I'd been using charcoal to mix new ink. You crumbled some in your hands and began to smear it on your cheeks and arms.

'He was a good king,' I said as I watched you, and even though it wasn't true, I realised then how much I had liked him.

'He wasn't the worst,' you said.

I stepped towards you and reached out my hand to touch your head. Ran my fingers through the coarse, tufted bristles that spilled out in clumps like the fur of a diseased dog.

'We have to get out of here,' I said. 'They'll be here soon. If we leave now, we can—'

'It's already too late,' you said, and looked up at me with eyes bright like newly blown glass. 'If we leave now, they'll kill us.'

'But the south gates – we could—'

'Anyone who left by the south gates is already dead,' you said, as though it were obvious.

'The canals—'

'Blocked by felled trees, I bet.'

'But the – we could—'

'We can't go anywhere. Sit down. Change out of those clothes if you don't want to be ransomed.'

I looked down at my gold-and-green sarong, felt the weight of the jewels in my ears. You were right. My hands were shaking as I unpinned my earrings. I turned my sarong inside out so its embroidery was hidden, and you sat back down at your cushion.

'Why did you write a poem?' I said, dazed. You shrugged. I wiped my forehead and sat down beside you. You didn't say anything for some time, so I read your poem again.

'You've made many corrections, many false starts,' I said. I had to strain a little as the light was dim, and the cuts in the paper hadn't been inked yet. 'You're using farmer's grammar here, but here – this line is very musical.'

You were silent for a moment longer.

'You sound so funny when you speak Tamil,' you said then. Our talk always seemed to go this way: I insulted you by accident, and you stung me back in revenge. You did an impression of my speech, puffing out your cheeks and putting on my accent. 'It makes me laugh.'

'I'm still learning,' I said.

'You speak the way a dog walks when it has a front leg missing.'

'Ha! Your language is difficult, all lips and roof of the mouth. Pa-ha, la-ha, ba-ha – all breath.'

Our words trailed away into silence.

'Don't be afraid,' I said then. What a useless thing to say.

'I'm not afraid,' you said, but your voice was tiny. Out of habit, I took your hand and ran my lips along the valley of your palm, up to your long fingers, your broken nails. Today, it's these details that paint you into my memory.

'Half these mainlanders speak Tamil, anyway,' I said. 'You'll be fine.'

You shrugged, took an ink cloth, soaked it, and dabbed your poem with black. The ink soaked into the cut letters, and they bled into sight, leftover globules wobbling on the waxy paper. Then you smeared the remaining ink on your forehead.

'They'll be kind to us,' I said. 'On my way to the palace, I saw an omen.'

'An omen?'

'Yes, and a good one, too. Unmistakeable. You know that tall paper palm by the guardhouse?'

'The one where the monks sit to beg?'

'Yes. Well, it burst into flower as I walked past it. I know, just like that, cascades of yellow, white, orange,' I said, pretending to mistake your doubt for wonder. 'I wish you could've seen it. Then, when I passed that old wheel maker by the canal, I saw that by some miracle all sign of his disease had disappeared – he was out stripping saplings in the sun. He even waved to me, and then when I looked down into the canal, I saw a lotus growing, with a bee trapped inside the flower.'

You looked up, parted your lips and kissed me.

'You're such a good liar,' you said. 'Tell me more. Why don't you tell me about our wedding?'

I breathed in the slight scent of sweat on your skin, and the attar the queen sometimes let you try on when you brought her water in the mornings.

'I can't lie about something that's certain,' I said. 'We'll still have our wedding. I bet my wife's already returned to her brothers in the countryside. I bet she'll never come back. It'll be a marvellous Deepavali.'

Deepavali was two whole seasons away, and I knew neither of us even expected to see the dawn. You wrapped the charcoal, ink palette and stylus, stood up and hid the writing materials back in your wall, kneeling to slide out the loose bricks near the floor one by one. I could never see what else you kept inside: you always concealed the hollow's contents with your shoulder, replaced the stones with care. When you stood up, you brushed the brick dust from your hands.

'Will there be drummers and dancers?'

'What kind of wedding would it be otherwise?'

You sat down on the bed. 'What kind of food will there be?'

'All the best kinds. Peppered mangoes, coconut daal, five kinds of rice.'

I sat beside you, ran my hand through your shorn hair, my fingers coming away black from the charcoal and ink. Then we lay down, and I let you curl up beside me and burrow your head into my chest. It was then that a deep sound shivered up through the floor: the Hanuman Gate opening in the north like a pair of gigantic wings. I tried to breathe away the quaking that rushed through my body, and went on in my loping Tamil.

As I described how we would say our vows, how I would tie a white sash around your waist and remove your anklet, a voice inside me spoke in Sinhala, asking all the questions I had never dared to ask you. I wondered who your parents were, and why they had left you without dowry; why you had come to the city of Polonnaruwa from whatever rich earth had given birth to you; where you went on those nights you disappeared into the forest; why you risked punishment and disgrace just to learn how to write; and whether you told the truth when you spoke about the Buddha or whether in the cool black water that sits at the bottom of every person you believed in the old gods, the gods of your people, and their ancient wars. I knew that now I would get no answers.

'It's not important where I came from,' is all you would ever say, or 'It's not important where I go. Are you taking a census, taxman?'

I'd long ago learnt not to ask questions. As my thoughts chased each other through thick jungle, my mouth seemed to work on its own. I was telling you that on Deepavali you would wear a skirt of blue water lilies, that we would live together in a grove of rosewood or perched somewhere high up in the hills. I didn't know if you were still listening. I felt the cool of tears leaving tracks along my temples, felt the weight of my exhaustion and your breathing on my chest. And then – wasn't it the strangest thing? Despite the heat and the shadow of death that hung over the city, we both drifted to sleep. The deepest, most dreamless sleep.

We would wake to the sound of screaming.

Chapter Two

Shrieking is perhaps more accurate. I blinked awake, and my first thought was that I had slept through the morning, that I was late for a meeting with the King, and that my newest poem wouldn't be completed on time. It took a moment for that old, wonderful life to fall from me like water.

Memories of that day return to me in flashes, like a shadow puppet-show illuminated by a fierce fire. There was the smell of smoke, and you were shaking beside me. I jumped as a man's piercing scream, broken halfway by sobbing, came from a room some way down the terraces. There were the barks of foreign voices, shrieks, and then a cruel eruption of laughter. I realised then. We'd fallen asleep, and the enemy had stormed the city. Magha was here.

From the street outside your window, there was shouting, the clatter of chariot wheels and hooves. Through the floor, I could hear a man chanting the Dhamma Vandana in terror, getting louder and louder, then cutting out with the sound of something clay breaking against a hard surface. Dozens of feet pounded the steps to the terrace, leather on stone, and I tried to enclose you in my arms and cover your ears. Your curtain screeched on its rail, and a swordsman came inside, dragging a laughing spearman with him. They were bearded, with patterned sashes, and they had the yellowed eyes of men who have caught the sweating sickness more than once.

'Get up! Get up!' the swordsman laughed in Sinhala, then Tamil, with a mouth born into speaking neither. The men strode across the room to our mat, tearing down the curtains as they came, feet thumping on the boards and straw. You sprang up as though you would fight them with your fists, but the swordsman, with a great long plait swinging behind him, grabbed you by the wrists and laughed as you tried to strike him.

I tried to stand too, but the spearman struck me in the chest with the butt of his weapon and used his knee to pin me back against the floor. I kicked my legs like a crushed mosquito until I felt a cold, sharp point press into my throat. Then everything seemed to stop.

My whole life I'd read and written poems of heroes, of battles and wars, but I'd never before had a weapon held against my neck. At any moment, I expected to feel a searing note of pain open my insides to the air, blood warming my chest like spilt sauce. I tried to call out to you, but the spear blade dug further into my throat, and I spluttered on my words. A pot beside your bed fell and shattered.

'What are your names?' the man on my chest demanded, and the pressure lessened on my neck. A hundred lies flooded my head, but only the truth came out.

'I'm Asanka,' I said, my voice cracking. 'I'm nothing, just a poet to the King. She's Sarasi, a servant girl. Please—' but at the mention of my name, the swordsman growled, and before I could beg them for our lives, the shaft of the spear crushed into my windpipe. I felt my eyes bulging. I could smell the smoke of campfires and half-cured leather, the rancid sweat on the man's body, the smell of horses. He said something to the swordsman in a mainland tongue, perhaps Kalinga, and they laughed, looking first at me, and then at you.

'Don't touch her!' I tried to shout, but gargled like a man drowning. The swordsman nodded down at me, and said something else in his language as screams and barks harrowed the air from outside. I heard the word 'maharaja'. My heartbeat filled my head, and the spearman lifted his weapon so I could gasp for air, then dragged me along the floor and out into the light of the corridor. The whole time I could hear someone nearby squealing like a pig going to slaughter, and it wasn't until they pressed me against the pillar outside that I realised it was me. They tied my hands behind my back, a line of fire on my wrists. Then they dragged me back through the servant quarter.

Men and boys with all kinds of weapons were going from room to room on both levels. They tore the curtains from the doors, threw people out of their rooms, wrapped women's braids around their fists and pulled them along like goats. I was mewling, pleading. Tamil words were babbling from my mouth.

'I have money,' I kept saying. 'I'll give you money. You don't know what you're doing. I eat dinner with the lords every day. I've touched the King!'

This much increased their taunting.

'Have you ever been brought before a maharaja?' they crooned in dislocated Tamil. 'Magha of Kalinga has summoned you, monkey child, and now you will appear!'

I howled and trembled as they dragged me across the King's Highway, where the gutters were running crimson and brown. I felt myself faint, swimming in black water, and the warriors took my weight between them. Then we were in the palace. The world passed by as a blur of granite and plaster, angular entanglements of limbs, the sound of breaking wood and pots. We were moving at speed, and I remember detesting the bunches of flowering jessamine that hung everywhere, their bright orange petals immodest amid the horror. I scrunched up my eyes as the screams rose like a tide closer to the palace. As the soldiers carried me up the palace stairs, the tops of my feet tapped against their sharp edges, step by step by step.

Soon, I heard the sound of a large door opening, and I was dragged into a room full of hot, copper-smelling air. When they dropped me, I opened my eyes and saw that I was in the throne room for the second time that day. Cushions were scattered everywhere, an ornamental dais overturned and one of the curtains had been slashed with a sword, gaping like a laughing mouth. Tall foreign soldiers stood silently along the walls, with a line of bound and sitting lords, some weeping, some trembling, on the floor. I recognised the chiefs of Matara, of Gokarna, of Mahatale, among others. They looked the way I knew I must: pale as drowned men.

King Parakrama Pandya was kneeling in the centre of the chamber, a swordsman on either side, his hands tied behind him. I forced myself to stifle a scream at the sight. Blood was pouring down his cheeks, caking his neck and matting the plaits of his beard. It was still seeping from the meaty sockets where they had gouged out his eyes. He was murmuring softly to himself. He turned at the sounds of our entry, mouth gaping, and I'm sure that he looked right at me. I'm not a strong man, either in my muscles or in my stomach: if someone showed me a grievous wound today, I wouldn't be able to look at it – that's why I could never be a physician or a medicine man. And the face of the King in those few moments – I will remember that sight if I live to be a thousand.

Standing over King Parakrama was a man in armour made of leaf-shaped plates, and a spired helmet in the Persian style. He turned his head as I entered, flushed as if from some intense task, and when he smiled it wasn't the kind of smile that some men flash like knives, but a smile that cracked his whole face. This man, I knew immediately, was Kalinga Magha.

I still have a coin from those times. Even today you can appreciate the skill of the mould-casters in capturing the sharp lines of the Kalinga's face, the mouth framed by that moustache, and almost full with teeth. Of course, what you can't see in copper is his most commanding feature: that pair of thick eyebrows, black as charcoal, the bushiest I have ever seen.

There was an exchange in his language, and the lords were all kicked and dragged from the room by their braids. Once their cries receded outside, the soldiers who brought me bowed to their master, and one of them spoke. The Kalinga prince nodded, and looked at me.

'You,' he began in accented Tamil, and it surprised me that his voice was as smooth as coconut water. 'You're Asanka the poet. Am I correct?'

He placed each syllable like a game piece. I nodded, all words gone, and the soldiers pushed me towards him so that I stumbled. I was sure that I was going to die, and I shrunk from him when he turned to face me. Then he said, of all the things he might have said, 'It's an honour to meet you. I'm a great admirer of your work.'

Time seemed to stop. The Kalinga prince drew his sword with a flourish, let it catch the light, and placed it across his index finger. It teetered there for a moment.

'It has perfect balance,' he said. Then he snatched up the sword with his other hand and gave it to one of the soldiers beside the King, who I noticed was mopping blood and an inky fluid from his hands. The man put a whetstone into the cloth he was using, took the sword and began to sharpen it. There was no expression on his face, nothing. On the floor, King Parakrama shook with every scraping note the stone played. The prince walked across the room to the throne, and the King's table.

'I imagine these are yours,' he said, and raised the pages that I'd left there the night before. Leaf veins, light through paper. He took my shamefaced silence as a yes.

'My name is Magha,' he said, 'the youngest prince of the Kalinga line, and, from today, ruler over this island. You should have seen this King, this man, come out to welcome me. He came out to give me his crown. How could he be so—' the prince turned to me, for effect '—blind?'

There were dark chuckles from the soldiers around the room.

'Tell me,' Magha said, 'have you ever heard of the poet Sri Magha?'

I didn't know what was happening. I tried to say that of course I had heard of Sri Magha, but as the sharpening of the scimitar continued like the scraping of a string instrument, and my gaze fell to King Parakrama, I could say nothing. The thought of you swam unbidden into my head – that you might already be dead or dying somewhere while I stood there and choked on a question that wouldn't even make my dullest apprentices sweat. Where was the Queen? Where was my wife? I felt my knees almost buckle, and knew that if I collapsed with hands tied I would fall painfully.

The Kalinga went on. 'Magha was the poet who immortalised the court of King Varmalata in Gujarat. He is the author of the holy Sanskrit epic, the *Shishupala Vadha* – surely you've heard of it. Magha. He has the same name as me.'

The way he said this made it seem a credit to the artist.

'Yes,' I managed. 'I've studied it.'

'Aha! He can speak!' the Kalinga said, his smile returning. 'Always a useful skill for a poet. The problem is, Master Asanka, I can't read Sanskrit. It's a language nobody speaks but priests and philosophers, and I'm a man of action. I speak Kalinga, the language of my fathers, and Tamil, the language of my soldiers. But I've heard so much about this Magha and his poem. They say it's the story of how the great Krishna defeated an evil king, how he saved his bride and won the world. Your name,' the conqueror said. 'It's Sanskrit, isn't it?'

'Yes.'

'Do you speak it?'

'Of course.'

'Read and write too? As well as Tamil?'

'Yes.'

'And you're sure you've read Magha's poetry?'

'Yes.'

'Excellent. Then you,' he said with much ceremony, 'you will be my royal translator. You will translate the *Shishupala Vadha* into Tamil in my name, so that I can give it to the people of this land, this bud I'm here to bloom. Thus we may achieve the King's pleasure and the greater good of the masses in a single move.'

These moments I will remember for the rest of my life, but they happened so fast.

'A noble cause,' I remember saying, and King Parakrama, bleeding on the floor, turned his face towards the sound of my voice. I imagine that if he still had his eyes, he would have wept.

'No no no,' Magha said. 'There aren't noble causes, only noble men and their destinies. You'll learn that for yourself.

What a day for lessons! Now, since we're to be friends, why don't you ask a favour of me? I'm to be the King soon enough. I can grant you anything you desire.'

He gestured down at the bleeding King Parakrama, as though I might ask for his life. This prince was so strange, laughing and smiling in a room that stank of blood, so kind and cruel at the same time. Before I knew it, more words were tumbling past my lips.

'My lord, great king from the mainland,' I said. 'My lord, there's a woman. A servant. She has hair cut short and a red-brown robe, with charcoal on her face. In the servant quarter, across the highway. In the room with the flower lattice. Please, your soldiers, please don't let them hurt her.'

Magha stood there for a moment, his bristly eyebrows arching. And then he smiled. 'Anything you desire, Master Asanka.' He waved at a soldier wearing a fox skin. 'Go on, tell the fools to leave the woman alone.'

The man nodded and slipped out of the door. The prince turned back to me, face crinkled, teeth showing. 'And now we're friends, see? But you'll have to prove yourself before I can trust you. You can start with the poem's title, the *Shishupala Vadha*. Translate it for me.'

I looked up at him, and saw a spark in his eye. He already knew what the title meant.

'*Shishupala Vadha*,' I croaked. 'The Slaying of Shishupal.'

Magha smiled, showing his perfect teeth.

'The death of a king,' he drawled. 'That *is* a fitting way to start, don't you think?'

There was an almost imperceptible movement of his hand, and the soldier's arm unwound like a snake. A flash of the sword, a spurt of red mist, and the old king fell forward. Blood glugged from his throat the way water glugs from a toppled jar.

I am Shishupal

Aha! By the look in your eyes I can see that you know me – and by the way you avoid my gaze, I can tell that you already know my story. Well, don't look so proud of yourself. Men spend their lives wishing to live for ever, but I am one of the few who have achieved it – and what a torment it is! Since the cursed poet Magha wrote my story all those years ago, I have suffered the indignity of being brought back from the dead over and over, billions of times, just to die again. My death is all people remember now: brutal, humiliating and immortalised in song.

We lived centuries apart, the great Sri Magha and I. He is here too if you look for him, somewhere in this hall of dark corners, probably scribbling some nonsense into the dust. Perhaps you could ask him something for me – 'Why,' ask him, 'why did you write your poem about King Shishupal?'

I have always wondered, but I can only guess. Was my tale always his favourite? After all, it has everything a poet could wish for: love and lust, violence, betrayal and murder. Perhaps a blind grandmother recited it to him when he was only a bamboo-thin boy, curled up on a reed mattress. Perhaps it was the only chapter of the *Mahabharata* that his family could afford, and so he learnt to read and write from its pages. He dreamt it one night, perhaps, or saw it dance through his head in a vision after knocking himself out with bhang. Sometimes I imagine him jumping up from his bed to write naked in the darkness. The immense desert night outside. Other times, I imagine that King Varmalata chained him to his writing tools the way gypsies bind their bears.

I have only guesses. All I know is that without this ancient poet and the masterpiece he made of my murder, I would be just another of Krishna's slaughtered enemies, a brief name among thousands in the *Mahabharata*, like a speck of lotus pollen in the ocean. Such bliss that would be, to be forgotten.

Sometimes I think that Sri Magha saw his own life reflected in my story. I know poets are not brave like swordsmen or quick with words like courtiers. Perhaps there was some woman he pined after. Some woman like my own Rukmini – the sorrow of my life. When I think of my promised bride, I want to tear out my own hair and fingernails. I anticipated our wedding night for months. Those long evenings, I grew mad imagining her tenderness in my arms, the taste of her lips. But my young virgin, my golden princess, was stolen from me.

The night I found out that Krishna had taken her, I smashed furniture with my feet, cursing and spitting. I stamped and howled and tore at my skin. I went to the empty room that lay waiting for her and hacked at the bed with my sword, feathers and straw flying through the air. That night, after executing nearly a hundred prisoners in a drunken daze, I summoned the concubine in my harem who most resembled her – same dusk-coloured eyes, same round, supple shoulders – and dressed her in the princess's wedding sari. The girl guessed my purpose, I think, even before, in the moment of climax, I murmured 'Rukmini'.

Over the coming weeks, I summoned my boundless armies. I employed assassins, invoked gods and their dark brothers in the world of demons – I ordered my ten thousand war elephants to be gorged with liquor, to have lemon juice dripped into their eyes and sabres strapped to their trunks in immediate preparation for battle. I resolved to destroy Krishna, to make him bleed from a thousand wounds. Deep down, all men are at war with their gods.

Of course, none of it would bring Rukmini back to me. At the end of my story, only death and shame awaited this one-time king. Wait a moment – I fear I have something stuck in my throat, and a mote of dust in my eye. Do you not feel the dryness in the air? Such – such dryness. It is becoming difficult to speak.

Chapter Three

The soldiers dragged me out of the throne room as the executioner began to hack off the King's head. I was fainting and mewling, and they carried me most of the way down the stairs, out of the palace and into the gardens, where flocks of people knelt with their hands tied. Peacocks were wandering brazen and oblivious among them, and foreign soldiers walked up and down swinging kicks and blows into the crowd. I managed to walk a little once the breeze washed over me, carrying with it the cool air from the garden's many pools. The men supporting me loosened their grips, but as we passed the King's bath, and the lion-ringed pavilion where he used to lounge and listen to my poems, my legs became boiled bamboo again. The soldiers caught me by my armpits and dragged me on.

It was my fault, I kept thinking. By not begging for his life, I had killed the King. Each time I shut my eyes, I saw those gouged sockets, the tendons of his neck tightening like rope, his own blood coating him in a steaming garment. A man most people would go their whole lives without touching. My face was sticky with sweat and tears.

The soldiers dragged me to the shade of the flame tree beside the pavilion, and dropped me painfully to my knees. There was a chorus of muffled sobbing, the sounds of the canal nearby, and the wind rattling the seeds in the tree's dry pods. Once the men left, I felt brave enough to look around for any sign of you. Hundreds of people were huddled there: servants and palace workers, scribes, washermen and cooks, all the guards of the gate watch. People were being brought in loose huddles with their clothing torn, weeping, and bleeding from fresh wounds.

Kalinga scribes were walking about with fresh fans of paper, cutting little marks for each person they passed. Magha's spies had been busy. The scribes would motion at some, and they were dragged away, their howls echoing against the tall citadel walls. I couldn't see you anywhere. I didn't know if the Kalinga would keep his promise, or if the soldier in the fox skin had got to you in time. You could be dead or beaten or raped. I searched every group of new arrivals for your face. As I looked around, I noticed that there were no nobles in the garden, no courtiers or generals, and I realised with a rush of anger that I'd been placed among the servants. As I watched spear butts strike the backs of heads, I became sure that you were dead. I wept pitifully.

After a long time, Magha came down from the palace with the highest ranking of his generals and began a tour of the gardens. He'd changed into the royal sandals and had washed King Parakrama's blood from between his toes. One slave walked behind him carrying the Umbrella of Dominion, another swinging at flies with the royal whisk. The Kalinga was coming right towards me, gazing up at the citadel walls that hemmed in the garden on one side, peering at the carvings of crouching lions that ringed the King's bath, smiling broadly all the way. For every one of those thousand-year moments I roasted in the fire of my own disgrace. I knew that if he spoke to me, if he singled me out, everyone would think me a traitor. We were friends now – that's what he said. *Asanka the poet*, I thought, *friend to the demon king*.

Magha walked past me without even glancing my way, talking animatedly in his language to the crowd of generals following him. I breathed in the fresh cloud of perfume that wafted in his wake, and the trembling in my body gave way to convulsions. It was then that the weight of his order descended. A translation. Sanskrit, Tamil. Shishupal. How could I write for a man like that?

Everything in the garden was flattened by the heat.

'An impressive palace, and a beautiful garden!' Magha announced, once he'd performed a quick circuit. He didn't seem to be saying it to anyone in particular. He washed his hands in the air and stepped into the sunshine falling among the trees.

'Maharaja,' a young soldier said to him. 'This man says he's in charge of supplies.' He gestured at Shona, an old man who had spent more than half his life as Chief of the King's Stores.

'Cut his ropes,' Magha told the boy, and then to Shona, 'Take my men to the storehouses – have them bring up the siege rations and prepare a feast. I want meat, fish, eggs, beans, as many kinds of rice as you can find.'

Shona crept forward with his beard trailing between his knees and touched the new King's feet. A guard barked an order, and ropes began to be cut all around the garden. People got to their feet, stumbling on bloodless legs, fainting where they knelt. Everyone's eyes were like the eyes of fish. There were warriors everywhere, shouting, cuffing people about the head and standing guard for no reason at the doorways to storerooms and latrines.

Once my ropes were cut, I went to look for you in the kitchen yard, but it was empty, sickly with the smell of rice water and wet ash. I headed back to the servant quarter, but found guards crossing spears at every gate.

'Go home,' one of them said to me. 'If I see you again, I'll cut off your ears.'

I fled, and took my most circuitous route home, through the gardens and along the canal where bodies were floating eastward, past storehouses being pitilessly ransacked by soldiers.

It was cool beneath the canopy of my villa, though the place was a mess. Our food and wine had been looted, along with some of the ornaments on our veranda and the snake stone in our gateway. My wife was still there – I saw her as soon as I crept through the gate. She was sweeping potsherds in the courtyard with abrupt, violent motions. When she saw me, she puffed out her cheeks.

'Where – where have you been?' she demanded in a bruised rage.

'Madhusha, I didn't – the soldiers, they—' but she was already storming towards me, holding the broom like an axe. She fixed me with a stare, smouldering with silence.

'Madhusha—'

'And what if I'd died?' she said, and swung the broom as she said it. The palm fronds scratched at my face, and I tried to fend off the blows as they fell one after the other. '*Aiyo!* What if I'd died, and you found me lying here? How long before your whore would be sleeping in my bed?'

She threw her broom at me and marched out into the street as she sometimes did, crying out so the neighbours could hear that I'd left her to die alone to be with my mistress, that I'd brought her to live in a cesspit of a city only to betray her, and so on. She was always so full of life when in a rage.

I stood there in the courtyard for some time, then stumbled upstairs, full of the overpowering thought that I was the worst man I had ever known.

The King's Highway beneath my balcony was filled with soldiers, brilliant in their bronzes, marching in spear-porcupine packs that stretched all the way down the road, past the servant quarter and through the open Hanuman Gate in the distance. So many of them, each so large and well armoured, shouting 'Triumph to the King! Victory to the Maharaja!'

They were driving the men of King Parakrama's army, naked in chained lines of twenty, and for hours afterward as I lay curled in my bedclothes I could hear the crack of whips, the howls of the struck and the music of their shackles chiming on the cobbles.

By the time the temple bells next sounded, and the servants beat the dinner drums, I walked to the wide, glittering tank, the great manmade lake, with a terrible sense of dread. It was that hour when the sun grows low over the water, turning everything gold where it bleeds through the trees. Magha had ordered his feast to be held in the old three-tiered council chamber near the King's baths, and the court was gathered at its entrance.

'Why here?' the chief of Gokarna was muttering to someone behind me, scuffing his feet on the moonstone carvings. 'Why not the banquet hall?'

'I hear he's going to give a speech,' some minor lord replied, and I felt hot water in my veins. Would Magha mention my name? Would he tell everyone that I had let the old king die?

We filed up the steps, all as pale as cave lizards: some senior diplomats, consuls, officials and myself, all robes and sarongs in the plum-pink combination, as it was nearly the New

Year. Then, when I got to the top of the steps, I saw you. You were there among the thirty or so servants kneeling and standing with parcels of food, arranging the flowers and hangings. I nearly laughed. I nearly wept like a child. You were alive – this was the moment I knew it – and after that I began to appreciate the beauty of the hall, the smell of the lamps, scented oils and gum resin. As I walked to my place between the pillars, you glanced up at me.

On the high lion throne, beneath the umbrella, the new king from Kalinga sat with many garlands hanging from his neck. He looked the way some birds do when they puff up their breasts to sing. I remember he sat with one hand on the lion's braided mane, and the other on the tail coiled over its rump so that triangles of rosy sky were cut out behind him. Foreign priests oiled patterns into his scalp.

'Increase the age of our king to five thousand years,' they were whining in Sanskrit, 'increase it as long as the sun and moon last and as long as the heaven and earth exist . . .'

The rest of the court took their places, having left at the foot of the throne the tributes they had secreted away for this eventuality: baskets of guava from the hill town lords, shells from the coast, jewels from the south and turmeric water from the plains. Many lords wore swollen eyes and lips.

'. . . until the crow turns white, until the hen's egg grows into a plant, until brick and mortar bear leaves . . .'

On and on. When they finished, before the eating began, Magha rose from the throne and began to speak. I was coated in sweat.

'A day of such glory,' he began, raising his hands, 'hasn't been seen on this island since the days of Rama. In the first age, Rama came here to claim his kidnapped wife from the demon king Ravana, as is told in the *Ramayana*. I also came to claim what is rightfully mine: this land, and all its people, who were once ruled by my great-uncle, King Nissanka Malla.'

He was a good rhetorician, in the classical way. What was wild and unsettling about him in person translated before the crowd into an admirable energy, and the bones beneath his face looked brutally sharp in the slanting evening light. As he went on, I recognised many of the same phrases he had used with me, and became sure that he would speak about the translation, as his voice was taking on that same manic tenor. I sank into my cushions, waiting for the arrowheads of a hundred eyes.

'We need two things to make this land great again,' Magha was saying. 'Just two things. The strong hand of a king, and the transforming wealth of high culture. Like the two wheels of a cart, these will carry us in a straight line towards the future.'

At this point, as I was trying to stretch the tension from my neck, a bright sunbird flew in on the entrance side of the hall. Did you see that happen? It fluttered in panic through the rafters and then disappeared through the colonnade on the other side. Magha's voice didn't even waver in the commotion, didn't falter, but his eyes darted after it as it went.

'I am in need of good men if my plans are to be achieved,' he announced near the end of the speech. 'Those who join me will grow strong the way vines flourish in the sun.'

The eyes of the lords didn't meet, didn't even rise from the floor. When the Kalinga began to say a final series of blessings to his gods, I let out the breath I hadn't realised I'd been holding. All around me, the eating began. I was so grateful to Magha for leaving me out of his speech that I could have wept, and perhaps this is what he intended. He glanced at me before sitting down, and I felt cold. Around the hall, people reached forwards to take handfuls of rice, and the servants began handing out the sauces. My gaze followed you around the room as you went, and I could hardly wait until you reached my spot between the pillars.

Magha and his generals were eating hungrily, gorging on the fine food after months of chickpeas and millet on the march. The King's ration of fine red mountain rice had been found, and along with urns of dried river fish and game, one lord had turned up a preserve of rich molasses. The cooks had made many fine sauces, but I could hardly bring myself to mix them with the rice, even to lift my hand to my lips. I picked at the food and scanned the hall, counting missing faces.

No one spoke. The two plaintive notes of the peacocks outside were the only sound to puncture the silence, along with the sickly chewing of a court full of mouths, and the heavy breathing from the chief of Matara to my left. I thought he might ask whether the poem I was writing for him had been finished (it had not), but he simply nodded at me and kept his eyes on the floor. When you reached me and leant down to place the parcels on the floor, I smelt your perfume through the scent of the food, and my head felt light. The pinks of pomegranate juice blushed the light palms of your hands, hinting at the course to come.

'Sarasi,' I whispered, and touched your foot with my little finger. You moved hastily away, the tiny bells on your anklet making a 'tss' sound as you went. I tried not to watch as you made your way around the hall, tried not to check you for bruises. When I looked down at the plantain leaf decking my seating place, I noticed that my hands had been working without thought, tearing it to ribbons.

Once the rice was finished, the servants brought in the pomegranate seeds with honey, and we left with stained and sticky hands.

There were horrible whispers spreading through the city. On my way home after the feast, I passed the Shiva temple outside the citadel gate, and heard a Tamil wood-carrier called Vatuka murmuring there that even the wives of the lords had been spoilt by the Kalinga's men. Vatuka was well known to exaggerate his stories, and all wood-carriers are notorious gossips, but you ignored me at the feast. I needed to see you smile, to hear your voice, to know that Magha had kept his promise and the man with the fox skin had got to you in time.

I headed to the kitchen yard as dusk fell and the lamplighters began their work. I was shaking like a warrior going into battle. When I got there, someone in the yard was cursing the lamplighters in Sinhala.

'Hurry, you brothel spawn! We can't work in the dark.'

'Ha!' one of them called back. 'Your children will piss on your pauper's grave!'

Such uneducated language was common there, unknown to the Tamil overseers: not many people in Polonnaruwa have learnt our snappy southern language. I ducked under the bunches of herbs they used to hang near the doorway, felt the heat of the enormous iron pans on my face, smells of wood smoke and curry leaves.

Doesn't it feel like you're back there, when you imagine it? It was reassuring then to see its industry already revived, the everyday rhythms of coconut husks scrubbing at clay, of mixing staves thumping the edges of urns. I found you kneading coriander and cumin on one of those smooth stones in the corner. When you saw me, you stood, smeared the crushed leaves from between your fingers and gave a quick bow. I could feel everyone watching us.

'I'll ask for some rest,' you said, and called to the old Tamil man overseeing the work.

He eyed me, and shouted 'Only for water!'

Someone whistled. We walked to the well, and the sounds of the men and women pounding kurakkan and heaving the pepper-grinding stones were enough to drown out our conversation on the way.

'The soldiers came in here and beat Niranjan,' you said, and motioned to the overseer with your head. 'That's why he's acting like a kicked dog. Most of the others fled last night, and the apprentices can't even smoke fish without setting their sarongs on fire.'

'At the feast—' I said, but you cut me off with a gesture as a boy no older than ten passed us, balancing an urn on his head.

At the well, you let the bucket plunge to the bottom, and whispered to me.

'I'm sorry I ignored you. I'm scared of these foreigners. Everything's being turned upside down and inside out, and our – our lessons – they were dangerous to start with. We need to be careful, is what I mean.'

'I understand,' I said, but knew only that I was supposed to understand. I was Sinhala, you were Tamil. Still – the Sinhala men in the bathhouses may have insulted me in my absence, the Tamil women may have murmured that you would one day give birth to a dog or a monkey – but Magha, the Aryan from the north, didn't even seem to notice the difference.

Your forearms looked knotted like a hunter's as you pulled up the rope, and washed your face and hands in the water.

'You're not angry?' you said. The lamplighters still hadn't reached that corner of the courtyard, so I leant over and touched your hand. Your skin was cold from the water. You smiled, in that shy, pursed-lip way you used to, but I saw you glancing behind me for disapproving eyes. I wanted to reach out and stroke the shorn patches of your hair. You washed again, drank from your cupped hands and then brought up a bucket for me.

'What happened to you?' I asked, washing the dust from my face. 'The soldiers – did they hurt you?'

'It was strange,' you said. 'They kept me there, tied up, and argued over me for a long time, shouting and shaking their weapons. Who would get the first go. That kind of thing. They were nearly fighting. All the while I sat there with my hands tied, watching them, and then my hands found a shard from the broken pot on the floor behind me. A nice long piece. Slightly curved, so it fitted the shape of my palm. I was getting ready to jam it into one of their eyes.'

I stared at you.

'They would've killed you.'

'Maybe. Maybe not. Anyway, just when it looks as if the swordsman's going to cut off the other man's head, a soldier with this animal skin bursts into the room all out of breath, and starts screaming at them. I mean, shouting like a madman, going red in the face. They start bowing to me and cutting my ropes, and even when I drop that long, curved piece of pot on the floor, right in front of them, they just look at it. They don't do anything.'

You were staring at me really hard now, with those piercing dark eyes. You ran your hand through your patchy thatch of hair.

'These foreigners are strange,' I said, and avoided your gaze.

After that we began the walk back to your stone.

'I saw them dragging all the inner court to the servant quarter,' you told me as we went. 'Made them line up in front of us. They wanted some women to watch, I think. To humiliate them. They stripped them, even the royal ones. Made the King's brothers crawl around and bark like dogs, made them beg Magha for their lives. Some of them refused,' you said, and when you told me how they had been tormented we were both silent for a little while.

'In the end they were chained and put on carts to the mainland, people are saying. Did you hear what happened to the King? The demons took his eyes.'

I wonder if you noticed some flicker in my expression.

'I heard,' I said, and put a hand over my own eyes as though exhausted. 'May the Buddha bring us mercy.'

'What happened to you?' you asked as we neared the stone.

'They wanted money,' I said. 'They marched me back to my villa and broke the gate, stole the snake stone, the wine, some rice and beans.'

Your eyes sifted me for secrets. I knew I had to move the conversation in a different direction.

'Do you know anything about the Queen?' I said. 'Is she still alive?'

'Just some rumours. I heard a wood-carrier say they'd tied her to a rock and drowned her in the lake. The wheel-makers are saying she's been shipped to a port in Kalinga as a dancer. Half the wine-tappers are saying she's been sent to work in the city tanneries, the other half say in the brothel-goers' district.'

'Nobody knows anything,' I said. 'They're making it up.'

'That's what you said about the invasion, too,' you said as you sat back down, but there was no bitterness in your voice.

'Will you come to the canal tonight?' I asked. 'Or I could come to your room?'

'No,' you said, and crushed the coriander with your palm. 'It's too dangerous.'

The heat of the kitchen wet my cheeks and forehead with sweat. I made my excuses and left.

I didn't want to go home, not to the scorn of my wife and the black mood she always put me in. I imagined her to be still stalking the neighbourhood, destroying my reputation at the top of her voice. That, and of course the serpents that had no doubt been swarming into the house since the snake stone was taken. But I was hardly relieved to be stopped by a foreign soldier on my way out of the palace, the type who always wears his hunting costume and doesn't even tuck it under his knees when he sits.

'His Majesty wants to see you,' he said.

I fell right back into the craw of terror, of course, but I remember a very specific feeling come over me: the kind that must fill degenerate gambling types when they realise that their shells are finished, that their money is gone, and it's time to live with their losses.

I walked up the palace stairs to the throne room with the expanse of the city stretching out on every side. Even in the dusk I could see my villa far down below, with its tall peaked roof, and the lantern-lit carts trailing along the King's Highway down to the canal and the servant quarter – the thread that connected my world and yours. There were lamps reflected in the canals, the first stars in the lake. The spearmen guarding the throne room knocked and announced my name when I reached the top of the stairs. There was the smell of strange incense from inside, and I felt that I was entering some creature's lair.

Magha wasn't in the throne room, but in the King's bedchamber, alone, examining the mechanical peacock that peered out of one of the alcoves. This toy, and the heavy golden inkwell on the desk, were all that remained of the old King's belongings. I entered, and my eye was drawn to a long, rectangular object on his table, wrapped in a red satin cloth.

'You sent for me, Your Majesty?'

'Ah yes,' he replied, as though he had forgotten. 'And you will call me "Maharaja".'

'Maharaja,' I repeated without thinking, and the foreign word tasted foul as rancid curd.

'Isn't it ingenious?' he said, peering closely at the jewelled feathers of the peacock. He turned its handle so that it performed a half-rotation and let out a strangled cry. I had always found this favourite of King Parakrama's possessions profoundly disturbing, so I said nothing.

'Quite beautiful,' Magha said, and then turned suddenly to me. 'I hope I haven't made you afraid of me. You're not, are you?'

There was no safe way to answer this question, I was sure of that. Without his armour, the Kalinga's arms and legs looked too long for his trunk, but he had a glow to his fair skin. He smiled as though to reassure a child.

'When a man feels himself in the heat of battle, he can often . . . let things run away from him. It's a sort of madness. You understand, I suppose.'

He reached up and smoothed the hairs of each huge eyebrow with the heel of his palm, one after the other.

'I understand, Maharaja.'

'We have to burn down the forest to grow rice, isn't that right?' he said, as though it was impossible to disagree. 'Anyway, I brought you here to discuss the translation we spoke of. I don't want any delays with something so important, and I wanted to make sure that our agreement was—' he fanned his hand around, searching for the word '—agreed upon, I suppose. Anyway, I have with me a copy of Sri Magha's poetic masterpiece, the *Shishupala Vadha*. I've been looking forward to showing it to you.'

He reached down and drummed his fingers on the object beneath the red satin. There was an intense expression on his face as he unfastened the thread.

'My father, the Emperor of Kalinga, read Kambar's Tamil *Ramayana* to me and my brothers over and over as a child,' he said, and unfolded the cloth to reveal a book as thick as two fists, as long as two forearms and bound in black leather. 'If you want a soldier to fight for you, you have to speak his language, you see. And the Tamil speakers in the south are some of the bravest fighters in the world. You heard me talking about Rama at the feast. To me, the *Ramayana* was the perfect story, simply perfect. A triumph over adversity on an island of demons.'

Magha lifted the cover of the *Vadha* and some of the pages fluttered upward, dancing on their bindings. I watched the inlay on the book flash in the light – curlicues of ivory, mother-of-pearl, polished silver. He kept his eyes on me as he spoke.

'My father always used to say that while Kalidasa is famous for his similes, Bharavi for his insight, and Dandin for his resonant words, the poet Magha was a master of all three. His poem sounds so marvellous, but I have never read it. Your duty will be to keep his mastery alive,' he said, 'even in this language. How versed are you in the poetics of Tamil?'

I felt a well of pride suddenly, from somewhere unexpected. I fell easily into this trap.

'I've read all the great anthologies,' I said. 'It's quite a passion of mine, my lord. I've studied them thoroughly, and I know their theories. I've got quite a collection of the great texts, and the whole . . .'

Those tufted eyebrows raised very slightly, and I found myself trailing off.

'I need you to translate the poem as truly as possible,' Magha said, and moved the book towards me. 'And that means it will require . . . balance. It must be written in Tamil, a common language, a language of soldiers and merchants, but it must keep the noble character of the Sanskrit original. You can't let this island, and the influence the Tamils have here, seep into your work. No, the *Vadha* is a story from the *Mahabharata*, the greatest tale ever told!' he laughed, and wheeled towards the window. 'Written by our most pious master. You have to retain its purity, its integrity, but—' and here he broke off again, and turned back to me. 'But people must love it, too. The way they love that Tamil *Ramayana*. They have to see in it everything that makes the Kalinga Empire great. Do this, and you will be truly rewarded.'

'Fulfilling your wish is my only reward,' I replied, reeling with his demands.

'Indeed. How many parvas could you translate in a month?'

I looked at the book and numbers flooded into my head, but I could think only of the names of each number, in every language. My arithmetic has always been poor.

'They're long, dense chapters,' I said. 'Perhaps three each month?'

'Impressive!' he declared, and struck his hand against the peacock with a clang. His eyes flitted upward and he counted on the joints of his long fingers.

'Twenty parvas, three each month,' he murmured. 'Then it will take six months, if you put in a bit of extra work towards the end. It's almost a month until the full moon of the New Year: that's when you'll hand in the first three parvas. Only then will I choose whether you're truly worthy of the task.'

He picked up one massa from the King's table.

'What do you call these little copper coins?'

'A massa, my lord.'

'Good. You'll receive two hundred of them each month if your work pleases me.'

My head spun. It would be the best-paid commission I'd ever undertaken. I nodded, afraid even to smile, and considered asking him what had become of the Queen. His eyes, black as the heads of ants, darted up to meet mine.

'That's all,' he said. 'And make sure that you're diligent, that you keep your head about you, Master Asanka. I'm in the habit of testing all of my servants, eventually.'

He folded the red satin around the book and handed it to me, watching my eyes as I reached out to take it. It was as heavy as stone, and felt cold even through the cloth. I backed out of the chamber, bowing and, for not the first time that day, I felt sick. The Kalinga terrified me.

'Six months', I kept murmuring to myself on the way back from the palace, like a prisoner fresh from the courts. As I passed the masters' lodge, trying to find an easy way to hold the enormous book, I came across Pushpakumara, the fat master ink-maker. He was on his hands and knees in the doorway of his room, grasping after papers and belongings that had tumbled out on to the terrace. A pot of ink, maybe one or two seers in volume, had broken and coated the floorboards in a lacquered pool.

'Are you going to Matara again for the New Year, Master Pushpakumara?' I taunted him, as he was clearly in a state of panic, and it helped soothe my own fear to mock him. He shot me a look of hatred, but his eyes didn't linger on what was in my arms.

'I'm sure you'll do just as well under this king as you did under the last, Master Asanka,' he snarled. 'You idiot child. If you had any brains left in your head you'd leave too.'

But Pushpakumara was always saying foolish things, and I wasn't sorry to see him go. When I returned to my villa, I found my wife sleeping on a coir mat in one of the empty rooms we'd always set aside for the children we hoped would one day come. All the servants were gone, the floor unswept. I watched for a moment as my wife slept, snoring slightly, the rise and fall of her chest. The poor village girl I'd married back when I was just a poor village boy. How the years can change us!

I went up to my bedroom and dropped the *Shishupala Vadha* on to my desk, unwrapped it from its cloth. It sat there like a blood-fat tick, and I took in its size, the length of its pages, the gold on its cover. It smelt of old dry leaf and ink, of cavernous temple libraries and the perfumed beards of scholars.

I could burn it, I thought. *I could throw it in the canal.*

The moon was already showing, a perfect shell in the blue. The evening temple bells hadn't yet rung.

I sat down. They say of some men 'he escaped into his labour', and I tried to do this. In normal circumstances, it would be easy. The *Shishupala Vadha* is one of the most famous of all poems, and even common people have heard of it. They call its author Sri Magha, Magha the Poet, Bell Magha, even, after that one line they all love, where a great mountain is compared to an elephant with the sun and moon hanging from its ears like bells.

It's an ancient story. The princess who chooses to marry Krishna, despite being promised to a king. The abduction on the night of the wedding. The rage of King Shishupal, her groom-to-be. As famous as it is, we hardly know anything about the poet who wrote it. I always imagined a man of strange dreams, composing while walking the bright bazaars of Gujarat's walled cities, brushing the sand of the Thar Desert from his pages, singing his work to a marble hall full of all the princes of India.

His rhyme and metre are interwoven as intricately as the Chinese weave the worm's threads, so I've always imagined him in conjunction with fabric – with the complex designs of the carpets, the tapestries and robes that I'm told fill the markets of the mainland, that fill the ships sailing here from Malabar, Kerala, the Comorin Cape. Before the coming of Kalinga Magha, I'd dream of leaving my wife and sailing with you to walk those cities and their libraries, to breathe the same air as men like that great poet. I always promised myself that I'd bribe a shipmaster and go at the next blossoming of the kurinji flower.

Sri Magha's words are difficult to understand sometimes, as they're old Sanskrit, and the gods of the mainland, the gods of your people, perplex me. The language is hard, filtered through five hundred years the way water seeps through rock. Often I don't understand what the poet is referring to. He uses strange words, and the names of people and places that are unfamiliar to me. He's been dead for so long, and this world is such a fast-moving place.

When I despaired at the task, and this happened countless times over that half year, I would remind myself that it would take only eight weeks on a northbound barque to walk those far sands, and only eight aged men, their lives forming an unbroken chain, to join Sri Magha's life and mine. When I think in this way, the whole of history feels as fleeting as sudden rain. And six months? It feels like nothing.

Chapter Four

After that first day, my memory becomes a blur. I have an impeccable memory, as you know. Sometimes I'm sure I can remember my own birth – the hot water, the smell of blood and smoke, the paper-dry hands of the midwife – and of all my life, I remember the year that Magha came better than any other. But memory is also like a fabric, wearing thin with age, tearing, coming unravelled.

Some things I'll never forget, like the sight that met everyone on the second day of Magha's reign: the twenty grisly trophies speared along the ramparts of the Hanuman Gate.

'Looks like the generals have met a King they can't swindle,' one washerman said to me after I found the spots of the old king's blood on my good sarong and went to get it scrubbed. Soon vultures came to take the generals' eyes, to peel away their lips and cheeks too, until the skulls were bare and teeth began to fall to the cobbles below like nuts.

Later, the foreigners hefted King Parakrama's beheaded body on to one of the iron impalement spikes beneath the south wall. No one ever found his head, and I don't need to tell you the rumours about what they did with it. Those days were grim and unsurprising, and I went about them in a kind of dream, as did most of the city's people. That was, until the rumour about the Queen began to circulate on the fifth day.

Meanwhile, Polonnaruwa crept back to life. The streets were filling every day as stall-keepers returned, as businessmen swept the broken pots and urine from their doorways and lit their fires, as the barges from Gokarna began unloading in the dockyard. I bought a new snake stone, and put it in its gateway alcove with a feeling of relief. Shopkeepers chanted out from their hills of dry kurakkan sheaves that when times are hard, when the rice crop fails, there is always kurakkan. It was an old song. The rice crop hadn't failed; it had been requisitioned to feed the soldiers who now filled every traveller's halt and sleeping house in the city, whose tents had begun to spring up outside the walls. People grumbled over their bowls of sloppy brown meal, something I haven't eaten for many years. Kurakkan growers did well, that year. On the night of the fourth day, soldiers came for the merchant Arul who lived in the house next door, and always gave handsomely to the temples. I watched from behind the edge of my window as the warriors ransacked the house, smashing pots, beating servants, and finally dragging the merchant from the house with his wife and child crying after him. A scribe accompanied Magha's men, a man whose tongue hung out of the corner of his mouth the whole time. When all was done, I saw him run his finger down the list on his piece of paper, and make another cut next to what must have been Arul's name, before following the soldiers off into the night.

You and I met secretly, twice. Once, we met beside the canal and walked some distance in near silence, barely daring to touch each other. The second time, I went to your room and tried to give you a writing lesson, but the soldiers we could see wandering around in the courtyard frightened us too much, and I didn't stay long. The days were long and tense, and I could never bring myself to tell you about the arrangement I had come to with the new king. My wife punished me with silence.

Then the fifth day came, and everyone's favourite rumour was about Queen Dayani. It was clear by the topknots still clinging to the skulls on the gate that none of them were hers. Even the group of degenerates that used to gather outside the south wall of my villa could be heard putting shells on when it would happen: this week, tomorrow, this afternoon. Even so, as I went about my business in the city, or walked south to the library temple, or tried to sweat out my fear in the baths, I heard a certain rumour circulate. It was one of many, and I didn't believe it at first, until after sunset on the evening of the seventh day. It was the half-moon day, when the King summoned me to the royal theatre to see a dance.

When I arrived, the hall was only half full, with a large fire burning in front of the stage. There were some Kalinga generals and princes in the stands, some foreign dignitaries I didn't recognise, some Sinhala and Tamil lords of Lanka and Magha. The King was sitting on the high throne in the centre, between the thick wooden pillars carved with birds and flowers and leaves. He was drumming his fingers on the arm of the throne, but he seemed in a remarkably good mood.

'Asanka!' he called as I came in through the main door. 'Asanka, it's so good to see you.'

I felt my forehead prickle as the lords I knew looked around at me and frowned, seeing the new king address me like that.

'Come and sit beside me,' Magha said, beckoning me to an empty cushion next to the throne. I walked around the amphitheatre and the eyes of the court followed me as I went.

'We're going to watch a play,' Magha said as I sat down. The fire was casting tall, leaping shadows against the back wall, and the air was full of the smoke of fine hojari frankincense.

'A play, Maharaja?'

'Yes, a play – of course. I thought you deserved some entertainment to refresh you during your labour,' he said, loud enough so that everyone could hear. 'How has the translation been coming?'

'Excellently, Maharaja,' I said, feeling the colour rise to my face, wishing I could sink into the cushion beneath me. I'd still written nothing, of course. Seven days, and nothing. I felt the way a child in school would feel if their stern teacher could have them impaled with a single order.

'Good, good,' the King said. 'Get the poet a drink!' he called, and a Sinhala servant with a white umbrella hurried forward with a large cup of frothing palm wine.

I didn't feel like drinking at all.

'Thank you, Your Majesty,' I said, but the King motioned for me to be quiet as some drummers came out on to the stage of stamped earth and palm leaves and sat down in front of a rabana drum. I recognised them from the old king's theatre troupe: two thin men and one round as a dumpling. A man with a thin moustache came out on to the stage too, as the musicians tested their drum skins with their thumbs. He bowed to the King.

'My lords and ladies,' he said, though there were no ladies present. His voice echoed, and a certain kind of expectant silence passed over the crowd. 'This evening we are all here to sit in the same room and dream the same dream. It is my pleasure to announce a one-time performance of a story you may know.'

I shifted in my cushion, wondering how long this would take. The man flourished his hands above his head, and took a dancer's pose.

'Tonight, lords and ladies, the esteemed royal Kolam troupe will perform the story of Shishupal's death for our new King!'

Magha looked down at me, and nodded with a smile. I felt my heartbeat rising, and my throat was suddenly dry.

'My father would always bring me to watch plays in the great arena in Dantapura,' Magha said. 'Such a magnificent place it is, with tall towers and fountains. Perhaps I'll take you there one day, Asanka. Did you ever see plays with your father?'

I took a long gulp of the wine. 'Never, Maharaja.'

As the dance began with a slow beat of drums, my fingers wandered along the shape of the wicker mould imprinted in the clay cup.

First on to the stage was Krishna, with his yellow dhoti and crown of peacock feathers. The dancer was talented: he perfectly captured the immense, bliss-like bravery in Krishna's stride, and I was reminded of a saying that was a favourite of my old teacher Bhikkhu Baabu: 'Krishna plays the actor, not the other way around.'

The crowd of nobles muttered as he appeared. Krishna is one of the legends from the mainland that are as much in demand here as the merchants' stamped jars of saffron, their sandalwood and frankincense and fine horses. Krishna is brave and strong and always does his duty. The drums went *gatta gatta gatta goom* as he strode around the stage.

Rukmini was next. She was beautiful. I'd seen that dancer before in some of the troupe's other performances, as joyful Radha in a badly performed pastoral romance, as tragic Sita in the *Ramayana*. She had wide dark eyes and tiny lips, the sort of woman the lords are always sending poetry to. Rukmini danced slowly towards Krishna. They were in love, the princess and the hero. She was singing: 'O lotus-eyed Krishna! If I cannot achieve even the dust of your feet, then I will destroy my life.'

The pair danced together to a beat like a heart, and the drummers watched them carefully. The dance was fast, and soon the paint on their bodies ran and caught the firelight. Afterwards, the pair fled the stage, and someone behind the curtain blew a conch.

The foreign lords sitting in the stands were cheering and clapping, and even the Lankan nobles were forgetting that they were watching a play in the same room as their cruel new king. They too must have been drinking deeply from their cups of wine. Everyone hissed and clucked their tongues as the villains of the play walked on to the stage: Rukmi, the princess's brother, and Shishupal, King of the mighty Chedis. They both wore masks painted with recognisable expressions of evil: sharp teeth, bulging eyes in lurid colours. Shishupal wanted to marry the beautiful princess Rukmini, and her brother Rukmi promised to arrange it. The lovers, Krishna and Rukmini, would be parted. Shadows joined the dance, the drums throbbed. Some drunken lord shouted something at the dancers.

The man who had announced the play came back onstage, and warned the audience that the next scene would leap back in time. Some of the men around me seemed confused by this. They were used to stories that begin at the beginning and end at the end.

'The years peel away,' he told us, 'until we can watch the birth of Shishupal, a birth unlike any that came before.'

The Chedi King Shishupal was born with three eyes, and four arms. The child the actors were using was perhaps only a year old, and I wondered if he belonged to the Rukmini dancer. He cooed and burbled, a third eye painted on his forehead, and two extra arms in balsawood fastened to his back. On stage, the King and Queen grew mad with fear. They held the child and swayed like reeds.

'What evil omen is this?' they sang. 'To have a baby so deformed?'

They were ignorant like country people sometimes are. Afraid, they prepared to drown their child in the river. They carried him to the brown, rushing waters of the River Betwa (a stretch of fabric rippling in the hands of two stage helpers) but as they lifted him over the edge of the bank, a mysterious voice as deep as cracking marble called out.

'Stop, you cruel parents!' the voice boomed, and people in the audience jumped. 'The baby's deformities are not permanent,' it said, 'but they will disappear only when the child is touched by the man who will one day be his death.'

The King and Queen looked at each other as that final word echoed around the hall. They returned to the palace determined to cure their newborn. They invited every man they knew to touch the child Shishupal and see whether he would become normal. As the actors came and went in different costumes, each touching the child in turn, I stole a sideways glance up at Magha. He was chewing one of his fingernails, the sharp angles of his face lit up by firelight. One of his thick eyebrows was twitching. The scene went on for a long time, and it wasn't until Krishna stepped onstage to much applause that the truth about the little boy's fate was known.

I liked this troupe's Krishna especially. He had a strong but peaceful expression on his face. When he took his baby cousin on to his lap, there was a crescendo of drums. The crowd laughed at first, since the carved balsawood limbs dropped from young Shishupal with a clatter, and his third eye only partially rubbed off under his mother's sleight of hand. Krishna looked at the child guiltily, as if he was a broken pot.

The laughter died down in patches, until everyone onstage, everyone in the audience, was silent. If the prophecy was true (which, in stories, all prophecies are), then one day Krishna would kill the infant that he now held in his arms. Shishupal's mother raised her hands slowly to her mouth.

'Don't fear me,' the hero declared, getting down on his knees. 'Shishupal is my family. No matter what, I will pardon your little son even one hundred insults.'

Magha looked down at me, and pointed at the stage as if driving his finger through a plank of wood. I nodded as though I understood.

The dancers fled from the stage, and the years gathered like clutter: trees burst through rocks; rivers ebbed and flowed, until Shishupal was a grown man again, strong and handsome. When he spoke, I realised that he had been the deep-chested voice from behind the stage, that in the strange universe of the dance, he was the one who had saved himself from the waters. His hair flowed out from beneath a golden-painted crown on his head; his chest was rubbed with oil and he sang beautifully.

Promised in marriage to King Shishupal, Princess Rukmini was heartbroken and furious. She secreted away some paper and a stylus, and wrote a long and beautiful letter to Krishna. She begged him to come and rescue her before the wedding. Forgetting the prophecy, Krishna rode to Magadha and abducted her on the night before her wedding. On stage, Krishna's chariot was a decorated handcart with an umbrella on top. An impressive touch. As the lovers rode away, Rukmi and Shishupal chased after them, gnashing their teeth, firing streamers that were supposed to be arrows after the escaping lovers.

At this point, Magha noticed that I'd finished my wine, and snapped his fingers at the servant, who hurried over with another. My head began to swim as I took a sip of the second cup. Scene blurred with scene, and before I knew it, the play had reached its climax. The wise man Yudhisthira was holding a sacrifice to return balance to the world, which he would do by making himself its king. In the future loomed the greatest war ever known, that would strip the earth to its bones and lead to the deaths of all the epic's heroes. None of them seemed particularly worried.

Yudhisthira's crown was far too large for his head and the wiry frame of his body.

'Without my friend Krishna, we would not be here today,' he told the assembled crowd. 'He is the noblest man alive.'

This is where the trouble began. For a few moments of peace, Yudhisthira inhaled incense as he spoke, and his words of blessing curled in blue ribbons of smoke from his mouth.

Suddenly, there was a cry of fury from the back of the theatre, and everyone jumped, turning their heads to look. Shishupal had crept up and hidden behind the audience. Now he was howling like a wounded bull. Magha swung around and laughed out loud, slapping the arm of his throne in appreciation. Shishupal looked murderous. His lips were curled, his eyes wild, holding one crooked finger out at Krishna. He staggered forward and people scattered out of his way, jumping up from their seats.

'You wily, filthy cowherd!' he screamed. 'You sit like an undeserving dog and lap up the praises of this man – you lecher, you pedlar of lies, you thief and dishonourable peasant!'

It went on and on as he stumbled towards the stage. Insult after insult. The actor was so absorbed in his part that beads of spittle flew from his lips as he shout-sang at Krishna, as he broke into more and more dance the closer he got to the stage, finally whirling like a leaf in a series of river eddies.

'You dog, you thief, you elephant turd!'

His insults fell to the beat of the drums, and Krishna counted on his fingers as each one came. Then, with the drummers raging against the skins and the crowd shifting in their cushions, Krishna counted Shishupal's hundredth insult. He smiled, and raised his golden discus to the sky. Then he hurled it with a lightning movement at the King – who staggered, struck – and sank his head into the neck of his heavy robes. The illusion was convincing. The performer produced a small melon through some sleight of hand, and dropped it to the ground where it bounced and then rolled into the firelight. I saw that it was painted with a face, with gnashing fangs and fiery eyes. The crowd laughed, then cheered. Magha smoothed the hair in one of his thick eyebrows, deep in thought.

Blessings to Krishna made the air hum. It was over, and servants began to heap sand on the fire. People filed out on either side as smoke filled the hall, and Magha turned to me with bright points of light in his eyes.

'Excellent, wasn't it? They are such talented performers, such passionate dancers. And that Rukmini – what a beautiful girl!'

'It was magical, my lord.'

He nodded.

'It's such a wonderful story. Which is your favourite part? The birth? The abduction? The sacrifice?'

'It's so hard to choose, my lord.'

'I can't wait to hear the first part of the poem, once it's translated,' he said. 'Three weeks, isn't it? Just under three weeks until I can read the first instalment?'

'That's right, my lord.'

He took a deep breath, then, and clapped his hands once, pursed his lips.

'Wonderful. Asanka,' he said, but didn't look at me. His eyes flitted after the lords who were crowding out through the door, and waited until the last of them had left the room before speaking.

'Asanka, will you come to the throne room tomorrow morning, before the first bells? I have something very . . . sensitive that I want to ask you.'

I felt my skin crawl.

'Sensitive, Your Majesty?'

'That's right. A rather delicate matter. About your queen.'

My heart gave a little skip. My queen. Queen Dayani, who I had last seen walking to the arms of her doomed husband. A noblewoman in every way, tutored in mathematics and logic, a lover of poetry and music. A lady whose habit it was to murmur each of my lines after they had been sung, and roll them on her tongue like candied jujube berries. Did this mean she was alive?

'Of course, Your Majesty,' I said. 'Whatever you wish.'

Magha stood up and cracked the bones in his neck, then swept past me and across the room.

'Good, good. We are friends, after all? Tomorrow, Asanka. Before the bells.'

He left, and let the doors swing shut behind him. The boom they made sounded around the empty hall that smelt of ash, where I sat and steadily began to tremble.

I hardly slept at all that night. When I went to see Magha the next morning, I found him waiting for me in the throne room, doing nothing except leaning against the balcony and watching the sun rise over the city. The air still held the cool of dawn.

'Asanka!' he said as I entered. 'Good to see you again, as always.'

I bowed. Magha seemed nervous.

'How's your health?' he asked. 'How's your family?' and other such questions, but he didn't seem to hear the answers. Then he paused for some time, saying nothing. His eyes wandered across the sun-gold rooftops and the smoke plumes of cooking fires and fluttering prayer flags in the city below.

After some time, he said, as though with little thought, 'I've spent the last week investigating the loyalties of the court, you know: speaking with all the lords, testing their resolve for change. I found many who were stuck in the old ways, clinging to their worship of rotten old teeth and so on. All of these crooked places, I've made smooth.' He made a motion like flattening a crinkled cloth. 'You won't have seen those men at the theatre yesterday.'

A pregnant silence stretched out for some time.

'But the pretender queen, the empress consort,' he said. 'You might wonder why I've left her alive.'

I said nothing at first, so great was my joy. The Queen was still breathing. Even now, so many years later, the idea seems so fragile, so beautiful that it's difficult to write down. When I heard it from Magha himself, I felt as though a tiny lamp had flickered to life in a dark corner of my chest. I tried not to smile, cautious of betraying a weakness.

'That's most merciful of you, Maharaja.'

He laughed a little, turned and showed his teeth.

'You know, I heard stories of her beauty from as far away as Kalinga province,' he said. 'The travellers that passed through our palace used to describe her as the equal of Sita. They were right – isn't she beautiful?'

I tried to keep my expression stable. I said nothing. Queen Dayani only ever appeared publicly for important festivals like the New Year, Vesak, Poson and Deepavali, and of course remained veiled. I assumed that these travellers had in fact been Magha's spies. He ignored my silence, and began listing similes.

'Her eyes are like lotus flowers,' he said, starting with the old favourites. 'Her bottom lip is like a young mango leaf.'

As he spoke, the temple bells began to sound.

'My older brothers,' he said, 'all have queens of great beauty. A king of Lanka, such a jewel itself, needs an equal jewel as a queen.' He looked out over the city and stretched himself against the parapet like a cat. 'Her eyes have made me mad. She has devoured me, Asanka, but she constantly rebuffs me.'

'Is that so, my lord?'

'Sadly, yes. I hear that you share some confidence with the lady, Asanka, that she speaks to you often. Is this true?'

'I've spoken to her on occasion,' I said, wondering who had given up such information. 'The Queen was always kind to me.'

'Do you think she could ever return my love?'

'It's not impossible,' I croaked, and wondered if anyone had ever told him the truth about anything.

'Speak to the Queen, poet. Use the magic of your words, if necessary. You must have wooed a lady or two in your time, am I right?'

'Only my good wife, my lord.'

'Of course. But I'm sure you're up to the task. Or at least, I hope so. I've told the Queen that I'll marry her, and a king's word is law,' he said, wistfully. He was still gazing out over the balcony, watching the dawn over his kingdom. 'But I'd prefer her to love me. The men outside will take you to her.'

I stepped outside and walked with two large swordsmen through the palace's cool patchwork of light and shadow, men who looked like they could hurt you with their eyes, just with the things they'd seen. Servants jumped out of our way with heads bowed, and even lords avoided my gaze as I went. I tried to look like a prisoner, rather than a messenger. I was to see the Queen – I held on to this fact – I was to see her alive and breathing, but making my way to the Queen's chambers, Magha's orders weighted me as if I were dragging a plough, and I listened to the footsteps of the soldiers as we went, like the beating of a wooden heart.

Queen Dayani was being held in her summer chamber, on the palace's eastern wing. Here the tamarind trees sent their branches into the terraces of the lower floors, and somehow no one had cared to cut them. I remember you telling me once about a group of monkeys that had climbed up those trees and into the palace in search of food, and how Shona had chased them with a switch until his face went purple and he had to lie down flat on the floor.

A pair of soldiers with wide-brimmed helmets guarded the Queen's door. They were inspecting the leaf carvings on its surface, spears slack by their sides, and they didn't see us coming. As we approached, one of the warriors escorting me shouted what was clearly a curse, and the men jumped back into position with their weapons at their chests. They unfixed the latches and pulled the door open, bowing and mumbling to their superiors on either side of me.

It was dim inside, but I could see the Queen right away, sitting by the window and peering through the slits in the bolted shutters. She was dressed in the white of mourning, her face veiled. When I stepped inside, the soldiers stayed outside to berate and strike the slacking guards, and did nothing when I closed the door behind me.

'Asanka—' she murmured, in disbelief.

'My Queen,' I began, bowing as low as I could.

I noticed that the small plants she used to grow in the light from her balcony had dried to paper without sunlight.

'Asanka, how are you – how did you—' she began, but then she seemed to laugh and sob at the same time. 'I expected the worst. I thought—'

'I'm not hurt, my lady.' I burnt with shame and anger, and wished suddenly, above all else, for a lie that made my situation seem less absurd. I could think of nothing. 'It seems the Kalinga is a reader of poetry,' I said, with a sense of defeat. 'He wants me to translate a poem for him.'

Beads blossomed in the corners of her eyes. She hadn't slept. On the wall a painting of Rukmini's marriage to Krishna caught the light in eggshell blue and gold leaf, and the half-smiling faces of all the tiny courtiers seemed to mock me and the message I brought.

'Asanka – they killed him,' the Queen said. 'They killed my husband. They cut out his eyes.'

'I heard, my lady. I'm sorry. He was a great man,' I said. 'Those who witnessed it – they said that he died well. Bravely. He'll be in the gardens of heaven now, waiting for us.'

She wiped her eyes with the hem of her sari and looked up at me for a long time.

'You know,' she said then, 'when I was growing up, the person I admired most in the world was Queen Lilavati, the old queen. She was the first *mahesi* of King Parakramabahu the Great, do you remember her?'

'She was before my time in the city, my lady. But I heard stories, in the countryside.'

'You should have seen her. She was so beautiful in her day, and so strong. It's been nearly thirty years since the Great King died, and since then she sat on the throne three times.

The first queen to rule Lanka in a thousand years, and she did it three times. Did you know that?'

'I had some idea, my lady. An apprentice of mine mentioned it.'

'Ruled three times, deposed three times. And each time, she used her wit and her strength to survive. When my husband deposed her, and made me his first *mahesi*, do you know what I thought? I thought, "I'll be just like her." How stupid does that sound?'

The Queen screwed up her face, and brushed away another rush of tears.

'It doesn't sound stupid at all, my lady.'

'I was just a girl. A child. You know, all the omens of my life fell together favourably,' she said, with delirious exhaustion in her voice. 'I was married to a man I grew to love. I was his first *mahesi*, a queen, and I never wanted for anything.'

I knew even then that telling one's life as a story is a sign of thinking towards its end.

'First *mahesi*, and last *mahesi*, my lady. You were his only queen,' I reminded her, and she hid her head in the crook of her arm. People were always gossiping about King Parakrama, and his appetite for only a single wife. They gossiped

that he preferred the touch of beautiful young men.
that he was a eunuch, castrated during the war for the crown.
that his life of peace and poetry had weakened that same organ for the rigour of married life.

I wished that I'd had the courage to ask him the truth before he died. The Queen hadn't spoken for some time, and I could see that she was holding back tears.

'I've always been one of those who sow their life like a seed.' She looked up at me. 'This Kalinga brute – what did he say to you?' There was surprising calm in her voice. Her eyes wandered across the room, dark pools of rainwater. 'I've been waiting to die,' she said.

I hesitated, and looked at the floor.

'Magha wishes to marry you, my lady. It seems he wishes you to be his wife.'

She closed her eyes. A warm breeze blew through the spice garden below the window: even at that height, cardamom swept through the room, spiralling up from the city on warm updraughts, along with the smell of prawns, freshwater crab and burnt mustard oil. Here, the smells of ordinary life seemed aberrant and stale.

'I told him I'd marry an elephant before I married him,' she replied with a resolve I'd never heard in her voice.

'He'll kill you if you don't, my lady,' I said.

'He'll have to. With his cruelty, and his sneering voice and those hideous eyebrows. He'll have to.'

I said nothing more. I wanted to praise her bravery and plead against her foolishness all at once, but I saw then that either would be useless. I know you always admired the Queen. I think all the girls who worked in the palace did, and many of the men. As I stood there, one memory came back to me with such clarity: three years before, standing before the King for the first time, with the Queen sitting beside him and all the lords gathered round. Just a village boy, trying to keep the shaking from my voice as I sung one of my inconsequential village poems, so small in the throne room's vaulted cavern. The way she leant over to her husband and touched his arm, as if to say 'he's the one'.

'It's been the greatest honour to write for your husband,' I said. 'And for you, Your Majesty. I know if it weren't for you . . .'

But one of the guards who had escorted me opened the door then, letting in a strip of light.

'Come,' he said, tugging at his beard, and I bowed goodbye to the Queen. She tipped her chin up at the foreign soldier, and pursed her lips.

On my way back through the palace, I felt as heavy as if I were carrying a stone. By the time I returned to Magha, two of his servants had arrived, and were picking him for lice. An army on the march, I'm told, is worse than the poorest slum for the filthy crawling creatures. He sat on his cushion and watched me come towards him as the fine comb shuddered through his hair.

'Asanka! How did your meeting go?'

'My lord, the Queen has given me her decision,' I told him, in a tone that I thought would convey my regret.

Perhaps it was chance, or perhaps he turned his head slightly as I spoke, but either way it was at that moment that the sharp edge of the comb nicked his ear. He sucked air between his teeth.

'Imbecile!' he bellowed at the man holding the comb, and sprang up from his cushion to strike him once with the palm and once with the back of his hand. The man didn't duck or raise his hands, only let out a whimper as the two sharp cracks echoed in the rafters. The King's face had turned pale as dough, and he sat back down as the men continued their work.

'They've got one task,' he said to me, and the struck man sniffed as the marks rose on his cheeks and he continued to comb with shaking hands. 'What were you – ah, forgive me. What did the Queen say? Were your words beautiful enough to win her over?'

I felt a great rising terror.

'She said – my lord, the Queen said that she would marry you. I convinced her that, in time, she might come to love you as she came to love her husband.'

His smile showed all of his pearly teeth, his face a crinkled mask. I didn't know what I was saying. I would need time – time to sort out this mess.

'The Queen, my lord – she asked for only one thing. That she be allowed a period of mourning, to honour her vows in the proper way.'

'How long?' he asked, as the pinching thumb and forefinger of the unbeaten servant worked their way down the parting in his hair.

'She asked for – I believe it was two weeks, Maharaja.'

'Excellent, then it's settled!' he announced, clapping his hands once. His eagerness made me think I could have asked for more.

'Is there anything else I can do for you?' he said then, with genuine graciousness. 'Anything to make your work easier? Any pleasure you desire? Women?' He paused. 'Boys?'

Opportunities would arrive in those days like apples falling in the dark. I didn't know him, then, and took the chance.

'My lord, your soldiers – they are always taking note of things, writing down people's names. I see the scribes with their books whenever they take someone away.'

The King looked coolly at me, and his eyes flashed wider for just an instant. My voice wavered.

'I request a guarantee of safety for my apprentices. They wish only to learn, and I can assure you they're loyal to your just rule. All of them. Their names are written in a roster. Shona, the Chief of the King's Stores, will have it, so you can add them to the list of those loyal to you.'

Magha tilted his head forward as the servants combed the nape of his neck. 'Is that all?'

'Yes, my lord.'

He looked at me from under his lids. 'Hm. Of course, no harm will come to anyone on that list.'

‘Thank you, my lord.’

He stretched out his neck, then his arms and shoulders, and the servant with the red cheeks began to oil his scalp.

‘And so finally I will be like Rama after all,’ he said, with a note of satisfaction, and a laugh like crockery crushing into a wall. ‘Come to Lanka to claim my wife. I’ll have to send word to my father and all my brothers, that they should sail here to join me in celebration.’

On my way out, I told myself that I’d done well. Once the Queen had grieved for her husband, I thought, once the two weeks were up, she would marry the new king. Perhaps by then the chieftains would have massed their forces, retaken the city and driven the foreigners into the sea. Perhaps a greater army would land from the Tamil lands to save us, or put us in different chains. Perhaps one of Magha’s own men would kill him. Two weeks, after all, can pass like two years in Polonnaruwa.

That night, I tried to begin my translation, but I wrote nothing. In fact, I think it took me three days to actually begin the translation of the *Vadha*. I remember the day it happened most vividly and painfully, and I’m sure you remember it too. If you ever read this, it’ll be strange for you to see your memories through another person’s eyes.

The air was heavy with the mists of the late season. It was the day of my first class since King Parakrama’s death, and I dreaded the thought of trying to teach my apprentices in the afternoon: all of their faces slack, with empty eyes, dreaming of girls they knew and trees they wanted to climb. I tried to work through the morning, but I was distracted, and went to the lake. On my way out, I absent-mindedly left my palette by the window, and when I returned from bathing I found my ink dried to that black, grainy paste. Since Pushpakumara the ink-maker had fled, I needed to go to the storeroom and mix some more myself. This would be the perfect opportunity, I thought, to add your name to my list of apprentices.

I headed to the shaded wing where Master Shona kept all his records in neat and well-ordered piles. Shona, the Chief of the King's Stores, was the kind of man who had served twenty kings and queens, all of whom came and went while he sat and kept his books, measured the distances between villages and grazing lands, tracking the tributes owed between the castes, the yield of crops and workshops and brick-makers. His beard was as long as my arm, and he had pale, watery eyes.

'Another apprentice, Master Asanka?' he said to me when I told him why I was there. 'Is this really the time for new commitments?'

He gave me the book anyway, and I wrote your full name in small, cramped letters so that Shona wouldn't be able to read it.

'Poets,' he said wistfully as I left, 'always choose the worst times for everything.'

I left satisfied, and headed to the scribes' storehouse for ink materials. It was only a short walk from Shona's office, but the streets were busy, and the heat made me dread being close to other bodies. There were soldiers everywhere, too, and elephants, so I took my preferred route through the garden of Nandana, which bloomed in the wedge between the west wall of the citadel and the Grand Canal. There, only members of the court and palace workers were allowed, and the master of gardens would never have let an elephant trample all over the manicured lawns. On my way, enjoying the shade of the palms, the white champaka and mango, I saw you sitting in the pavilion, with a large jar of water leaning against the flame tree's trunk. I walked over to you. Your remaining curls of hair wrote the whorling symbols '*va*' and '*dha*' in Sanskrit countless times across your shorn head.

'Sarasi,' I began, but you didn't look up at me. I sat down, but still you didn't move. You were rigid next to me so that when I put my arm around you, the embrace was clumsy, and after some time I let it fall. To my horror, tears began to slide down your jaw, lining up like the beads of an abacus.

'Sarasi,' I said again, although I had nothing to follow this.

'In the marketplace,' you said at last. 'His soldiers—'

'Whose?' I asked stupidly.

'Magha!'

Your eyes flashed at me, and the growling syllables bounced off the tall citadel walls. Your eyes were stones.

'He's digging defensive works along the road,' you said. 'Diverting canals, building a camp for his soldiers near the river. They've been rounding people up to dig the earth – the poor, the low castes first – but anyone fit to work is being taken.'

'*Anay*, Sarasi, you mustn't worry about his evil,' I said. 'There's nothing we can do. So long as we tread quietly and carefully, we won't be harmed.'

Your voice cracked.

'What if I don't want to tread quietly, Asanka? I saw them punishing the families of the men who resisted them. They're flogging them in the Sal Bazaar right now. Have you ever seen a child being flogged, Asanka? A little child?'

'No.'

You brushed the tears from your eyes, and seemed ashamed of them.

'I hear you're writing a poem for him,' you said, and I felt guilt and panic flow into me like a stream of scalding water. 'Is that what you mean by treading quietly?'

I searched your face for some pity. Through the trees and hanging clusters of flowers, a Tamil servant was setting little lamps afloat in a stone bowl of water. I felt myself drift like one of those lamps. Untethered.

'There's nothing I can do, Sarasi. King Parakrama – they made me watch him die. I was there. They cut out his eyes, Sarasi. Magha said I had to work for him, or he'd cut off my head.'

You listened as I went on, and said nothing. When my words ran dry, and I finally looked up at you, I saw in you what I had always suspected: that your taste was for braver men, and that I was too much of a coward for you ever to love me.

'Do you know what they say during harvest season, where I'm from,' you said, 'to men who talk too much and do too little in the fields? They say "poetry makes nothing happen".' You laughed, but the sound had a bitter edge. 'Do you think that's true?'

'Of course it's true,' I said. 'Poetry's beautiful. It whiles away the hours. It tricks people, thrills them. It makes us forget our lives for a few minutes – but that's all.'

You looked up at me with a face empty of all hope and happiness.

'Is that what you've always thought? All the time you've been teaching me?' you said, and I felt a little ball of anger ignite inside me. I flicked the jar leaning against the tree. A hollow clay noise.

'It's just my trade,' I said, regretting it instantly. 'Just like you carry water for the king, I write him poetry because neither of us are exactly heroes, are we?'

You took a sharp intake of breath as though I'd splashed you with cold water, and stood up.

'Sarasi,' I said. But you were already going, swinging the jar on to your back. I was left alone with the sounds of the garden, the footsteps of soldiers walking along the high walls and the first scatterings of afternoon rain. I knew it was useless to chase you, and after some time I remembered the ingredients for my ink, and left.

I was angry with you at first – I remember that. I thought bitterly that I was as much of a slave as the men being dragged from their homes to break rocks and carry earth in the sun and rain. I believed it, too.

Soon the dark of the storehouse saved me from the wet heat outside: the rows of pots, the glass ampoules catching tiny points of light, the sheaves of curling paper. A place of calm. I turned my anger against Magha, against the gods, and against that bastard Pushpakumara, who had fled and left me to do my own ink-making. The only consolation was that I didn't have to see his face, distended and pustuled like a bitter gourd, or talk him into giving me the right ink.

'I'm sorry, Master Asanka, no soot and goose-fat oil. Not this week,' he would say, or 'If you want more dummala resin you'll have to talk to Shona. Do you eat it with your rice?'

I took about a hundred carobs of charcoal in a cloth, and cursed his name as I spooned a generous amount of dummala oil from the large urn in the corner, even a little of the expensive kakuna oil to thin the mixture out – something Pushpakumara would never have allowed me, as he used it to keep the leeches off his ankles.

I went home and dropped the ingredients in my room, and went to bathe again before the rain got too heavy. Soon, I was sure of another explanation for your behaviour: you had grown tired of me. Your interest in me had died, and you wanted any excuse to leave me for ever. I thought long, tortuous thoughts about what a fool I had been, to have thought for even a moment that you could love me.

When it was time to teach my apprentices, I walked to the workshop I used to lease near the south-west tank wall. I entered its warm dark with my sarong steaming and sticking to my body, and found the place empty. They'd all fled, I suppose – along with most of the rich families of the district: Ainkaran, who always spilled his ink stone on purpose so he could go to the well to wash up; Mayuran with the limp; Sampat, who couldn't recite anything from memory without crossing his eyes. All of them. I waited for some time, in case any of them turned up. Then I took some paper, a new cloth and a palette of dried ink I'd left there, swept the floor and went.

At dusk, when the day flowers in the canal began to close and the rain thinned, I went to your room and peered through the curtain. Adhi, the old Tamil woman who lived next door to you, had returned to the city, and she came to the door, pursed lips, red-brown sari.

'She's not here!' she hissed at me, and I might have thought this a lie, had she not begun immediately to scold the two of us. She implied that I came from a village that had forgotten its festivals, that the ghosts of your parents cursed us from their stones, and she turned back inside, murmuring some words to do with your people's complex ideas about chastity.

'Where is she?' I called after Adhi's retreating form, 'where does she go when she's not here?'

But she didn't come back to the door. You slept in that cramped room most nights, but some days I would see you walking southward out of the city and through the fields, becoming a bright-coloured dash on the landscape, then disappearing into the trees. Sometimes I was sure that if I followed you through the forest, I would find a village where your husband lived and a clutch of smiling children, mouths greasy with butter. It wouldn't surprise me. After all, there are all kinds of reason for a girl of your station to attach herself to a court poet.

As I passed back through Nandana and the low sunlight that fell through its foliage, I splashed my hand in the lotus pool to disturb its calm.

I returned to my villa and lit a dried fruit skin to keep the evening insects away. I sat cross-legged on my writing cushion, put my elbows on the table. I'd wasted too much time already. With my new ink materials, I began the usual ritual, thinking of other things. While the oil spread to fill the palette, I crumbled a nugget of charcoal, crushed it to powder in the cleft of the grinding stone. I spored the dust across the gleam of the oil, thickened the black until it was the black of a deep cave. I breathed in the comforting smoky smell of the ink, and tried to hear the wails of flogged children among the sounds of the city at dusk. There was nothing, only the barks of dogs, the hoof beats of patrolling soldiers.

I stared at the first blank leaf, and traced its leathery veins with my stylus. I always do this when I'm lost at my desk. The *Shishupala Vadha* was fanned open, propped against the wall. It was magnificent, such a fine manuscript. The penmanship was perfect in each sharp Sanskrit letter, all lined up like demons' teeth, like a forest of spears turned earthward. The human and non-human figures of its illuminations, the patterns of curling vines and flowers caught the light the way only gold can.

I thought of what you'd told me in the garden: 'poetry makes nothing happen'. I said it to myself over and over, a new mantra. I stretched the muscles in my stylus hand. Since I still had no appetite for writing, I began to read the poem first, and since I hadn't read anything so rich since my days of study at the college in the hills, I gorged myself on all seventy-five of the first parva's verses. It was just as I remembered: brilliant and ornate, a great hall filled with echoes.

It's strange how language moors itself to memory. The sharp downward strokes of each Sanskrit letter – how can such a thing take me back to the thunder of waterfalls and the smell of kuduru wood masks? For a moment as I hummed a line, I felt I was walking the rust-coloured path to my old college. I thought of Tamil, of the words that would replace this poem, and these sounds brought me different memories of your voice, of the folk rhymes that King Parakrama would murmur to himself as he bathed with his harem girls, of the songs the cart drivers sing on the roads. Of the allotment children – such a distant memory – and the games we played.

I read on and whispered some of the lines to myself, to feel them against my tongue, cool as pearls.

'The snowy mountains.' I whispered the words to myself. I've never seen snow, but I've often dreamt about it. A blanket making silence of everything.

From the very beginning, I knew that translating the *Shishupala Vadha*, with its grand stanzas of marble and gold, would be impossible. There are so many languages in the world: Tamil, spoken by the countless people in the south of the mainland and what seems like half the people of Lanka; Sanskrit, spoken only by priests and philosophers. There is the Kalinga language of our conqueror, and Sinhala, spoken only on our island. There are the languages Muslim sailors speak, and the languages of the Vedda wild men who live in the deep jungle, all the languages of the tribes that stretch across the wide pan of the earth, each with its own taste and rhythm. A poem written to be beautiful in one language shouldn't be bent and buckled to fit into another. That seemed obvious to me.

For instance, when Sri Magha describes the heat and fury of the battle in the nineteenth parva, you can hear the breathlessness of war hiss from every line: '*rasahava*', the sound of exhalations from beneath a helmet, breath wetting bronze. The songs of blades and the hooves of the horses, the elephant footfalls and conches all clamour from the tumultuous '*sakarana narakasa kayasada dasayaka*', but these lines are part of a verse that can be read as a palindrome in all directions – not just left and right, but up and down as well – the most intricate poetic device ever created.

sakāranā nārakāsa
kāyasāda dasāyakā
rasāhavā vāhasāra
nādavāda davādanā

It translates into Tamil as: 'Loving battle, the army was formed of allies who struck down their various enemies, the cries of the best horses contesting with the music of instruments.'

It makes me feel ill even to tell you this. What about all the tortuous verses in which each line is a palindrome? What about the verses that can be rearranged into the shape of a sword, a drum, a jagged crack of lightning, and contain different hidden messages? What about the verse written in the form of a wheel, with 'This is the *Shishupala Vadha*, a poem by Magha' hidden among the spokes?

I would translate the poem. Certainly I would – just as Queen Dayani would surely marry the new king. Because everyone does what they can to survive.

And so I began. The story of the *Vadha* starts with Krishna, the best of men. He is the mighty god Vishnu the preserver, born as a mortal, come to protect the world. One day, a sage called Narada descends from the thunderclouds as a falling star. He is a pale-skinned man with golden, braided hair, wearing a black antelope hide. Krishna meets him; they sit on their high seats and praise each other. The sage says that

Ravana, the monstrous and powerful demon king of Lanka, Ravana the grand evil of the *Ramayana* and scourge of the three worlds, has been reborn as a man named Shishupal. 'The character always follows the man,' he says: Shishupal is a cruel and arrogant king.

Before meeting Kalinga Magha, I might have based my Shishupal on Ravana himself, who built his golden city among our southern mountains. I could have borrowed phrases from the Tamil *Ramayana* that Magha loved, worked hard, and those six months might have passed like days to me. But I began to write in Tamil that night, and between the words I scratched in my finest calligraphy, a picture of King Shishupal emerged, with a smooth voice and pearly teeth, a smile that cracked his whole face, and thick, black eyebrows that snaked like pepper vines across his forehead.

I am Rukmi

Do not hiss! I can see that curl in your lip, the readying of a clucking tongue. You've heard the tale before, fine – you've heard about my sister Rukmini and how Shishupal died; but don't judge a man before you've heard it from his own lips. The truth is that I am helpless, a victim of a strange and frightening disorder. Sit, cross your legs, and permit me to explain.

I was born prince of Vidarbha in Kundinapuri. It was a good life, but I was restless, and enjoyed escaping into the countryside. I would climb the palms that lined the goat paths and pretend that they were the masts of great ships, Vidarbha's basalt rock formations like the backs of sea monsters. On clear days I could see all the way out to the Rikshavat mountains, blue and wreathed in cloud.

The first time my disorder surfaced, I was playing alone on the banks of the Wainganga, building a city from mud with the shells of freshwater crabs as the gates and windows of the palace, mud-hoppers as my teeming citizens. Perhaps I was pretending that it was Indraprastha the Golden. It was mine, anyway. Some mud-hoppers I would honour, collecting them in my hand and placing them within the palace – others, I would place in the poor district of my city, returned them if they ever hopped over its high walls.

As I played, a gang of older children emerged from the jungle and began to taunt me, throwing handfuls of mud, and then stones that struck me, crumbled my kingdom and brought hot tears popping to my eyes. Mud-hoppers danced in the muddy pile where the city had stood, and I could no longer tell which were the rich, which were the poor. We were far from the nearest village, and I knew that no parents would come crashing through the jungle to save me.

'Stop that!' I shouted up at them. 'I am the prince of Vidarbha! I will have the gate watch lock you in the dungeons!'

They did not believe me, of course. I clambered up the bank, muddied and bruised, with putrid palm fronds sticking to my hair, while the whole congregation laughed. Their leader, a tall boy with a dog-bite scar on his cheek, grabbed me and twisted my ear. He was much stronger than I was, and jeered: 'Look! Here is a cowardly monkey boy who claims to be Prince Rukmi! Look how he doesn't even fight back!'

You see, this is where the madness I spoke of took over. As the taunts and blows rained down on me, I lost control of my body. I swam deep in a lake of shadows, a cool black water from which I fought to surface. As though from far away, I heard the screaming of the children, and then the darkness sucked me under. After shrieking and thrashing through the worst nightmares I have ever experienced, I remember finding myself back in the palace, curled up and sweating beside my mother, father and sister, wondering at the strange darkness of my dreams.

The next morning, I shook myself awake, took an early daal and found my way back to that village by memory. I needed to return, to find out what had happened. I navigated the mesh of goat paths that criss-cross the forest, following the bulge of the

Wainganga until I found where the spires of my mud city had risen. There was a hush in the trees. I soon found the path by which the children had come, and followed it through the forest.

I could smell smoke before I reached the village, and a sickly stench in the air. When I got there, I found a funeral pyre burning. I remember the shiver, like moths' wings brushing up my spine. When I asked what had happened, the elders of the village wailed: with eyes pinched from weeping, they told me that wild animals had butchered a child the previous day. Some of the children recognised me from the river, and they ran behind their squalid huts or to their mothers, as though I were leprous. They told their parents that I had killed the child, that I had torn him apart with my bare hands and that as I did so, my face had 'changed'. They kept whispering a word that was created to be whispered: '*rakshasa*'. A demon.

The adults told them not to lie. Nothing but a tiger or a leopard could have done that to the poor child, they said. That was not the work of a boy.

When my sister Rukmini refused to marry my friend Shishupal, I lost control again. I felt the dark water rising around me, watching from afar as I threw her against the balustrade of her pagoda. I hit her in the stomach, and held her out over the pool as though I would throw her in. Then I saw my reflection. The village children's voices came back to me through all those years, vague as though from the very end of a dream, whispering that my face had 'changed'. They were right. It was grotesque. My eyes were wide and bulging, and a grin split my face from ear to ear.

After that, I remember nothing. It is worth noting that even in the throes of my madness, I did not beat my sister's face: presumably I still wanted her to remain attractive to her future husband. I am only glad that I did not do to my dear, stupid sister what I did to that boy on the bank of the Wainganga.

Now if there has to be a villain of this story, let it be whatever causes these fits in me. Whatever it is that wakes me some mornings with feathers and blood on my pillow. Or the time I awoke covered in lurid cuts and bruises, in a pool of my own blood, my mind heavy with dreams.

If you ever find out what it is that afflicts me, please tell the scribes what you know. Then maybe they can find a cure, or at least change their histories, and give me the peace I deserve. It is common for men to lose control of their demons. I am not evil. I am helpless, I think.

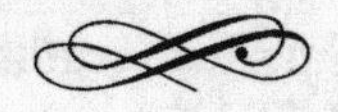

Chapter Five

In the dream, I'm standing in a city with walls snaking to both horizons; the spires are clustered like loom needles, the rooftops peppered with doves. This is Indraprastha, the great city of legend, but it's also Polonnaruwa, in the way that places in dreams can be two places at once, or one place but not at all. Here's Magha, but he's also King Shishupal. He's grinning with his perfect teeth and arching his black eyebrows as he drags Rukmini away to be married – she turns, her veil slips, and I see that she is Queen Dayani.

I still have this dream all these years later, though now one of the faces is different. Every time, I wake up believing that Krishna has arrived and sliced off Magha's head in a blaze of light, that only sand poured from the stump of his neck, and that everyone present laughed until tears made riverbeds of their cheeks.

The first time I woke from this dream, I blinked in the bar of morning sunlight that had been crawling up my bed, and realised immediately the true state of things. Three weeks after his arrival, the barbarous Kalinga still sat on the lion throne, and as I lay there and stared up at the flies crawling over the silk canopy of my bed, he was in the palace being readied for marriage. I wanted to scream curses and break things.

I'd heard nothing that whole two weeks, no sign or clue of whether Magha had met the Queen himself or what had passed between them. I knew that if she spat at him and sent him away, my life could become very difficult. Still, I heard nothing, and I wondered as the days went by if the Queen had accepted the chance I left open to her. Even when Magha himself finally announced a grand procession and ceremony for the occasion of his marriage, I couldn't predict what was going to happen. The realisation made me nauseous. My own invitation to the festival day came through a servant who called at the gate of my villa the next evening.

'The lord of the three Sinhala lands, the king who conquered the world, invites you to be present at his glorious wedding', and so on.

In the theories of Sanskrit poetry, the pandits speak of something called '*rasa*'. In Sanskrit this means 'juice'. It's the emotion of a poem that swallows up all smaller, more delicate feelings, that stands alone and cannot be broken down. You may not have heard of it. Perhaps if we had had another year together, we might have reached such a point in our lessons. My point is that I felt no such thing. That morning, perhaps the most uncertain of my life, I felt no single dominant feeling, but a great broth: the red juice of shame and fury; the blue juice of disgust; the grey of sorrow; the fresh green juice of love and pity; the black juice of terror. I thought almost every moment of the Queen, and the endless nights behind her sleepless eyes. I didn't believe that she'd go through with it.

I pulled myself out of bed, and performed all the dull ceremonies that allow us to face other people. I washed my hair in the basin and combed the expensive oil through it with my fingers. The sweet scent didn't improve my mood, though. I stepped into my newest cloth and knotted it tightly to my stomach, put on jewels, and all the while my throat was parched. I didn't pay attention to the view that morning, but all the time I bathed, the rooftops outside the window must have been turning from ochre to fawn to gold, scales on a lizard's back. The early bells began to ring.

Where were the omens? A gecko falling from a ceiling rafter, maybe, or a parrot perching upside down to nibble a thorn pod – something, at least, could have warned me.

I said goodbye to my wife, who sneered at my finery, and then I went down into the city. The procession was beginning in the Sacred Quadrangle, where the Vatadage temple once held the tooth of the Buddha, before the priests took it to be hidden.

When I drew close, I could hear the sounds of instruments and singers, and once I'd climbed the steps, I saw that a litter was waiting for me in front of the great temple. There were dozens of huge elephants, which sent shards of fear into my stomach. Ah, the elephants: huffing and shitting all over the holy ground. I suppose I should have expected them. Huge, hideous and cruel creatures.

I found out afterwards that all the servants had worked through the night to have the food ready for that day, so you didn't see the morning procession. It was as loud and bright as you can imagine, an expensive clamour with many skilled acts and chained beasts. My litter swayed along the parade route between the breathing hulks of two huge elephants, otherworldly in their jewelled caparisons, and I felt as if I would throw up from fear. I've heard many mahouts say that elephants are as clever as men, that in the shade of the forest they speak in their own language, that they remember all the endless winding elephant roads they cut through the trees, and even mourn their dead. The thought fills me with horror. I tried to keep my back to my seat so that no one in the crowd would see my face coated with sweat. I made a list of detestable things.

Pieces of grit and husk in a bowl of rice.
The western wall of a house.
An extremely fat person covered in hair.
Being caught in the rain so that your sarong and travelling coat stick together and steam.

Musicians, dancers, whip-crackers and soldiers followed ahead and behind, the music too joyful to bear, the beating of many demon drums.

Then I saw the Queen. She rode at the front, resplendent in a red-and-gold robe, though my view of her was obscured by the fan of peacock feathers that spread from the back of her throne. I couldn't see her face, but I felt my stomach plunge at the sight of her.

The city houses had been topped with thick thatches of new cadjan and hung with flags, the stones that lined the road were painted white. The soldiers chanted as they marched: 'Long live the king who conquered the world! Long live, long live!'

The whole lively mess of the procession moved south down the King's Highway, passing over the bridges of the southern districts, the canals named after the great rivers of India. You must have crossed them every day: the Yamuna, the Betwa, Kaveri, Godavari, Jayaganga. Soon my litter passed through the King's Gate and out into the countryside, under the succession of archways that frame the road south.

Thorny wood-apple trees cast starved shadows over the procession, and as we moved further from the city and the shore, we saw workers toiling in the verges on either side, clearing the ruined sesame fruit from the fields. I was told later that the rain had fallen in a sudden late deluge, and darkened the skins of the fruit – they had rotted, and that accounted for the fallow smell in the air. The workers didn't stop their work to watch our procession pass by.

It took an age to reach the wide grove of talipot palms where the poruwa platform stood, flanked by dragons. The grove was at the top of a slight elevation, and the countryside spread out in either direction through the trees, broken only by Gangadoni Hill across the river, and the white smudge of the city behind. Magha stood with one of his holy men beside a large fire, patient and smiling. He wore many jewels, with Vishnu's yellow clay markings surrounding a ruby *tilaka* on his forehead.

Throughout this final stretch of the march, I watched the feathers behind the Queen nod like courtiers with each movement of her mount; my litter moved close behind the animal as it followed the tug of its mahout's hooks around the crowd, and drew alongside the poruwa with steady, crunching steps. Soldiers surrounded the crowd in their wide-brimmed helmets, their histories of violence scrawled into their skins, their horses trembling as they smelt the water on the breeze. Servants scattered white sand and rice on the ground.

I expected the Queen to jump down from her mount at any moment, to make a run for the trees, or call on those still loyal to her husband to take up arms and cast out the invaders. I expected men to burst from the forest with bamboo spears and rescue her, to cut off the head of the Kalinga usurper and hold it up to the cheering crowd. I don't know what I expected, but I expected something.

I didn't watch as the Queen slowly dismounted. The whole time, I was staring into the black eye of her elephant, trying to see cunning in its depths. My litter lurched to a stop.

'What a happy matching,' muttered a Sinhala man behind me as I got down, pressed a massa into one of my bearers' palms and joined the crowd.

It seemed the ceremony would never end. It was long and exhausting and conducted in Sanskrit, which few but myself could understand. By the time the sun had reached its highest point, Magha and Queen Dayani were walking around the fire, containing it in a helix of their steps and throwing offerings of puffed mountain rice to the god in the flames.

'May this couple be blessed with an abundance of resources and comforts,' the priest droned. 'May this couple be eternally happy . . .'

Had I saved the Queen, or betrayed her? I changed my mind countless times as the ceremony dragged on. I watched her eyes, and they never once left the fire. Beside her, Magha's expression was complex, like a boy who has nearly won a game. Once the circling had stopped, the attending holy man asked them both to hold out their fingers, so they could be tied together with the golden thread. As Magha's finger hovered there, the Queen just stared, with an expression that said she would rather be tied to a tiger than to him. I felt my breath catch as time seemed to slow and the muscles around Magha's mouth twitched. But then she raised her finger, and the priest's shoulders sagged with relief. He tied the fingers together with hurried movements, as though the Queen might pull hers away at any point. The priest chanted a joyous hymn as he did it, but it hung in the air over our heads and turned mournful there like the sesame fruit rotting in the fields.

Once the ceremony ended, a feast was served: fried gram egg, I remember, giant prawns and peppered mangoes served on almond leaves. The platters and piles of food packets were brought from the city by a line of a hundred servants, and I saw with a rush that you were among their foremost, hair a little less patchy, but face no less hard than when I'd last seen you. The attendants ate little, and I certainly didn't eat. The Queen and Magha sat together at the apex of the crescent, but I couldn't see her eyes through her veil. I spent the time watching you and tracing the shell pattern stamped into my platter. When the chief of Naga Dipa pointed enquiringly at my empty plate, I said that I felt sick, which was true. He made the sign that wards off the upasagga plague, and returned to his gorging. I saw my face in the brass dish, and I did look sick.

After the feast, it was customary for all the lords to gather and congratulate Magha. They flocked around him and sang his praises, bowed to him, offered their wedding gifts. At one point, he sidled over to me, glowing with puffed-up pride.

'I'm so glad you could be here, Asanka,' he said. 'So glad. I assume the translation is progressing nicely?'

'Wonderfully, my lord. With only a brief pause to attend this day of joy.'

'A day of such joy,' he echoed, and beamed in gratitude as a lord from the gem fields of Ratnapura presented him with a polished coconut shell full of rubies.

'Permit me, my lord,' I said, looking around. 'Did your father and your brothers not come to see your wedding?'

Magha seemed not to hear me. He kept smiling as he took the rubies and touched the head of the lord from the south coast, but something cracked behind his face. He didn't speak to me after that, or look at me, although he laughed and talked with the other lords for a long time.

As the guests filed away from the wedding, I waited at the edge of the clearing. When you passed by in the line of servants, I began to walk subtly beside you.

'Sarasi,' I whispered. 'Please speak to me. Don't be so cruel.'

You didn't even look my way.

'Sarasi, where do you go those nights? Why don't you sleep in your room? If there's someone else . . .'

You hissed: 'Leave me alone!' and hurried away to the front of the line. I thought I heard you murmur the Tamil word for 'traitor', too, but perhaps this was only because I expected to hear it.

The *Shishupala Vadha* was waiting for me when I returned to my room. I sat down and tried to begin the second parva, but as the sun beat on and my room grew hotter, carving out the vast architectures of Tamil words became an unbearable task. The very design of the language, the aroma of the sounds, the way the emotion of the verse falls flat if the tempo and the tune of each word doesn't properly resonate – it all seemed a conspiracy to vex me. Soon my wife began deliberately performing noisy tasks in nearby rooms, and I suddenly reached a verse in which the poet mentions Shishupal's name. I found myself, almost before I knew what I was doing, making changes to the poem. Eyebrows. Smile. That laugh.

The late afternoon heat was intense – all the peacocks were taking shelter in the trees, querulous, calling me down to the lake. Dogs were sleeping in the shade. I was desperate to escape the close air of my villa, the chattering of cooking knives and bashing of pots and tuneless singing, to escape Polonnaruwa and the shadow of the two Maghas who now ruled my life. And I had to escape the poem, too – this poem that kept warping and changing like potter's clay in my hands. I didn't know what shape it might take if I stayed.

For all these reasons, I set out for the lake. It shocked me to find two spearmen posted at the gate to my villa, and they began to follow me as I walked down the King's Highway, shouldering their weapons, swinging their feet. One of them had a crescent scar on his cheek, and the other periodically spat great, wet blotches of red betel on to the floor, his teeth orange with chewing. I could feel their gazes drilling into my back as I walked, and I imagined what they might be ordered to do to me.

They followed me past craft shops and chanting halls, past one of those fashionable new manuscript workshops full of young apprentices bustling about the business of destroying poetry for ever, through market streets and the labyrinth of caravansaries loud with horses, along the high wall of the elephant stables, past the low archways of the servant quarter, and over the green waters of the Grand Canal, thick with a traffic of barges. All the while, I considered darting down any one of the alleyways we passed, into the palm-lined rookeries, but I didn't doubt that they would kill me if I tried.

Instead, I stopped at the stall of the old mango seller at the north edge of the servant quarter and joined the crowd waiting to buy one. The warriors sidled nearer as I waited for the seller to stop arguing with a man who wanted a discount. From atop an overturned wicker basket, a royal singer in plum-pink robes was chanting that old song to the crowd: 'The King takes taxes for the good of all, just as the sun takes spilt water.'

The spearmen came up close behind me, and I pricked up my ears to gain some clue about their plans for me. They were just talking to each other. Tamil was their common language, and the one with the deeper voice, whose mastic breathing identified him as the betel-chewer, was complaining about the heat.

'Any heat's better than the rains here,' said the other. 'All the way from the coast we couldn't light a fire. Every day, cold and wet, and now look at this. Where was this on the march? All those wild places we passed through, festering with spirits and bandits and animals, all hidden in the mist.'

The other one, the chewer, murmured in agreement, and I heard the squelch and spatter as his spit hit the ground.

'These people live like pigs,' he said.

Once I'd climbed the high bund of the tank near to the north wall and the lake yawed into view, the men fell back and watched me from the shade of a banana palm. I climbed down to the edge of a flat wash rock beneath the trees and ate my mango, trying to enjoy the cool that rose from the water. The tank was full after the rains, and bathers were scrubbing themselves in the shallows. Washermen, many of them from the palace, rinsed clothes along the banks beneath the walls, beating them against stones to dry and laying them out like colourful artworks.

I thought of bathing, but some distance away a herd of work elephants were rolling and plashing, their handlers swimming fearless among them. Over the water were the bright flashes of cranes, white-headed fish eagles. My thoughts followed them, forming themselves into couplets, but I had no words to fill the lines and they sat in my head like empty cups.

The King was dead. The Queen had married his murderer. And I had a hand in both these tragedies. You were right: everything was being turned upside down.

A pair of Sinhala fishermen passed by.

'*Aiyo!* Did you see the slave market of nobles? They brought them all out into the Sal Bazaar, beaten, wearing only cloths,' one was saying.

'What do you care about the nobles?' the other said. 'What about the monks? They killed a monk from my temple for singing the *dharma* in public. We found his body by the canal, with his vocal cords cut from his throat. Haven't you seen them sharpening the stakes outside the walls?'

I hugged my knees, tried to climb into myself. I remember there were plumes of smoke rising over the treeline on the far side of the tank; ten, twenty, breaking the line of blue hills in the distance. Too black to be campfires. I curled up against the stone, which was the temperature of flesh in the shade, and closed my eyes. More people passed by – fishermen, bathers and driftwood gatherers – and as I lay there I caught snatches of their conversations. Incomplete stories: torture and deliberate disfigurement, houses searched and looted and burnt, Sinhala and Tamil soldiers found hidden and executed where they cowered, the taking of slaves from the countryside and the city, everywhere disrespect for the Buddha, the looting of temples, image houses and monasteries. Some, like you, spoke in hushed voices about the flogging of children, some of the blinding of uncooperative monks, the hunting of rebel chieftains, the rape of the nobles' wives.

I tried to think about poetry. I crawled like an animal into deeper shade, and watched between my eyelashes as a kingfisher preened on a low branch. After a little while a group of Sinhala men began walking along the shore and climbing to collect the last of the coconuts that had clung on to their stems through the rains.

'Monaragama was burnt to the ground,' came a snatch of Sinhala, dotted with Tamil slang. 'All the men impaled along the sides of the roads, everyone else just thrown into the fires. Sahadevan the clothier says some of King Parakrama's deserters were hiding in the forest nearby, that the villagers fed them.'

'I knew a hunter from Monaragama,' the other said, with a lead voice.

There were so many smoke plumes. Had more begun to rise as I was lying there? I sat up, held my feet against the bottom of my thighs and watched them billowing from the earth like trees of smoke in a titanic forest. I think now that this was the omen, the one I missed. At the time, I thought only of how easily a breathing, laughing person – a person who told stories, who argued about the boundaries of chena land, who had secrets and loves – how easily they could turn into smoke and disperse on the wind. Whole villages of people. I find there are times in my life, and that day beside the lake was one of those times, when I sit and ask myself in all bewilderment, 'Well, how did you get here?'

I thought of my wife, on the day I told her that we were moving to the city. Her young face free of lines, her sarong wrapped in the countryside style.

'The city swallows people up,' she said to me. 'Swallows them whole.'

She cried for days, in secret. I could hear her sobbing at night as we travelled through the hills, with the rain hissing off the carriage roof and tapping at the walls. I comforted myself with the knowledge that we were going to the great city – the city so many speak about but never see – where the women are beautiful, the men are giants, and the buildings are taller than the trees. A new life.

When I saw Polonnaruwa for the first time – the white palace seven storeys high, with its thousand lights like the palace of the gods, the buildings of the city climbing on top of one another and leaning over the streets, the ecstasy of people and noise – I did not believe that such a place could exist. Sometimes, even after living there for three years, it still felt strange. Something would catch me off guard – the hubbub of a busy market day, the vertiginous feeling of standing beneath the palace walls, or the unending selection of fruits and vegetables and spices that could not be found all together in even the most abundant part of the forest – a moment would catch me off guard, and the city seemed like the strangest place in the world.

I thought of how at ease you seemed in Polonnaruwa, how well you knew its many languages, its hidden paths and signs. I thought about the day I first left you a poem written on a scrap of paper, how I left it in the folds of the banana leaf you'd laid down at my seating place so that it would fall out when you lifted it. Your eyes when you first met me outside the palace, in the shade of the palms. How you bowed, very formal, and said only 'Master Asanka.'

At the time, it put stones in my throat to think about you. I sat and watched the smoke rising from the forest and tried to find reasons to detest you.

You were lucky to have found me, I often thought, a rich, important man, and still young – and you, a girl without a dowry. Hadn't I saved you from Magha's men on the day the city fell? Hadn't I safeguarded your life by scoring your name into my roster of apprentices? How could you dare to spend such scorn on me? My anger gave way in waves to sorrow, and at those times I felt glad that for even a moment, you had found it useful to love me.

It was evening by the time I tore myself from the stone. The sun began to set without show over the lake, and soon it was what uneducated people call 'cowdust hour', when the merchants and farmers lead their bullock carts back to town and the red dust from their wheels fills the sky. Do you remember how beautiful it could be? People were leaving the tank, wringing water from their hair; the washermen were peeling clothes from the rock. Then I realised that soon Magha would be enjoying the pleasures of love, that his new queen would soon have to do him a wife's service, and I couldn't bear the place any more.

I cast my eyes back over the vast tank, from the lakeside audience hall and the island pavilion, up to where the lines of the hills rise across the water, tricking the eye, making mountains of the undersides of clouds. I swept my gaze round to the jungle in the north, and all the onion-domes of the stupas white above the trees, to where the walls levelled the high bund and hid the chaos of the city evening within. I tried to encompass it all in one movement of the head, all that Magha now owned, and I spun.

In Tamil, you don't have a word 'to have', just as in Sinhala we don't have a word 'to be'. Your language suggests mere association with the object: 'it is to me'. That's how I felt – that you had been 'to me' perhaps, but you had never been mine.

Magha's pair of warriors, leaning on their spears in the shade, were still waiting for me. They glared at me as I reached the top of the bund and turned back towards the gate; the chewer looked as though he had finished his bag of nuts, and was flexing his hand impatiently. I pretended not to notice them, but when I was a certain distance ahead, they began again to follow. A troop of ash monkeys leapt in the branches overhead, screeching and stretching their long limbs.

'Worse than dogs!' one of the men shouted, and I heard the whoosh as he swung his spear like a switch after them.

It was dark when I reached the streets, lamps in the niches and alcoves of buildings, hanging from gables, in neat rows along window ledges. It was only when I made my way through the elevated plaza of the Sacred Quadrangle, with that sal tree shifting in the night air above, that I noticed how empty the streets were. Almost deserted, even. As I came through the citadel gate, I heard shouting up ahead, bellows of anger and frightful sounds, coming from the direction of the palace. The beating of metal on metal. I started to feel cold creeping up the backs of my knees.

There were no guards at the gate, or on the wall. I went some paces further into the citadel, and then, as though in a fearful dream, people were running past me, breathless and wild-eyed, and the nearer I drew, the greater the castrophony that boomed from the palace courtyard up ahead. As I passed the Golden Hall and the House of Incantation, I became aware that the two spearmen behind me were babbling among themselves, throwing gestures at the running people. They seemed as confused as I was, and scared. I thought that perhaps, as had once happened before, a band of commoners had gathered enough courage to try to enter the palace, tempted by the smells wafting from the kitchens.

The terror arrived when I came into view of the nightmare in the palace forecourt. Its walls were lit from beneath by torches. All around the courtyard, servants and lords and women and children huddled in scared and half-naked bunches, their faces bloodied. There were soldiers everywhere, beating their shields as they strolled among the people, snarling a constant flurry of insults and commands in fiercely approximate Sinhala and Tamil – 'Get down, get back, stay still, stop your sniffling!'

Ten paces away, two soldiers were beating a skinny Sinhala man, screaming about what they would do to his mother, telling him that they would kill his god. The light from their torches sent shadows dancing against the walls and flower pillars, it glinted on the moonstones, it lanced up the blades of the soldier's swords. The night was thick with furious foreign speech and sobbing.

I froze. I didn't know if I should run away or remain, but before my thoughts could clear, some foreign command was issued, and the men who had been following me all day grabbed me by the arms. They pulled me up to one of the groups of quivering servants, and I begged clemency between breaths. They cuffed me twice on the side of the head – once for daring to buy a mango on their watch, I thought, another for the long wait beside the tank – and threw me among the weeping, white-haired men, the young girls, the thin boys that staffed the palace. An old man with skin like gum, dressed only in a cloth, huddled beside me. He was sobbing with fear.

'What's happening?' I asked him, dazed and smarting from the blows, the world teetering, but another guard barked in his own language and the servant shrank away from me as though I were cursed, wailing prayers to himself. My thoughts were burning white. I caught sight of you among a group of turbaned kitchen servants, your expression stony, though you hadn't seen me. You'd been in the kitchens, by your clothes. I thought that this was it: that Magha had simply decided to put us all to death.

'You can't kill me,' I wanted to shout to the warriors. 'There's been a mistake. I'm writing a poem for the King! I helped arrange his marriage – I carry messages for him, I'm his servant!'

But then from the main gate of the palace, surrounded by a circle of the largest soldiers I have ever seen, Magha entered the courtyard like a typhoon coming in from the sea. He was limping and dragging something of considerable weight. He screamed some Kalinga at his soldiers and his eyes flashed in the firelight, his hair sticking to his scalp, one hand clutching his side. By the time he reached the centre of the space and dropped his burden, there was silence but for a chorus of soft sobbing. The guards around him drew apart with their hands on their swords, and I saw that what the King had been dragging was Queen Dayani. She lay in a heap of red and gold on the flagstones, her chest heaving, her sari torn. My stomach dived into the centre of the earth, and the Kalinga, with wild and fiery eyes, began to speak.

'Behold!' he announced. 'The whore, your queen, who tried to kill me as I slept!'

He raised a tiny dagger above his head, the metal rosy, and when he lifted his arm, I saw the dark red lily on his robes, blossoming from a point just below his ribs. I had underestimated my queen.

Chapter Six

'My father once boiled a man,' Magha told me, the next time I saw him. He was surrounded by soldiers, lying on a feather mattress as he said it, pale and with a cruel thinness to his voice. 'Boiled him like a rabbit, just for plotting against him. Sneaking about. My father – now there was a man who knew how to deal with traitors. Tell me, Asanka, tell me why I shouldn't do the same to your queen.'

Those hissed words sounded over and over in my head as I walked to the dungeons deep below the guards' barracks abutting the citadel wall. Three soldiers came with me, dragging their feet and kicking up dust as they did. I felt a desperate, bottomless emptiness, once again bent low under the weight of news I had no wish to deliver. The guards led me down the row of dark cells and stopped at one door with a small barred slot at head height. They opened it, and let me go in alone.

Queen Dayani sat slumped in the centre of the cell, still wearing the torn sari of her wedding day. Her hair was dirty and unoiled, and a purple bruise flowered across one cheek. The cell was exceptionally narrow, and floored with sand that sloped up the walls.

'Asanka,' she whispered as I entered, although the clank of the door closing drowned this out, and I recognised my name only by the shape of her lips.

'My lady,' I said, bowing as though I were entering the throne room. In that instant I knew why King Parakrama had taken only a single wife. This Queen, this young Sinhala girl from Rohana, was so much braver than I was. She was braver than anyone I had ever met. They had given her only the water she could suck from a doused rag, and her lips were white and cracked.

'Did Magha send you?' she asked, but there was no accusation in her voice.

'Yes,' I said, feeling hot tears in my eyes. 'He has set a date. He has ordered you to be executed on the full moon before the New Year.' She didn't react. 'It . . . will be a quick death, Your Majesty. Everyone at court has been ordered to attend.'

She breathed out then, in what might have been a sigh of despair or relief. She was shaking a little, but held one arm in the other to hide it. You would weep to see it.

'I wish I'd killed him, Asanka,' she said, and her voice was as cool and sharp as a copper blade. 'I didn't know what I was doing. That's the worst part – that's what I regret. I hid the knife in the lining of my clothes before he summoned me, but I wasn't going to actually do it. I didn't know what I wanted to do. I felt it there as he spoke to me, as he slid across the bed towards me and called me his wife, his tender lotus flower. When I refused to lie with him, he became angry.'

Her hand moved to touch the bruise on her cheek, but she didn't look away, refused to apologise with her eyes.

'I knew if I struggled, he'd find the knife there, and he'd kill me. So I didn't struggle. When he'd finished, he slept, and I crept from the bed to find my little dagger in the folds of my clothes. I sat beside him in the dark, watching him. He breathes like a snake when he sleeps. All nostrils. His lip twitches, sometimes he murmurs in Kalinga. Sometimes he laughs. Sometimes his face falls and he looks afraid. He looks monstrous when he sleeps, but I couldn't kill him. Even after what happened to my husband. Even though I've heard everything he's done, what he did to the noblewomen – my friends, their children. I'm not Rama, Asanka.' A whimper escaped her throat as she said this. 'I'm not a hero.'

It was a long time before her eyes left the floor and she continued.

'He woke up slowly, frowned in his sleep, the way dogs do – he frowned as though a mosquito had bitten him, and opened his eyes – like this. At first, he thought I'd returned to make love to him, but the dagger must have caught the light. When he saw it, he leapt at me. I stabbed him in the side when he grabbed me. I stabbed him in the side, but he was too strong and pinned me against the bed. His blood made my hands slip. If I could have done it, Asanka, if I sank the blade into his heart or slit his throat while he slept, I could have avenged my husband. I could have saved so many others.'

Her story over, she visibly sagged.

'The King would be proud of you,' I told her, but she was crying now.

'Write me a poem,' she said.

'A poem?' I was taken aback. 'What kind of poem?'

'Something beautiful. Something I can take with me to my death. Short enough to memorise, so that I can repeat it to myself as the sword falls. Write me a love poem.'

I took a moment's thought. If she had asked me this a month before, I would have begun composing like a spider spins its web. Now, I felt unable to write even the first line of a verse that wasn't the *Vadha*. I felt in the folds of my cloth, and found a small piece of wrapped charcoal that I kept there to thicken ink. I began to write in Tamil on the stucco wall:

O man of hill country, where in winter
it rains heavily with sweet thunders—
all living beings sleep at midnight.
The fathers of hill-dwelling maidens,
with pretty jewels and fragrant hair,
have searched for a resting place during the chase,
but returned home to sleep on a bed of tiger hide.
When we are separated,
I suffer whenever I think of you.
When I wait long for you outside,
during the night, while all are asleep,
facing the cold and unfriendly north wind
in our garden, and stand embracing a tree
and pondering over your return—
such standing and waiting is sweeter than
embracing your body so as to press
my well-shaped and heaving breasts
and to surround you with my bangled arms.

It took some time before I had copied out the entire poem, and the Queen watched silently as I did it. It was an excerpt from one of my favourite Tamil collections, *Akananuru*. I chose these lines because I knew the Queen wouldn't have heard them, and would believe that I'd composed them all for her. She may have heard Sinhala folk rhymes as a child, but on the throne neither Queen Dayani nor King Parakrama had ever concerned themselves with the poetry of the common languages, poems written in the voices of the common people. Like most people in Lanka, when the King and Queen weren't reading the scriptures of the Buddha, they looked across the sea to the epic poems of the north: to the *MahabhMahabharata*, the *Ramayana*, to the love poetry and drama of Bharavi and Kalidasa. I knew this Tamil poem would seem utterly new to her, with its mysterious shades, its aroma of wood and water.

The poem's *rasa* is also the grey juice of sorrow. The lover is waiting for her beloved to return through the dry and dangerous wasteland; the Queen was waiting to join her husband in the beyond. The poet, whoever he may have been, articulates perfectly how I imagine the Queen must have felt in that cell: that as miserable as it is to cross the wasteland, it's worse to be left behind alone.

When I finished writing, I turned and bowed. I saw that the Queen was reading the poem with glistening eyes.

'"It rains heavily with sweet thunders",' she murmured, and I felt my heart glow as she recognised my favourite line. 'That's beautiful, Asanka.'

I nodded, squirming inside.

'Thank you, my lady. I hope it's what you desire.'

Before she could answer, there was a banging on the door. My time was up.

'I have to go, my lady. I'll visit you again as soon as I get permission,' I said, though I think we both knew that no such permission would be granted.

'My Queen,' I said, feeling my heartbeat in my head, feeling my mouth dry. 'Why did you choose me? Out of all the others?'

She looked up, as though surprised by the question, and took a moment to answer. When she did, it was as though saying the most obvious thing.

'Because you loved poetry,' she said. 'That's the way it seemed to me at the time. That you loved it more than anything else in the world.'

I felt a great weakness spreading through my arms and legs.

'Thank you, Your Majesty.'

I bowed once more, and left. The bearded guard outside leant in to draw the door closed, and I heard the Queen reading the poem back to herself: '"All living beings sleep at midnight",' I heard her murmur, and then the door slammed shut behind me.

When I look back on those days, it's not that I don't remember them, but rather that I find it hard to separate one from another. They were all hot and without rain and spent in torment. The image of the Queen, alone and parched in her dungeon, sat in my head like a warm stone, and still you wouldn't speak to me. Even if I went to see you in the evenings, to apologise or explain, I found that you had disappeared into the forest, leaving your room empty. My wife knew what was happening, I think, and was enjoying my ill temper. I could see in her face that she thought this a fitting punishment for the months I had abandoned her, left her alone with the servants in an empty villa in a city she didn't know. I began to find pieces of charcoal in my morning curry, and grit in my rice.

My nights were a frenzy of candlelit writing as I tried to make progress with the first three parvas of the *Vadha* before the first full moon. I walked through the city and already the koha's two-tone warble could be heard from the acacia groves, and the scarlet, trumpet-shaped flower of the erabadu tree was blooming. It was the season of the New Year. The moon was only days from fullness, and soon Magha would read what I had written so far, and Queen Dayani would die.

I knew that my life, too, was in question. I knew that there were other poets – and Hindu poets at that – who would love to see the Kalinga's patience with me run dry, his protection expire. Poets who would clamour all around court for the commission. *The Kalinga must continue to find me useful*, I thought over and over as I knelt in the temple on idle days, as I bathed in the lake, as I sat and flaked away at the paper with my stylus, cursing under my breath. My three anxieties, about you, the Queen and the poem, felt like a trio of elephants chained to my arms and legs, each about to be seared by a white-hot iron.

Every night, I tried to imagine what Magha wanted my translation to be. The lamps gave me kathakali dancers for shadows, the temple garden across the road always aflame with the sound of cicadas and frogs. I wrote my translation with an urgency I hardly ever felt for anything; I brought the terrible King Shishupal to life with similes that hit their targets like darts. I sifted the Sanskrit the way commoners in Ratnapura pan the rivers for precious dusts. I paced the room incessantly.

If only you would talk to me, I thought, then I could ask you every time I grasped and fumbled for one of these words – the certain slant of light that falls through waterfall mist, for instance, or one of the eighteen different ways of describing the smell of a durian. You could help me knot together the suffixes that are the threads of your tongue, and weave into each verb the amount, the mood, the tense, the voice of what I was trying to convey. But thanks to Magha, I had lost you for ever.

I wrote magnificent work. I wrote work that Magha would applaud, but with each simile I unpicked and restitched into Tamil, my Shishupal became an ever more detailed tapestry of my King.

In the second parva, when Krishna's elder brother Balarama is encouraging him to march to war, I even gave these words to the famous mace-carrier: 'Shishupal has conquered a kingdom and enslaved its people, bought its lords with his foreign gold, flogged its children in the streets.'

The *Vadha*, you see, is structured like a palm tree – it's large and asymmetrical, with many fronds, filled with divergences and tangents of a hundred different kinds. I was confident that the Kalinga wouldn't notice my small changes, and I was careful: for every change I made, I balanced it with twenty or so verses of immaculately rendered work.

Still, my hand shook whenever my restlessness and anger found this release. I knew the look that would cross Magha's face if he ever saw through it. The hours he would spend planning my death. How much he would make it hurt. I couldn't stop myself – that's all that matters. When I became too afraid to continue, I would step out on to my balcony and let the night air cool me, let the soft sounds of the city draw me back to earth.

The day of the full moon, the day of the execution, was oppressively hot and unusually cloying. It was a good day for brick-makers, I imagine, a good day for pig-herders and pepper-farmers, palm-tappers and potters, but in all other respects, it was a day of sorrow.

I found a spot on that gravelly rise up against the western tank wall, between the servant quarter and the Sal Bazaar, and watched them build the platform. It seemed hours that the lashing of beams and split planks clattered around the square, and the soldiers' backs steamed in the heat. Unable to watch, I looked down at the dust and loam beneath my feet, at a single stamped okra finger and a pink rambutan skin, a blood-splatter of spat betel juice. There are such enormous termites in Polonnaruwa, so large you can see the dust on their backs. I remember following their lines to where the mounds rose between the buildings, homes for cobras, monuments to their own futility.

The market was filling. Lords were arriving in litters, with their entourage; robed courtiers with peacock feathers in their turbans; palace servants and artisans; copiers and philosophers squinting in the bright sun; priests and clothiers, all in silence and pale as unpounded dough. No one spoke as the storekeepers threw mats over their wares. It was like some sorrowful festival: a lightless Deepavali, or a colourless Holi, like a Vesak without drums. An ascetic tottered through the crowd, avoiding the shade of the bo tree and wailing. His eyes were bloodshot with bhang. Then things started to happen.

A dignitary stepped up on to the platform, and began to read from a long piece of leaf. You know the kind of man: a long, full-bottomed robe, wearing his side-whiskers braided on his cheeks, and his cap pulled over his forehead.

'These are the crimes and the sentences of the traitor-queen Dayani,' he read. 'An attempt on the life of the King. Death. Acting against the peace of the land. Death. Being a whore in the first degree.'

And so on, in his reedy voice: death, death, death, and before long that wailing ascetic took up the chorus at the back of the crowd.

'Death!' he started shouting, and cackling as he shouted it, and I watched the mist of the word settle over the crowd, over the caved-in rooftops of the old buildings, the clusters of ruined temples, the disused devales and ancient dry bathhouses that had filled that district of the city for a hundred years.

By the time the platform was complete, the square was stifling and crowded. The loose ends of turbans snatched at the breeze, and I was glad of my raised position beneath the wall, where the breeze could wash over me. There was the pounding of staves on drums, and then the low mourning of a conch ran a thread through the air.

'Clear a path for the traitor-queen!' cried a Keralan soldier in Tamil and then Sinhala. The crowd parted, and a horse cart made its way through the people. The Queen was slumped on top, finally stripped of her sari and wrapped in sackcloth. I couldn't see her face. On the platform that waited up ahead, a bearded man leant on a curved bar of sunlight.

I'll not dwell on the events of the execution. I'm not one of the bloodthirsty idlers who loiter at crossroad gallows, nor one of the men of science who are hoisted up to the prisoners gurgling on the stakes to ask them: what colour are the flowers of heaven, have they yet been shown their past lives? By that time I was already worn thin with the weeks I had spent immersed in the *Vadha*. The resurrected demon, the war for dominion over the world, the battles in which hundreds of thousands died, Krishna's army marching through the glorious countryside to war, and always the spectre of that final, terrible beheading. That Sri Magha's descriptions are those of a man who wrote from imagination, that he probably never saw with his own eyes the likes of such bloodletting – on that day only this redeemed him in my eyes.

It will do to say that there was no daring rescue, nor cunning deception to save the Queen, as there might be in a poem. Still, I expected the beheading itself to be different. I imagined the scimitar rising slowly into the air, catching the light at the apex of its arc and then falling as though through water into the nape of her neck. I expected to catch a glimpse of her sorrowful gaze just before the blow fell, a gasp from the crowd as the last breath escaped her throat. The tolling of a faraway brass bell. This, at least, is how I would write a poem of the scene.

None of this happened. I was a long way from the front of the crowd, and although I was glad to be spared the sight, I felt that of all the people there, I should have been close to the Queen when she died. The swing of the sword was so quick that I didn't see its journey, and her hair hung down over her face so that I could almost pretend that she was some other woman. The executioner had to strike twice through the substance of her neck, and her head hit the wood three times before coming to rest. The whole thing was as unspectacular as the breaking of a jar. The crowd was silent throughout, but when the Queen's head rolled to a stop and the streams of blood gushed, flowed and then trickled, the silence intensified until the marketplace was like a wasteland devoid of even the smallest signs of life.

Outside the city, the funeral pyre burnt for hours. I stood there, beside the road, and watched the black outline of the Queen's body swimming in the flames. I watched until her charred remains were indistinguishable from those of the camphor and reeds that burnt beneath her, the pile of mangoes and cassia flowers that had been laid on her body. Hundreds stood along the highway, watching with bowed heads. Some chanted prayers, some murmured darkly among themselves.

Even the servants were allowed from the kitchens to mourn. The girls of the palace, who had loved the Queen, threw garlands into the fire. Their hair, their saris were whipped about their bodies by the hot whirlwind that lifted spirals of dust into the air, which made a mirage of the countryside behind and set the leaves nodding. I saw you among the crowd, weeping, but couldn't bring myself to try to talk to you again. I lifted my eyes to where the steep lines of Gangadoni Hill crested the horizon across the river, its twin granite peaks like a cup to hold the sun. To my left, a Sinhala chieftain with a glittering sash muttered to his friend through chewing: 'What hope do we have now? The rebel lords are fleeing south. Now Magha has garrisons at Kottiyar, Anuradhapura, Padaviya, Valikagama, Pulaccheri . . .'

'I knew some of the chiefs they sent into slavery,' murmured another, and he stared into the fire as though it were a far-off hill. 'They were good men. But only the fool struggles against the stronger. Isn't that how the saying goes?'

The first spat his betel into the red earth. '*Aiyo*,' he sighed. 'Even the bravest man doesn't go down the path where a devil lives.'

People left the pyre, one by one, bowing their respects, but I stayed. I stayed until my hair was thick with soot, until my eyes welcomed the cool insides of my eyelids with every blink. I thought of the stories of the *Jataka*. I remembered how the Buddha-to-be had once lived as a cobra, how he bore the torments of a brutal snake charmer, danced for the crowds and endured.

I will not say that the rains fell for the last time on that day, that drought descended immediately and completely, as some have said. That seems too neat, too like a poem or a story. But it was close enough. Even when everyone began blaming the Tamils and the Muslims, they still said that it was the Queen's death that stopped the rains, and they would go on saying it for a long time.

Later that evening, I carved the final mark of the *Vadha*'s third parva. I took my time dabbing ink across the cuts, and watched each word drink in the black one by one. For the first month, my torment was done. I bound the pages and readied to take them to the palace, murmuring a chant under my breath.

I took my route through the gardens, and the canopy of Nandana was thick with cheeping parakeets that night. When I arrived I found that Magha was away. I left the book with the captain of his bodyguard, and walked home infused with a glow of hope. Perhaps the King's wound had turned bad, I thought. Perhaps he was already sweating the last of his life into a mattress. I even spoke fondly to my wife when she encountered me at the door, though she met this with no little disdain. I returned to my bedroom feeling happy, feeling drained, but already the next parva was unfurling in my mind – an army on the march to destroy evil, passing through the land's beauty. The bare, mist-wreathed pinnacle of Mount Raivataka in the distance.

When Magha returned from his absence – not riding, but carried in a litter – and all my hopes for his death evaporated, it took him several days to read what I had written. It was evening when he summoned me, perhaps a week after the Queen's death, and the day's heat still rose from the stone.

I presented myself at the royal quarter and found him pacing the throne room in distressing good health, but with a definite limp distending his stride. He was speaking rapidly in his own language to two of his generals, but broke off what he was saying as I entered. There was a powerful aroma of medicine in the room: ginseng and wine, tar and burnt skin. He stopped his pacing and turned to me.

'Do they teach you the word "*dharma*" here?' he asked, and I could hear his voice hardened by an edge of pain, still thin and reedy. I murmured a yes. 'It means duty,' he said, ignoring me. 'That's how my father would explain it. It means a man's duty, his destiny, obeying his fate – it's difficult to explain in your language.'

'I think I understand, Maharaja.'

'Do you?' he said, and went over to his desk. He stooped with a small grunt, and picked up the solid gold inkwell with the shell pattern that had belonged to King Parakrama. Then he walked towards me.

'Do you know what this is?' he said.

'An inkwell, my lord.'

'Let's say for a moment that this is your *dharma*,' he said, and his eyes were fixed on me. When he was less than an arm's reach from me, he suddenly lifted it above his head in both hands. I flinched, but he did not strike me. He only placed the inkwell on the top of my head, and I felt the cold metal pressing down on my skull. It was heavy. He slowly took his hands away, and I felt the amused eyes of the generals watching me.

'Don't let it fall,' he said.

'My lord?'

'Don't let it fall.'

He sidled back to the desk, where I saw the pages of my first instalment of the *Vadha* were lying fanned open. I felt the inkwell wobble on my head, and my breathing began to come in little gasps. I looked at the generals, but they were only watching and smirking.

'When I ordered you to translate this poem for me, Master Asanka, do you remember what I asked of you? The *dharma* I gave you?'

He gave that same pained grunt as he bent down for the pages of my translation, and his eyes moved like a saw blade as he skimmed back through the verses. I willed myself not to tremble, not to let the inkwell fall.

'You told me to translate as truly as possible,' I replied, trying my hardest to keep my head still, and taking short breaths when I could. 'To make it both Tamil and Sanskrit. Both popular and beautiful. Both glorious and sacred. To make it – balanced.'

'Balanced,' he repeated, and looked up at me. The inkwell wobbled. 'And? How do you think you compare?' he asked, dropping the cover of the book with a snap.

I didn't understand why I was being punished. Then, with a rush of needles, I realised. It was my idiot joke. I had given my King Shishupal Magha's eyebrows, like a child's chalk drawing of a schoolmaster on the wall. *He noticed*, I thought, and those words sounded again and again in my head. *He's too clever not to have noticed.* All I could think of in that moment was: *Help me, Buddha, what a foolish way to die.* Where were the guards? Was the royal torturer waiting behind one of the tapestries or curtains, toying with his knives? I began to quake, and the inkwell teetered dangerously forward on my head. I felt a little whine in my throat as I struggled to balance it.

'Well?'

I felt my voice shaking. 'Please my lord, a poet – a poet can never translate in isolation. I have to – the words of the two languages are very different. There are compromises to make – everywhere compromises – and yes, my lord, some of these may be tinted by my own – by our own—'

I felt my life drain away like milky rice water, and closed my eyes, felt the cold weight press down on my scalp.

'I can only – only try to keep Sri Magha's spirit alive in my translation,' I pleaded. 'I wanted to mock what he would find absurd – to hate what he would find hateful.'

'Hrm . . .' the Kalinga grunted, eyeing me. 'And you have done magnificently!'

I opened my eyes, a shudder passed up through my body, and the inkwell fell forwards. I caught it in my hands.

'Ha! Not a man with natural balance, I see!' he laughed, and his generals laughed too, both at once. 'But your translation has pleased me. I was unconvinced that a Lankan poet would have the sophistication to translate such a great work of Sanskrit poetry. I thought you might not be worthy of this *dharma*.'

I didn't know what to say.

'His Majesty – my lord – liked it?'

I came close to tears. Like the Ganga bursting its dam of arrows, relief flooded into me. It stunned me with the recklessness of what I had done, laid open to me the miracle that my changes hadn't been caught. I swayed a little, but remained upright.

'Your mastery of Magha's similes is impressive,' he told me, and he sounded very far away. 'Here, where he describes the glow of Krishna's teeth shining on the sage's white skin as the light of the moon falling on the walls of a whitewashed palace.' He sighed, shaking his head in admiration. 'And here! Where Balarama displays his fury towards the heretic Shishupal, the beads of perspiration on his body are like stars in the reddish evening sky – magnificent!'

I nodded, feeling the cool heft of the inkwell in my hands, the pain still fresh on my crown.

'He was a truly accomplished poet,' I replied. 'It has been an honour.'

He ignored me.

'Surely now you see why I've brought this epic to your shores,' Magha said to me. 'Why I chose it as the fine example that the people of Lanka need to be set.'

He brushed his hands as though they were covered in dust.

'Yes, Maharaja. I am sure they will follow it,' I said, and a servant hurried from behind me to take the inkwell and put it back down on the desk.

'With the will of Ganesh,' he murmured, 'all obstacles are removed. That's all, Master Asanka. Leave us.'

I stared at him. He wasn't mad – I saw the intelligence in his eyes and knew that for certain. I bowed to leave, and when I stepped out on to the terrace, with the sun setting like heated bronze in the lake, everything seemed sharpened and more brightly coloured. A new world. Then Magha's voice sounded again from inside, unnaturally high.

'Master Asanka!' he called. 'Step back inside for a moment.'

I shuddered, the fear crashing back down on me. I turned and re-entered the throne room. The generals hadn't moved, but now Magha was sitting on his cushion, pulling out his maps.

'Asanka, I have to mention it before I forget. I know you were close to Queen Dayani. And you were, after all, the man who told me that she would be happily remarried. Let me ask you – could a woman working alone plan and carry out a deliberate attempt on the life of a king?'

He let this question linger as he smoothed out his maps and the papery sound of his hands on their surface filled the air. He let it turn to accusation in the heat. Suddenly there was the smouldering look of a beaten child on his face.

'"All living beings sleep at midnight",' he mused without emotion, and I felt the blood rush to my face. When he spoke next, it was in the tone he also used to suggest new levies on chena cutting, or a new system of weights and measures in the marketplace.

'If your translation were not so much to my satisfaction,' he said, 'I assure you that my torturers would already have you in their hands. I advise you to give me no more reason to suspect you in the future.'

'I understand, Maharaja,' I replied, and I was ashamed to hear my voice jump a note higher in mid-sentence.

I left the throne room, and the breeze funnelling through the palace corridors kissed the hollows on my neck and face where sweat had gathered. The sun was almost completely set, and darkness crept into the halls. I walked down into the shadows of Nandana to cool myself among the shifting leaves, then along the canal to my villa, where my wife was already asleep in her empty room.

Inside my chamber, I balled my fists and pressed them into my eyes. A powerful shaking passed over me, and I moaned. I lit the lamps, making many attempts to bring flame to the tinder, and took the *Kuruntokai* collection from my shelf. My breath was still heaving. Without stepping away from the bookshelf, I read through the verses of *Neytal*, the seashore section, and then moved on to my favourite, the mountain section. I imagined watching the mountainsides of the mainland as the rains washed them and the sun turned them gold, waiting twelve years for the kurinji flower to bloom and turn the whole world blue. I read until my breathing softened into tiny gasps. I let the Tamil voices settle into my chest like blossom.

Once the shaking had subsided, I felt my exhaustion and prepared to sleep. I stepped out of my clothes and kicked off my grass sandals, but as I watched them skim across the floor to the bed, I saw it. I felt the same sudden start as when one expects an extra step in a dark flight of stairs and finds only flat ground to meet one's foot: pressing a soft indent into the straw mattress, a thin bundle of bound pages sat on my bed. I hadn't left them there. I knew I wouldn't have left poetry in any proximity to where I sleep, for the tale of Shishupal and Krishna was already seeping into my dreams. No, someone had been inside my room.

I crept towards the book as though it were an injured grey monkey, as though it might leap at me with claws and teeth at any moment. My name was written on the cover in Tamil. I picked it up, felt its weight, explored the paper with my fingertips, tested the give of the sinew binding. The paper was familiar, perhaps even of quite inferior quality – the binding in the fashion of these new workshops that are popping up everywhere – but the ink was very fine, and smelt of faraway places, of strange earth. It wasn't the simple charcoal and oil I black my own writing with. I took another breath, and thought that the strange ink smelt like rain, falling for the first time on dusty stone.

I read this manuscript dozens of times over the coming months, and I caressed it like this each time, as though its secrets could be coaxed out with gentleness. The book was made up of three sections tied together with cord. That night, I let the tied leaves unravel, and saw a single line of Tamil script at the top of each section. As I read the titles, I felt my stomach boiling, frothing like a pot of rice forgotten and left to sputter on the flames. They said:

'I am Shishupal'

'I am Rukmi'

'I am Ilvala'

I am Ilvala

No, do not step back; I will not hurt you. I have been asked to tell my part of the story. I am the *rakshasa* inside Prince Rukmi. The spirit, the demon – whatever the commoners are calling it today. I was listening when he told you about me (I am always listening), but in truth, he's lucky I don't take his body all the time. It's such a strain to inhabit a man from morning to dusk: all the sinews and muscles always moving, the glands that make me hiss with disgust – how does a sweaty halfwit like Rukmi even manage to keep it all going, keep it all secreting, even for the eye blink that is a human life?

Day to day, I let the prince have control of his body, of those various secretions and oily oozings. I let him sit through conversations with Brahmins longer and duller than a front-to-back reading of the *Mahabharata*, I sit through all the quarrels with his disobedient sister, and I do nothing. But sometimes history calls, or at least some tremendous fun. The little boy beside the river – that's exactly the kind of thing I mean. This – look at this – these bodies of muscle and skin and jelly disgust me so much, it is liberating to tear them apart like canvas sheeting.

I was furious to find myself trapped in the oozing body of a prince. Under the constant gaze of his father (with his strangely instinctive sense of good) and sister (her disobedience and clever eyes) and all the servants and soldiers and priests and Brahmins and scholars, I could never sate myself. There were many times that Rukmi does not remember. Some pigeons and rats that

I pulled apart with his fingers, for instance. You see, I must keep myself amused, like any prisoner. I leave him clues: he awakes some mornings with feathers in his hair or blood on his bed sheets, and the fear that clings to his sweaty forehead is like sugar to me. That day beside the Wainganga, I painted myself with blood and howled.

Sometimes I consider taking control of the prince and jumping him off the palace's highest tower. I imagine plummeting him through the air, the incandescent moment of weightlessness, then his bones snapped like sticks against the rocks. Fun, perhaps, but I might be reborn into someone worse – a cripple or an untouchable or an orphaned brothel girl. After all, at least a prince has cushions to sit on and does no work, but still, I was so bored. This was until the business with Rukmini, Shishupal and Krishna.

My brother Vatapi would be proud. I remember his favourite sport when we were young was to murder Brahmins. He would transform himself into a goat – listen to this, it gets better – he would transform into a goat, and I would slit his throat, slice him up and roast him into the finest dish you have ever tasted, dripping juices soaked to cochineal by turmeric, cumin and a thumb of ginger, garnished with tears of coriander.

We would invite the Brahmins to eat with us, fat, obnoxious ones – the kind we knew would walk past a starving orphan girl in the street and pretend to be blind, the kind who say to the people 'read our stories, forget your language and your festivals, serve us, worship us and pay us levies!' The kind who burn down villages, and then write great poems about how they defeated armies of demons.

Corpulent, sweating, they would eat until they had finished every scrap of my brother, licking their lips at his tender parts, gnawing at his gristle. The mess they made was disgusting – the slime and spit, the slobbering mouths that split their jowly faces. I would sit and watch the shadows of the plantain palms shifting across their skin, trying to ignore the mortal bodily functions that they did not seem to know they were performing.

Once they had finished, I would ask 'Sri Brahmin, oh wise one, have you enjoyed your meal?'

As they sat back and began to blather their praise, massaging their swollen bellies and dabbing their mouths on their dhoti, I would call to my brother deep within them. I would call to him and utter the Sanjivani mantra, the mantra used to make the broken whole. Vatapi, that little trickster, would hear the mantra, and would rend his way back to life through the lining of their stomachs, would burst out into the room in a fountain of blood and bile. Oh, how we laughed!

Afterwards, once we had both bathed in the river, Vatapi and I would watch the fireflies circle the areca palms, and he would tell me stories. I loved Vatapi's stories. Stories are like words: they change what they mean every time someone tells them, but they belong to no one. In the end, that's the only reason I tried to force Rukmini into a marriage she did not want, why I brought Krishna and Shishupal into such spectacular conflict. For the story. Have you ever trapped two beetles in a box, just to see which one would kill the other?

Now it would be a good idea for you to step back, for I feel the old mischief boiling in my blood. It would be wise to run, even. Get away from here as fast as you can!

Unless, of course, you are hungry?

Book II

Ink

Chapter Seven

The mystery of this mad poet's work drove me half insane. The day the first bundle arrived, I barely slept. I stayed up half the night reading and re-reading those pages, and when I finally fell into bed, it was only to dream in a confused jumble of images and names I didn't know, all wreathed in the smell of that ink.

When it was morning, I went to find my wife making breakfast, cracking eggs beneath our little kitchen canopy.

'Madhusha,' I said, and she didn't turn around. 'Madhusha, did you see anyone around here last night?'

'You mean Janani, Sumeda, Gayani?'

I didn't know any of my servants' names.

'No – someone different. Someone not supposed to be here. Some hooded figure in the street, or a shadow in the courtyard?'

She turned and looked at me the way someone looks at a horse they are buying when they are sure the price is too high.

'Who knows who sneaks around this place?' she said, in a voice leaden with meaning. 'I was out all last night, with the women from the tank. I didn't see anything, husband.'

Obviously no respectful Sinhala wife would ever use her husband's name, but Madhusha had a way of making the word 'husband' sound like the name of a rice-spoiling fungus. Was it the way she crunched an empty eggshell as she said it? I considered inventing a trinket that could have been stolen, so she might take me seriously, but I knew she'd only have one of the servants whipped. Probably the girl she didn't like, whichever one that was.

I retreated to my room to re-read those vulgar Tamil manuscripts: King Shishupal, Prince Rukmi, the demon Ilvala – the voices of the dead, telling their stories. I had no idea what they could mean, or who could have left me such a thing.

Whoever did it, they were clearly unhinged. Their stories were crude, written with a complete lack of style. An insult to the poetry to which I'd dedicated my life. Each one was told as though from the mouths of these characters: I am, I am, I am. While the old Tamil poets might use their poems to speak in the voices of hill maidens and village boys, the villain who left these pages for me wrote about the heroes and demons of the Sanskrit masters the way the Sinhala wives gossip in the marketplace – well, what then? Shall we have drunks in the street claiming to speak in the voice of the Buddha? Shall we have books written in the voices of gods? I could imagine few greater blasphemies, and knew that if the Kalinga ever found these pages, I would be butchered for someone else's crime.

The ink was my only clue, that strange sharp smell. It brought me back to some of the fine books I'd touched only once or twice in the temple library where I learnt my craft. It was such fine quality, in fact, that I thought with suspicion of the Sangha priests and the lords whose betrayal I had mocked in my translation; of the rebel chieftains in the hills and forests, who hated Magha's rule and must have thought me his servant. Then I thought of you, I admit, of my wife, of all the people I'd betrayed. I thought of my rivals, but were they capable of this crime, even in the heights of their jealousy? To infiltrate my home and threaten me, mock me, perhaps to incur the King's wrath against me – all of this seemed beyond even the desperate depths to which I knew they would sink to see me fall from grace.

I even wondered if Pushpakumara the ink-maker had conceived this as some elaborate joke from wherever his exile found him. The story told by Shishupal, for instance, was I to see myself in the poet chained up like a gypsy bear? Even Rukmi's visit to Rukmini, his attempts to convince his sister to marry, seemed a mimicry, if a grotesque exaggeration, of my meeting with Queen Dayani. It was just the kind of thing he might do: write a story so lacking in any poetic convention but written in the finest ink he could find. I clenched my fist thinking of his jowly face laughing at me. But who else knew about the poem, and the Queen? Who had Magha told? Who among all the people I knew was already talking about how I had been the one to cause her death? I re-read what Ilvala said about those stories, the stories I had loved all my life, and felt that I detested all of my being.

The chest of two hundred massa arrived in my courtyard several days after the mad poet's papers. I didn't immediately realise who had sent it to me, and after opening it I stared at its contents in mute awe. The dull shine of copper pieces in the sun. Then I noticed that they were all new coins, edges unclipped, and on each of them Magha's face had been newly stamped.

With that sum I paid off all my outstanding debts, which had become sizeable. My tailor, for instance, was owed a great sum, and was apparently busy trying to destroy my reputation around the bathhouses. You still wouldn't speak to me, and at times of the deepest desolation I thought of buying a whore's services – and not one of the cheap consorts in the doors of the brothel-goers' district or the wall shadow, either. Thankfully, fear of market talk and disease, in equal measure, prevented me from such foolishness.

Instead, I poured my frustrated energies into the poem. For the next three weeks, I toiled at the *Vadha* until I could hear the termite sound of stylus-scratching even after I had stopped work for the night, and every morning ink smudges made maps of different coastlines on my palm. When I read of Krishna riding past the great mountain Raivataka, all the seasons manifesting at once, its trees wound around with snakes, its glittering jewelled slopes bursting into flower and fruit, all this seemed more real than the everyday substance of my life. Seeing my wife, writing love poems for the lords, eating rice and bathing, working in my room, sitting in the palace garden: everything around me became flat and prosaic. I noticed only the discomforts, the unpleasant sides of every thing and person.

Terrified as I was by my last encounter with the King, I didn't make any changes to the poem. Not for a week or so. But every night when I returned to my room, I would take out the bundle of pages from beneath my mattress, breathe in the smell of that ink, and read back through the terrible stories. Shishupal, Rukmi, Ilvala. Ilvala, Rukmi, Shishupal. Trying to tease some sense from them. They were so vulgar, so far from anything I had ever read before – but the more I read them, the more I felt something strange. I began to find these artless scraps exciting. I began to look forward to coming home in the evenings and reading them to myself by the light of a single lamp. My secret; my mystery.

Slowly, the changes began to creep back into my translation – and I think now that it was those dead voices written by that mad poet, above all else, that led me down the path I eventually followed to the end. One night, with the moon re-emerging as a toenail clipping in the sky, I realised that whenever I imagined King Shishupal, it was Magha's face that swam into my mind.

For the longest time, I didn't see how far I had strayed from the original poem, one simile at a time. It wasn't bravery. I was never brave. I awoke many nights peeling from my mattress, sticky as papaya with sweat. I would hear the sounds of rats beneath the boards, the sound of flies thumping against the ceiling, and the noises of the city at night, and become convinced that my alterations had been discovered, that the guards were coming to break down the gate of my villa and torture me. To take my eyes. I would jump out of bed and read poetry to calm myself, then step out on to my balcony, into the dark and the mosquitoes, and let my poor body breathe.

The obvious place to continue the story is the next time I saw you, some days after the New Year's first moon, and because it was such a dark and lonely month, I'll pass over it in my story. At times it seemed like my normal life had returned. The chief of Gokarna came to me one day and told me that a poem I'd written had lacked all feeling and warmth, that his beloved had only shrugged as she read it. I gave him half his money back, promised to write another for him, and sent him on his way. My wife dismissed the youngest and prettiest of our servants, on the pretext of her having stolen something. The price of rice went up by two-thirds. The price of a water skin doubled. My tailor took back some of his more outlandish accusations in the bathhouses, blaming a disingenuous wood-carrier. The fig tree in Nandana gave fruit, and dropped its sweet purple figs on the lawn so that flies and wasps circled all day, and the servants had to clear them away with their heads wrapped in muslin hoods.

When the moon swelled to full size, the air of the season making it as white as a sliced disc of rose apple, I handed the second instalment to the King. He took five days to read it and summon me to the throne room. He was still bedridden, but his mood was up. Throughout our meeting he was eating oysters, into each of which the servants had placed a fine pink pearl. He read his favourite similes back to me, and between each one gulped down another oyster whole, head jerking back like a wading bird.

'This was my other favourite,' he said, towards the end of the list. 'When Krishna finally reaches the holy mountain, and stops his army there: "On one side the mountain wore clouds coloured white from rain showers, like the glow of a newly washed gown". It's beautiful, isn't it?'

'Yes, my lord.'

He gulped down another oyster, smacking his lips.

'"Upon that mountain, a tree grew upon a boulder of silver, its opened leaves like a thousand eyes",' he read. Then another oyster.

'And what about this? "All men despise the thick-eyebrowed King Shishupal for their own reasons – for his murders, for his greed, for his cruelty – just like the twitter of different accents pronouncing the same word."'

The breath caught in my throat. You might have guessed that you would not find that line anywhere if you read the *Shishupala Vadha* today. Magha's tongue moved slowly across his teeth.

'It's wonderful, isn't it?' he said. 'But that part with Rukmi having some kind of demon living inside him, that's not in the *Mahabharata*, is it? I've never heard it before.'

I hesitated. 'I believe it's not, Your Majesty.'

'Then Magha was a man of imagination, too. Not content to slavishly march along the story's old path – I admire that, Asanka.'

'Yes, Your Majesty. Although some say Rukmi lived as a demon in his past life.'

'Ha!' Magha laughed, a sound like a flock of crows taking flight all at once. 'Didn't we all, Asanka? Didn't we all?'

He dismissed me then, still chuckling, and downed another oyster.

The next time I saw you was a few days after that. It was a bright evening, and I was sitting alone in the Nandana pavilion. I didn't want to go home, because in the first days of the New Year, the astrologers are always walking from door to door selling their *awurudu sittuva*, the little strip of palm-leaf paper containing forecasts for the year: all the auspicious days, news of the harvest, the weather, the favoured dress and the chances of success for prospectors and merchants. At the time, news of the future was the last thing I wanted to hear, and they tend to be persistent salesmen with wide smiles.

Instead, I sat in the garden and re-read the mad poet's ravings for what must have been the hundredth time. By then, I felt that I was beginning to tease out some kind of pattern. A man under the spell of a demon, a whispering passenger, beyond the prince's control. A king brought low by the peasant Krishna. The chained poet. There was some message in this madness, I was sure of it.

It's always been my tendency to become so wrapped up in reading that I forget my surroundings. How long did you stand there beneath the flame tree before I noticed you? I became aware suddenly of the tourmaline sari you wore on evenings off work, and when I looked up from my reading I saw you half-hidden by the tree, just watching. By then, we hadn't spoken for six weeks, and I'd spent that time trying to conceal my shame as an excess of pride: avoiding corridors where you might walk, and not meeting your gaze whenever I did pass you; staying away from the palace when I could, and keeping up conversation with some lord whenever you passed me in the banquet hall. Your hair had grown back to cover the bare patches, and now you had a short, glossy thatch like a young man.

I became conscious of how ill I must look, having eaten and slept less with every day that went by. I tucked away the offending manuscript so that you wouldn't see it, and tried to appear thoughtful but melancholy, the way I imagine the poet Kalidasa must have looked as he sat and composed in the gardens of Ujjain. Then you walked towards me, ducking beneath the boughs.

'Asanka—' you said. It was as though you didn't recognise me, as though I'd returned from a journey through the wasteland, older now and with my fortune made. I didn't reply, barely dared look at you, but then you came towards me and put your hand on the top of my head, softly, as though touching a wound. I hid my face, unable to speak or think, but I remember that as I did so you pressed my cheek against your stomach so that my temple touched your sari and my cheek your skin, and so blissful was that moment that I rested against the warmth of your body with your fingers moving in my hair.

You dropped down to my level and kissed my neck, placing each kiss as though with much thought: first in the hollow above the collarbone, then just beneath the angle of the chin, then on the tip of my Adam's apple. If I touch myself in these places now, if I wet the tips of my fingers and press them lightly against these spots, I can conjure those moments with such clarity. Finally you pressed our lips together, and placed your forehead against mine. I felt the weight of your skull; I believe I was weeping. I am sure I murmured something, but what?

'*Aiyo*, Asanka,' you whispered. 'I'm sorry. It's so wonderful what you've done.'

I let those words settle into me. Then I looked at you.

'Wonderful?' I croaked. I had imagined, even in my moments of greatest optimism, only a period of slow reconciliation, a month or two of purgation and apology before you would even look at me kindly. I felt the work of strange forces. 'Sarasi,' I managed. 'What's wonderful?'

'Your poem!' you laughed in that same whisper, and your nose ran a line up my forehead.

'What?'

'The *Shishupala Vadha*!'

A hint of accent showed through suddenly in your pronunciation of the name, elongating the vowel sounds. The *Vadha*. I tingled to hear you mention it, the accursed labour, but I didn't understand. As you embraced me, my arms were protruding from your back like the tusks of an elephant, caught halfway between holding you and pushing you away.

'I thought you were a coward,' you said, 'or a traitor. Asanka, I thought so many things.' You fixed the full strength of your eyes on mine. 'But last week Magha had a copy of the first two instalments sent to every village in the Raja Rata, with orders to hold readings. Now it's all anyone is talking about down in the city.'

I felt suddenly faint. I remembered what the Kalinga had told me about spreading the poem throughout Lanka, about teaching the peasants virtue and *dharma* and suchlike. Why hadn't I thought to take his meaning so literally?

'There were horsemen sent out with three hundred copies,' you went on, perhaps registering the way my gaze had become untethered. 'Now the whole kingdom is talking about how you're defying the King even while living inside the royal city!'

'What do they mean, "defying"?' I managed, reeling. You looked at me as though I were mad.

'Your King Shishupal. He's a perfect imitation of Magha! He has the same cruel, selfish nature. He commits the same crimes. Asanka, you even gave Shishupal bushy eyebrows!'

You giggled nervously. I tried to smile, but it was a taut mask: terror turned my feet numb, crawled up the backs of my legs like scorpions.

'And people have – they've noticed this?'

'Of course! They come together in large groups to listen to readings. I've seen them, Asanka, all gathered round as though watching a festival dance, listening in silence and then cheering every time you describe him. Sometimes the soldiers keep watch nearby, and they never suspect a thing!'

'This is . . . unbelievable,' I managed, and felt an uncontrollable trembling spread throughout my body. I was going to die. I knew it with such certainty in that moment.

'I'm sorry I doubted you,' you said. 'When I heard that you were writing for him . . .' You pressed your lips against mine again, and it took a moment for me to return the kiss, to catch up with the world and prove to myself that this wasn't a dream. I kissed you like a thirsty man drinking, but I was still shivering. Dusk was descending on the garden, lamps were being lit. You glanced up at a murmur of voices on the balconies above, then an explosion of laughter from the vicinity of the noble quarters. You stood, glancing upwards.

'Come with me,' you said. 'I have something to show you.'

You took my hand and we left the palace, hurried down the avenues slowly filling with moonlight, through the lamplit pools of faces and turbans arguing outside the wine houses. I felt the weight of the dead voices in the folds of my cloth, and prayed that they wouldn't fall. You led me south through Polonnaruwa's yawning Chandi Gate, and in the moonlight all its brightly coloured paints seemed different shades of blue.

Thankfully, Magha no longer sent soldiers to follow me, and those stationed at the gate didn't bother us. I think the King had already guessed what I had come to realise: that I didn't have the courage to leave. Every halt and rest house was guarded, people said, every village was inspected and filled with informers.

The country was a huge black sea on either side, banana palms and thatched watch huts picked out in moonlight. The fields bristled with frogs and crickets, the calls of night birds and the occasional screech of a monkey from the forest ahead.

'Where are we going?' I asked.

'You'll see,' you said, and began to run, as I'd never seen you run. I hurried after you, but not so fast that the mad poet's book would come tumbling out of my sarong. I was laughing for the first time in weeks. Had I already forgotten about the poem? Maybe my fear changed shape: in my night blindness, I saw leopards everywhere, and every black boulder became a bull elephant waiting to make pulp of our bones. I stayed close to you. There was the sound of eels swimming in the rice waters, a distant herd of elephants.

Then, as we rounded a grove of tall rain trees, I thought I saw lights glittering in the south-east. That's why I stopped, and you called out for me to keep up. I didn't believe what I was seeing at first, but there they were. Glittering orange lights flying, or at least hovering, across the river, suspended as though by black medicine above the horizon. All I could think of was Ravana's fiery chariot, the miraculous vehicle of legend that he flew to the mainland to kidnap Sita.

'Sarasi—' I said weakly, 'Sarasi, there are lights in the sky.'

But you were walking on ahead, and I hurried on to follow. When I caught up with you, you were leaving an offering for safe travel to the old jungle gods: a twig suspended between two branches. I felt delirious, and said nothing about the lights. I felt in those moments as though I were living in the world of those old tales, where the hero of a story might reclaim his beloved, where chariots might fly above the clouds.

Soon you were leading me by the hand again. The river was nearby – I could hear the chuckle of rocks – and as we reached its banks fruit bats screeched overhead as they began to feed. The water was black, and riddled with shifting light. At intervals, the star-filled emptiness of chena plots loomed on either side, watchtowers in the forks of high trees. The smell of ash. Termite mounds lined the path, and at one turning the shape of a roadside shrine insinuated itself in the darkness, a bronze Buddha with garnets for eyes. As we passed it, a troop of monkeys began bickering and mocking nearby, and I jumped at the sudden chatter.

How long was it? I don't remember, but some time later I began to feel a hush of drumbeats through the earth, and before long a light filtered through the trees, put a dust of orange on your cheeks as you turned and grinned at me. The treeline opened out on to paddies, a moon in each, and the hedged island of a village floated at the end of the path, surrounded by thirty fathoms of open land. As we got closer, I saw ten or so thatched houses, and I could have been home, so similar was this place to where I had grown up. A fire threw spokes of light through the legs of thirty or so people who were dancing around the flames, singing and jumping over them as a drum throbbed in the air: *gatta gatta goom, gatta gatta goom*. Some of the gathered wore kolam masks, but I recognised others as servants from the palace; half a dozen washermen, a lamplighter and a pair of cooks.

'Welcome to Aliyagama,' you said, and pulled me towards the dancing villagers. *Elephant village*. I didn't even have time to think about whether that meant there were elephants nearby, tethered somewhere out of sight, or roaming the night jungle. This was where you came from, I thought, watching the quiet touches that you laid on the others' elbows and shoulders. I was stunned. I bowed my respects to the girls and mothers of Aliyagama, and they accepted me without question. They began to tell you market talk about a man who had beaten another man for letting his goat run untethered through the chenas, about a monk who had slipped in wet plaster while repairing his temple. As I watched you receive their excited talk with a private language of laughs, gasps and sighs, an old man with a moulded-clay face threw a garland of yellow flowers over my neck – he smudged my forehead with a *tilaka* of sandalwood paste and vermilion, chanting low and tuneful blessings.

'Thank you,' I said, and he wobbled his head.

'How do you like it?' you said to me when you turned back.

'It's like my village in the hills,' I said. 'Isn't that strange? Were you born here? Is this where your parents lived?' but you shook your head with a smile and pulled me on.

Even the villages around Polonnaruwa seemed wealthy to me when I thought of my childhood. Beside one house, a large pile of green coconuts waited to be cut open and pressed or scraped. On a bed of palm leaves, a young villager sat chewing betel and peeling the bark from wands of cinnamon, apparently sulking at the festivities. The people were dressed colourfully, but I began to feel very glad that I hadn't worn a fine sarong or jewellery that day. The villagers spoke a dialect of Tamil I heard a lot in the area around Polonnaruwa, dotted with Sinhala words. They laughed and talked without restraint.

'Are there elephants nearby, then?' I asked, as though simply curious.

'Why do you care about the elephants?'

'Never mind. Would you like to dance?' I asked.

'I never dance,' you said, and for an instant I felt that you betrayed a glimmer in your eyes, like a distant lamp at night.

'No, me neither,' I said.

We stood and watched for some time, and when the music had gone on so long that I began to feel the beat of the drums tingling through the earth, the dancing stopped. The people gathered around the fire and sat squatting in a crescent, shouting:

'Kitsiri! Kitsiri! Read it to us!'

A young boy with fine bone-structure stood up from the crowd, and people whooped. He had nervous eyes, a bound sheaf of pages in his hand and a necklace of leopard's teeth strung around his thin shoulders. I didn't think that he had killed the leopard. You explained that this was Kitsiri, who was the pride of the village: he had studied at a *pirivena* in Polonnaruwa, and had been taken in as an apprentice in one of those fashionable scribe workshops I so detested.

Silence settled over the villagers as a series of blessings and invocations were spoken by the village headman, and for a while the only other sounds were the crackle and pop of the fire, the calls of birds. Jugs of palm toddy were passed around, and I watched you take a deep sip. Then the boy began to read.

'This great poem is a gift to the people of Lanka from King Magha the conqueror of the world, the lord of the three Sinhala lands and legate of the Empire of Kalinga, so that they might learn and better themselves. Praise Vishnu the preserver!'

There was much jeering as he read out the dedication, but the voices fell silent as the poem began. Kitsiri read slowly, and stuttered over some of the longer words and more difficult names. He wasn't an accomplished singer, and the notes of the simple song he laid over the poem weren't what I would have chosen, not even an evening *raga*. Even so, my heart beat quickly as the story went on.

By now I knew the poem well enough to know always which word would come next, but hearing it like this, sung aloud in Tamil, changed it completely: the florid intricacy of the metre, the high tone of the poetry, were gone. It was a poem that I had never heard.

We stayed until the boy had finished. He didn't read much of the parva he chose, but it took several hours. We listened as Narada delivered his warning to Krishna: the demon King of Lanka has been reborn! He is a pale-skinned man from a distant land, a man of terrible cruelty, with eyebrows like moss-furred creepers! There was a grumble of affirmation, and when Kitsiri read out my description of Shishupal's eyebrows, a bubble of laughter.

When I described Shishupal kidnapping King Babhru's wife, and dragging her behind him 'like a sack of tender jak', those who had seen or heard about Magha's treatment of Queen Dayani cried out in spontaneous anger. Finally, when I described Shishupal carrying out inspections of livestock and crops, increasing his punitive levies and wiping out the villages that opposed him, the boy paused for a long time while the audience cheered and hissed in equal measure. A bowl of roasted jak seeds spilled as the old man who greeted me leapt to his feet, clapping above his head.

Each time one of these allusions was read out, you leant closer to me, and squeezed my hand. The firelight caught the flecks of your irises, veined them like polished tiger eye, and I remembered with a painful hunger the touch of your lips in the shadowed garden. When the boy finished, the people of Aliyagama burst into applause. After some moments, you stood. I could see the palm toddy you had drunk in your polished eyes, a slight darkening of your cheeks. I smiled to see you so at home, that you would speak aloud in front of these people.

'See how powerful Magha's armies are now!' you said, and the crowd whooped. You were beautiful, your cheeks painted by firelight. 'Think about it, sisters and brothers: why do the mahouts carve their goads out of madara wood? Because it's the wood of the tree beneath which elephants lie down to die. It's their weakness. This poem,' you said, 'written within the walls of Magha's citadel, is his madara wood. It has made us laugh at him.'

I felt the hard edge of the mad poet's stories, his dead voices, beneath my cloth, unnaturally warmed between my thighs.

'*Anay*, Sarasi!' one of the women called above the chatter, pronouncing your name strangely. 'But tell us who your man-friend is!'

You laughed and hurled a flurry of colloquial Tamil at the older woman.

'He is Asanka the poet,' you said, to my horror. 'The man who has translated this *Shishupala Vadha*.'

There was a sudden quiet, and a burst of confusion as they turned to get another look at me. They stood and clapped and said many blessings. People approached me as the night drew on, bowing and kissing my hand. They traded insults against Magha. They told me how brave I was for defying him. Despite the terror that spiked in me with each exaggerated praise, I felt my face crease into a smile as they came.

Of course, my poetry had seen success. I was King Parakrama's royal poet for three years, and there is no greater honour, but none of my work had ever been taken out to the countryside, to be read to peasants. It occurred to me that I might be the new Kambar, adored by rich and poor alike. Perhaps I would live for ever. I felt conscious of the softness of my hands as they were grasped in calloused palms.

You and I spent the night in a room conjoining one of the headman's houses. The air was warm from the heat that rose from the cooking stones in the corner; the smells of old palm leaves from the roof above. We lay together and murmured about our month apart as though we had been separated by some long journey. We talked and talked, and you let my hands wander across your stomach and your hips. If I ever strayed too close to the hem of your cloth, your body tensed, and you gently pushed me away. I felt the hunger of a long separation sapping me.

'The King must have a bitter gourd for a brain,' you said as we lay there, 'to order the poem in Tamil. Why not Sinhala? Why not Pali?'

'He's like King Kumaradasa,' I murmured, distracted by my yearnings and feeling sleep weigh me down. When you poked your finger into my ribs – which is what you did when I said something you didn't understand – I said: 'The King of Lanka who wrote his own telling of the *Ramayana*, and wrote it in Sanskrit. Did your priests never teach you that?'

'Never mind what my priests taught me,' you said. 'What's Kumaradasa got to do with anything?'

'Magha wants mainlanders to read it,' I said. 'He wants the whole world to think he's a great artist, for people to admire him.'

You blew air through your pursed lips.

'More like King Saddha Tissa, stuffing his mouth with jambu fruit.'

'So they did teach you something,' I said, and you bit me.

'Will you start teaching me to write again?' you said.

'Of course. I won't even ask why, this time.'

'If you can write, you can do anything,' is all you said. 'Like the way you made all these people stop being afraid of the King, just for one night. Why did you do it, in the first place? What made you change the poem?'

'Sometimes men lose control of their demons,' I said. Those words came to me ready-made. They'd been playing through my mind for days. There was silence then, full of frogs and the night insects.

'Do you remember that poem you gave me?' you said, after a while. 'Back in the early days, when you used to pass me poetry in secret? Do you remember it?'

'The one from *Kuruntokai*? Of course.'

'You're a liar! Say it again.'

It's the most beautiful of all of *Kuruntokai*'s poems. I recited it in the darkness.

How did you and I ever meet?
In love our hearts are like red earth and pouring rain:
mingled beyond parting.

It's easy to be brave for a short time. I don't remember being afraid, at least; I remember that night as a womb of laughter. We talked forever, as sleep crept up on us both. As you began to drift beside me, I told you in hushed tones how I had written the passage that Kitsiri read that night, delighting in describing each poetic gem that I had lovingly and cunningly distended into Tamil.

I told you about the languorous, luxuriant chapters to come, and as sleep pulled me down as well, I felt my dreams mingle with my descriptions, until I was afloat on dark pools beneath starlight, and all the laughter of the gods playing at love wound a wreath of flowers around my neck.

Chapter Eight

During this time, Magha paraded his elephants and flower-garlanded soldiers through the streets only once, for the festival of Vesak: the day of the birth, the death and the enlightenment of the Buddha, which the priests assure us all happened on the same day, though of course in different years. It's true that the Kalinga hated our religion, but he loved to hold parades, to dress his soldiers in the full mainland style and march them through the streets, fully armoured like rows of brass bottles, their feet stamping down with every step on our prized holy day.

I watched the parade from a vantage point on the citadel wall, beneath the shade of the tall corner watchtower, and tried not to think of my childhood among the festival smells of frying fish, roasted gram and burnt sugar, the plucking and striking of many instruments. The crunch of the soldiers' boots sounded on the path of palm leaves and white sand laid out along the King's Highway, the thuds of elephants' footfalls, and the steady beat of the war drums beneath it all.

There were no figures of the Buddha, of course – only the multi-coloured and many-armed statuettes of Magha's gods –

and the King took the front of the procession, where the monks and elders of the Sangha would usually march with fans and umbrellas in hand. Magha was riding his army's largest elephant, a thick-set, yellow-tusked bull called Airavata, who walked with loping, unsteady steps. Beside him was the young dancing girl from the royal troupe, the girl who had played Rukmini in his dance, veiled and covered in jewels. The latest gossip was that Magha had taken her as a mistress since the recent dissolution of his marriage. She looked sad and small on top of the huge black elephant.

Pandals and shrines had been set up throughout the city, festooned with flowers. Though the verges of the road that snaked between the citadel and the tank wall were filled with people, no one cheered. They barely even spoke, all staring impassively as the parade passed by – first the whip-crackers, then the fire-spinners, the elephants and the soldiers from the mainland, from Malabar and Cape Comorin and the Cardamom Hills, then the Lankan regiments who were now the most hated of all. Next went the units for night-fighting, the burglars and tunnellers, the skirmishers in their animal skins, and the Vedda wild men who still live like jackals in the forest. These were followed by drummers and dancers and a cage in which two leopards paced.

I noticed that the crowd had been split into separate pockets according to their profession and status. That must have been Magha's order. He often spoke poorly of the lower castes: the bamboo-workers, the sugar-millers and the weavers, for instance. He sometimes asked who had touched a certain stylus or drinking vessel, before taking it in his hand. I've heard from merchants that this is normal on the mainland, that a potter, for instance, would never be allowed to touch even the hand of a seal-bearer or a bronze smith. Here in Lanka, I've seen earringed accountants share the back-scratching pillar in the bathhouse with even the lowliest brick-maker. I've never been to the mainland, but I hear poets are held in high esteem.

It was when Magha's elephant drew him beneath the balcony of a shuttered toddy establishment that someone in the crowd shouted 'Death to Shishupal!' above the noise of the instruments. Some heads turned, and there was a flutter of nervous laughter – soldiers moved quickly into the crowd after a quickly retreating shape – but Magha didn't hear, or pretended not to. I nearly threw myself from the wall. The lines of elephants and gleaming soldiers passed beneath me in a haze, and some men I recognised as palace servants began throwing petals and grains of rice from the walls.

For the two weeks since that night in the village, I had entertained all the possible ways that you and I could escape from Polonnaruwa. It hadn't rained for more than a month, and the persistence of the dry heat, the sun beating down every day from the cloudless sky, made me feel as if I were being baked. The roads were of a good condition – hardened by the heat but not yet cracked and dusty – so the time would soon be right.

I'd spoken to some cart drivers in the marketplace about leaving, too, but they could tell by my beautiful golden skin tone that I was from the palace. They would always begin to murmur about the increased dangers of bandits, the tolls that the Kalinga had placed on the roads, all things contributing to the great cost of the journey. I hadn't yet received the second instalment of two hundred coins from Magha, and since my last payment had gone to settling my many debts, I found myself almost without means. Even the lords had begun to avoid the extra attention that amorous affairs could draw, and had found no use for my poems. The chief of Gokarna had come back only a few days before and told me that my rewrite of his love poem had been even worse than the first, and that as a result his beloved was now courting the lord of Dambadeniya. He demanded the full cost of the poem back, which I gave him with little argument.

My skin crawled as I watched the bands of soldiers marching in their animal skin headdresses. Now half the country, all those tired eyes in the crowd, were waiting and watching to see what would happen. You were wrong when you spoke in the village: Magha still had the power of his armies, his torturers and spies, and no amount of poetry would ever change that.

I knew one thing for certain: if my mockery were discovered, the King would have me killed in ways that would exercise the imagination of his cruelty. The Kalinga might take inspiration from the legend of King Jarasandha, who was torn in two by the mighty Bhima. He might tie me between two pegged-down palm trees, have them released and watch them tear me apart. Or have some of his elephants do the job. I looked down at the parading animals, at the muscles tautening beneath their loose, dusty skin, and the footfalls of the parade began to sound like the popping of sinews. I remembered the fathoms I had seen in your eyes, deep as the sky is deep.

I watched for a few minutes longer as the procession wound out of sight over the canal bridge and past the sluice gate of the island park, between tiled workshops and almshouses. I watched as the crowd dispersed with barely a murmur, some thin spectators getting down on hands and knees to gather the thrown rice grains from the cobbles, and then returned to my room, fleeing the heat of the sun. I sat cross-legged at my desk. I thought of the fate of the Pandavas, those who had slain their brothers on the battlefield of Kurukshetra, the weight of whose sins dragged them down from the mountain of heaven. Perhaps Magha would chain my arms and legs to round boulders, and roll them down a hill.

I took up my stylus and worked like a dog until the bones of my knuckles ached.

After Vesak, the hot days began: days of searing sun and empty skies, days of flies and thirst and fruitless trees. The tracts of paddy land became flat sheets of mud, broken sometimes by shoots, cracking in places like the dry skin of a foot.

During that time my translation continued slowly. I was occupied every day with bathing at least twice, seeking the windy spots along the walls and beside the tank waters. You were often busy with the running of the palace, keeping the place cool and watered, keeping the gardens green, and I didn't see you often. The next two-hundred massa arrived just like the first, in a fine calamander chest. I took some of it and paid off some more debts. Then I put fifty coins aside for our escape, barely half of what most cart drivers were asking. I bought a new sarong, and left the rest of the money in my wife's room, so she could take as much as she wanted. The chief of Dambadeniya came to ask me for a poem to give his new beloved during that time. I took his money, but with everything else going on I had no patience or energy for writing a new poem. Instead, I gave him the same poem I'd given the chief of Gokarna. I only realised some days later that the woman receiving the poem was the same one as before. Needless to say, this hurt my reputation no end in the bathhouses, and when the chief came back with his face purple and his moustache bristling, I blamed an apprentice's error and returned his money without question, thankful to be rid of him and left alone with my fear. He muttered as he left that due to my error, the woman in question was now courting a minor bureaucrat from Anuradhapura.

I remember sitting in my room and breathing hard after he left, staring at the blank page in front of me as I mixed my ink, watching the light play on the gold lacing the *Shishupala Vadha*'s pages. It's important to mix your ink regularly, to stop the charcoal and resin separating from the oil, from becoming two distinct substances. Such a deep black. I felt like the man who is sentenced to death but allowed to choose the method of his execution. I pinched my stylus, rinsed out my ink cloth and began once more to write of the shaded awnings and rich carpets spread throughout the gardens of the gods, the beautiful music of stringed instruments. A mention of King Shishupal came just a page or two later, and I let it slip past me, unchanged.

The stories say that Nisumbha was torn apart and eaten by the goddess Devi's lion. Perhaps Magha would have his leopards slash and rend me to shreds.

That whole month, I made no changes to the poem. When I finished the third instalment, I collected up the pages, bound them with cord and took them to the palace. I placed the bundle on the Kalinga's desk, and he nodded, without looking up at me. His head was turned to where light streamed in through the balcony curtains. There was an interminable silence.

'The Demon King,' he said then, his voice cold. 'Do you know that's what they call me, in the markets?'

I froze. His lips were pursed.

'No, my lord. I had no idea.'

'Don't you go to the markets, Master Asanka?'

'No, my lord. A job for servants, my lord.'

He grunted.

'The briars of rebellion are sprouting up everywhere,' he said, and he didn't seem to be speaking to me, but to the balcony, and the land that spread out between its arches. I shifted on my feet, waiting until he picked up the pages, and waved his hand for me to leave.

On my way back to my villa, I saw a crude message scrawled on the wall of a temple in chalk.

'Death to Shishupal!' it said, and there was a picture, too, of an angry face with thick, furry eyebrows and a crown. I checked that no one was looking before hurrying over to smudge it out with the hem of my favourite sarong.

Soon after that, the poya day came with its bright full moon, and we arranged to go walking by the lake in the first days of the new month. In the days leading up to it, I imagined us finding some cove of round stones, hidden from view by scrub, where you would let me undress you again. I was beginning to forget how certain parts of your body looked, let alone how they felt.

I waited for you beneath the high-towered Serpent Gate, listening to guards playing dice with knuckle bones in the shade, and the gossip in the air. A village of washermen had fallen out with a village of blacksmiths, apparently – the washermen were supposed to supply face coverings for the dead as part of their ritual duties, and the city guild was investigating them for failing to do so. Some cattle-herders had let their animals drink at the water tank of a village of lapidaries, too. The daughter of an accountant wanted to marry the son of a weaver. A farm village hadn't paid enough grain to the drummers and brick-makers. All the complexities and banalities of daily life, overlaid with stories of Magha's cruelty, and the battles he had won in the south.

When you finally arrived, you were guiding an ox cart, and looked like you had spent a hard day at work. I should have told you straight away, the moment you approached me out of the crowd of people, that this month I hadn't changed the poem – but the sight of you with the cart threw me off. As soon I saw you, I regretted the cowardice I'd shown in my translation. I don't know what I'd planned to tell you.

You drew your cart out of the flow of traffic and touched my hand furtively by way of greeting.

'Asanka, I'm sorry, but I have this job to do. The villagers asked me to do it just this morning. We'll have to go to the lake another day.'

I tried not to show my disappointment, but my face must have fallen.

'*Anay*, Asanka,' you said, 'you can come with me. It won't be fun, though. Before the rains we took out a loan of a month's kurakkan from a melon village in the north, and they called it in suddenly. I have to take this load up the North Road and along the canal.'

There were sacks of rice and green coconut in the cart. I walked with you through the city, and out of the tall Hanuman Gate, past the stalls that have lined that road for so long that they have brick walls and guttering between them. The market wasn't as busy as usual. We talked a little as we went, but all I could think about was how my next instalment would disappoint you, and how I could tell you about it. I kept imagining that cove of round stones, and kept my mouth shut.

You flicked at the animal's haunches with a switch when it strayed from the path, but it wasn't a strong ox, and the journey was hard. The air felt swollen with heat; sand sprang out of the dunes beside the river and blew across the fields, covering every leaf and bamboo shutter with red grit. Outside the beautiful Lankatilaka temple, with its cavernous hall and towering Buddha statue, the women pulled their sashes over their mouths to keep from swallowing the dust.

We turned off and walked a path above some parched, empty melon fields.

'You should come and see the poem being read again, when Magha sends it out,' you said, and I felt my stomach dive.

'Yes, I should, but I might have to work that night. The chapters are getting longer and more difficult as I go.'

'I'm sure you can spare one night. You could even be the one to read it this time,' you said, as though this were what I wanted most in the world.

As the ox tired and the incline of the path increased, you took a rope and helped bear some of the load. I pushed from behind and watched the muscles in your back move beneath your skin, marvelling at how different we were. I remember thinking that rain and red earth might mix, but it takes only a day of fierce sun to separate them.

At a traveller's rest we stopped, glazed with sweat, and you gave me some nelli you bought – the small, hard gooseberry the farmers are always chewing, so sour and bitter that after chewing one, everything, even water and the air you breathe, tastes as sweet as an oil cake. We sat and chewed them by the verge, and watched the travellers pass by.

'Is she really so bad?' you said as we sat there. 'Your wife, I mean.'

I squirmed a little to hear you mention her.

'It's complicated, Sarasi. A long history. Why are you asking about her?'

'I don't know. You always talk about her as if she's so terrible. Like some kind of witch.'

I remember trying to shrug off the question, but you were persistent.

'I want to know,' you said, and stuck out your lower jaw. 'Weren't you in love once? Did her parents give yours a dowry they couldn't resist?'

'It wasn't such a big dowry,' I said, and flicked a nelli seed into the ditch. A traveller from somewhere up north was filling his water skin nearby. Some monks were standing by with their bowls out, as it was their begging hour.

'We weren't unhappy, though,' I said. 'Not at first. There was a time – years, even – when I didn't think about it. It was just the way it was. Then King Parakrama appointed me. We moved to the city, and everything changed.'

'How?' you said.

'I think she wanted children. She would have loved children. We tried, but none came. It happens, sometimes. Some women just can't conceive.'

'Only women?' you said, but I stood up and brushed the dust from my sarong. 'Anyway, lots of people never have children. They still love each other.'

'I don't want to talk about it,' I said. I enjoyed saying it, too, since it was something you usually said to me. How could I explain the way it feels to have your own happiness built on another's misery? To go off to the palace every day while my wife stays at home and cleans and gossips and cooks. How rancour builds up between two people the way sickness grows in a wound, until one day you look at one another and each finds a different person looking back.

I took your hand, and we went back to the cart, where a monkey alpha was trying to gnaw his way through one of your rice sacks while his harem looked on from the trees.

'Get away from there, you little shit-eater!' you shouted at him, throwing pebbles at him as he ran, and I felt laughter bubble up through my mood.

By the time we reached the town, the midday bells of the city were a distant murmur. The place was full of thin Sinhala melon-growers, who fell upon the cart with the quick anger of the hungry. They shouted at each other, they cursed each other's mothers and snatched at the polished green coconuts. A man they called 'hook-nosed Tissa' was pushed to the back of the crowd. A woman sitting against the wall of one house shouted at them to behave themselves, and I noticed that she was cooking the kernels of jak fruit on a pile of embers.

'Magha has taken all the melons,' one man said, 'pierced our tank, cut down our fruit trees, filled in the canals,' and though we asked many questions, we received answers from no one.

'General Sankha will save us,' one old woman kept wailing. 'He will protect us,' but no one was paying her any attention, and I assumed she was mad. Soon suspicious glares began to shoot in your direction, and there was one comment to the effect that the Tamils were Magha's servants and spies. We left the village in haste, and I thought that you struck the ox's sides with more strength than necessary for an empty cart.

Our explanation for the villagers' behaviour came when we took the second road out of the village, down through the forest paths. The air became full of the noise of many flies, and it became clear from the smell that something had died on the road ahead. As the sight came into view, we slowed, and the empty cart knocked to a halt behind us. Beside the road, Magha's soldiers had nailed the bodies of three men to a grove of coconut trees. Their skins were dried leather, their mouths yawning open. Beneath them, someone had painted the word 'rebels' in Sinhala and Tamil on a split plank. A terrible dryness rose in my mouth, and I saw your eyes turn wide and hard as glass beads, but what put stones in both our hearts for many days was the woman nailed between them, with a different sign beneath her.

'Taking down the bodies of rebels is an insult to the King,' it said. 'An insult to the King is treason', and I wondered if

Magha himself had ordered that this warning should be written in Tamil, in a perfect metrical couplet.

I didn't see you for several days after we saw the bodies by the side of the road. I'd promised to go to Aliyagama to see the reaction of the villagers to my cowardly instalment, but luckily I didn't have to invent an excuse. The day the copies were sent out to the countryside, Magha ordered me to see him in the throne room.

I told you that I couldn't attend the reading with a tone of deep regret. We spent that day in my room, you talking and writing and lying in bed while I sat at my desk, translating and listening to you, too nervous even to count the days since I'd last unwound your cloth.

'Asanka, what's wrong?' you asked me at one point. 'Why do you keep wringing your hands like that?'

'Am I wringing them? I didn't notice.'

'Yes, you are.'

'I'm just nervous,' I said, and put my hands on my knees. 'Nervous about seeing the King. And about you. I don't think you should go to the village today. It's too dangerous, Sarasi. I saw omens.'

'How could it be dangerous?' you challenged me. 'And what omens did you see?'

'Well, I – I didn't see any exactly, but that herdsman who always comes to the temple with his cows told me that two of the guards' horses have – have eaten each other.'

'Eaten each other? Asanka, that's horrible – did that really happen? And what's that got to do with me?'

'I just – Sarasi, I don't want you to go.'

'Everyone's expecting me,' you said, and pursed your lips. I knew that if I pushed the matter, you'd start to question me, so I dropped it.

When the hour approached, you left me with a kiss, and although I felt desperately alone once you'd gone, I at least no longer had to maintain the lie. Each breath of that dry air was like a cupful of sand. It was uncommonly hot.

I paced my chamber alone, and awaited the summons, imagining you walking through the jungle. I'd translated the poem so accurately that month that I wasn't even afraid of my meeting with Magha. I watched dark koels flit between the flowers of the mango trees that lined the citadel wall, and imagined you reaching the cow path, leaving your twig offering suspended from a branch. I paced round and round, stopping on each circuit to run my fingers over a quartz Buddha statuette in one alcove, something bought the previous year from a tradesman travelling from Anuradhapura. A lizard crawled across the ceiling, then down the wall, then behind the mess of cushions and vases and silver boxes that littered the space behind my writing table. I imagined you walking down the field path to the village, each step a step closer to learning the truth about this month's instalment.

Despite my confidence in the King's reaction, my stomach still gave a little dance of fear when finally a servant rapped on the door and told me that Magha was waiting. The man had a jackal look, like an old hunter who has only recently left the forest. I walked with him along the terraces to the throne room, and the few palace workers still tending to the gardens looked up at us as we passed, tipping large urns of water on to the hard ground with anguish in their faces. Several times, my escort looked as though he wanted to speak to me, but it wasn't until we reached the stairs to the second highest floor that he told me his name.

'I am Janaka, my lord. Listen – I should warn you,' he said, with the sympathy of a conspirator in his eyes. 'The maharaja isn't pleased.'

I felt very hot suddenly.

'Not pleased?' I enquired, careful to use the man's own words. 'Because of the rebellions? Or the heat?'

'No, my lord,' he said, shaking his head. 'The maharaja keeps shouting about your poem. About Shishupal, and his eyebrows. All the servants are scared.'

My toes caught in the hem of my sarong and I stumbled forward. The servant put out a hand to help me.

'Are you all right, my lord? You look sick.'

I was blind with fear. The only notion in my head was that my caution, my reticence in the writing of the third instalment had been for nothing. Magha had found me out. My cowardice had come too late. Perhaps in ceasing my mockery of the King I had merely drawn attention to it, the way one sometimes only notices the chirp of the cicadas when they stop.

My first impulse was to run. I wanted to gather my belongings and escape the palace for ever, out into the forest. I could hide in your village. The people there had liked me, whatever they might think of my latest instalment. There, you and I could spend every day together, in the shade of the forest canopy – we would walk and hunt, forage for food; we would build a house hidden among the palu trees.

But I knew that there were soldiers at the city gates, guards at the doors of the palace. I looked up at the concern in the servant's face, and thought that perhaps the hardness in his features was that of a soldier. Perhaps he was one of Magha's spies, there to test my guilt: the King might already have ordered him to apprehend me if I attempted to leave.

Escape plans flew through my head: the windows were too high, and the dry ground too hard; I hadn't the strength to test the sewage chutes. I imagined feigning a sudden, natural death, but they would surely cremate me with lime, and I didn't know how to stop my heartbeat at will, the way I have heard some yogis can.

Even if I could escape, there was nowhere for me to hide. Now that Magha knew what I had done, he would hunt me down like a boar, burn every village until he found me. He would torture all the palace servants for information, and one of them would tell him that you and I were lovers. Perhaps he already knew – perhaps you'd been arrested as you tried to leave the city, and were already in the hands of his soldiers. He would have you tortured, and the thought was like having white termites burrow under my skin.

There was no escape. I had no choice but to follow this servant to my death, up through the shaded upper galleries of the palace. I looked out at the city for the last time, at the flags snapping in the wind and the smoke making its shapes over the walls. A wave of nausea passed through me, and when the throne room was fewer than twenty steps ahead, I vomited twice over the parapet, on to the roof beneath. A servant below cried out in disgust and disbelief. I knew that my face must have been as pale as a demon.

My escort gave me a pouch of sugar crystals and fennel seeds, which I chewed gratefully to take the taste from my mouth, and he made the sign to ward off the upasagga plague.

We climbed the remaining steps together – I, staggering like a drunk, the servant bearing some of my weight on his shoulder – until we reached the door to the royal quarters and he left me with a kind look. The guards opened the door and nodded as I passed. Magha was inside, the shutters and curtains drawn. There were bodyguards half-hidden in the corners, and he had his back to me.

'Ah, Master Asanka,' he said in his milky voice, turning around. 'Please come in.'

'Yes, Maharaja,' I replied.

Magha had recently commissioned a large and expensive map of Lanka from an expert brought in from Persia. It was draped over his table, the island a bulging, distended thing, spilling down the cloth. Mountains in the south. Plains in the north. The three great rivers. My entire world. Magha sat down at the map before he spoke.

'In the last age, Asanka, the men were as tall as giants,' he said to me, using his thumb and forefinger to measure out a giant beside one of the ink mountains. 'Did you know that?'

'Yes, my lord.'

He leant back.

'Giants. In the age before that, they were even taller. And in Krishna's age, and Rama's age, they were unimaginably huge. Imagine seeing Rama stand before you,' he said softly. 'Towering above the trees. Imagine how small you would feel.'

He stretched himself over the map then, casting his shadow across it. Oil sputtered in a lamp. He ran his finger from the tip of the teardrop, along the trickling land that joined us to the far shore in the north. A broken baby's cord.

'A man so large he could build this bridge, with Hanuman's help. Large enough to conquer the demons who lived here, whom Ravana gathered in a nightmarish horde throughout the jungles.'

'He was a mighty man,' I said, my throat dry.

Magha leant forward so his palm splayed on the map.

'I've read the latest instalment of the poem. The similes were beautiful, your poetry was skilful. But I noticed that you've made a mistake, Asanka. Do you think I'm the kind of man who tolerates mistakes?'

'No, Maharaja, please, Maharaja—'

He cut me off.

'Asanka,' he said. 'I'm very angry.'

He didn't seem so angry. Still, I saw my whole life spinning before my eyes – not my past, but my future, disappearing into nothing like unbaked mud bricks in the high monsoon. Warm evenings with your head on my bare chest, children clapping and laughing as I read out clever poems that I had written for them, the smells of food drifting from the house where we would live together among the palms. I thought of you then, sitting in your village and listening to my poem without changes, and knew that everything was lost.

'Ten million apologies, Maharaja. My shame is burning like a billion suns,' I began to mutter, and he raised his hand.

'Do you know what your mistake was, Asanka?' I said nothing, and Magha stood up. There was a soft laugh playing beneath his voice. 'Then how can you apologise?'

He stood up from his map. A bodyguard moved in the shadows.

'I loved your rendition of the first parvas, Asanka. When Sri Magha writes about King Shishupal. Throughout those pages, the King's foolishness and hypocrisy were wonderful. The poet's description of Shishupal as a corpulent, sweating oaf who would eat a demon disguised as a goat without even realising – his enormous eyebrows – all this made me laugh out loud. I never realised that a poet of Magha's skill and majesty could also be so—' he paused, 'humorous.'

I felt the last of the blood drain from my face, and Magha laughed to himself again, Shishupal's eyebrows bouncing above his eyes.

'But now,' he said, 'now it seems that this foolish, evil king is quite a misunderstood character. In fact, he's barely been mentioned at all in the last three parvas. Can you explain this? And what of his majestic eyebrows? Have they disappeared? Did some jealous lover shave them from his face?'

'The poet – he must have changed his mind about Shishupal,' I managed.

The King frowned again, just a little, and then exploded.

'No poet of Magha's mastery would change a character so suddenly!' he shouted, thumping his fist down on the map. I jumped at how quickly his outburst came. 'I noticed right away that Shishupal had changed,' the King screamed. 'So either Magha is a small-coin poet, and I am a fool, or you are translating the poem incorrectly! Which is it to be?'

'You're right,' I whimpered, ashamed that I couldn't speak aloud beneath the intensity of his rage. 'It was an inconsistency I didn't notice. I must have misinterpreted some of the more complex adverbs. I can try harder, Maharaja!'

He puffed out his cheeks and seemed to shrink slightly from his fury.

'Yes you will, Master Asanka, or I may become as tired of you, as . . . as . . .' his eyes burnt as he floundered for a simile; 'as I am of the disgusting onion lentils that pass for food on this rock!'

By way of punctuation, he grabbed the golden inkwell on the desk and hurled it to the floor with a crash like the sound of a temple gong. It was at this point that the world went black.

I am King Jarasandha

Which of my stories do you want to hear? Is it the story of my birth: how I was born in two halves and fused together by the demoness Jara, my namesake? No? Well what about my death? When that cowherd Krishna told the secret of my birth to Bhima, who ripped me back in two after twenty-seven days of battle?

No? Then what about the story of how I conquered . . .? No, not that either. You want to know about the trivial goings-on in Vidarbha. You have summoned me back from the dead – me! King Jarasandha! Scourge of a thousand kings! Lord of the almighty Maghadha Empire! – and all you want to know is the gossip of one of my vassals. Very well, although I will be brief, and I will not guard my language, whether there are women present or not.

King Bhishmaka was nothing but a Brahmin who inherited some territory and called it a kingdom. I have no respect for the whiny, bastard son-of-a-whore. I never spoke much to the king, in truth, but to his son, Rukmi, who seemed to be the real power there. Rukmi was the typical prince: overfed, spoilt and selfish – he probably had a servant in charge of wiping his arse – but there was also something unsettling about him. Something about how intensely he looked at you. The way he never looked like a fighter, but would turn up wearing strange wounds. Sometimes, even though he had travelled to my palace, and was standing in a room full of my soldiers (some visible, some concealed behind curtains and false walls), I felt afraid of him. A chill ran through me whenever he arrived. There was something inhuman in his eyes.

His sister, Princess Rukmini, was a true beauty, the kind you could use for months and never tire of. When I heard how eager Rukmi was to marry off his sister, I thought immediately of my good friend Shishupal, who had been moping around like a dog recently, trailing his fingers in my lily pond. I thought a young virgin wife would kick some spine into the wet roti.

I didn't think it would be difficult, such a small kingdom! I told Shishupal: 'Take your ten largest elephants, and your ten finest carriages, and fill them with gold, riches, incense, jewels. Send five hundred of your finest men with them, and march all the way to Vidarbha. When they let you into the palace – and they will let you into the palace – break open one of the chests and let the riches spill out over the floor. Then you'll have your bride.'

It helps, as a king, to have a sense for the theatrical. When Rukmini refused Shishupal's offer, I had half a mind to invade the draughty little corner. I would have too – but my soldiers were all posted to distant lands, stamping on insurgencies across the empire. Without constant reminders, you see, the citizens of my more distant conquests forget how large a Magadha elephant can grow – how fearsome it can be when we tie a cleaver to its trunk and funnel an urn of palm liquor down its throat. My elephant stables had been empty for months; my stable-cleaners were all gambling and idling around with women rather than shovelling my elephants' shit. And war with Krishna? That is something you do not want to try without a good number of elephants. I told Shishupal he would have to solve his own problems – and you know how well that turned out.

Perhaps if I had known that Krishna would be the one to have his crony, that fathead Bhima, rip me back into the two halves in which I was born, I would have been a little less cautious about displeasing him. After you die (and you will find this out for yourself in due course), you look back with disdain at the depths to which you sank in life just to stay alive a little longer.

That is all I have to say about the messy business of that pathetic king, his unsettling son and beautiful daughter. I told you I would be brief. Now get out of here, and do not turn your back on me! Walk out of the room backwards, and bow before you leave: just because I am dead, does not mean you can throw etiquette out into the Yamuna!

Do not look me in the eye! Have you already forgotten who I am?

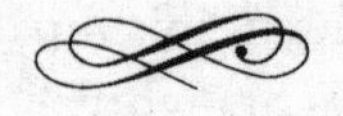

Chapter Nine

When I awoke in my villa, the late temple bells were ringing. Half the day had passed. I had fainted in the throne room, the attending physician said, and had to be carried from the palace by one of the King's bodyguards. I had been unconscious for many hours, and had resisted all attempts at resuscitation. There was the ghost of a smirk on his face when I handed him a few massa and sent him on his way.

In the courtyard, my wife met me with a similar expression.

'You used to be tougher in the heat,' she said, and then went off to the well for water before I could reply. 'But then you used to be a lot of things.'

Thankfully, news of this embarrassing episode didn't seem to reach your ears, but I'll always remember the way you looked at me when we met the next day, the day after the reading. The soft clang of the temple bells were announcing midday. I was walking home through the palace, having spent the morning in the image house, thanking the good Lord Buddha for once again fending off my death.

After hours of prayer, my head was full of the cycle of suffering and rebirth, the colourful paintings on the walls, the kindly, closed stone eyes of the statues. You were carrying a water jar to the lords on the upper levels, but when you saw me, you took the jar from your head and put it on the parapet, where it sat painted with coins of light. Your eyes were large and sad.

'What happened, Asanka?' you said, and a strand of hair fell down over your forehead. I knew immediately what you meant.

'What do you mean, Sarasi?'

'Your poem. We read it last night in the village,' you said. I began to feign innocence, but you spoke over me quickly. 'Everyone waited to hear about Shishupal! Some of the children – they took mud from the riverbank and mixed it with soot so that they could paint themselves bushy eyebrows. I sat there and told them to wait, that something would come. We read right to the end,' you said, your voice lowering to a hiss. 'It took the whole night. At one point you compared Shishupal to a lion!'

A pair of Sinhala nobles hurried past, and pretended not to notice us speaking to each other. You looked coldly at me, betrayal in your eyes.

'You made a fool of me in front of the whole village, Asanka. What happened? Did Magha find out?'

'No, I—'

'If you were too scared to keep writing those things, you should have told me,' you said, and looked long and hard at me.

I struggled to speak for a moment, and it was as though I could actually see the love draining from your eyes. Lies began forming in my head, about how I had intended to convey the viciousness of a lion, the fact that the lion is known as 'the king of the world' only because it rules over the herds of gazelle like a tyrant. I felt like a man trying to hold water in his hands.

'I was – Sarasi, I was saving it,' I said, cursing myself even as I said it. 'I was saving their laughter for next month. What I have planned is so big – so big, that I can't risk drawing attention to myself.'

'Big?' you said, frowning. 'What do you mean, big?'

My mind ran fruitlessly through possible modes of escape, just as it had the previous day on my way to the throne room.

'The next instalment, they will never forget,' I said, feeling all the colour drain from my body. And then, as though I hadn't piled my funeral pyre with enough dry wood, 'I promise.'

You looked hard at me for some time, but then seemed to find what you were looking for in my face, and smiled. I basked in that for a moment. You kissed me on the cheek and picked up the jar with a resonant scrape, telling me: 'I knew it. Be careful, won't you? Don't lose yourself.'

When you turned the corner – and I watched as you went – I fell against one of the satinwood pillars that lined the parapet. I thumped my head against it several times and listened to the sound reverberate through the rafters.

Over the coming days, the *Shishupala Vadha* ate up my life. I found myself scoring pages late into the night. I ate at irregular intervals. Slowly, so slowly that I didn't notice it at first, I truly began to hate the poem.

I have already said that I took no pleasure in distorting such a work of art, that I hated working for Magha, and that I found the violence of the story unsettling, but I had at least enjoyed the simple beauty of its sounds, the golden aura of its words. Suddenly, everything about it enraged me – even the similes.

'Why does everything have to be compared to something else?' I remember gasping to myself by candlelight, wringing the cramp from my hands. 'Why can't something just be like itself?'

I felt Kalidasa and Bharavi recoil in horror from the books lining my alcoves. Even the scribes in the new workshops, grinding out their copies in months for small-time trading families, filling them with their cramped illuminations and thinning out their gold leaf with paint – even they would gasp to hear me say such a thing.

In truth, the poem's rich similes were starting to affect my sanity. Mountains became elephants and elephants became mountains. A man's teeth became a ring of city wall towers, and bees the messengers of the gods. When I tried to eat the steaming rice and curry that Madhusha brought to my room that morning, I caught myself musing that it could easily be a rain-glazed mountain rising out of the mists; the garlic and ginger slices clinging to its sides like the houses of hill people; the curry leaves nestled like grazing beasts on its slopes. I felt sometimes that madness was the inevitable conclusion to this venture.

Since the latest instalment had been published, I had become obsessed with walking the marketplace and overhearing the gossip that passed from head to head. The windy season was arriving with force, and I would stand in line for kurakkan merchants, holding my sarong about my knees, and listen to the market talk; I would go to the *ambattaya* to get my hair and beard cut, even when I didn't need it, and I would buy food for beggars and skins of water for woodcarriers, and each time I did, it was only to have my worst fears confirmed.

'Asanka the poet,' came the whispers, 'Asanka the poet has betrayed us all.'

I once overheard a group of turbaned Sinhala merchants who were marking stacks of jars with their stamps and talking about my most recent instalment.

'The King probably threatened him with the spike,' one said, pushing his index finger through a hollow fist.

'No need,' another said to laughter. 'I wonder how much it costs to buy a poet!'

A wood-carrier named Bimal told me one of the worst rumours: that the first two instalments I had written were a ruse to expose traitors for the King's spies. I began to see murder in the eyes of hooded thugs and the bandit-types lurking in the alleys. I kept away from narrow streets.

Thankfully, my face isn't well known to the people of the city. When I went on these walks in search of rumour, I looked like just another citizen of Polonnaruwa, if a little thinner, with skin more delightfully golden than the men who spend all their days in the fields or the markets. I was subtle. I only asked about the poem after much meandering through subjects, or many cups of wine.

One other name kept coming up in conversation, that of a rebel chieftain called Sankha who had been troubling the Kalinga's army in the nearby villages. I didn't give much thought to it at the time, so distracted was I by the fear following me everywhere more closely than my shadow. I awoke many nights breathless with this fear, certain that the fronds of the palm shifting outside my window were a forest of weapons raised to the sky by a mob – a horde of thugs with a thousand torches – come to claim the life of Kalinga Magha's court poet. I began to see the soldiers as friends.

On the dark night of the no-moon, I didn't sleep at all. The month was half-spent, and I had written nothing. I had no idea what I could write that would be big enough for my promise to you, nor how I could do it without being caught. I sat slumped on my cushion and bent over my desk in misery. I prodded the lank muscle in my left forearm, tugged at the skin, ran my finger along a pink childhood scar. I remembered playing and slipping in the tank behind my town, the sting of water in my nostrils, a hot sensation as my arm caught a flint, and seconds later, blood curling through the water like smoke.

I was too soft to be cut open – to be blinded, like King Parakrama. I could never have been a physician or a medicine man. I remembered the fingers of blood spreading across the floor of the throne room, the three thuds Queen Dayani's head had made when it hit the wood. I wept into my arms: the drops drummed dissonant against the pages, and I had to re-ink some of the letters that they smudged.

Still I had nothing.

Anyway, this is how the idea came to me.

Over the next few days I felt like a squirrel skin being stretched. I made significant mistakes every time I tried to begin the instalment, and repeatedly had to crumble the expensive pages to flakes and start again. One night I tried hiding a message about Magha in every other word of the poem – but it was too obvious. I tried arranging each line of text so that 'death to the tyrant king' was spelled out down one edge of the page, but that was even more obvious. I wrote a story about Shishupal screaming at a servant so hard that his eyebrows caught fire, but it sounded like something a child would write. I wrote 'death to Magha' backwards, and pretended that it was the name of some ancient city. I wrote a pair of paragraphs that could be read in the shape of two bushy eyebrows – but I knew no one would notice. Each time, I tore up the pages almost the moment I had finished, and threw them out of my window into the howling Poson winds.

Between my mistakes and false starts, I had soon torn up all the paper I had left in my villa, and when I went to the storehouse and found the usually well-stocked paper chest empty, I knew that I was severely behind schedule. I could have sent a runner to fetch another shipment from the workshops in Talgama near the river – it would've cost only a massa or two – but I couldn't bear the thought of sitting and waiting for the boy to return while the winds buffeted my room and I wrung my hands. I decided to go myself.

'Madhusha!' I called from the top of the courtyard stairs. 'Madhusha!'

My wife didn't appear for some time, but when she did her hair was wet, she was wearing her bathing cloth and she looked furious. 'Madhusha, I need you to make me up a food parcel. I'm going on a journey.'

'Make yourself a food parcel!' she shouted up at me, knowing full well that I couldn't cook.

'Will you at least fill a seer of water for me?' I said. 'I need to get ready.'

She only laughed, wrung out the long skein of her hair so that water spattered on the flags, and went back to bathe. I found a skin seer in the kitchen, and when I went to the well to fill it I found my wife stepping through the water trough in her bare feet, with her cloth pulled up above her knees. She was pressing down hard with each step so her toes splayed against the stone.

'That idiot girl forgot to empty the trough,' she said, between a mouthful of betel. 'The mosquito larvae are teeming.'

She said it as though she was angry, but I knew she loved that job. I brought up a bucket, filled my seer and left, glancing only once at the muscles working beneath the flesh of my wife's ankles.

'Madhusha,' I said to her, and she turned to look at me.

'What?'

But what was there to say? I'm sorry for bringing you to this city? I'm sorry for leaving you alone in our villa for days on end while I lived a life of luxury in the palace? I'm sorry for making a fool of you with another woman?

'Nothing,' I said. She shrugged.

I went back up to my room to get my travelling sandals, and as I did, I caught sight of the bulge under my mattress where I'd hidden the dead voices. My mind began working. The workshop in Talgama, the whole village even, was full of commoners who could tell the origin of paper just by its feel, or the way it bent to the touch, what tree the leaf had come from, how old it was, where it had been cured. I pulled the bundle of pages out from under the mattress, wrapped them in a cloth and pushed them to the bottom of my satchel. Perhaps someone there could tell me something about its origin. I shouted goodbye to my wife, but she didn't answer. You were working, so I set out alone into the heat and the violent winds.

On my way to the Serpent Gate in the east, I passed the stucco houses of the poor district, squat and cool in the shadow of the wall. The winds funnelled through the streets, sending up flurries of litter first one way, then the other, the shutters of windows banging. The air was sharp with the smell of urine and the stench of the dysenterics, the cloth over the doors billowing like the sails of ships.

I remember very clearly that as I passed a whitewashed district temple, Magha's soldiers were throwing its ornaments and statues into the street, where labourers were filling a cart. One statue, which was too large for them to move, had bright sapphires for eyes, and one of the soldiers was working the jewels loose with the blade of a knife. I thought of King Parakrama, and began to sweat. I was glad when I turned a corner and the gate loomed overhead. But before I could leave, one of the guards stationed there held up his hand, moustache twitching.

'Stop. Order of the King,' he said lazily. 'Asanka the poet, right? Let me see your bag.'

'I don't – I can't—'

'Order of the King,' he said again, slower this time, and one hand slid to the handle of his long knife. 'To check for weapons, contraband or travelling supplies, should Asanka the poet try to leave the city. Give me the bag.'

I felt the weight of Shishupal, Rukmi and Ilvala's stories in the bottom of the satchel. It was so stupid of me to take them. I thought about running, but two other guards were sidling down the gatehouse steps, another lounging against the wall behind me. I could do nothing.

I handed him the bag. He took it, threw it open, and his hand darted in and out, rifling through the contents. There was the tinkle of coins in the purse inside, the grunting noises he made as he searched. Then his hand stopped.

'What's this?' he said, and his eyes widened.

'It's nothing, I promise you, it's nothing,' I began to blather.

'It doesn't look like nothing,' he said, and drew out the seer of water I'd packed. Glugging sounds came from inside when he squeezed it. 'They don't give us much for standing around here all day. You don't mind if I—'

'Oh. No, please, I don't mind.'

'No, of course you don't.'

He took a long swig, his Adam's apple bobbing, the skin deflating. Then I was past him, holding my bag and my half-empty skin seer in my hands, not quite believing that he had let me go. There were children climbing the grille in the wall through which the Jayaganga canal threads, and cranes were fighting the wind in the fields.

Shaken, I headed on eastward and then south, following the sea winds and keeping the twin summits of Gangadoni on the horizon to my right. Gangadoni: the hill of the river daughter. As the shock of my encounter faded, a memory returned to me: the night you took me to your village. The strange lights in the sky. They had been to the south-east, and in daylight I realised that my miraculous vision had been nothing more than torchlight on the ancient hill. I wondered about this for some time as I walked, whether bandits had made their camp there among the ruins of the old monastery, whether Magha had ordered a fortress to be built on its heights. Strange, I thought, that I had heard nothing in the markets.

The journey was tiring. I stopped beneath every shady tree to let the battering winds cool me, and listened to the whining of the *bambarayas*, the little windmills with reed whistles on their sails to scare away the birds, and the shells and stones clattering on strings. I made a list of unsightly things.

The inside of a cat's ear.
The seams on a fur robe that has not yet been lined.
A swarm of hairless baby mice when they come wriggling out of their nest.

Talgama village sits on top of a low rise above the river's flood plain, and I climbed up through the fields exhausted and smeared with dust. Men were walking up and down in the rice mud, throwing charmed white sand on the delicate shoots to keep the worms and flies away. Women were winding long skeins of coir rope from the bundles wrapped against their bellies.

From the top of the hill I could see over the tops of the trees, all restless and bent the same way by the wind, the snapped stalks of banana palms. I could see Polonnaruwa in the distance, with the palace like the stone at the heart of a fruit, the whipped smoke of city workshops, the flat glass of the lake. From that distance, the city looked bright, empty and still, like a jewel, but it's nothing like a jewel. It occurred to me that if someone inside the palace were to look out of a window, I would be able to see them as a grain of brightness among the roofs, but they would never be able to see me.

I carried on up to Talgama. The workshop on the village outskirts was a wide but low building, open to the air and thatched. The workers were all gathered outside the veranda in a crowd, drinking rasam soup like Tamils, sweat beading on their faces from the spice, all laughing at some joke. I didn't pay them any attention.

I made my way between the tall pots of leaves drying over fires, and ducked under the strips of hanging paper waiting to be moistened by the dew, trailing like prayer flags. The Talgama headman was standing near the back of the crowd with his arms folded, laughing along with the men. He was of average height and build, but with a rice-fatness that gave him a strange femininity; he had a mole on his lip that, from a distance, looked like a large fly, and his bright yellow sarong looked as if it had once belonged to a Sinhala noble.

They were watching some performance, though I could hear nothing over the battering of the wind. I assumed that a ragged kolam troupe was passing through the area after food or trinkets: the speakers behind the crowd were Sinhala.

They were doing cartwheels, backflips, and people were clapping and whooping. I approached the owner, and he turned to greet me with tears of laughter glistening in his eyes. Then, when he registered my good sarong and earrings, his face flashed with fear. He put his arm around my shoulder and led me hurriedly away from the crowd.

'Ah, good sir – what a pleasure! Please please please come this way. You have to see this new paper, fresh from the pots – come, take a look! The leaves have been dried and softened a dozen times; the King – my lord, the King will love the feel of it to his fingers. It's smooth as your sweetheart's skin – yes, you have a sweetheart, or a wife? No offence meant, my lord, we're all made of flesh after all – how about this kind? It's been smoked in frankincense so the pages will be fragrant for years. Tell your grandchildren – tell them, this paper was sold to me by Nimal of Talgama – he's dead now, but his paper still smells like the foot of a god . . .'

Sinhala tripped off his tongue like the rattle of a spinning wheel. He was frightened, obviously thinking I was a scribe or some royal envoy sent to collect the shipments. As he swept me into the shade of the workshop, I asked what was happening.

'What is that they're watching outside?' I said, my eyes drawn to a yellow gecko poised on one of the rafters. 'What's the clown saying that's so funny?'

The workshop owner went pale and started fidgeting with his hands. When he spoke, his voice cracked.

'Please, my lord,' he said, 'don't be angry.' He placed his hands together and bowed as low as he could. I didn't know what was happening. 'Everyone has been reading it, and laughing,' he went on. 'We saw the men in the Tamil allotment gathering to hear it, and we only wanted to know what they were laughing at. We're just fools, poor fools who can't even read. Please—' he whispered, and I was startled when he moved forward and took both my hands in his. 'Please don't tell anyone. They don't mean to laugh.'

I was silent. There were only the sounds of the wind in the trees, the workers' laughter, the high voice of the speaker. The headman's breathing came quickly, and I thought that he might weep. I allowed the sounds of the Sinhala words outside to settle in my ears, and recognised what the performers were reading. The *Vadha*. In Sinhala, my own language. One performer was bounding about the stage to uproarious laughter, holding his hands over his eyebrows the way children do when pretending to be a cow.

'They cannot speak Tamil,' the headman said, his voice shaking. 'This dancing troupe offered to read it for us – you know what the dancing folk are like, I'm sure. Rogues, sir, scoundrels! We're loyal to the King, my lord – if any rebels came here we'd drive them out with sticks and matchets, I can promise you that, my lord.'

'Don't be afraid,' I said, as softly as possible. An explosion of laughter outside accompanied a sketch – which I stole from the *Mahabharata* – in which Shishupal is tricked into thinking that a still pool of water is a floor of black marble. He steps into it and drenches himself to his neck. He sputters lamely as he struggles to swim. This was in the second instalment, I believe, and I couldn't help but think that whoever had written this Sinhala translation had made some vulgar additions of his own.

'I won't tell anyone,' I told the workshop owner. 'But your prices are too high – I want a discount.'

'But my lord, I haven't told you – ah, of course my lord, thank you, my lord, thank you,' the man said again and again, kissing my hands and backing away. I paid him for another month's worth of paper, and noticed the distaste in the corner of his mouth as he registered Magha's face stamped on the new coins.

I gathered my things together, but then turned as though I'd remembered something. I took the pages of the dead voices from my satchel and unwrapped them, trying to appear as if their contents were of little interest to me. I handed them to him.

'What's this?' he asked, and I flushed hot as he opened the first page and wrinkled his nose at what he read.

'The captain of the guard wanted you to look at this,' I told him. 'A certain notorious bandit left this at the scene of one of his crimes, a terrible massacre at one of the forest villages. The captain wondered if you could tell us anything about it.'

The man's eyes darted up at me, checking my face. I'd thought hard about this lie, and tried to hold my expression still.

'The captain of the guard gave you this?'

'That's right.'

He sighed, and ran his finger across the paper, brought his nose to the page, smelt the ink, and tilted it to the light.

'Very strange,' he said.

'What is it?'

'Well, the paper is common; I can't tell you anything, I'm afraid. Tal leaf, poorly cured. It wasn't expensive, not bound in a temple house. But the ink—' he breathed in its smell again.

'Yes?'

'Well, it's unusual. I've never come across anything like it – certainly not around here.'

'Is there anything you can tell me?' I asked, and the man's face hardened a little as I realised that I was leaning forward, losing my veneer of disinterest.

'I'm a paper man,' he said. 'I'm sorry. Tell the captain to speak to Pushpakumara, the master ink-maker. Perhaps he could help you.'

I felt the whole hopeless stupidity of it all bear down on me, that the only person who could help me had disappeared from the city long ago. I thanked the man and began to walk back down through the terraces with three new bundles of paper in my satchel. As I went, I heard the headman mutter something about the real bandits being found in the guard-house, not the forest.

He shouted at his workers to move the lazy sacks of guts they called bodies, and they all began to disperse, groaning as he shooed away the protesting dancers. Some of the villagers shimmied up the tal palms for the leaves, some stoked the fires, and others used nuggets of pumice to polish the surface of the paper. As I left, they were all talking and laughing. I realised I was shaking a little.

When I returned home, I found the word 'dog' smeared in lentil broth on my gate, dripping down in great gobbets. *This is it*, I thought, panic rising. *They've come for me*. The peasants had finally come to punish me for my cowardice. I rushed inside, expecting to find my wife in tears, or hurt somehow by the thugs who had done this. The courtyard was empty, though, and as I dashed from room to room, I couldn't find her anywhere. The cooking fires were cold, and the floor was unswept. I was convinced that she'd been kidnapped by whoever had smeared that word on my gate, that before long a message would come, demanding money. Then I realised the truth.

A little while later, I found the note.

'You are a man at war with yourself,' is all it said. 'You have made me a fool and I despise you. I have taken the money in the calamander chest. These are the last words you will ever hear from the woman who was once your wife.'

At the time, I believed that Madhusha would return once her rage had burnt out. I went into the kitchen beneath the Persian lilac in the courtyard and quickly ate the remaining lentil broth clinging to the bottom of the iron pot. I thought about my wife crushing mosquito larvae with her feet, the one strong image that still remains of her.

I took my time over the last meal she'd ever cooked me, crunched the cumin seeds one by one, and ran my tongue along the day-old tamarind seeds, smooth as the smoothest tooth. Then I went up to my chamber and watched as evening settled over Polonnaruwa, and the buildings of the Sacred Quadrangle sprayed complex shadows across the rooftops. Now I was alone with the *Vadha*, open in front of me, flourishing its fine calligraphy, its glorious illuminations. I felt as though it were strapped around my neck.

I closed my eyes and tried to meditate. I tried to picture symmetrical gardens and clear days in the hills, a sea of milk perfectly still, with a lotus flower the size of a mountain rising from it. Myself perched on the tip of the flower, master of everything. I couldn't keep my head clear for more than a moment. I thought that perhaps if I had been brought up to believe what the Kalingas believed, in giants and warrior gods and fighting heroes, then I wouldn't be such a coward. This is when I had the idea of how to fulfil my promise to you.

It struck me suddenly, like the flash of a coloured bird in a canopy of trees, and as soon as it came to me, I threw down my bowl and went to the table to sharpen my stylus, smiling, my fingers shaking. I poured myself a small cup of arrack from a skin I bought in the market.

Magha's gods. Rama, who had once come to Lanka to defeat the Demon King Ravana and win back his wife.

Krishna, who danced on the hood of the King of Snakes, who lifted mountains over his head. In translating this poem, Magha wanted to bring his gods back to Ravana's kingdom. And this – this, I realised, was where I could strike him.

I took a choking gulp of arrack, and coughed. I would fill the fourth instalment of the *Shishupala Vadha* with drunken, arrogant, violent gods, rife with more vices than a Gokarna brothel. I would make the heroes of the invader as much of a joke as I had made him. I smiled to myself, the smile of an unrepentant man climbing the platform to execution, and began to scratch at the paper, keeping my left thumb against the stylus for accuracy, using the parallel lines of the leaf veins to keep my writing straight.

The first parva of the next instalment was a luxurious description of a festival of love and drinking, verses that are some of the *Vadha*'s most polished jewels. To fulfil my plan, I invited all the heroes of the *Mahabharata* to that festival – all the Pandavas and the Kurus. Each of them represents some grand wisdom: Krishna's bravery; Arjuna's loyalty; Bhima's strength.

Even now I feel guilt at the things I wrote that night. I drank a lot of arrack. I took Arjuna first – loyal, beautiful Arjuna – and made him as cruel as our Kalinga king. As the courtiers and courtesans drank together beneath pavilions, Arjuna counted his gold, and stole anything left unguarded by the others. He picked the wings from fireflies and snuffed their brightness beneath his thumb. It was monstrous, and the rush of rebellion that passed through me filled me with the desire to continue.

Bhima came next, the mighty Pandava brother – lecherous and lustful, he clutched at other men's wives. His tent had the largest bed, with the most cushions and a spread of tiger hide. He used his strength to seize whatever and whomever he pleased. I paused, searching for a simile, and wrote 'like a grey monkey stealing garlands of sweet jasmine flowers'. Yudhisthira was a gambler, of course, and used the weaknesses of men and women to bend them to his will, while Balarama was a glutton and a liar – telling stories that would even cause burning faces in a Persian coffeehouse.

One by one, I passed over all the heroes of the epic. When I reached Krishna, though, I did nothing. Krishna, who would behead his own cousin before the poem had reached its end. I went over to the balcony and stared down into the street below, which reeled in front of my eyes. I gripped the balcony edge as if it were the bow of a ship at sea, and shouted down at a pair of stumbling drunks on the King's Highway.

'Why would you kill your own cousin, you bastard? You said you'd forgive him!'

'He slept with my wife, and didn't pay me a single massa!' the man shouted back, and his friend gave a whooping laugh before they stumbled on. I staggered back to my cushion, and slumped down heavily. I wrote with one cheek on my desk. Cutting slowly.

It was nearly dusk by the time I finished, and the skin of arrack was dry. I read back through my debauched, immoral account, and imagined the smile that would spread across your face when Kitsiri the little workshop boy read this out, the pride that would fill your eyes. Even if Magha found out, and had me poisoned with croton seeds, scorpion venom or neagala root, it would be worth it to have you smile at me so brightly. I stretched and knocked back my last cup of arrack. I breathed in the smell from the cinnamon bark being stripped outside, and got up to take an evening walk.

Still drunk, I walked along the canal at cowdust hour, and followed it through the east of the city and the Tamil districts, through the bright bazaars, where charmers played flutes to their cobras and touted their snakebite charms, where bright paintings of the god Murugan glared out from the peeling stucco walls.

The murals reminded me of a time that you and I journeyed to the ruined rock fortress of Sigiriya. It's a beautiful sight, jutting from the forest like a ship in a stormy sea, turning red at sunrise. High up on that rock, the luminous buff glaze of the ancient Mirror Wall is scrawled with graffiti, some of it hundreds of years old, written and signed by the likes of 'the merchant Kitalu', 'Sagal the guard', or 'the Lady Nal, wife of Lord Mahamet'.

All would-be poets, they say, must visit Sigiriya and add a verse to the whispering rock. That day I marked my short poem in small and unassuming black paint, but as I finished, another man's message caught my eye. It was fresh and dark compared to some of the older inscriptions.

'I am Budal,' it said. 'I came with all my family to see Sigiriya. Since all the others wrote poems, I did not.'

Chapter Ten

It's easy to imagine ruin happening suddenly – there's a crack like thunder and then the walls of the palace collapse, the roof falls in, and pieces of stone are pelting the earth like rain before you can even cover your head. But this isn't the way it happens. Ruin happens slowly. Rafters sag and soften. Tiles fall, and saplings push their roots through brick. Even before that, it all begins with the falling together of omens.

Once I'd finished the fourth instalment, I handed it over to Magha. When I arrived at the throne room, he was speaking with all his generals in grave tones. I'd never seen the lot of them together in one room, and I took in all the glittering decorations as I entered – their sashes in the Tamil Nadu and Kalinga and Keralan styles, the shining scar tissue on their skins, their earrings and ornaments. They were standing around the map, on which the King had drawn a jagged line in charcoal, splitting the country. The map was large, and he couldn't reach its furthest edges – they draped over the sides of the table and on to the floor. He was speaking gravely in Tamil.

'—recruiting malcontents from the villages to loot supply lines, sack towns, attack patrols and garrisons. The vermin are breeding everywhere. I've already sent half a dozen messengers to the mainland, but my father—'

He switched fluently into his own language then, and I let my eyes wander over the map. I could see some names scrawled across the island, with the word 'rebel' written beside them: General Subha at Yapahuwa, Chief Buvanekabahu at Govindahela, and General Sankha on the hill of Gangadoni, so close to Polonnaruwa that on the map their names almost touched. I felt a slight quickening of my heart. Suddenly the lights I'd seen on the hill that night took on a new and exciting significance. The King's forehead was dotted with sweat by the time he came to the end of his speech. As what he said seemed to sink in around the room, he looked up as though noticing me for the first time.

'Oh, Asanka. The poem – of course. Put it down over there,' he said, and I could see that he was looking for an excuse to shout at me in front of his men. His eyes followed me to the shelf, and he gave a tired sigh. He said something else to the room in Kalinga, and some of the soldiers laughed. Then he asked me in Tamil: 'Do you have any questions before you begin the next instalment?'

I was taken aback.

'Questions, Maharaja?'

'About the poem – any uncertainties?' he said, and I knew that I should quickly think of a question and allow him to tutor me in front of everyone. I had no questions, though, and could think of only one thing to say.

'Yes Maharaja, permit me—' I said, my voice weak. 'Why did Krishna kill King Shishupal?'

Chuckles ran through the line of generals, and Magha fixed me with a stare of accusation for some time.

'When I am translating,' I went on quickly, 'I find I have to know the wants of the characters, their reasons—' I began to say, simply wanting to divert his intense gaze. He cut me off again.

'Because Shishupal insulted the Lord,' he murmured, returning his eyes to the map. 'You've not been taught the proper meaning of *dharma*, but that's not your fault. There's a cultural sickness about this land,' he said, and waved his hands to suggest a vapour in the air. Some of the generals nodded. 'Shishupal was a reincarnation of the Demon King Ravana, and a devotee of Shiva. Krishna is perfection, and an incarnation of Vishnu. It was Krishna's *dharma* to slice off Shishupal's head, once he had been insulted one hundred times.'

I hesitated with the pages in my hands, the words I had written therein surfacing through the cloud of arrack. I tried to think of a way I could make an excuse, take them away and change them. But it was too late.

The generals turned back to the map, and Magha began once more to speak in Kalinga. His hair was thinning, and he reminded me momentarily of Parakrama Pandya in his final days.

'Thank you, Maharaja,' I said, and placed the book down on the shelf.

I left the throne room and walked back to my villa, where I sat on my bed and stared at the *Vadha* from across the room. I thought about beginning the next parva, but when I heard the second temple bells sound, I put on my sandals and went to meet you for our walk together. You didn't want to walk by the canals.

'No, we have to find somewhere private,' you said. 'I have to tell you something.'

'What is it?'

'Not here. Everyone's talking about this General Sankha,' you said. 'This chief who's built his camp on Gangadoni.

Look – Magha's soldiers are everywhere. They've doubled the garrison.'

They were everywhere, and not the boys and thugs in armour who usually patrolled the streets but the men from the elite regiments with thick black beards and bodies like wrestlers. They were walking along the canals in groups of ten, with horses and long spears and their heavy copper armour gleaming in the sun.

'What about the great ruin – the Tamil stupa?' I said. 'We could climb up there, and there'd be no one around to hear us. No one goes up there, except the monks, sometimes.'

The thought of going somewhere so isolated with you brought an urgent and hopeful sensation to life low down in my belly. You shrugged.

'We'll need a matchet,' is all you said, so we stopped by my villa on the way to get one. I noticed your eyes wandering around the place with a sad look on your face, taking in the finery, the climbing flowers, the rich hangings.

Then we walked north together into the forest, past the temple complex where the tangerine shapes of monks snoozed among the strange rock formations, curtained by roots. Soon the huge hill of the old stupa rose up out of the forest ahead, with trees growing up its sides. The Demala Maha Seya. The largest building on earth – so great it could never be finished.

Soon after we began to climb, a sudden, precious rainstorm broke. It was hard going. The bricks of the stupa are crumbling and loose, they came away in our hands, melted beneath our feet. Thorn scrub was growing abundantly on its slopes, but the trunks of saplings made good handholds, and once we were halfway up, the slope levelled out. I watched the muscles in your calves flexing as you climbed. I tried to breathe away my longing, chatter it away with frivolous talk.

'If Parakramabahu the Great had finished building this stupa,' I called up to you between breaths, 'it would've been the largest monument to Buddha in the world. He wanted it to be visible from the far shore. Can you imagine? It would have taken half the island's clay to encase it in brick.'

You were a little ahead, striking down thorn scrub with the matchet. Raindrops made bright patterns on your skin, wove your newly grown hair into ropes.

'They should have built a wall instead,' is what you said, and you didn't seem out of breath at all. 'It took ten thousand Tamil slaves to shift all this earth and brick. When the workers died, they just kept building around their bodies. This isn't a monument, it's a burial mound.'

When we reached the top, we sat down and ate the food packets you brought: millet, lentils and tender jak curry. We looked out over the less ambitious but completed stupas, the Rankot Vihara, the Kiri Vihara, rising like white suns from the forest. The sound of rain. Then we made for the small stupa dome at the apex of the great mound, which the great King built as an admission of defeat. Even this is crumbling after a hundred years of disrepair, and we climbed up on to it as rivulets began to pour down its sides.

'From here the trees look like an ocean, don't they?' I said, just to say something. 'Crashing against the city wall.'

You didn't seem to feel like talking. We washed our hands on the wet leaves, and you let me kiss your neck as the rain fell around us, as the chirp of frogs grew into a chorus. The skies soon cleared and the heat returned and we lay together in the moss and stone and earth, breathing in the fresh smell of the forest after rain. Love seemed to be the last thing on your mind. I shivered as you ran your fingers through my sodden hair, and imagined the bones of Tamil slaves in the earth, right down to the base of the hill.

'Sarasi,' I said. 'Why did Krishna kill King Shishupal?'

'What?' you said. '*Aiyo*, Asanka – I don't know. They're characters in a story – they don't have lives of their own.'

I watched you closely, and small lines appeared on your forehead as the thought burrowed deeper.

'He forgave him a hundred times,' you said quietly.

'But why kill him? Are words so dangerous?'

'Yes,' you said, and flicked the matchet blade with your finger as you said it. *Tong*. 'It's an evil story, Asanka. Don't let it worry you.'

I ran my thumb along the soft valley of your lips, and they parted slightly. You pushed me away.

'They're stories people tell to make themselves feel better,' you said. 'Like Rama – people say he came here and slaughtered an army of demons. When did you last see a demon, Asanka?'

'That's not – it was another age, Sarasi – when men were giants and demons walked the earth. And anyway, there're none left because he killed them all.'

'That sounds familiar, doesn't it?' you said, and rolled away from me to sit up and hug your knees. I didn't know what to say.

'What's wrong?'

'I'm sorry, Asanka. I'm scared,' is what you said.

'Scared? *Anay*, Sarasi, why?'

I thought that you might be talking about the spiders, the cobras and scorpions that could be crawling through the leaf litter, and I stood up quickly. You stood up as well, and sliced a sapling's head clean off with the blade, then turned and began to descend along the trail we had come by.

'That beast,' you said, 'that Kalinga has been speaking to me.'

'Magha?' I breathed, and the heavy, wet air seemed suddenly cold. You lashed out at another tree, and stumbled as the blade wedged in its trunk.

'He spoke to me in the hall,' you said, 'asked me my name. Every time I set food down for him, he speaks to me.'

I slipped a little as I followed you, loose brick falling beneath me. My heart was beating like a bird trapped in my chest. I had been eating alone in my chambers for several days, trying to finish the fourth instalment before the full moon, and I'd seen nothing of this.

'You told him your name?'

'I had to,' you said, and pushed at my shoulder. 'How could I not?'

All I could think of was the roster in Shona's records, your name cut there in my cramped, scratchy Tamil.

'I thought he had some dancing girl?'

'He's a boar,' you said. 'I'm sure he considers half the servant girls in the palace to be his sows.'

You probably intended this to be reassuring. We stopped for a moment in the crook where a large tamarind tree broke the slope. I lifted your hand to kiss your fingers and breathe in the comforting kitchen smells, but caught only the smell of ink. My fingers were soaked with it, I thought; it was clogging my senses, seeping into me, mixing with my blood.

I thought of my blasphemous instalment, which Magha had yet to read, and my blood felt like fire.

'We have to escape,' I said, and you squeezed my hand.

'I know. Why not the next time you come to the village? We'll wait until after you've met the King, and that way he might not notice for weeks that we're gone.'

'They'll notice when you don't turn up at the kitchens,' I said, and you smiled.

'I'll tell Niranjan I have to take my mother to touch the Buddha footprint at the holy mountain.'

'You don't have a mother,' I said.

'Everyone has a mother. Anyway, tell me what it is, this big thing you've done. What've you written about Magha?'

'*Anay*, Sarasi – wait and see.'

'Have you shown him raising the levies – or ruining the crops?' you guessed. 'No, Asanka, did you make him ride the palm-stem horse?'

You laughed at the thought, and bumped into me playfully as I laughed along with you – a genuine laugh that I felt relieve the tension in the air.

Do you remember that joke? In the *Kuruntokai*, the male lover often threatens to feign madness and declare his love while riding a horse made of palm fronds through the streets, garlanded by stinking erukkam buds. At the time, the thought of Magha naked, bucking and howling with those stinking buds around his neck, bubbled laughter in me like spring water through rock.

We continued our descent.

'When will the poem be sent out?' you asked.

'He's taking longer and longer to read each instalment,' I said. 'It was five days last time.'

'Five days. That's not long, and we could be gone from here. Out of this dying city. I'll get supplies for us and hide them.'

'Where? In your room? In that hole in the wall?'

'No, that's not safe enough. I'll gather it all together in my village, so the guards don't see you leaving with a bag. We'll need food and water skins, blankets, forest shoes and this, of course.'

You hefted the long knife in your hand.

'Yes, all of that. And bring lots of flatbread, if you can,' I said, 'and travel clothes. And not the millet-flour flatbread. I hate that kind.'

As we left the forest and made our way back to the city, we stopped in front of the northern rock temple, the Gal Vihara, to see the large granite Buddha that lounges there. On the floor, wreaths of flowers and candles shifted in the breeze. The veins in the granite create the illusion that he's lying in dappled shade, and the sculptors of a hundred years ago even had the skill to make the stone of the pillow look soft, as though you could press your hand into it. You and I sat before him for a while and prayed.

I stared into the Buddha's face for some time. I wished, as I had many times before, that he would help me. I wished that he would bless our plans of escape. When I looked into his peaceful face – and it is bliss caught in stone – I knew that he couldn't hear me. I looked into his closed eyes, and knew, too, that he wouldn't help me, even if he was able. It's said that the last thing the Buddha said was 'Be a light unto yourself. Seek no other.' These words formed silently on my lips as the prayer flags snapped overhead in the growing wind.

In fact, it took nearly two weeks for Magha to have that month's three parvas copied, bound and sent out, and for a while I was terrified that he would reject the blasphemies I'd written – that the long delay was due to his indecision over my manner of punishment. *I have gone too far*, I thought many times, *and I will pay*.

Those weeks were torture, as you reported back to me the supplies you had gathered in the village, and I had to tell you every day that I had heard nothing from the King. The rare rainstorm that had drenched us on the slope of the great stupa gave way to a fortnight of choking, relentless heat. The price of water skins doubled again. A minor bureaucrat from Anuradhapura came to my villa, very well dressed, and asked me for a poem for his beloved. I told him that the girl was trouble, that the lords of Gokarna and Dambadeniya could tell him so if he didn't believe it from me, and closed the gate on his surprised face. Each day was hotter than the last. Dogs began to die in the street.

And then it happened. The copies went out. A messenger came to my villa, battering on the gate one morning, and told me that the riders had gone out to the village, but that there would be no meeting that month. The King was preparing to leave on campaign the morning after next, off again to slaughter rebels in the south, he said, but I should continue the translation without his guidance. I wondered if Magha had even read it this time.

Suddenly, all at once and without warning, it was the time of our escape. Magha was leaving the city to go and fight his useless war. It couldn't have been more perfect. I told you as soon as I could meet you outside the kitchen quarter.

'Tomorrow night,' you said, and squeezed my hand. 'We'll go to the village tomorrow night, and then—' you looked around. 'Then we're gone from this place. Meet me by the tamarind tree outside the Chandi Gate.'

I hardly slept that night, and the morning of the next day I couldn't sit still. I went to the lake, and rushed around the city doing errands to keep myself busy. The one thing I didn't do was work on the *Vadha*, that accursed poem that I would never have to see again.

As the afternoon drew on, I went to the Sal Bazaar to pass the time and wait for evening. The air was thick with the smells of fruit, of smoke and sweat and cooking food. Cooks rattled knives against their chopping boards with the sound of a battlefield – *sakarana narakasa* – and thin-limbed men missing fingers chopped coconuts in their hands.

The streets were broad rivers of people of every race, buying and selling. At every streetside, stall-keepers plied their trades, selling oilcakes, garlands of flowers for the temples, scented powder and betel paans, while men sung to the music of tortured strings. There were women making bangles of conch shells, using their sarongs pulled taut between their knees as tables, goldsmiths crouching in the shade of their workshops, cloth-dealers measuring lengths, copper-smiths, flower-sellers, painters and weavers, vendors of sandalwood paste. Poets were sitting in the shade and contemplating the rhythm of things.

I was sad to leave, which surprised me. I saw Polonnaruwa that day as though in a dream: a city of so many languages, where people of all religions shared the ghats of the irrigation canal, whose children played in the streets, whose clothes dried on the same trees. It's easy to pass by something every day and never look at it – but when it's the last time you might see a place again, you look at it and think – 'Ah! So beautiful!'

I passed many houses painted with bright murals – and noticed that one showed Krishna dancing on the hood of Kali, the many-headed Prince of Snakes, another of Krishna serving as the Buddha's most loyal disciple. I thought of all the terrible things I had written. I made many circuits of the betel stalls without realising it. It was hot, and my back was cool with sweat.

Then the third temple bells began to ring, and it was time to meet you outside the gate. I left the city, and the guards searched me as usual, riffling through my clothes and my bag. Satisfied, they let me go, and I went to sit beneath the tamarind tree and wait. While I waited, I saw a whistling crowd gathered beside the cool green waters of the Yamuna canal. There was a man there who had trained a monkey to perform acrobatics. He lounged in the shade of a mango tree, holding the cord that collared the animal as it danced and cartwheeled in the dust.

I waited for some time, but still you didn't come. I looked up at every person who passed through the gate, and every time I saw a red-brown sari I thought it was you. But you never arrived. Rumours buzzed past me as I sat there: the tooth relic was being moved to a more secure hiding place on Mount Kotthumala, for instance; two separate rebel chiefs had declared themselves king over all of Lanka; Magha had grown bored with the dancing girl who played Rukmini in his play, but no one knew what had happened to her.

As the sun got closer and closer to the lake, I realised that perhaps you had already gone to the village ahead of me for some reason, and I set off walking on my own. I knew the way by now, but I was still frightened in the forest. I listened out for wild boars, bandits, lone elephants and leopards above the innumerable forest sounds, watching the floor for cobras, ducking beneath the bough-arches of banyans, between acacia and mustard trees laced with the vine that the people call 'the creeper without beginning or end'. Soon I was on the forest path. The river had shrunk in the heat, leaving red banks exposed and cracking, the cinnamon trees losing their leaves. When I passed the village tank, I saw that it too was only half full, with frogs jumping in the shallows.

When I arrived at the village, I found that you weren't there either. I was greeted with warmth, though. There was an atmosphere of great excitement about the place.

'We heard what you've got planned,' an old woman with a permanent smile and crinkled eyes told me. 'We can't wait to hear it.'

A small group of men were sitting on their haunches beside one house, and I started when I saw the curved blade of a sword at one of their sides. I looked around to see if anyone else had noticed them. There was a sweet murmur of talk and laughter, and children ran and chased the tame jungle fowl that pecked in the dust around the houses. Were they Magha's men? Were they assassins, sent to finish me off if I tried to escape? I began worrying a loose thread in the hem of my sarong, and watched the swarthy-looking men uneasily.

It was a beautiful evening, with rosy sky and thin clouds in strips like a ploughed field. I sat down on a mossy trunk and watched the villagers dance as usual. I recognised Krishna among the dancers, and Shiva – a young man with matted hair, and a cobra painted around his blue throat. Some of the children had painted dark smears of charcoal and mud on to their eyebrows, just as you'd told me, and they were fighting with sticks.

A pot of daal bubbled over the fire, smelling of velai leaves, tamarind and white sesame paste. The villagers tore strips from several huge rotis laid out on a flat stone and dipped these in the pot, talking excitedly, using local words that I sometimes didn't understand. They treated the armed men as brothers, and offered them food, which calmed me a little. I wondered when you would arrive.

Kitsiri sat down next to me after a little while, and I became conscious that I had been sitting on my own for a long time. I felt grateful for his kindness, but didn't feel like talking.

'I'm glad you came today,' he said, and his eyes were full of a kind of admiration that I have come to recognise in the young.

'I wouldn't want to miss it,' I said. 'But Sarasi isn't here yet. Do you have any idea where she is?'

The boy shrugged, and put a betel paan in his mouth, beginning to chew enthusiastically. He offered his bag to me, but I declined. The smell of the areca nut and betel leaf, the sweet tang of lime paste seeped into the air around our heads.

'She'll be here if she says she will,' he said, or at least, this was the gist of the Tamil proverb he muttered, which I had never heard before. I considered asking him more about you, about your life and past, but then felt dishonest since I never had the courage to ask you myself. I said the first thing that came into my head.

'Who are those men?' I asked, gesturing to them. 'The ones with the sword?'

'The less you know about them, the better it is for you,' Kitsiri said, shrugging. 'They're General Sankha's men. They got separated from a raiding party last night, and we gave them shelter for the night while Magha's men went tramping around the jungle looking for them.'

General Sankha. I murmured the name to myself, holding it out in front of me like a torch in a dark room. I felt like an ungracious guest for having asked. For a few moments, the young man's chewing was the only sound between us.

'I've always wanted to meet you,' Kitsiri said then. 'Ever since Sarasi began to talk about you. I didn't believe her, at first, that she'd been talking to the royal poet. I hear you've been teaching her to write. She's lucky to have such a good teacher.'

I murmured something about it being the teacher's honour to have such a fine pupil, but then a girl among the crowd called Kitsiri's name.

'*Hai*, wait!' he called back to her.

I noticed the yellow sarong he was wearing, and realised that he had been dancing as Krishna. In order to change the subject from you, I said, 'So you're going to kill Shishupal, are you?' and he laughed through the betel, showing a row of small teeth stained orange. Then, though I don't know why the question still plagued me, 'Why do you think he does it? Krishna, I mean. Why does he kill the Chedi?'

The girl in the crowd called again, and Kitsiri stood up and looked at me as though tormented by the most acute embarrassment, making a face as though he had no choice but to go. His mind wasn't on my question.

'Wouldn't you do it?' he said, by way of answer. 'Wouldn't you kill Magha if you could?'

And he left me, sending the question off into the evening like smoke. I sat and watched the villagers dance for a long time, though I think I may have fallen asleep at some point. I hadn't slept properly for several days, and my eyes became as heavy as stone with the thrumming drumbeats and dream-like movements of the people. General Sankha's men didn't dance, and sat outside the circle of people, squatting against the mud wall of one house, talking among themselves.

Soon the sun began to set. The dance slowed, and once darkness had fallen and the torches were lit, drawing clouds of insects from the trees, the village headman stood and said meek-voiced blessings to the gods. I looked around at the forest behind the houses, expecting any minute to see your figure cut out by the orange firelight, walking through the trees. I asked the villagers on either side of me whether they knew where you were, but they only shrugged and said that you came and went like a *yaksha*. This was true – and I knew better than most – but I was still afraid.

Kitsiri stood up and grinned at me, the village gathered around him, the fire lighting up his cheekbones. The pages of the copied *Shishupala Vadha* fanned out in his hands, and he fingered his leopard-tooth necklace. He began to read, with an evening *raga* this time. He took some time to warm up. I mouthed the words along with him, and he sometimes looked up at me nervously over the crowd.

As he sang, the villagers all seemed to be holding their breath, to be waiting. The men with swords murmured to one another and twined their moustaches in their fingers, chewing. I felt a rush of anxiety as I watched their faces.

Nods and whispers went round as the men of Krishna's army and their wives drank wine as fragrant as freshly chopped mango shoots, as the reflections of the ladies' faces wavered in the flower-scattered surface of the wine, and the blue-black bees settled over everything in swarms.

When the poem finally reached the bulk of my own unworthy and vulgar contributions, as the gods began to arrive and exhibited their own exaggerated vices, the villagers began to laugh – at first nervously, looking around, and then, one by one, they collapsed into uncontrollable, whooping laughter. Even Kitsiri had to stifle himself in order to read about Arjuna's drunken rages, Yudhisthira's foolish wagers, and Bhima's lustful exploits. The young boys who'd dressed as the characters in the story nudged each other at the descriptions of their new scandalous personalities. I glanced over to where the men with swords stood, and saw with relief that they, too, were laughing.

Kitsiri had to stop his recital for a full minute, clutching at his ribs and crying with laughter at another of Balarama's outrageous lies: the great maceman told a palace servant that King Shishupal scratched his behind like the silver monkeys because he ate too many spicy curries. The poem took twice as long as usual to read: the villagers demanded again and again that Kitsiri re-read certain lines so that they could laugh at them anew. The laughter went on and on for fear of stopping.

They enjoyed my description of Arjuna, who 'counted his gold like a monkey counting rotten fruit, wishing to hoard rather than eat it, jealously batting away flies as they descend'. Someone shouted out the name of what I gathered to be a local levy collector, and there was more laughter. I smiled along with them, pleased that I had such an effect, but filled with a growing fear. I rounded off the instalment with the old favourite of Shishupal's eyebrows, and there was applause and the clucking of tongues.

'Poetry makes nothing happen,' I murmured to myself, and wrung my clammy hands. Hearing the poem back, hearing the way I'd written the gods, filled me with a kind of deep and desperate sadness. You still hadn't arrived, and the trees of the jungle, cut out in black before the stars, were beginning to shift and whisper in a rising wind.

Before long, panic overcame me. I made hasty goodbyes and walked back through the forest at speed, all notions of our escape gone. The thought possessing me was that Magha had imprisoned you. He must have discovered our relationship, and forced you to reveal our plans. Or perhaps you had never loved me. You had lied to me all along, and now you were gone – fled from the city, or eloped with some thick-armed wine-tapper.

The moon was a sliver, and I stumbled many times. In that darkness I tricked myself into thinking that I could see, but I saw only what wasn't there. Your words rang through my head again and again, like a temple bell: 'I'm scared, Asanka.'

I tracked my way along the river, and tried to follow the worn cow paths using only starlight and the winking eye of the moon. Kitsiri's question was still hot in my mind: 'Wouldn't you do it? Wouldn't you kill Magha if you could?'

Yes, a voice in my head hissed, *Yes, I will kill him if he touches her!* and somewhere in the trees, a monkey screeched. At the edge of the forest, the sandal on my right foot caught on a vine or a root. It flew off into the darkness, and I knew I'd never find it. I hurried on, feeling thorns and stones on my sole. It's a miracle that I didn't step on a scorpion or cobra, or walk right into the side of a bull elephant in that dark. I tried to make a list of peaceful things, but it was impossible.

When I finally saw the palace's sloping roofs through the trees, Polonnaruwa's tall white walls and the thousand flickering lights, I hardly believed that it was real. The lotus-stalk pillars of the Chandi Gate passed on either side of me, and all the guards only laughed at my missing sandal. I went on, lurching through this city of ghosts in darkness. There were soldiers everywhere in the city, getting drunk and preparing to leave for war the next day. Shadowy figures hunched over in alleyways, and packs of dogs lurched through the streets after their leaders.

On my way to the servant quarter, I passed through an empty market square, the cobbles strewn with the refuse of the day, lit only by the lamplight that spilled from a few open windows. I passed a pile of green coconuts waiting on a bed of palm leaves to be split, and noticed the curved blade of a knife sticking up from the ground beside them. I took it. Gods know why, but I took it. As it slid from the earth, the red clay stuck to the metal, and I wiped it on the edge of an anvil. I felt its weight in my hand, then cold and heavy in the folds of my cloth, a reassuring weight against my hip. To this day, I don't know what I intended to do with it.

I went first to the servant quarter, my footsteps going 'tap, slap, tap, slap', and peered through the lattice into your room, then looked through the curtain. No lights. Nothing. I called your name and listened for any answer or sign of movement. There was no sound from within – not even the women in the other rooms shouting at me to disappear and call back in the morning, as I expected. My left hand nursed the wooden handle of the knife, worn as smooth as bone with age. *I will kill him*, the voice said, over and over. I felt the blood drain from my extremities.

I wandered to the palace, then. I knew that if there were guards, I'd have to turn back, hide the knife somewhere and find my way home along the canal – but there were no guards. I climbed up the servants' stairs through the wall, and then into the halls, past water-carriers and lamplighters and all the beautiful women of the palace who I believe are there simply to be beautiful, like the flower-carved pillars, tapestries woven with gold and the incense-thick air.

I wondered how late it was. Some people inside the palace were drunk. They called to each other up and down the staircases, and some lords were chasing women through one of the halls, shouting and laughing after them. The palace always got like that on the day of a big march, when men realise that some among them will soon die.

I muttered reassurances to myself. Perhaps you'd returned to your village after all; perhaps we passed each other in the dark of the forest, each thinking the other to be some animal moving through the undergrowth. Perhaps you had been kept in the kitchens, preparing some enormous feast for the day of the army's departure.

On some mad urge, I climbed all the stairs to the top of the palace. Still no one stopped me. When I saw that there were no guards at Magha's door, I even crept up and listened against the thick wood, every inch of my body on fire with terror. I didn't know what I expected to hear, but I heard nothing. Such madness! If I was found one-sandalled, listening at the King's door with a knife tucked in my robes . . .

I turned away and hurried back down the steps. I stretched myself against the terrace's balustrade, looked out over the shadowy mass of the garden. You were safe, I told myself. I was acting like a fool, and I was going to get myself put on a spike over nothing. I took a deep breath and leant over the balcony, took the knife out of my cloth. I leant out and let it fall several storeys down into the darkness of the forecourt below – it bounced off some roof tiles, shattering them, and then lodged with a slicing sound in the earth. I hurried back to my villa, shivering in the night's cold, with the laughter of the lords chasing behind me like the voices of ghosts.

You were in my room. I jumped for fright as you came out of the darkness towards me, your face wet with tears.

'Sarasi!' I yelped.

'Asanka,' you said, and I took you in my arms. Your wet cheek was cold against my neck.

'Sarasi,' I hissed. 'What's wrong? How did you get in here?'

I was glad that I no longer had the knife under my clothes.

'He came to my room,' you said. 'Magha. He brought me a gift. He sat down with me, tried to kiss me, touch me . . .'

My fists clenched of their own accord. I found it hard to speak, as if there was a lump of cold rice stuck in my throat.

'You . . . did you?'

'No!' you shouted, and pulled away from me, hitting me on my chest with the flat of your hands. 'I would never—'

'No, of course,' I said, pulling you towards me again so that I wouldn't see any waver in your eyes, if it was there. I thought of the coconut knife lodged in the earth of the palace portico. I wouldn't be able to find it again in the dark.

'He said that tomorrow he was setting out on a campaign to win glory against the rebels in the south. That he wanted – wanted— Asanka, what if – when he comes back? What if he forces me, like the Queen?'

'I don't know,' I said. I couldn't shake the thought from my head: the Queen, slumped in her dungeon in a red-and-gold sari, a purple bruise mapping the veins in her cheek. I remembered what Magha had said to me, then: 'I'd prefer her to love me.'

I remembered the part that I played.

'I'll kill him if he touches you,' that voice said, but this time I realised that I had spoken it aloud.

That night, we made love for the first time since the invasion. I close my eyes when I remember it, so as to bring these memories back with sharper clarity. I hardly knew myself, that's all I'll say. We were dragonflies stuck together in the wet season. I was blind, without language. Breathless with love and terror.

I remember with such clarity the way the light fell against the walls of my room afterward. Was it torchlight, or starlight? Surely the waning moon wasn't strong enough – I forget where it came from, or its colour, but I remember the way it slanted across the room and fell over our bodies, cut to the pattern of the shutters, making henna patterns of light across our skin.

I felt you breathe beside me. I thought in those moments that this final act of freedom had passed between us because you already knew, somewhere hidden, that we were both going to die. There was silence but for some vagrant coughing himself to death in the city below, the noises of frogs and birds, the wind hurling particles of sand against the window shutters. In the crook of my arm, your voice was tiny in the darkness. 'Someone left a book for you,' you said, and I crawled back from the bleary precipice of sleep.

'A book?'

'It was on your bed. It looked very strange, Asanka.'

I felt my skin as a hot cascade of needles. You rose from the bed, your body a totem of shadow, and when I struck tinder there was the sudden tang of burning oil. When you passed me the bundle of pages, I knew immediately what it was. I lifted the first page, and the smell of the ink drifted up to me. It was as if the air of Indraprastha was seeping out to me from the pages – rain on dry desert stone, acid and fresh.

'I am King Jarasandha', it said. I turned a page. 'I am Rukmini.'

'This is important,' I said, though my throat was dry. Your eyes contained many points of light as you looked at me. 'Sarasi, if I don't read this by tomorrow I'll fall behind on my work for the king.'

You didn't ask questions. I stroked your riverine hair, and you settled back down beside me.

You could never know about the dead voices and the mad poet – I was anxious of that – not now we were so close to escaping. I knew that if the pages of this volume were to be as vulgar as the last, then they were not for your eyes. The works had become my personal mystery. My obsession. And now it had happened again. Now I had another chance to unravel their secrets. My fingers were shaking with excitement. Before long, the rise and fall of your chest became regular, your breath soft and deep against my arm, and I opened the manuscript to the first page.

My life changed on the day the messenger from Chedi arrived with his dozen carts and spilled his gold on to the palace floor. I watched from the shaded galleries as the coins caught the light like fish scales, and sweat beaded on the backs of the courtiers' necks. When I saw my father that evening, he seemed extremely tired, and I knew that he had been talking to Rukmi.

'Oh, Rukmini,' he murmured, and massaged his temples. 'What a future you have in store for you.'

I hear you have also spoken to Rukmi. I overheard him telling you about the beating he gave me in the pagoda. But stories change every time they're told, and each one is full of secrets.

True, Rukmi is stronger than I am – years of martial training has seen to that – and his blows left bruises that did not fade quickly. If I were a field mouse, and some women are, I might have sent for Krishna's help. I would have asked him to cut off my brother's head with his chakra – and I considered it, in the days when the bruises were still ripe, blotched with blue and yellow, and it hurt to walk up the palace steps. But I am no field mouse.

I waited. Days passed, and my bruises faded as the wedding drew nearer. Then one night, my darling brother collapsed drunk in his bedchambers after an evening in the city. The night was hot and thick with the clicking of bats. I stole into his chambers in darkness, crawled into the bed and lay next to him for some time, breathing in the reek of bhang and spirits that rose from his clothes, the stale sweat and smoke. I remembered how, when we were younger, he would pull strands of hair from my head with his muddy hands, running away and out of reach before I could strike him, how he had always known that he would be king when father died. I remembered the blank look in his eyes when he beat me, his whole face slack and grinning.

I rose from the bed and took his heavy bronze doorstop from the floor. I lifted it above my head, held it there for an instant, and then I struck him with it. Perhaps I only intended to hit him once, but once the first blow had landed I did not stop. I struck him again and again all across his face and body, until the beginnings of bruises blossomed across his skin like the dark flecks on the full moon, until blood dotted the straw of his mattress. I split his top lip like a grape and knocked out one of his teeth – I brought the metal wedge down on to his face, and one of his eyebrows began to bleed. He woke up momentarily, still drunk and unable to blink the blood from his eyes, so I swung the doorstop hard against the side of his jaw, and he collapsed back into the mattress. I fled, thinking that I had killed him.

In the morning, I think he assumed some drunken fight, or a tumble down the palace steps, since he never mentioned his injuries to anyone. He had them quietly seen to by Father's physicians, and locked himself in his room until they faded. He has had a scar on his brow ever since, and I conceal a smile whenever I see him fingering it.

This small act of vengeance aside, the wedding was drawing closer, and I was desperate. Again, I thought of asking Krishna to come for me. I knew that if I asked, he would lay waste to our palace at Vidarbha, rain fire down on its rooftops, shake the earth beneath it until it crumbled to nothing but a scatter of soot-black bricks. I thought of the women in the palace, my relatives and my poor, weak father, and knew that I did not want this. After all, some people want a god who doesn't carry a sword.

Luckily, there was another way.

On the evening before a wedding takes place, tradition dictates that a grand fair is held, and the bride travels out to the temple at Girija. No soldiers are allowed to follow the bride up to the high altar. I wrote a letter to Krishna, telling him of my plan, and gave it to the Brahmin Sunanda, whom I trusted beyond all others.

The day of the festival came after much preparation. I sat in my bedchamber and stared out of the window as servants wrapped me in a sari the colour of rain-washed leaves, looped jewels through my hair, fetched rings and bangles and anklets, and covered me in as much gold as a royal horse. It was heavy, and noisy to walk. They painted me a delicate bindi and darkened my eyes until I looked into the mirror and did not know myself.

The temple at Girija is a white pagoda on a tall promontory overlooking the river. My family spared no expense that day: everywhere, the bells, conches and drums of celebration were playing. My father and brother were watching the ceremony from afar. I could see the look of defeat in my father's eyes, in his sagging shoulders. Rukmi had the same cool, cold look he always had.

When I walked up those hundred and eight steps, garlanded and covered in gold, with the warm breeze blowing through me and all around, I was more afraid than I had ever been; I would rather have died than live as Shishupal's wife. As the priests anointed my head with oils and moaned their hymns, I began to believe that my love had abandoned me. But I had not noticed the sky flushing red behind me.

When Krishna swept through the flame-coloured dust in his chariot, the drums stopped – people screamed and ran in all directions; soldiers began to rush towards him, shaking their weapons. The chariot thundered past them, shattering their spears, wheels screaming on the cobbles. Then my love lifted me up, away from the priests' clutching hands, and set me down beside him. I looked down over the edge of the chariot, and saw my brother Rukmi in the distance, shaking with rage. I saw him holding my father's crown, and as I watched, I saw that change come over his face. That distortion I cannot even describe. He smiled with that wide, demented grin, and then he began to chase us.

The horses whipped the chariot back through the crowds, brushing away spears, arrows and closed gates as though they were made of dry grass. The sudden acceleration made my stomach soar. Arrows thudded into the sides, sailed past us like swallows. Krishna tied down the reins, then reached over and wiped the paint from my face with his hand.

'Did you think I wouldn't come?' he said.

But this is not the story that reaches the market-place.

This is not the story they write in the books.

Book III

Rain

Chapter Eleven

I read the manuscript many times before falling asleep, and dreamt that dream, of an Indraprastha that was also Polonnaruwa, a Polonnaruwa that was also Indraprastha. Around us, the city crumbled. Its roofs fell in, and trees put roots down into its bricks. I dreamt that, even in Sanskrit, Sinhala or Tamil, I couldn't write a single word of the *Vadha* without corrupting it with the first person: I, I, I. In my dream, I saw the word written in Sinhala, '*mama*', those two whorled seashells, then '*naan*', the way the Tamils write it: a trellised vine, a black sun.

I dreamt that the rebel chieftain Sankha had sent the dead voices to me, that he was a man more terrible even than Magha, and that his sharp, yellowed eyes could spy me out from his roost on the peak of Gangadoni. The acid, rain-fresh smell of the ink was the cord that bound together the pages of my dreams.

I woke before dawn at the sound of shouting coming from outside. It was still dark, but I could see the sun's early light through the palms cresting the rooftops; my nostrils flared at the smell of the first cooking smoke rising from the street. You were curled up next to me, your face resting on my shoulder. You frowned as you slept, and your lips tickled my skin as you murmured in your dreams: the recipe for kiri hodi, the words of some Tamil rhyme, the names of gods.

I watched you for some time, knowing that sleep wouldn't return. The idea of Magha visiting you, sliding towards you in his fine robes, cooing like a parakeet, was like a blockage in my throat. Our first attempt at escaping the city had failed, and the vulgar Tamil pages had returned: King Jarasandha and Rukmini. I felt something had changed in the work of the mad poet, too – something that any poet can tell just from reading another's work: that he had begun to enjoy it. That perverting the great old stories had become a kind of thrill. But what did it all mean?

There were mosquitoes whining in the air. I curled a strand of your hair around my fingers and wondered if the King knew that I loved you, whether he had read the names on my roster of apprentices more carefully than I had guessed, and whether this was his revenge for the blasphemies I'd written. I thought of going to my bookshelf to read, but my mind was still fogged by sleep.

The strange shouts that woke me were getting louder: a distant ululation, pierced by whooping and triumphant laughter. The first temple bells hadn't yet sounded. It was early, and I made use of this small mystery to lift myself out of bed. I tied on my clothes and went to my balcony, but there was nothing unusual on the King's Highway, only the pale blue of predawn light. I took a last look at your sleeping form before I wandered outside.

I went barefoot like a commoner, since now I had only one sandal. I was like a day lily half-opened in cloudy weather – not awake, not asleep, drifting through the city in a daze.

In the courtyard, the stone beneath my feet was cool enough to make me shiver, and I could feel how soft my soles had become since the start of my sandal days. I was still clouded by sleep and dark thoughts, and when I opened my gate I jumped at the sound it made, loud as the screech of a mountain monkey. As I walked, the wind brushed through the wide streets, carrying with it the smell of smoke and chopped onions and rotting mangoes. The shouting was coming from the south, in the direction of the holy quarter and the citadel. I followed the noise through an empty market square, round a narrow passage and past a kottu seller already heating his pans, all the alleyways cool and crooked as the tunnels of a termites' nest, then past the warehouses where shirtless Tamils had begun stacking rice.

Everything was normal, in fact, until I climbed the steps into the courtyard of the Vatadage, the Temple of the Tooth. Here, I found a large fire leaping from the flagstones in front of the magnificent pagoda, beneath the great bo tree. It was crackling and popping, filling the air with sour smoke. Some of the holy tree's leaves were seared by the arcs of flame; the bronze Buddhas all around the courtyard glinted in the light, and the dragon carvings on the banisters came alive in the space where the blue dawn and the tangerine firelight met. Thirty or so men were gathered around the fire, shouting: 'Lo! We are the giants of Kerala! Long live the Maharaja! Long live the King who conquered the world!'

They were Magha's soldiers, enormous, bearded men like the giants of Mara, heaving fuel from great piles into the flames. I crept nearer, and made sure to follow the line of the low image house so that I wouldn't be seen. Smoke blurred everything, and I stifled a cough. I didn't understand what I was seeing.

Then the wind whipped the smoke curtain aside, and the heat of the flames washed over my face. Horror – such horror I felt at what I saw. All around the courtyard were books, piled in hills as high as men. Their pages were torn, the cords that bound them snapped. All of them screaming in pain. It looked as if the temple library's entire collection had been emptied out into the courtyard. The soldiers strode to and from the fire with armfuls of books, scattering the manuscripts into the flames, or one by one, like children throwing stones into a river. Their laughter filled the air, filled my head – I felt a great shriek rise inside me as bound volumes of Tamil and Sinhala curled and popped, grey moths' wings fluttering to the rooftops.

I ran – stumbling, delirious – back to my villa, back to my bedchamber, and as I ran, the burning stories seared in my mind clear as a white-hot brand. *My collection*, is all I thought, *my collection is in danger*. As I ran, I saw bands of soldiers moving through the streets with torches and great canvas sacks, thumping on doors or simply walking in through the curtains, shouting out to the people in the houses.

When I got back to my villa, I bolted the gate, and ran up the stairs. I burst into the room, and you started, wrapping yourself in the bedclothes.

'Asanka! What's wrong? Where did you go?'

'The books!' I gasped, my chest heaving, 'they're burning the stories!'

'Asanka!' you shouted and sighed at the same time. 'You terrified me!'

But I was already at my shelves, flicking through the exposed edges and pulling out anything that I thought was in danger. Sinhala books, Tamil books. All the common languages were in danger. I knew the books without opening them, by the colour and feel of their bindings: the *Bodhi-Vamsa*, with its lacquer trim; the red cords of the *Siyabaslakara*, our most ancient poetics textbook; the worn vellum of the Tamil sangam works, *Kuruntokai*, *Purananuru*, *Akananuru*; even the musty *Mahavamsa*, our great island's history, and the fresh, thin fan of the *Chulavamsa*. I was blind with fear, and threw them all down on to the bed next to you.

'Here, help me put them in this bag,' I said. And then I remembered the dead voices, those heretical Tamil manuscripts. If the guards found those, that would be the end. I could see the bulge of them beneath the mattress, but you were still sitting on the bed.

'Quickly!' I said. 'Can you go and lock the door?'

You got up, throwing your clothes on as you went. There was a crash from the courtyard outside, the sound of my gate being forced open. I dived to lift the mattress and grab the pages while your back was turned.

'They'll be here soon,' I said. You helped me bundle the last of the books into my satchel. Your hand met mine on the cover of *Kuruntokai*, and I looked up at you as feet sounded on the stairs.

'He can't have my books,' I said. 'Sarasi, I can't let him have my books.'

There was a rap on the door, and a foreign voice demanded in Tamil that I open it. I thanked the Buddha that my room was built with a closing door rather than a curtain, but it was rattling on its pins. My blood ran hot, but you spoke calmly to the door, in the accent of a Tamil maid: '*Aiyo* – wait a minute – I'm indecent! I need to get dressed!'

This seemed to give them pause, as somewhere in all men's hearts must cower a scolded village boy. In those few seconds, I managed to close and tie the satchel's cover over its bulging contents. I cast my eye around the room for hiding places, but found nowhere that the soldiers wouldn't immediately look. I cursed myself for not having found some hollow, some crevice behind the bricks of my wall in which to keep secrets, but my room wasn't like yours: the walls were smooth and impeccably plastered.

I headed to the balcony, but the King's Highway beneath had gradually filled with traffic and sunlight and shouting soldiers, so I went to the window on the other side of the room and flung it open. A pair of foreign soldiers were patrolling the side street below, but their wide-brimmed helmets made them blind from above, and now the giants of Kerala outside the door were rattling at the latch. I knew the bolt wouldn't hold if they forced it.

I closed my eyes, and lowered the bag out of the window so it swung above the tiles and the heads of the soldiers below. If I swung hard, I thought, I could reach the wall of the district temple, the one with the bristling palm leaning out over the other side of the street. I was terrified – I didn't want to throw the bag, but above the rooftops I could see smoke rising not only from the courtyard of the Vatadage, but from the plaza before the dome of the Shiva Devale, and perhaps six other places. I would later find out that there were eighteen large fires.

I swung the satchel once, twice, and then let it loose. It arced across the street as if through water and crashed into the branches of the palm. It teetered there, caught in the fronds, and I had just enough time to close the window shutter before you opened the door and two large warriors ducked into the room with a thin scribe between them.

'Order of the raj!' one of the soldiers declared in thick mainland Tamil, as though he was capable only of shouting. 'Show us your collection of books!'

'Of course, sir,' I said, in formal speech. I tried to stop my chest from heaving as I motioned to my emptied shelves. The scribe smiled, and descended on them hungrily.

I didn't know what had happened to my bag. Was it still stuck in the tree's branches, or had it fallen back into the street? Had it toppled over the wall? I remembered with a pang that the monks kept a small ornamental pond, and I imagined the pages of my books littering its surface like leaves, the ink washing out, the paper disintegrating. Perhaps it had struck someone as it fell, and the guards were already gathering around the body of some crushed wood-carrier, or one of their own. There was no way to go to the window to check, and I felt my sarong cling to my back with sweat.

The men ransacked my alcoves book by book, the scribe pulling them out and flicking through the first few pages, then throwing them on to the bed. He was a man who looked as if he was made of knives. I stood by in silence, and you were completely still in the room's corner. They showed no sign of leaving, scouring through the *Ramayana*, chapters of the *Mahabharata*, books of Bharavi's and Dandin's poems, Kalidasa's plays.

Once they had looked through every book, the scribe turned to me, and said, 'This is it?'

'Yes,' I replied, and saw you nod too.

'These are all Sanskrit. Where are your Lankan books? Your Tamil books? The maharaja told us you had many.'

'Me? No, not at all,' I said. 'I gave those books away when we were freed from that tyrant Pandyan. Much better to read the poetry of the far shore, don't you think? So civilised, so cultured . . .'

The man narrowed his eyes, and turned back to my largest alcove. He ran his fingers along its edge.

'There are marks left in the dust,' he said. 'There were books here not long ago.'

I could hear my voice shaking with an equal amount of rage and fear.

'Sir, there's dust everywhere. No one has cleaned this place, since – since my wife left,' I said.

The man glanced at you, with a knowing look. He ran another finger along the windowsill. I could see that he didn't believe me. Then he peered out through the shutters, and my heart nearly stopped. He paused. Turned back. Then he grunted and turned to the soldiers.

'Search everywhere,' he said, and stood by the door, watching as the soldiers ransacked my room. They rifled through my chests and the alcoves where I kept styluses, ink and candles. They broke a glass jar, and disarranged all of my writing materials. One of the men even found my small quartz Buddha statue, and tucked it into the folds of his cloth, giving me a lean and meaningful look that said 'Now it's mine.'

They even peered at the first page of the *Vadha* lying open on my desk. They searched under cushions and bolsters, in the tiny space beneath the heavy mahogany writing desk, under the mattress and bed boards, until all of my possessions had been moved from their places. Finally, they shrugged to each other and made to leave.

'I'm sure we'll see each other again,' the scribe said to me, pulling his hat down.

'I hope so, learned one,' I replied, bowing. He screwed up his face, and the three of them satisfied themselves with drawing their eyes up your body as they went.

They didn't leave, though. The banging and clattering of a clumsy search continued downstairs for a while longer, and I watched the muscles in your shoulders tense with every loud bang from the courtyard. I edged to the window, and peered out through the slats of the shutter. I couldn't see the bag anywhere – not in the tree, not in the street. I waited, holding my breath, until the sounds subsided, and I heard the noise of the servant on duty closing the villa gate. Then silence. The whole time, you didn't speak, but watched me closely. I took a deep breath, begged the Buddha for strength, and ran outside.

The scene in the King's Highway had changed completely: now there was a pile of books scattered outside every door, all thrown into the gutter, cords straining, pages splayed like gutted fish against the dust. All the rich merchants and lords who lived in my district had large, ornate collections. They boasted about them at gatherings – who had a pearl-studded *Ramayana*, or a century-old copy of Kalidasa's play, *Remembering Shakuntala*. I staggered through the street, stepping over the piles.

Through doorways, I caught glimpses of noblemen struggling with the Kalinga's men over beloved volumes, or standing by as the contents of their shelves were swept into the street. As I turned into the alley I saw my neighbour Mohan the jeweller chasing a soldier carrying an armful of books out of his door. Mohan screamed as the man tore off the cover page, and pearls came loose from the bindings, cascading into the street.

I darted off down the narrow side street that runs below my window. I was still barefoot, and my feet slapped against the cool dust as I ran. The patrolling soldiers had left, and now the sun was rising over the rooftops, painting all the window shutters gold. The men who always lounged under a rush bivouac beneath my window were already, or perhaps still, drinking arrack; a few pigs and a large water buffalo wandered about apparently without owner, and an old ox cart lay on its side against the high temple wall. My bag was nowhere to be seen.

I looked up at my window, and tried to follow the arc it must have taken. There was no doubt: it must have tumbled into the garden of the district temple. The gate was on the main road, in full view, and so I'd have to climb over the wall. I walked up and down that stretch of the road twice, my ears straining for the heavy footfalls of soldiers, the clatter of horses.

I climbed on to the ox cart, and the degenerates under their bivouac began to laugh at me. It was difficult to balance as the thing shifted and rocked beneath my weight. It took a lot of courage to continue. I jumped up and grabbed the top of the wall, the mud brick crumbling slightly in my hand, my feet scrabbling up its side. The laughter of the drunks chased me all the way up. When I got to the top, and swung my leg over, my sarong caught on the edge of the wall, and I almost lost my balance. I noticed that a couple of neighbours' children were watching and pointing, too, leaning out of a high window.

I looked down into the garden on the other side, and saw a group of monks standing beside the pond in a circle some distance away. They hadn't seen me, and I tried to drop down the other side quietly, so that I landed behind a trellis propped up against the palm. I hit the ground among an arrangement of jessamine at the foot of the palm, and shivered as the flowers scattered dew on my arms and face.

I bent low and looked around for my bag, but it wasn't in the undergrowth beneath the wall, so I crept forwards and peered through the trellis at the monks, appreciating the way their robes rhymed with the tangerine temple flowers around the garden. They were gathered around a dais where a golden Buddha had once sat, all looking at something. It took me a few moments to realise that what they were looking at was my satchel.

I didn't know these monks, as I frequented the richer Lankatilaka temple outside the city. These poor district priests could already have sworn their loyalty to Magha, I thought. How else could they stay here, filling their bellies with rice? I watched the elder among them take the bag from the novice, and begin to open it. A wave of panic filled me, and I knew I had to act.

I hurried forward into view, and called out to them in Sinhala, 'Listen, my friends – thank you for finding my bag for me. It fell from my window by accident. How lucky you found it!'

If the monks were startled by my sudden appearance, they didn't show it. The elder hesitated, and I saw his hand tighten on the leather. After a moment, he bowed and handed me the bag without question. I noticed beads of dew had settled on the close-shaved hairs of his head, and I thought that perhaps he had once visited my temple with begging bowl in hand.

'Of course, Master Asanka,' one of them said softly. I didn't know how they knew me. 'That's quite a collection of books you have. All the Pali chronicles: a complete history of Lanka, and every one of the sangam collections. I'm afraid the cover of the *Mahavamsa* has been bent by the fall.'

I felt colour rushing to my face. They had already looked inside the bag.

'You're a brave man, saving them from the flames,' another added, and I felt my stomach crawl. I thought of Krishna, and the idea of bravery made me feel sick.

'Come with me,' said the elder. 'There's a back gate through our stables, you can leave that way.'

I followed him, and when I looked back at the novices dispersing, I noticed that some were bruised and cut, with burns the shape of knives on their faces and necks, that one small man's shoulder dropped off abruptly where it should have become an arm. My forehead prickled, and I felt guilty for my previous thoughts.

'You shouldn't stay here, hamuduruwo,' I advised the old monk in quiet, urgent tones. 'You have to flee Polonnaruwa before they kill you all, and this whole place becomes a ruin.'

The old man smiled, and recited some lines from *Kuruntokai* in cool, hesitant Tamil:

As part of their work,
farmers leave water lilies piled high by the field edge.
And yet the water lilies do not say
'These men are so cruel;
we will go to another field to live.'
Again they bloom
in the field from which they were weeded.

At the stable gate, I mumbled thanks for finding my bag, and shrank away from him. Despite his kindness, I hated him for not being afraid. He watched me go with head bowed, as though he knew the darkness to come in the days ahead.

Chapter Twelve

I found you at the gate of my villa, sweeping together all the shards of broken things with my wife's broom. When you saw me, you threw it against the wall.

'What happened? Your books – where did you find them?'

'Some monks, in the temple, they – never mind, it's not important. Look, I have to hide these. We can put them in the kitchen, under the pile of coconut husks.'

'They'll come back,' is all you said. 'That's exactly what they're hoping for. If you don't want the books to burn, we have to hide them.'

'What about in your secret place – the loose brick in your wall?'

'They won't fit,' you said. 'We have to get these outside the city.'

'The village?'

'Too dangerous. They might be searching the villages as well – and you know no peasant would ever have all those books. Look, follow me. We'll go north. I know where we can hide them.'

We walked through the streets, dodging the bands of soldiers sidling from door to door. Everywhere the air was still thick with the smoke of burnt paper. Though the soldiers were shouting and beating people and kicking down doors, we got only disdainful glances cast our way, and arrived without incident to where the King's Highway threads north through the Hanuman Gate. It was the day of the big market, and people and carts were flowing through the gate in an unbroken stream in both directions. It was easy to disappear among them, and we stayed close to the wall of the gate, kept our faces down. I remember catching the mischievous eye of one of the cartwheeling dwarves carved into the gatehouse. People were shouting at each other to move, oxen were huffing.

A band of Magha's swordsmen were stationed at the guardhouse, and as we passed them, their captain fixed me with a stare. I inadvertently shifted the satchel on my shoulder, and his eyes darted towards it. I almost stopped in my tracks, heart pounding, but you grabbed my elbow and pulled me on under the gate.

'Don't give them a reason,' you said to me as though to a child. 'They're bored – look at them. They'll stop you if they can.'

We passed all the stone-walled market stalls on the North Road, where more people were arguing and a drunk man was staggering about. Monkeys watched from the rooftops and in the trees, baring their teeth. Then we left the road and cut through the temples. It hadn't rained properly for weeks. The dust choked everything, coated the smooth white domes of the stupas and the surfaces of the leaves, the lacquer of doorframes.

Monks in undyed robes were walking from the university to their residential cells, to the temples and the meditation chambers they built on the outcrops of rock formations, fluttering with prayer flags. Then we walked off into the dry forest scrub, and the shapes of deer darted through the trees. For a long time we followed an elephant path through the forest, one of those highways that criss-cross the jungle just like the roads of men. I was afraid for my life as we followed the trail of shattered tree trunks, sidestepping the imprints of monstrous feet and the heaps of fibrous dung.

'It's here,' you said after a while, pointing to a copse of trees growing into the shoulder of a rocky hill.

'Here? What's here?' I said.

'You'll see.'

We pushed our way through the thicket of undergrowth, tangled with creepers and thorn scrub, and when we burst out through the other side, I saw a sunken pool, ringed with trees and the ruins of a small temple. There were walls and steps crumbling everywhere like sugar, bricks clamped together by roots, and a beheaded Buddha statue lying on its back close to where we were standing. The water level was low, and swarms of flies orbited the lilies that were rotting all around on the mud. A group of monitor lizards lurked in the shallows and trained their yellow eyes on me as I stepped down the crater's sides.

'They hardly ever bite people,' you said. 'But watch out for their tails. They'll lash you, and it hurts.'

I held my bag close, and edged down the sides of the crater, using tree roots as footholds, until I stepped on to the dry bed of the pool. Here and there, the exposed earth had warped in the heat, cracking into large hexagons. I went over to the headless Buddha statue, the treasures hidden beneath its feet long-since plundered, and placed the bag in the crook of his outstretched arm, so it looked as if he was holding them. I tore up several handfuls of ferns to cover my secret, and might have hidden it more thoroughly had one of the monitors not at that moment slipped into the deeper water of the pool, unsettling a muddy scum. I bolted, and scrambled up the bank. I got mud all down the front of my fine sarong, and you laughed at me for a long time.

'Scared of a fat lizard,' you kept saying. 'The man who mocks a king! Don't worry, they won't eat your precious books.'

We walked back to the city, and you held my arm as we went. On our way, we passed a dead monkey – a corpse picked to gristle, its fist-sized ribcage a rigging for flies – and I thought of it collared and dancing.

'You said Magha gave you a gift,' I said. 'What did he give you?'

You shifted uncertainly. 'I brought it with me yesterday, to show you. I left it on the table in your room.'

I felt my mouth getting dry. Heat was beginning to rise from the dry earth, and Polonnaruwa's limed walls were soon difficult to look at in the glare. When we returned to the smoky and busy streets, you came back with me to the Vatadage courtyard, where the black heap of the book bonfire still smoked. The soldiers had left. On the ground, curls of sinew and cords spelled out Tamil words everywhere, but I didn't know what any of them were supposed to mean.

The acrid smell of burnt lacquer and leaf and sinew was overpowering. I slumped down in front of the pile of blackened paper, and tears ran down my cheeks. The embers were still glowing in the heart of the fire. As I knelt there, the wind teased out a fragment of a charred page, and opened it out on the stone in front of me. A fragment of poetry. Some omens happen like that. They insist on being noticed. I reached out to take it.

Death's no new thing.
In grief we suffer patiently,
for we know this much-praised life of ours is a raft
borne down the waters of some mountain stream
that over boulders, roaring, seeks the plain.
Though storms flash from darkened skies,
descend, for the raft goes on as fates decide.

I sat and watched all the thousands of beautiful voices turn to ash, all the hundreds of years float skywards. I cried like a child, and you stood beside me and ran your fingers through my hair. Soon you had to leave for work, I remember – or perhaps that's just what you told me. You left me kneeling there in the ash.

When I returned to my bedchambers, I didn't wash my face or hands. I went to my desk and found the gift Magha had given you. It was a sari. Red and gold, in the finest fabric. With my hands shaking, I opened the *Shishupala Vadha*. I took out my stylus. There was soot on my fingers, in my hair. My nose was an inch from the page, and I wrote a long anecdote about King Shishupal burning the books of all the libraries he had conquered, in rage at Krishna's theft of his wife.

I described the bonfires as 'so numerous that they burnt like Vishnu's infinite, flaming eyes'.

It was perhaps two weeks later, with the moon thick in the sky, that Magha summoned me. He was back in the city for a few days, replenishing himself after his campaign in the south. There had been riots. Not full-blown riots like the city had seen during the days of the sixteen kings, when commoners had stormed the palace and been fought off at the points of spears. They were scuffles over water, mostly, and food, sometimes. But Magha evidently saw them as challenge enough to require his presence in the city. Or just thought the captain of the gate watch needed a cuffing around the ears. Around this time, I saw another charcoal drawing on a wall: Death to Shishupal. This time I let it stay.

On the morning Magha sent for me, I'd hoped to go down to the lake, to wash away some of the pallor that had been creeping into my face: the patches under my eyes were swollen and nearly purple; red lightning bolts lanced across the whites of my eyes. I was just getting ready to leave when I heard a knock on the gate. Outside, I found a palace servant. He looked bored.

'The maharaja wants to see you,' he told me, and by the way he said the foreign word, I could tell that he had been disciplined for his pronunciation. Magha had returned from campaign.

'I thought there would be no meeting this month?' I said to the man, the usual paroxysms of terror washing over me. 'It's been so long already.'

He only shrugged, and I began to panic. Had Magha finally got around to reading the blasphemy I'd written? Had someone seen us hiding my books? What about me and you? Did he know?

I made my way through the palace slowly. I took in every wall painting as I passed, the long tableaus of the great King Parakramabahu: his war in Bagan, the building of Parakrama Samudra, his healing of animals. I wondered if Magha might have these walls whitewashed one day or repainted with scenes from his own life. That painting, I imagine, would be hideous. The smoke from villages, from the forest, from the tall piles of books, would stretch down the corridor in an enormous cloud – the blood of the King, the Queen, of half the people of Lanka, I thought, would run in rivers down its bottom edge.

When I entered the throne room, I noticed that the pearls that hung about the place had multiplied so they now clustered everywhere like jasmine flowers. Magha was sitting on his cushion as usual, but now wearing his suit of golden armour. The map of Lanka was on the floor in front of him, and it was covered with hastily penned Kalinga script, shifting in the liquid light. I could read none of the words, but I could see that many of his additions had been scored out and changed, that arrows and crosses dotted our island. The map had been a beautiful thing. I felt my own helplessness seize me like terror.

'Ah, Asanka, it's hot today, isn't it?' he said. He looked tired, but all traces of his wound had disappeared. He rose from his desk in one quick movement, eyebrows arching. They'd become even more prominent as his skin grew paler. 'Let's take a walk down into the city,' he said. 'I have something to show you.'

I flinched a little when he swept past me, and hurried after him. He was a fast walker, and his boots drummed out a stern rhythm on the floorboards: heel then toe, heel then toe. The reactions of the people we passed disconcerted me: servants scuttled by fearfully, guards nodded at us as we went.

'I hardly ever read while I'm on campaign,' he told me. 'The fighting in the south's been fierce. The villages are betraying me all over the place – but the bandits will be beaten soon. And, more importantly, the mindset of banditry. My generals have everything under control.'

'Of course, Maharaja.'

'They're capable men,' he said, 'and brave, but the rebels know their country. When we come near them, they disperse on every side, and while we hunt them through the forests they penetrate back into the lands we've already brought under our control. It's like fighting an army of women. Or demons. While all that's going on, how can I find the time to read poetry?'

'It's hard, Your Highness. If only the days were twice as long.'

Magha sighed, and rubbed at his temples.

'You saw the fires, I suppose?' he said.

'Maharaja?'

'The fires. All the books, and maps and poems, from the libraries. I had to burn them all.'

He looked tortured and miserable.

'You had to, Maharaja?'

'The people are – they're reading the wrong things, Asanka. We've been translating this poem for – how long has it been?'

'Nearly five months, Maharaja.'

'Five months. And still, they can't see what I'm trying to give them. They're ungrateful, Asanka. They mock me, do you know that? They make fun of their king.'

He looked at me hard, then, and I could feel a knot tightening in my throat.

'Treason, my lord. Pure treason.'

He sighed again.

'It was your latest instalment that made me see it,' he said. 'It reminded me of the works of Kalidasa – that's how beautiful it was. And so true.'

We were approaching the steps down to the gardens, and spearmen at the gate nodded to us and uncrossed their weapons.

'Yes, you're correct,' I said, though in fact my work was much closer to the poetry of Bharavi, who influenced the *Shishupala Vadha*. 'Kalidasa was an influence of mine. Very astute of you, Maharaja.'

He looked pleased, and seemed to suck pride from the air. There was a malice and passion to his every movement, and

I couldn't help but see each shift in his body as a sign of danger. The garden was spotted with shadow, and full of servants tipping urns of water between the tree roots. Even here, the drought was sapping at the trees, and some leaves were yellowed at the tip.

'I was spellbound by Magha's description of the gods,' Magha went on, clearly in full flow. I sensed danger looming on the horizon. I couldn't tell if he was playing with me. 'Spellbound,' he said again. 'I've always wondered how the gods and heroes can be shown as so rigid and perfect in some texts, all glittering skin and white teeth, when all of them would stop at nothing to achieve their destiny. When Bhishma would seize the three princesses of King Kashi – or Krishna. Krishna would destroy King Shishupal because the man insulted him. He simply stood up and threw his chakra into the neck of a king. We all have these desires, don't we?'

'I think we do, Maharaja.'

'I've heard it said that a man who can control his desires merely has desires weak enough to be controlled,' Magha said. 'Don't you agree?'

I thought of you, and I did, although I said nothing.

'That's when I knew I had to burn all of the books,' he said. 'When I realised what Magha's message meant. We have to exorcise the past. We have to suck it from the world like a poison. I hope this isn't too subtle for the peasants to see,' he said, with a look of genuine concern on his face. 'They are so slow and so stupid – and that's what the bandits prey on.'

'I can only hope it isn't, Maharaja,' I said.

We walked through the gardens, and out through the gate into the canal district. As we went, a large contingent of spearmen that had gathered at the garden wall hurried to follow us – men with finely bound chainmail and bronze armour, with extravagant heads to their weapons. With this heavy escort, we moved among the workers and artisans clattering about their various noisy trades, chattering from kilns and warehouses, pottery wheels and livestock pens. When I thought about being the king, about never being able to simply walk the streets of the city without bodyguards, I felt desperately sad.

'My father will send me more troops soon enough,' Magha said, wringing his hands. 'Just as soon as he reads my messages, he'll send me more troops. I expect them in the weeks to come. More horses, too.'

Soon the wattle houses peeled away, the alleys became floored with palm leaves, and we were in the area of the city reserved for the guilds and workshops. Dried fish, herbs and sheaves of fat, black-dappled plantains hung from market stalls, with monkeys perched watchfully on the rooftops above.

'Look, this is what I wanted to show you,' Magha said, as if presenting me a rare treat. 'It's the place where the work you've been translating is copied.'

He led me through a clutter of mud-brick workshops and into a courtyard of shade trees before a wide, tiled building. He ushered me towards it, and one of his bodyguards lifted the curtain with his spear blade.

The place was windowless and lit by oil lamps. My eyes became accustomed to the gloom and I took a sharp intake of breath at what I saw. Inside was a large hall, where perhaps two hundred scribes sat on rows of mats along its length, each with their nose an inch away from the page. The sound of styluses scratching at paper filled the warm air like a hive of insects. The resin smell of cheap ink.

I'd seen workshops before: a dozen apprentices, the dust of the small hut, the old master. Even the largest of the fashionable new script houses employed no more than fifty men to churn out their poor quality manuscripts. This – this was monstrous.

As we walked down the aisles of desks, I saw the men hurrying over to a lectern where a large master copy lay open, murmuring the lines to themselves as they scurried back to their desks with their bowed backs. I could see at a glance that even this copy wasn't the one that I had written. Copies of copies of copies. I shook a little, but I had to walk quickly to keep up with Magha. Not one of the furiously writing men looked up as we passed. Their spines showed through their skin where they hunched – their beards were greying and beaded.

'The light has to be dim to prevent the copiers from succumbing to blindness,' Magha explained, as though I didn't know this. 'These copies will be taken down into the south, and handed out to the villagers there. Maybe it will finally teach them not to harbour rebels in their houses or in their fields. Maybe it will teach them to be civilised.'

We left soon after, but it seemed like for ever that we walked up and down those lines of scribes. From the twilight of the copy house, the brilliance of the sun made me squint. Magha led me back to the palace by a different route, past brick-makers taking advantage of the heat, cow-herders sweating and cursing the sun, monks gliding through the crowds and pretending not to notice the chaos of the world.

As we walked, the King insisted on discussing poetry with me, which was extremely dull, for his tastes were at best amateur, at worst bestial. While he talked, I wondered to myself at how confused the King was.

We drew closer to the palace, where the quartz-riddled earth was looser and the dust rose more insistently into the air. Then we passed the guardhouse and the courtesans that are always filling the opposite side of the street, and who I'd heard had begun accepting payment in water. I realised that we were approaching the palace dungeons, a squat but opulently decorated building that is the only visible sign of the warren of underground passages beneath.

We stepped inside. Magha ordered his soldiers to wait in the guardhouse, and a prison guard began heating some water for them as they waited. The jailer was a thin man with a dirty cloth. He led us through the series of heavy bolted doors, his footsteps musical with keys, and we descended into the coolness below ground. The sweat the day had brought to my back became cold. I wondered if I would leave this place.

The moaning of more than one voice rose from the bottom of the steps, and chain links tinkled against stone. I counted the rows of cells as we passed, to distract myself from the thin and grubby men that languished inside. We walked past the cell where Queen Dayani had spent her final days, and I felt the roti and onions I had eaten that morning rise up to my throat. I caught a glimpse of the Tamil poem I had written for her: 'O man of hill country', still dark on the cracked plaster.

At the end of the corridor, Magha stopped, and leant on the door of one of the cells, looking in through its small, barred window. I stood beside him, and peered in at the wretched man with a ragged beard and glassy eyes. Even in this state, I could recognise him. Pushpakumara the fat master ink-maker.

'Can you imagine what this man's crime is?' Magha asked me, as if this would be a good game.

'No,' I managed, although my throat was dry. The ink-maker in the cell didn't look up. His sizeable belly had shrunk, and he now looked like a crushed fruit, draped with folds of skin.

'When this man was caught fleeing the city five months ago, I gave him a second chance,' Magha said. 'I put him in charge of a whole division of copiers in the workshop we just visited. In every one of their copies, a batch of which were to be sent out to Gokarna, he made additions of his own. Hey you!' he shouted to the wretched man, 'Tell him what you wrote! Tell him what you told the slaves to write!'

Pushpakumara didn't move, and remained silent. Magha kicked the door.

'Death to Magha the tyrant!' the King shouted, and this echoed down the dungeon. I thought I heard a faint cheer from one of the cells, but if so it quickly faded to nothing. 'He hid it in the middle of one of the poet's stanzas in the master copy,' Magha said. 'He believed no one would notice it, that it would be disseminated among the villagers at Gokarna and would spread mutiny!'

'Terrible,' I murmured, unable to take my eyes off the man in the cell. 'Despicable.'

'Ha!' Magha laughed, and spat through the bars. 'To corrupt a masterpiece of ancient poetry is crime enough, but to corrupt it with treason?'

The King allowed this syllable to hang in the air for a long time. Let it settle like ash.

We left the dungeon and returned to the light of day, although the cold of that underground place remained with me for many hours afterwards.

I am King Bhishmaka

I always wondered, when I was alive, how people would remember me. Would I be 'Bhishmaka the Kind'? 'Bhishmaka the Vassal'? I often suspected it might be 'Bhishmaka the Weary'. But it happens that after all my years sculpting the kingdom of Vidarbha from those scattered, mud-scraping villages, I am remembered only as 'Bhishmaka, father of Rukmini'.

I think that of all my work, it pleases me that I am remembered for her.

I certainly know myself as 'Bhishmaka the Weary'. Gods know, I would have given up the throne years ago if my eldest son, Rukmi, didn't have a brain as small and misshapen as a bitter gourd. I wish Rukmini had been a man, and Rukmi's elder.

For years, I was afraid of my son. I saw the look that boy gets in his eyes: hard as black pearls, like wet river pebbles. There was madness in those eyes. I used to shudder at the thought of my kingdom and its army falling under his command – but of course, if we had much of an army, I would not have to bark after that bastard Jarasandha whenever he clapped his hands. They say King Jarasandha has an army of men merely to clean out his elephant stables every day. Maybe now you see why I am so weary. Please, pass me your cup – I am thirsty for wine.

On the day of the Girija ceremony, I secretly hoped that something would happen to put a stop to my daughter's marriage to Shishupal. I had seen my darling Rukmini spending more and more time alone, with that furrow in her forehead that means she is hiding something from the world. I saw her writing, once – and by the way she gripped the stylus with white knuckles, I knew it wasn't some love poem. On the day of the festival, I was prepared.

When I saw Krishna's chariot approaching in the distance, over the flags and streamers, my heart nearly burst for joy. Rukmi was standing next to me, watching the drummers and dancers with his eyes sharp. I knew I had to distract him.

'Here, my son,' I said to him. 'Will you hold my crown for a moment? It's itching my head terribly.'

Rukmi turned to me, his eyes flashing, and a hungry look came over his face. I knew he wouldn't refuse a chance to touch the crown. I'd seen him eyeing it more than usual recently, and even stroking it when I'd taken it off and he thought I was not looking.

'Yes, father, of course,' he said, and reached out to take it, a little too fast. I held it a moment longer, enjoying his impatience. In the distance, I could see Krishna's chariot getting closer and closer to the temple where my daughter stood and prayed. I delayed for as long as possible, breathing on the crown and buffing it with the hem of my robe before handing it to my son.

'It's . . . heavier than I imagined,' Rukmi said, his fingers running over the jewels encrusted in the band. 'And cold to the touch.'

It wasn't until the first soldier shouted that Rukmi swung around. It was already too late. My eyes welled with tears, watching my daughter being swept away in that chariot. Such happiness, I felt. Rukmi shot me a burning look, and his face, in that instant, had a deranged quality to it. I just managed to snatch the crown back from him as he dashed away with startling speed.

'Rukmi!' I cried after him. 'My son, don't be a fool!'

But by that time, he was already behind the reins of his chariot, and began to give chase. At that point I looked down at the crown. It was completely bent, crushed into the shape of my son's hands as though it were made of foil. The royal goldsmith, who tried for days afterwards to bend it back into its former shape, said that nothing but a vice could have done such damage. The first thing he did was to cleanse it with holy white sand and say some very serious prayers.

When Rukmi caught up with Krishna, I hear they fought for hours, battling with many weapons in the dust, as Rukmini looked on. They say that when Krishna's power finally prevailed, Rukmini rushed forwards and begged for her brother's life. Krishna agreed, but did not let Rukmi go unpunished.

That night, my son returned to the palace, and I hardly knew him. He sagged and wept like a little boy, bruised and defeated. Every hair had been shaved from his head, and all the courtiers laughed at him behind their hands.

'Father,' he said to me, wrapping his arms around my shoulders. 'Father, how will you ever forgive me?'

It was strange. I don't know what Krishna did or how he did it, but from that day onwards, the madness in Rukmi's eyes has faded. He is quite a different man, although – I regret to say – still has a brain like a gourd.

You will excuse me – just speaking about this whole tiresome episode has brought about my weariness once more. Begone, begone! Leave me to my rest.

Chapter Thirteen

As I walked back to the palace with Magha, he talked to me about *dharma* and duty, about the unquiet citizens of the city, the battles he had won in the south and the chieftains he had quelled.

'So we put them on bamboo spikes,' he said, and made a number of popping sounds with his lips. 'A warning. All along the road. To show the beasts what it means to choose the wrong side.'

I felt myself become physically weak. I still remember how I pictured the thing to myself, and it left behind a certain inner trembling. This is again why I could never have been a physician or medicine man.

'Tell me what the peasants see in this Buddha's tooth that they're always talking about,' Magha said to me. 'How can you worship a man's tooth like a god?'

'It's hard to say, my lord. I suppose because every word the Buddha ever spoke passed over that tooth. And it's his words that—'

'Ha!' Magha said. 'And that's why they've squirrelled it away somewhere in the hills. You asked me before – you asked me why Krishna killed Shishupal. Do you see it yet? It's simple: it's his duty – do you see the beauty of it? Every man has to fulfil his *dharma*; every man has to fight towards his destiny. That's what the rebels in Rohana don't understand. That's what that rat rotting in his cell back there didn't understand.'

Magha seemed agitated that day, and I was struggling to keep up with his thoughts. He always seemed to enjoy sharing them with me, since I never interjected or disagreed, but merely nodded and complimented him occasionally on his insight. To take my mind off the poor wretches in the south, I thought of the bruised face of Pushpakumara, his skin three sizes too large, and his great knowledge of ink. How they used to say he could identify even the most exotic inks just by their smell.

As we drew under the shadow of the palace's enormous wooden beams, with the lamps and prayer flags swinging high up in the rafters, Magha and I passed a ragged cohort of prisoners. They were naked and resting for water beneath the bowed stems of coconut palms. Their heads were shaved, and they had glassy, passive expressions, as though the world were a story being told to them. I knew them, if only by this, to be monks, and noted some of their horrific and fresh deformations. Magha gestured to them as we passed, as though they proved his point.

'Why,' he asked, 'would a man follow a god who won't even fight on his behalf? Who won't even make him brave?'

'Because some want a god who doesn't carry a sword,' I said, without thinking. The moment the words were out of my mouth, I realised where I'd got them from. I wanted to snatch them out of the air and stuff them back in. Magha looked very hard at me, and I felt the blood rushing to my cheeks.

'You're right,' he said. 'What idiots they are.'

We passed a temple courtyard as the afternoon bells began to ring, and the flock of pigeons pecking for spilt grain between the flagstones took flight all at once, wheeling around the courtyard in a cloud before settling back where they had begun. The King dabbed his forehead, which was bright with a sheen of sweat.

He was still wearing his armour and mail, despite the heat of the day. Desperate to change the direction of the conversation, I remarked on this: 'Is the maharaja preparing to leave for battle again?'

He looked uncomfortable suddenly, and cast his eyes over the passing monks and worshippers.

'Every day is like a battle for me, Asanka.' He drew closer to me, and whispered, 'A knife was found. Outside my chambers, in the palace's forecourt.'

I realised at once that the weapon he was talking about was the dull coconut knife I had thrown over the balcony. Cold scorpions scuttled from the base of my spine up to my neck. What if someone had seen me?

'I believe there may be plots against my life forming in the mind of every malcontent in the city,' he hissed, and tapped the scales of his breastplate. 'The Tamils, the Sinhala rebels, this Sankha upstart on the hill across the river – they think I've never met their kind before, but by the gods I have. There could be any manner of renegades hidden within my very servantry; they're swarming throughout the poor district, that den of filth and crime and treachery. It's always best to be vigilant.'

'Of course it is, Raja,' I replied. He was scared, I saw that now, and also saw that I had caused it – I who had spent the last five months living in constant dread of him.

'Assassins could be anywhere,' I muttered as an afterthought. 'You must be prepared, Maharaja. They could be hiding in every shadow.'

'Exactly,' he said. 'You know what it says in the textbooks of war? That the path to victory lies not in attack, but in making one's own position unassailable. That's what my father taught me. Yes – that an enemy can never defeat you unless you give him the means of doing so.'

As he said this, he stroked the leather thongs that held his armour together at the neck.

'He's a great king, my father,' he said. And then, as if from nowhere, he said, 'All these people living so close together. The modern life of the city. Don't you think it brings out such tensions in people? They way we live these days?'

'The tensions aren't so modern, Maharaja. I think they're very ancient,' I said.

He sighed, and nodded. When we reached the palace, he put out his hand and touched my shoulder, squeezed it slightly and held it for a long time.

'How is the fifth instalment coming?' he asked, looking me directly in the eye. 'It's not too much?'

'It's going magnificently, Maharaja,' I said. 'Like a bee's honey or a worm's silk.'

He gave my shoulder an extra squeeze, and let it go.

'I've brought you a gift, Asanka,' he said, and produced a little package wrapped in a cloth. 'Some treasure from the campaign. I hope it brings you good luck.'

As he walked away with his guards, I unwrapped the bundle to find the most beautiful golden stylus I had ever seen. The curling-vine pattern that wound up its side caught the sunlight in warm, bright streaks, and at the very top a tiny Buddha sat. I felt sick. I couldn't imagine what holy place Magha had robbed this from, and what had happened to the monk who owned it. On my way home, I threw it in the canal with a heavy plop.

The rest of the day I spent in the baths, trying to scrub out the sour smell of frightened animal from my skin. I went to the library temple, too, to look up some of the words that were giving me the most trouble in my work on the fifth instalment. I returned to my room after dark to find the ceiling bathed in a flickering orange light, making the kind of patterns you might see on the undersides of leaves that hang over water. I walked to the window, and saw streaks of flame striating the city to the east, belching a high pillow of smoke into the night and underlighting it in orange. I watched the poor district burning for some time. I didn't have it in my heart to feel more pity.

The days drew on, baking the earth, and Magha's men cleared the ash and debris from beneath the east wall. I passed them several times on my way to the temple, watched them kicking through pots burst open in the heat, prayer beads melted to pools of glass, the blackened ribs of houses. In the following days, once the area was properly cleared, they erected tents and pavilions on the debris, increasing the permanent garrison in the city. The people who had once lived there were gone.

It was one night after that, before the first half-moon, that you came to my room and woke me. I started awake as you touched your cold hand to my forehead, and your voice half-mixed with my dreams.

'Asanka, I can't sleep,' you said.

I remember the shape of your face loomed over me in the dark, and though I knew it to be you, your features rearranged themselves into a grotesque shape so that I sat up sharply and gasped.

'What is it?' you asked in a small voice.

'Nothing,' I said. 'A dream. How did you get in here?'

'It's not so hard,' you said.

‘Didn’t the servants bolt the gate?’

You pulled at my arm, and I groaned. ‘*Anay*, stop it. Get into bed, if you want.’

‘No,’ you said. ‘I want to go outside. Let’s go for a walk.’

You showed me how you’d tied the hem of your sari around your anklet so your steps wouldn’t make a sound. I felt sleep fall away from me, and got up to get dressed.

We left my villa and walked a little along the canal, where a perfect half-moon shone white in the water, and the dark mass of the citadel wall loomed on our left. Torches were lit in the guardhouses.

‘With the King back in the city, I don’t like to be in my room at night,’ you told me as we walked. ‘Hopefully he’ll go back to his butchery soon and leave us in peace.’

I didn’t know what to say, so I said nothing. When we came up against the wall of the Nandana garden, you pulled at my elbow.

‘Let’s go in,’ you said.

‘In?’

‘Let’s go into the gardens. We could do it – look.’

You motioned at a tree that was overhanging the wall, its lowest branch within grabbing distance of a good jump.

‘No, we can’t. We’ll be caught, and what then?’

‘Don’t be a coward,’ you said. ‘Give me a leg-up.’

Realising that it was hopeless to argue, I gave a long out-breath, and cupped my hands for you to step into. I brushed my cheek against your thigh as you did.

‘Hey!’ you said, and jumped up to grab the branch, swung yourself deftly on to the top of the wall. You reached down your hand to me, and I took it. You were so strong – that always surprised me. You gripped my wrist as I walked up the side of the wall, and with only a little scrabbling at the end, we both dropped down into the walled garden at night.

It was strange and beautiful. There were the sounds of cicadas, the light of stars and the moon giving everything that odd silver edge. We whispered for fear of waking up the servants or watchmen in the palace. As we rounded the groves of plantain trees near the pond, fireflies dipped and wheeled around in the air, and you murmured, 'The night before the half-moon, the stars grow wings and fly.'

Your normally golden eyes were opaque black. We kissed in the darkness, then moved on, listening for the sounds of other footsteps. When we reached the steps down to the royal bathing pool, you tugged at my hand.

'Come on, Asanka,' you said. 'Let's take a bath.'

'Are you crazy?' I hissed. 'If anyone sees us—'

'We'll jump back over the wall,' you said.

'I don't think I can climb that fast.'

'You don't have to – just stay here and say to the guards "I am the King's poet, and if you'll excuse me, I'm trying to bathe!"'

You laughed, that taunting laugh that drove me mad, and pulled me along with you.

The water of the bathing pool was as still as black marble. You shuffled to a halt at the top of the steps that disappeared beneath its surface, then knelt down and broke its perfect stillness with your hand. Ripples moved out over the pool and rocked the lilies growing at its edges, scattered the moon in its surface.

When you splashed me, as I knew you would, I pretended to be angry, and brushed the water from my chest and face: I feigned for a moment that you had hurt my eye, and when you advanced with genuine concern and outstretched arms, I pushed you into the water – do you remember? I hadn't done anything like that in a long time.

There was a crash of waves, and you shrieked so loudly that I worried someone might wake up, even though we had by that point travelled some way from the palace. You parted the curtains of your wet hair, and swam out into the centre of the pool, then back.

'Come in!' you said, and when you began to tease me, I slid into the dark water with my sarong billowing up around my stomach; it was cold, and I held on to the shallow ledge that ringed the pool. You swam over and kissed me. I could smell the water on your skin. Your cloth had come loose – I felt one of your breasts slide free of your clothing; your skin felt oily, your wet hair cold against my cheek. We were both shivering, and suddenly all laughter had left the air. The only sounds were the chatter of crickets, your breaths in my ear and the water of the pool lapping against the sides. *This is heaven*, I thought. *This is what it feels like to die*.

Afterwards, we lay on the grass together, allowing the warmth of the night to dry us. I was on my back, with your cheek on my chest. I stared up at the constellation of Prajapati, the sky god who in legend made love to the dawn. The mainlanders say that he was born alone in the vastness, and split himself to ease his loneliness: peeled himself apart into man and woman. The three stars in a straight line across his waist wink so beautifully that it's hard to believe they are the arrow that killed him.

'Did you hear about what happened on the south road?' you said. 'The men who attacked one of Magha's patrols.'

Word had been spreading through the markets.

'They left the soldiers dead in an irrigation ditch,' I said, wanting to change the subject. 'They're calling them bandits.'

'That's what the guard is calling them, anyway,' you said. Your voice was level and cool. 'But you know what they aren't saying? That all the soldiers were found with eyebrows painted on them. Big, thick, bushy eyebrows. I heard it from Kunjan.'

I swallowed hard. I felt silence creep up on us, a kind of thick inkiness, and felt an overwhelming urge to tell you something I had never told you before. I closed my eyes.

'When I was a child, my village shared farmland with three others,' I said. I felt as if the words were coming out of nowhere. 'There was one higher village, one lower – and a Tamil allotment. The children of our villages would gather in gangs, and all play games together. We would even let the Tamils play, when we played at war. They complained sometimes because there were so many of us, and we always chose where the battles were fought. Our parents beat us for fighting in their rice fields, so we went down to the chenas of the allotment children to fight. I remember being caught in the rains while stealing pepper from the tall vine in their garden, throwing stones at them as they chased us, splashing and laughing in the ditches alongside the hill paths. I find myself thinking about that time a lot. It was around then that my father died.'

I felt your fingers tighten a little on my chest.

'He was trampled by an elephant,' I said, hearing my own voice as though from far away. 'A great big, tusky elephant that had drunk up a jar of rice liquor stockpiled for a festival. I went home that night, with my mother and all my sisters weeping. One of my uncles got drunk, too – drunker even than the elephant had been – and told us all that when a bull elephant wants to kill a man, it lifts him up with its trunk, and then throws him against the ground so that every bone in his body breaks. Then it stamps him to a chutney of flesh and hair. I've – I've been scared of elephants ever since. Isn't that stupid?'

You said nothing, but the tips of your fingers tightened against my chest. For the longest time I thought you were asleep – but then you spoke.

'I was born on the far shore,' you murmured.

At first I thought you were speaking in your dreams, but there was a purpose to your voice that made me quiet my breathing so as not to miss anything you said.

'My parents were killed by Chola mercenaries when I was young. They were puppeteers,' you said. 'We travelled from village to village on the far shore, performing stories. The old Hindu legends.'

You went on in that low voice, and told me about your sisters, a family waking up in a different place each night, always beds of sacks and hay, living off whatever the villagers had to pay you.

'My parents,' you said. 'They always told me that once they'd earned enough money with their puppets, they'd send me to a temple school, and I'd learn how to write stories of my own. When they died, and my sisters were taken away, I begged for a time. Then I was adopted by the priests in the temple of Brihadeeswarar in Tanjavur.'

You described to me the building of sharply cut sculptures, gods and heroes and animals all climbing into the sky in a great staircase. How young you were when you first saw it. Dark corridors lit by lamps, flowers rotting to mulch on the altar.

'I don't remember much of my life before the temple,' you murmured. 'Or what my parents looked like.'

Your father was tall, you said. He did the voices for the male puppets. His favourite was the cunning trickster Shakuni, who casts spells on the other characters, and cheats Yudhisthira in the game of dice. Your mother had soft, quick hands, and she loved performing the old stories. The *Ramayana*, the *Mahabharata*.

'I remember them most clearly,' you said. 'The stories.'

You paused for a moment, and swallowed.

'When I went to the temple, I thought that this would be my chance to learn how to write, and tell my own. I would've settled for being a scribe, even. But the priests apprenticed me as a devadasi from the day they took me in.'

'You were married to the gods?' I said, and tried to keep the petals of laughter out of my voice. 'Magha's gods?'

You didn't find it funny. Perhaps if I had been more knowing of the world, I might have heard the stories about how the Chola priests treated their dancing girls.

'You said you never danced,' I said.

'I don't.'

The soft noises of the city outside the garden sank into our conversation for a little while. Then you went on:

'The devadasi are married to the gods in their hearts, but their bodies belong to the priests of the temple, and once they are old enough, they belong to any man who will pay.'

I felt a tingle pass through my fingers.

'You—'

'I don't want to talk about it,' you said. 'Not ever, so don't ask me.'

You told me about how you escaped that place, how you hid in caravans, walked dust roads and begged for food, all the way to the coast and Mylapore. You told me about nights spent sleeping under sacks waiting to be loaded at the quays, and how you eventually became desperate enough to stow away in the cargo of a dhow headed for Lanka, with an Arab crew. How you survived by stealing food from the crew – mainly some flatbreads that were a bit like rotis.

'I stayed hidden,' you said. 'If they found me, I think they would have sold me on to a brothel in Persia or as a slave in Africa.'

'Why that ship?' I asked, amazed and horrified by your story. 'Why Lanka?'

'I don't know,' you said. 'Chance, I suppose. I met a girl who told me that the ship was sailing the following morning, that the sailors were all drinking coffee in the port town. I wanted to put the sea between myself and Tanjavur. But there was another reason too: I remembered how my mother told me the *Ramayana* as a child. Perhaps some part of me soaked up the descriptions of Lanka: Ravana's golden palace, the bridge that the monkeys built.'

I felt your cheek move into a smile against my chest.

'I wanted to see it, I think. The place where the story happened. When I arrived at Gokarna, I found it a more horrible place than even Tanjavur, full of soldiers and sailors and thieves, so I left and followed the Mahaweli River south.'

You told me about how beautiful the river was at that time of year. A wide ribbon winding through the land. All the trees so green, the palu and banyan, with peacocks roosting in them. You told me how you foraged enough food to keep yourself moving. The hot days, the cool mornings.

'At night I climbed trees to be safe from leopards and bears,' you said, 'but I still imagined that Ravana the Demon King was lurking somewhere in the night, hungry for a feast of little girls. You could hear him, sometimes, in the rustle of the trees, or a palm squirrel gnawing its way through the young coconut husks.'

After weeks of wandering the forests alone and starving, you rounded a bend in the river and saw Polonnaruwa, white as a gem, with the lake a plate of bright steel. You knew in that moment that this was where you would spend the rest of your life. That you would never care to move from this place.

'But after such a long journey, I didn't have the strength to reach the city,' you said. 'I collapsed into the river, and a group of women found me washed up on the rocks as they came to rinse their clothes. They took me back to their village – Aliyagama. They took me in, taught me to peel cinnamon and weave cloth. Taught me how to honour the Buddha and pray to his trees. Some of the men worked as washermen at the palace, and they petitioned there for me. Because I was young, I was taken on as a servant. And here I am. Still lost. But at least now I can write, the way my parents wanted. And now I'm not alone.'

Your fingers clutched at my chest, and I shivered, tightening my hold around you.

'Why did you tell me all this?'

You looked up, and I could see that your face was wet with tears. Your eyes were still black in the moonlight.

'I am not a Princess Rukmini to be saved, Asanka. No poor Sita, either. If the Kalinga forces me to marry him, I'll run. I'll choose death the way Queen Dayani did. I'll escape somehow.'

Now I felt tears stinging my own eyes.

'We can't run away,' I said, my voice only a whisper. 'Not until the fifth instalment is finished. When he finds out what I've done, he'll hunt us across the whole island. We need a head start.'

'I've already stayed in this city once for you,' you said, as though you had thought it many times.

'Sarasi,' I said. 'If we escape before I've finished my translation, he'll find another poet to complete it. Then this other poet will tell him about all the changes I've made – the things I've written about him. He'll have guards at every port, patrols through the forests, and spies everywhere. He'll put bounties on our names. He'll send word to Kalinga and the Tamil kingdoms – he'll hire assassins, mercenaries! There's no end to that man's cruelty.'

'Do you think he'll let us go, if you finish it? Once you're no use to him?'

'No,' I sighed. 'But if we had enough time, we could make it to General Sankha's fortress on Gangadoni: they say the rebellion there is getting stronger. It'd take ten thousand men to seize that hill, and Magha won't risk a battle just to reclaim some worn-out poet. Once I've given him the fifth instalment, we'll have a month before I have to see him next. That should give us enough time.'

Another two weeks. That's all I had to put up with, before we could be free. But there was something else, too. The dead voices, and the mad poet who had left them to me. I had to know who was behind them, and with Pushpakumara rotting in the dungeons, I finally had some hope of working it out. I breathed out and let your story settle into me.

'I've never seen the sea,' I said, realising suddenly how much larger the world must seem to you. 'Only in poems.'

You reached up to kiss me, and I knew then that the next two weeks would feel like a hundred years. I didn't believe I could last that long without going mad with fear.

'It's Deepavali next month,' you said. 'Will you still marry me?'

'Of course,' I said. 'Even if we hold the ceremony in the forest, and the only priests are the monkeys in the trees.'

We lay on the grass until morning. Before I slept, in that halfway place between wakefulness and dreams, I thought to myself what magic it is to close your eyes and die for just a while. I dreamt of chasing you through the dark forest of Ravana's kingdom, but you were always too far ahead, and my legs were as heavy as water-filled urns. Then the Demon King swooped down and took you from me. I had the sense that I was Rama, but I didn't know where I was, or what I should do to save my Sita.

When I woke up, you were already gone, and I had to explain myself to the confused-looking guard who found me lying in the grass.

'I fainted,' I told him, 'last night, after reading a poem of such beauty you wouldn't believe. A poem by Kalidasa – you may not have heard of him.'

The man grunted, struck my leg with the butt of his spear, and sent me on my way.

Chapter Fourteen

The nights only got darker. In the day, the sun baked us all until our lips cracked like elephant skin, until the village waters were sunken mudflats and people flocked to Parakrama Samudra to drink and fill pots. The water shrank a little further every day. I bought a new pair of sandals. The heat forgave no one.

More than a week after that night in the garden, with half of the time until our escape behind us, we met at one of the rundown temples on the outskirts of the city to go through our plan. While not the richest of temples, it was one of the oldest in that district, and had survived Magha's pillaging well: its pillars were worn and grown with lichen; its bo tree had grown so large that the priests had to prop up its ranging branches with timber. Each temple in Lanka has a bo tree at its centre, and each tree is a cutting from another temple tree. You can follow them back, the way you follow noble families or rivers, until you get to the venerable cutting that the monk Mahinda brought from the mainland, from the tree under which the Buddha himself meditated.

You and I were muttering to each other as we prayed, leaving offerings of water, cut jasmine flowers and sandalwood to the little Buddha statue cross-legged in its alcove. We were satisfied that no one could hear what we were saying beneath the murmuring of the monks, the tolling of the temple bell and the general noise of the market road outside the compound.

'I have skins of water,' you were telling me, quietly, and covering your lips with your fingers tented in prayer. 'About five seers. Some rotis from the kitchens, too. And the matchet. They're hidden under some cadjan in the roof of my house.'

As you told me about all your preparations, the routes you thought we should take, the supplies you'd already left at key locations, I felt increasingly useless. What had I done but sit in the city and write?

One of the nearby monks, a man who was both old and ageless, like a tree clinging to a high cliff, was praying loudly.

'Keep the Buddha's tooth hidden from the King,' he was pleading in a cracked voice. 'Keep it hidden, keep it safe until it returns to us.'

For the past week, Magha had been away in his chariot, marching his army up into the hills. Rumour had it that he was trying to extract information from the peasants there about the whereabouts of the tooth relic. No King of Lanka had ever ruled without it: by that point I think Magha realised this, and he would do anything to find it.

'Fill any man's purse and he'll betray his chief, his kingdom, his friends, his children,' I said, under my breath. 'But these common people would endure any torment before they'd betray that tooth.'

'You have to love something more than yourself,' you said. 'It's how you go on.'

'He won't find it,' I said. I had to say it. After all, if Magha could find one man's tooth hidden somewhere among the endless caves and passes of Mount Kotthumala, then he would be able to find us, too – wherever we found to hide. Our fate and the fate of that tooth seemed in those days to be tied.

Soon, raised voices began to be heard outside the temple, and the official-sounding rattle of one of those annoying declaration drums. It looked like a crowd was gathering, too. There were jeers, shouts, the sound of armoured men walking and spears rattling together.

'Is there some kind of parade happening?' you said, although you didn't sound sure. I went to the doorway, where a young monk of maybe ten years was bowing, and blessing everyone who entered.

'What's happening outside?' I asked.

'The prisoners,' is all he said, and murmured his benediction to an old lady climbing the steps. 'They take them past here some days. On the way to the spike.'

I felt a crawling beneath my fingernails and stepped outside into the sun, where a crowd was gathering in the verges and on the rooftops. Soldiers were marching a skinny band of prisoners down the street, all chained together and marked with burns and bruises. You came up beside me and touched my arm.

'Asanka, we shouldn't watch,' you said, but your voice was quiet. Some in the crowd shouted insults at the soldiers.

'I . . . I recognise one of them,' I said, and shielded my eyes from the sun. 'That man, being marched apart from the other prisoners. He was a servant in the palace. He warned me one day, about one of Magha's rages.'

Janaka, his name had been. The man who had almost carried me to the royal quarters on the day I'd thrown up over the balcony. Now he stumbled along with one eye closed and swollen up like a plum. I remembered how he shared his bag of fennel seeds and sugar with me in a moment when I thought I would die.

A crier was walking ahead of the prisoners, rattling his fingertips between every declaration on one of those tight-skinned drums they always carried.

'All of these men have been condemned to die on the spike!' he was announcing over and over in a clipped, high-pitched voice. 'They have allied themselves with the thief and brigand Sankha, and made war against their king. The most treacherous among them was even a servant in the palace, passing secrets to the enemy! For this they will die in agony. All of these men have been condemned . . .'

Jeers began to sail in from the rooftops, and a purply mangosteen came flying through the air too, thudding against a soldier's shield. The culprit disappeared down the other side of the houses. One of the soldiers loosed an arrow into the trees as a warning, and people ducked for cover. From the alleys behind the buildings, I heard the cry I had learnt to expect: 'Death to Shishupal!'

You tugged at my elbow.

'Asanka, you look so pale. Come back inside. Was he a friend of yours?'

I followed you in, back to the monks and the cool of the temple courtyard.

'A friend of sorts,' I managed. You watched me with concern for some time. We took some water in a jug and walked around the bo tree three times before pouring it on to the roots, saying prayers as we did with chapped lips. The water mixed with the red dust in little rivulets, before seeping into the earth. The leaves shifted overhead, and their noise seemed unbearable suddenly, like the shrilling of a thousand insects. I was sweating and cold, even in the heat.

I don't know why this death stuck with me, among all the others I knew who were killed that year. By that point it had become normal for lords to simply not turn up for a meal one day, and never be seen again, or for monks from district temples to turn up dead and mutilated in irrigation ditches. Magha was slaughtering rebels in the south every day, and floggings and executions had become part of Polonnaruwa's daily life – as normal as the ringing of the temple bells at the allotted times of day, and the riots over food and water. But for some reason all I could imagine as we said our prayers that day was the poor servant I had met only once, who had shown me kindness, being hoisted high into the air over the long iron impalement spikes beneath the wall. Being slowly lowered, lowered, lowered, until the point where the executioners jumped and grabbed on to his feet, pulling him down the spike with their weight until it left his body through the throat. The screaming turning slowly to gurgling. They say some men take days to die. I dreamt about that for many nights afterwards – that he was still alive, legs twitching, glassy eyes still blinking – and I always screamed when I woke.

Amid all the horror of that time, one remarkable thing happened. I was struggling to sleep on one of those nights, and you had been called to work in the kitchens for the King's early morning return to the city. Our plan of escape was still running through my head, over and over. The thousand ways it could go wrong. I rose out of bed in darkness, and opened the door to my balcony to cool myself. I could just make out the shapes of bats threading between the eaves, and the city's jagged line of deeper black against the sky. A sea of tiny lights.

There were mosquitoes, and I soon retreated inside to peruse my half-empty alcoves. I lit a lamp, and in the corner of my vision I saw the gold on the sari Magha had given you catch the light. It was still where you'd left it; I hadn't had the strength to touch it, to move it out of sight. Turning my back to it, I pulled books from the stone one by one, and flicked through their pages. The *Ramayana* first: I read the passage where the demonic Ravana, disguised as a hermit, tricks Sita into offering him hospitality before whisking her into the sky on his chariot. I snapped the book shut. My fingers found the *Mahabharata* next, and I let the book fall open to a random page: the part of the *Bhagavad Gita* where Krishna reveals himself to Arjuna in his universal form: 'You are without beginning, middle or end; you touch everything with your infinite power. The sun and the moon are your eyes, and your mouth is fire; your radiance warms the cosmos.'

This, too, I closed. The *Shishupala Vadha* even swam into my head, but I batted this thought away. I paced my room for a while, and the floorboards creaked beneath my feet with the sound of an old barge. These grand Sanskrit poems did nothing for the itch in my chest, and I thought of the bag that I had hidden in the swampy ruins of the old stupa – the sad, waiting lovers of the *Kuruntokai*. I began making the walk in my imagination, out into the dark of the scrubland at night, and before long I realised that I had to go. I left my bed, tied on my clothes and my new sandals, and crept out of the door.

The night was a madman's dream. There was no moon, and the grey monkeys cackled in the trees and among the rooftops: 'aaach, ooch ooch ooch'.

I found my way by memory through the streets of Polonnaruwa. The night guards at the gate questioned me and rifled violently through my bag.

'Where are you going so late?' they sneered. 'Got a common girl in one of the lake villages, have you? I hope you're paying her parents well.'

'No, I – I have to see the sunrise from the temple,' I told them. 'For the poem. The poem I'm translating for the King.'

They exchanged looks as they searched me, but as I had no baggage, only a lamp, oil and tinder, they didn't stop me, only held their hands out for payment, not meeting my eye. I looked into my coin purse, and brought out a handful of coins of all different sizes and shades of alloy, with different kings and different signs punched on their backs, and dropped it all into their hands. They didn't count the money, just nodded and nudged me past with their spear butts. I wandered out into the countryside.

All sound was amplified in the darkness. I tripped often once the light of the guardhouse was behind me, and I imagined snakes and spiders creeping across the path. Soon I became convinced that I would step on any manner of unclean and deadly creeping thing, and trod like a man on a mat of thorn scrub. Parakrama Samudra spread into the night on my left, boundless and black, and I stumbled along beside its shore. At one point a black snake slid off the dyke into the shallows, and the moon in the water shivered. I made a list of rare things.

A son-in-law beloved by his bride's father.
A copper tweezer that's good at plucking out hairs.
A well-dressed ox driver.

I passed the statue of Buddha at the Gal Vihara sometime later, and though there wasn't enough light to see his features, I could feel rather than see his hulking form, and the cold in the air that surrounds stone.

I reached the copse sooner than expected, creeping along the elephant road with the utmost care and my ears alert to any sound. When I got there, I pushed my way through the undergrowth. Remembering the monitor lizards that lived in the pool, I sat down to fill my lamp with oil and strike tinder. I regretted it immediately: the light it cast did nothing but illuminate the wall of darkness around me, and I stumbled down into the crater almost blind. It was a nightmare wasteland at night. The ragged stones of the stupa rose out of the earth like teeth, the fronds of the trees like a sea of blades, and the dark movements of the monitors slopping about somewhere in the water. I tried to stop my body from trembling.

This was exactly the kind of place where *rakshasas*, demons, would lurk – that was the thought I was trying to keep buried as I stumbled about the ruins. Lanka was once their island, so the stories say, and perhaps if Vijayabahu had never come and driven them into hiding more than a thousand years ago, theirs it would have remained: venturing out at night to slake their dark lusts, disturbing sacrifices, desecrating graves and causing madness, changing shape and practising black medicine, spreading disease, scraping at window shutters with their venomous fingernails, feeding on human flesh and spoilt food.

There was the slithering sound of a monitor's tail sliding over mud.

'Poets can make people believe anything,' I told myself. 'They're just stories. Just stories . . .'

I said it many times until a flurry of bats took flight all at once in the trees, and a wave of panic passed over me. I ran to the stones so that I could put my back against them, and waited for the beating of my heart to slow. I felt ashamed of myself: quivering, scared of *rakshasas* in the darkness, just like a little boy.

'I am a man of learning,' I said to myself. Ravana's *rakshasas*, whoever they were, weren't demons. Probably just simple folk living out their lives in the jungle. In a thousand years, people will probably tell such stories about us, just to scare their children.

When I'd regained my breath, I made my way over to the fallen Buddha statue. The pool had shrunk even further since our last visit, and as I lifted my lamp, the bright eyes of the monitors glinted like yellow topaz in the dark.

I found the bag where I left it, wedged in the arm of the old Buddha. The blanket of ferns I'd covered it with was brown and brittle when I brushed it aside. I opened my satchel like a child does a gift, handling each of the books one by one, cradling them, feeling their weight in my hand. They were as beautiful and precious as newborn children. I opened *Kuruntokai* at its first few pages, and read:

In the darkest depths of night,
when all have surrendered
to sleep's sweet embrace,
their slander coming to an end,
and the broad earth itself slumbers,
bearing me malice no longer,
I alone can find no rest.

I slumped back against the old Buddha and drank in the night air, and with every breath I could feel the hornets in my head become drowsy. In the light of my small lamp, I sat and read all of *Kuruntokai*'s 'Poems of the Wasteland' section, and then moved on to the mountainsides, where the delicate blue kurinji flower blooms once every twelve years. The lover who journeys across the desert and finally returns to his joyful beloved, his fortune made.

When I'd finished, I closed the book gently and slid it back inside the bag. I sat and looked up at the sky. I love the Tamil *Kuruntokai* because it's poetry about waiting and longing in shaded gardens, poetry for people who don't have the wise Krishna to advise them before their battles, who don't have a monkey god ally to help them build a bridge across their seas, who have no chakra to hurl at their Shishupals.

As I thought these things, I caught myself nodding. I shook myself awake, aware that if I fell asleep, I would make a feast for the monitors. I felt the vulgar Tamil manuscripts lying loose in the bottom of my bag and I thought of Pushpakumara, of his lifelong knowledge of ink. But he was in a prison cell, and the dead voices were out here in the jungle night, with the guards at the gate between them. I felt that I would never find out who had sent them to me.

I prepared to leave, but when I replaced the bag and covered it in fresh ferns, I noticed something that made me freeze and almost drop my lamp in the mud. Some feet away, nested between a wall and a crumbling, half-sunken pillar, itself covered in fresh ferns, sat another bag.

For some time, I did nothing but stare. I became suddenly afraid, as though the owner of this other bag might be lurking nearby, creeping among the stones. The common people know the country around Polonnaruwa like they know their children's faces, and I wondered at all the things Lankan villagers might hide in this ruined place. I wondered, too, if my books were safe at all here, whether some illiterate peasant or criminal might get it into his head to use *Ettuthokai* or the *Mahavamsa* as kindling, to sell them for food or water.

I crept towards this other bag, made of some rough sackcloth – hemp, flax or goat hair – not as fine as my own leather bag. It was tied at the top, and it took a while for me to open with my shaking fingers.

Inside were books. I stared at them for some time, not understanding. I took one out and opened it. I actually half expected to open the pages and find 'I am Shishupal' or some other nonsense written there, but I opened their pages, and smelt ink that I knew well: oil and the charcoal of coconut husks – a very cheap ink. They were books of Tamil poetry, all of which I knew. I pulled them out in wonder, squeezed their bindings between my thumb and forefinger, laid them out on the pillar that hid them: *Pattupattu*, *Akananuru*, *Natrinai* – and here! Another copy of *Kuruntokai*. I opened each of them to their first pages and muttered the first lines to myself.

They were all poor quality, hastily copied and bound in the most basic fashion, probably in one of those fashionable new workshops, but they were Tamil texts. All of them books that Magha had tried to burn. Warmth filled my body as I imagined some villager or low-ranking temple scribe stashing these books away in the same place that I had chosen. It was as though in the darkness of the night, through the isolation of life under the Kalinga king, an anonymous hand had reached out and touched mine.

I made my unsteady way back to the city as an immodest blush rose in the direction of the coast. When I got back to my villa, I tripped over something that someone had left carelessly on the inside of my gate. It was still dark, and I was too exhausted to care much about what it was. I went upstairs, cursing the servants, and collapsed on to my bed fully clothed. I slept more deeply than I had in months: a black, dreamless sleep that lasted most of the morning.

When I woke up in the early afternoon and went down into the courtyard for some rice and sambal, I found that what I had tripped over was a bundle of bound pages, sitting just inside my gate.

'I am King Bhishmaka,' the first page said, in that same fragrant ink.

'I am Yudhisthira.'

My stomach took a dive for the centre of the earth, and suddenly I wasn't hungry any more.

It was always my destiny to be the king of all the world. But destinies lie at the end of long, tortuous roads, made longer by our weaknesses. My weakness is for gambling. When I lost a game of dice to the trickster Shakuni, our enemies cursed me and my brothers to twelve years of exile. Twelve long years of wandering the forests, preparing for war. For many of those years, my brother Arjuna performed penances the likes of which you would shudder to hear. He spent days submerged up to his chin in icy rivers. He spent a month standing on only one toe. For a year, he drank only the morning dew. Through his devotion, he won each of the great celestial weapons from the gods: the vayavastra, which could summon up a typhoon to blow away enemy armies; the suryastra, which can dispel any darkness and dry up any body of water; the parvata-astra, which causes a mountain to fall from the skies on top of enemies. When the twelve years were up, we would be ready.

When we returned from our exile, we knew that we had to perform a great sacrifice if we wanted to rule the world. The mists were coming down off the hills on the first day. The sun shone gold on the canals, glazing the fields and waterways. The priests were wrapping garlands and bright silks around the old bamboo pole in the courtyard. Then they brought the finest stallion in the stables before us, and whispered their mantras into its ear in ancient, forgotten languages. We took the horse to the gates of Indraprastha, opened to the wide countryside and morning breeze, and set it free down the cart-rutted road to the north. I and my four brothers – Bhima, Nakula, Sahadeva and Arjuna – set out after the horse with each of our armies.

The animal wandered for a year through the wild, irreligious lands around Indraprastha. In each kingdom it passed through, we demanded tribute. If the king refused, we laid siege to his capital. Our armies made camp when the stallion stopped for water or to graze in the fields, and when the beast moved on, we mustered our troops and followed it. Can you even imagine what it is like to trust in the gods so completely? Our soldiers whispered about it, muttering that the horse was only following its belly or its thirst, that it was only spurred on by the noise of the army behind it. But we knew otherwise.

Our influence spread like ink spilled on a wrinkled page – first in one direction, then the other – until we met only empty plains to the west, the Snowy Mountains to the north, and the sea to the east. The year of the sacrifice passed, and the conquest of the world was complete. We returned victorious for the final ceremony.

It was such a joy to see the city at last, after a year of battle and blood. All the kings and princes of the world were invited to see me crowned king, and so hundreds of luxurious pavilions had been built around the city, laced with gold netting, two storeys high, with garlands of flowers and pearls. There were carpets of such rich reds and golds on the floors, and tiger hides on the beds.

The guests began to arrive in the following days, friends bringing gifts, and our newly conquered enemies bringing tribute to match. Kings came from across the world: the Vangas, the Kalingas, the Tamraliptas, the Supundrakas, the Dauvalikas, the Sagarakas. The air was full of incense and hymns. The excitement was almost too much to bear when Krishna arrived, riding alongside his beautiful bride Rukmini, with gold, silver, silks, spices and precious stones piled in carts behind him. When Krishna dismounted from his horse and embraced me like a brother, I knew how far I had come, and I wept.

The day after Krishna's arrival, King Shishupal of the Chedis arrived. I could see even from a distance that his eyes were ringed with black, that he had not slept in days. He slouched on his slave-borne throne, and spoke quietly.

When the day of the sacrifice arrived, we lit a huge fire in the centre of the great square. All the kings of the earth watched from their pavilions as the ceremony commenced – as the Brahmins marked out the place and spread it with kusa grass, chanted their verses so old that no man alive even knows what they mean, and spread homa over the flames.

Then more priests brought the sacred stallion into the square, its coat still dusted with the sand and pollen of far-off lands, along with a great collection of other animals in a heaving, braying, half-stampeding mass. The blessed horse watched as the priests cut the throats of these beasts one by one. The poor animals foamed at the mouth and stared with glistening eyes. Their blood gushed and steamed across the flagstones. The priests carved their flesh from the bone, and cast this meat into the fire, invoking Agni to cook them through and keep them tender. Then we served the meat to the host of guests, along with a great many other sacred dishes. While the nobles ate, we tied the sacrificial horse to a stake; it shifted nervously as the priests helped me paint its sides with ghee, chanting: 'Steed, from your body, of yourself, be sacrificed and accept. Greatness can be gained by none but you.'

I stood painting its muzzle, and felt the hot breath leave its nostrils. The wet, black glass of its eye. It amazes me how an animal can fail to fear a blade. Then we offered this last long-travelled animal up to the gods. It died like all the rest, and we cast its body into a pit.

After the ceremony, several words were spoken; the guests stood up to offer their praise to me. It was embarrassing to hear them all speaking so highly of me as a scholar and a king, complimenting me on my piety and hospitality. But I didn't have time to enjoy their kind words: as soon as they had finished, it was my turn. I stood up and held out my hands. I informed them that the final words of the ceremony were about to be spoken. I had to offer one man present the cup of argha, the milk and honey reserved only for the most distinguished guest. Of all those present, who could I have chosen but Krishna?

The moment I spoke his name, there was a furious cry from one end of the courtyard. King Shishupal stood up from his pavilion and shouted over the heads of the gathered royalty that Krishna was not deserving of the honour. I do not know whether he was drunk, or merely intoxicated by the grief of losing his bride: his speech was slurred but he strode out powerfully, quaking with rage, to the centre of the square. He railed against Lord Krishna, screaming insults of the vilest kind, and even drew his sword and challenged him to fight.

When Krishna summoned the chakra to smite the king into the earth, I wager the Chedi king felt no pain. It was like a thunderbolt, like the shadow of a swooping bird passing in front of the sun. As his body lay twitching on the floor, storm clouds gathered in the previously clear sky and rain began to fall on the dusty stone. Its acid smell rose in the air. The new drops mixed with Shishupal's blood on the ground and washed it between the cracks. Some people there claimed to see a bright light rise from the Chedi's body and enter Lord Krishna through his chest, but I think that they were indulging too much in the wine and bhang. Shishupal's loose head rolled to a stop several feet away from me and stared up into the sky with a surprised look on its face.

The next day, my servants scrubbed the blood of the sacrificed animals from the square, but there is one stain that did not wash from the stone, and it is there to this day.

Chapter Fifteen

The new batch of the mad poet's writings that once more appeared in my villa put an end to all other thought. With so many possibilities, and so few clues, I felt like a man lost in a thick cloud of mist, following only the rain-stone smell of the ink. They were telling the story of Shishupal's death one piece at a time – and once again, it seemed like the poet was revelling in his madness. Like a man laughing as he breaks a beautiful carving with a hand axe, this vandal was once more enjoying smashing to pieces the poetic traditions I'd spent half my life to master. But one thing was different now: I knew that Pushpakumara was alive and where he was. Now I could visit the master ink-maker in his cell and find out what he knew before we fled Polonnaruwa.

Soon after, Magha returned to the city with the usual pomp, surrounded by cavalrymen with pennants flying from their spears, with musicians playing from the gatehouse and servants throwing petals from above. He returned like a victor, as though he had found the tooth, but the people said it was still hidden somewhere in the green hills. I expected to be summoned soon after he returned, but the summons never came. Every time I met you, I expected to hear that Magha had come to visit you, but for a while it seemed the King had forgotten all about his earlier interest.

I continued translating the *Vadha* as though the story and my life were the same, knowing that the sooner I finished the fifth instalment, the sooner we could leave. In these final parvas, Sri Magha was beginning to anticipate the end. I could feel his language becoming more ornate, his metrical devices more ingenious, his similes more elaborate. The battle and the beheading were nearing, but the tone of his writing gave no hint of the bloody end to come. Even the calligrapher of Magha's copy seemed to look forward to the conclusion: his penmanship became more elaborate, as though excited.

In these parvas, King Shishupal sends his messenger to Krishna to deliver a famous speech, riddled with double-meaning. Krishna understands its subtext and declares war. The battle is fierce and bloody; the language rich and many-faceted. The similes are perfect. As I worked during those days, I felt a strange competence in my task. It had taken me months, but I had mastered it. My written Tamil had become fluent and beautiful, my renderings of the Sanskrit meanings immaculate – and beneath that, my mockeries of Magha became ever more incisive, delving into his deepest flaws and failings with more and more inventive similes to describe his cruel laugh, his idiotic edicts and voluminous eyebrows.

On the day that I finished the fifth instalment, I ordered the pages carefully and bound them together with cord, leaning back and breathing deeply. Before going to the palace to hand it in, I went to the kitchens to meet you, and found you crushing pepper with one of those heavy stone pestles.

Kunjan the overseer eyed me suspiciously, but waved me through.

'Asanka!' you said, and gave the grains a final twist. 'What is it? What are you doing here?'

'It's finished,' I said. 'The fifth instalment.'

You looked around quickly, checked that no one was listening.

'Does that mean we can leave?' you hissed. 'We can get out of here? I saw Magha returning to the city already.'

'As soon as we can,' I said. When's your next rest day?'

'The full moon. The poya day.'

'Three days, then. That's when we'll go.'

'I'll get everything ready,' you said. 'At sunset we'll meet at the library temple to pray, and from there go to Aliyagama.'

'Yes, and then we'll make for Gangadoni and General Sankha's fortress. If we make it there, Magha will think we've disappeared.'

'It's high up, you know?' you giggled, and poked the belly that had been growing beneath my sarong. 'Lots of stairs.'

I batted you away and tried to insult you back, but the pepper in the air was beginning to make me want to sneeze, so I left you to your work.

So it was done. I would leave the poem unfinished, and in three days, we would disappear into the dark of the forest like *yakshas*. I imagined us huddling together for warmth in the forest night, begging for food from villagers, following animals to watering holes, fearing to light a fire in case it attracted soldiers. With you beside me, it wouldn't be so terrible, I thought, even though my stomach was used to the taste of the royal kitchen's rich curry, and my body had become soft from palace cushions.

I fetched the fifth instalment from my villa, and went to the throne room to hand it in. A betel-chewing guard there told me that the King was taking a bath near the sluice gate, so

I headed back through the city and across the bridges into the island park. There were guards everywhere. They were standing at the gate of the luxurious park, and lined its path of white sand, too, past all the private temples in the shade of the flowering trees.

Magha was bathing in the main pool when I arrived. He was clearly drunk, and was sharing a cup of wine with two beautiful young girls, the kind the lords are always chasing. When Magha saw me, he called me over, slurring my name.

'Asanka! What a surprise! What are you doing here?'

'The translation,' I told him, averting my eyes from the women, who looked at me blankly. 'I've finished the fifth instalment. I'd like to hand it in early.'

'Wonderful!' he slurred. He looked exhausted, even a little delirious. He waved at a guard, who came and took the book from my hands.

'Asanka, you must come in,' the King said. 'Come into the water. It's beautifully cool for such a hot day.'

'I've already bathed, Maharaja,' I said to him, and he laughed.

'Nonsense! You can never bathe too much. It's good for the blood and the mind. Come in, or I'll tell my guards to throw you in!'

He said it like a joke, but I heard the footsteps of a heavy man step closer behind me, and I didn't doubt that he would have them do it. Luckily, I wasn't wearing a fine sarong, so I hitched it up and lowered myself into the water. He was right: it was cool and refreshing, tapped straight from the great tank through an underground channel. Even with the lake drained so low through drought, the mechanism still worked.

'More water!' Magha called, and two servants high above the King cranked open the sluice gate. A torrent of foaming water crashed out through the thick bamboo pipes. Magha laughed in delight, and his hair clung to his scalp like a helmet.

'And more wine!' he called. A servant came to fill his cup, and he fixed his bloodshot eyes on me. 'Asanka,' he said with a knowing tone, his gaze untethered with drink. 'You're not a man of pleasure, am I right?'

'My lord?'

'You've never asked me for anything. Most people here, most people everywhere, they always want something. Women, boys, gold or fancy titles. And yet you, you don't seem to want anything.'

There was a strange hard and hurt edge to his voice, though he was still speaking jovially.

'We all have our pleasures, my lord,' I said. 'Mine is to write poetry. And to serve the King.'

'Serve the King, serve the King,' he parroted. 'That's all I hear from anyone! But Asanka, I want you to be happy. We are friends, after all, aren't we?'

'Yes, my lord.'

'I want you to have everything you want. What about women? You can have this one, if you like?'

He flicked the shoulder of one of the girls at his side, and she giggled falsely. I felt the blood rise into my cheeks.

'No, my lord, I'm a married man. I'm loyal to my wife.'

Magha laughed. 'But do you know what I've heard, Asanka? Do you know what my little spies have told me?'

He fluttered his fingers, to suggest an airborne swarm of bees.

'What, my lord?'

'They tell me that your wife has left you.'

I felt myself shiver in the cool water. My mind was racing.

'It's true, my lord. It's an unfortunate thing, to be betrayed by the woman you love.'

'Oh I know that well enough,' Magha said. 'But your wife – do you know she left the city six weeks ago? And you didn't even tell me, Asanka.'

'I was too broken-hearted at first, my lord. The fact of it was too painful—'

'Do you know why she told the guards she was leaving?' Magha said, cutting me off.

'Women's reasons for anything are hard to read, my lord.'

The King shook his head, and pointed an unsteady finger at me, drops of water falling from it and scattering the surface.

'She told them that her husband has a mistress,' he said. 'A mistress, Asanka!' he cackled and slapped one of the girl's hips in mirth. 'Asanka the poet has a mistress.'

I was trembling, now. I knew I had to get out of the water, had to escape the King's questioning.

'A brief thing, my lord, just a fling with a common village girl. You know how pretty they can be. My lord, I have to—'

'Ah, Asanka – don't worry. I'm only teasing you. It gives me such joy to see that you're a man of flesh and blood after all.'

He hiccupped triumphantly. I stood up out of the water, and wrung it from my sarong.

'I have to go, my lord. I should start the next instalment. It's long, and very complex.'

'Of course!' he said as I stepped out of the pool. 'And Asanka – if there's anything you want. Anything in the world—'

I stopped. There was the pattering of water drops on stone. In three days, we would escape. This was my last chance, and I took it.

'Yes, my lord. There is one thing.'

'Anything.'

'That villainous rat you showed me, in the dungeon. I want to visit him. I want to know what made him destroy such a perfect work of art with his idiotic treason. I want to explain to him what the *Shishupala Vadha* really means.'

Magha sighed, and beamed with pride like a father looking at a son.

'Whatever you like,' he said, and waved his hand. 'I'll let the dungeon guards know you're coming.'

As I left, I released a long breath that I realised I had been holding. The false, high-pitched giggles of the women followed after me through the trees.

I didn't sleep all that night. In the morning, the last-but-one I would spend in the city, I put the latest dead voices of Shishupal and Yudhisthira into my satchel, along with a seer of water. Then I walked through the workshops and district temples towards the dungeon. The weight of the voices in my satchel thumped against my thigh as I went.

When I arrived at the dungeon, I found that the soldiers there had heard about my request. Some brief mumbles about 'order of the maharaja' were enough to get me through the gates, and they took me below ground without saying more than a few words to me, leading me to the end of the line of cells. They unlocked the prisoner's door, and left me alone with him.

I stepped inside, and Pushpakumara looked up at me. His eyes, always sharp like the eyes of a boar, were now ringed with purple, puckered like a dog's anus. He was just sitting there, and I suspected that he had been watching the wedge of light from the high window crawl across the uneven ground. Perhaps that's all he did, for hours every day. He had blade-shaped burns running up his arms.

'You,' he said, as the door sounded shut. It wasn't an accusation or a curse. His pupils, among the folded wrinkles of his lids, were desperate and glassy, and I thought what horror it would be to be kept there.

'Hello, Pushpakumara,' I said.

'I won't tell you anything,' he wailed then, in a voice that was high and unlike a man's. He crawled further from the door, and what dislike I still had for him evaporated.

'Please,' I said. 'You have to help me. I can't trust anyone else.'

'You're here for Magha!'

'No,' I said, but he didn't believe me. I took the bundled pages from my satchel. This time I had no lie prepared. 'Someone has been leaving these for me to find. I need to know who wrote them.'

'You're a traitor, Asanka. A coward who'll work for whoever fills his pockets.'

'Pushpakumara, I need—'

'You've been that way ever since the old king,' he said, and his eyes filled with tears. 'Ever since you came here. You poets are all the same, with your fine clothes and finer words.'

I took a step towards him, filling suddenly with desperation.

'Pushpakumara, I want to help you,' I said. 'I want to hurt Magha. I want to bring him to his knees.'

And then, because he still looked at me with empty eyes, I whispered so that the guards wouldn't hear: 'The King would have me killed if he knew what I was doing here. I loved King Parakrama and Queen Dayani, you know that. I hate Magha more than even you could.'

I realise now that this was a shameful thing to say, and dangerous. I remember that he looked up at me with an iron contempt, and the thought came to me that perhaps his wife and children, his mother and father, his brothers and sisters hadn't escaped Magha's punishment.

'Please,' I asked him. 'Please look at these pages and tell me where this ink came from.'

He looked at me hard for a long time. I took out my seer of water and threw it into the sand in front of him. He dived at it, and drank long and deep, the lump of his throat jumping up and down as he did. Then he wiped his mouth and held out his hand.

'Give them to me,' he said. I gave him the pages, spread out in a fan. The ink's lustre caught in the shaft of light that slanted from the narrow window. He snatched them from me and looked over them, squinting, for some time. His lips curled as he read much of what was written, as though deeply ashamed to experience it. As my eyes grew used to the gloom and the man pored over the manuscript, I noticed that a verse had been etched in Sinhala on the wall behind him:

Oh, if only one could
go there alive, I'm convinced
hell would be fine.
With work, we could make it
a pleasant land.

Eventually, Pushpakumara sniffed at the ink, wrinkled his nose and closed his eyes. He breathed deeply and handed the pages back to me. Then he pulled at a loose strand of his hair.

'The paper of the book is palmyra palm,' he said.

'Like a thousand others in Lanka – I know!' I exclaimed, flushing in anger suddenly. 'But what about the—'

'The ink?'

'Yes.'

'The ink is of a type I've only ever seen on the mainland: burnt bone, shellac resin and oil. It spoils on the ships, with the salt and the motion of the waves.' He made a seesaw motion with one limp hand. 'Once it's unloaded from the boat, it has to be stored for years before the crystals properly dissolve and it's usable again. That's why you don't see it over here. It's a very fine ink.'

After he had spoken, I watched him crawl into a corner with what remained of the water, and regretted losing my temper. He looked like a beaten dog. Ink from the mainland that couldn't be transported by boat – I didn't know what this meant. Was it flown here, then, on the wings of a bird? On Ravana's chariot?

'Thank you,' I said, with an immense feeling of defeat. I left him, bowing as I went, and did not straighten until I was out the door. I felt physically weak.

That night, the night before our escape, I fell through a confused mess of dreams, in which the Shishupal poet was writing his mocking verses for me with a melon for a head, writing with ink made from the ground bones of a thousand Lankans; in which I was Krishna, but didn't know how to summon my chakra, didn't know how to strike down a Shishupal who loomed over me, twice my size, who rode on a drunken stamping elephant and who kept laughing, high-pitched and cruel, as I fumbled in my robes for the golden disc. I awoke in the night with my arms raised above me, as though fending off some attacker, and knew without a doubt that soon something terrible would happen.

The moon was almost full.

The next day, I went about the city performing errands. I paid off the last fifty massas I owed my tailor, and returned a book I'd borrowed from a monk down in the library temple. Even that was a hard journey in the heat.

The country was parched, the lake barely a skin of water at the centre of wide mudflats, with fish flipping and roasting in the sun. *Tonight*, I kept thinking. *Tonight I'll leave all this behind*. The heat would make our journey more gruelling, but also improve our chances of success. Hunters have told me before that it's more difficult to track footprints over hard, dry ground. We would need lots of water, though, and I bought two extra skins on my way back, from a shifty man selling them by the roadside. They cost ten times the usual price.

'Demand,' he said. 'Demand is what it is.'

He started arguing with some thirsty poor people as I left, about the price. There were stories going round the markets of bandits robbing people on the roads and taking only their water skins, leaving coins still jangling in their pouches. I took a sip of the cool liquid crystal from the skin, and walked back to my villa to prepare for that evening.

In that haze, nothing in the city seemed real. Not the men with headscarves making bricks in the sun, not the women of the city selling spices and herbs and livestock, not the bargemen with their long poles gliding along the canal and rocking the green waters. Everything had the quality of a ghostly image, like a vision or dream, as though soon it would all dissolve before my eyes and leave only stone, crumbling and fading into the earth.

On my way, I heard a woman at a stall talking about a gang of youths who had found one of Magha's soldiers on his own, visiting a prostitute in an alley, and thrown stones at him from the rooftops, calling him 'hook nose' and 'monkey head'. She chuckled as she said this, and the shopkeeper made a noise like 'ha!' and stroked his moustache.

Some of the market-goers spoke about more serious insurgencies. They talked about the elusive General Sankha, mostly, who still held his fortified encampment on Gangadoni, even after all these months. Apparently his men were defending stupas and libraries in the area from the King's soldiers, and I imagined a man like the statue of Parakramabahu the Great in the library temple – a kind-faced man cradling a book. Someone whispered that Magha had sent assassins to put an end to the man's insurgency, but they had no success.

'He's like a ghost,' the man muttered. 'Like a shadow, or a *yaksha*. You can't find him unless you know his full name, and call it three times in the very heart of the forest.'

The streets were as busy as usual, although I thought I noticed even more guards patrolling than usual. I leant down and pretended to smell a bunch of coriander, to test the firmness of some aubergines, white cucumber, snake gourd, while listening to the conversations of the shopkeepers and customers.

Some monks were arguing about a group of their brothers, sent to the mainland to enlist help.

'Ha!' one scoffed, 'The Pandyas? The Cholas? They're too busy fighting each other. And what if they do come? We'll have to watch their armies trampling through the land, more blood spilled, more homes burnt.'

A couple of women hurried past, flustered, complaining that the monsoon was late. They were right: the air was as dry as a kiln. I wandered through the chaos, between a shell-cutter's workshop and a mason, and into the cool quiet beneath the skin of the city. I sat among a ruin that had seen a hundred kings, on a cleft that had once been a window, and stared at the stones.

When I got home, I told my servants to take a long holiday for the full moon, dismissed them all and wandered around my suddenly empty villa as though I didn't know the place. I touched everything, the precious stones inlaid in the doorjamb, the wooden handle of the well bucket, worn smooth as bone, even knelt down and sniffed the smoky teak fragrance rising from the furniture. I wanted to remember it, all the climbing flowers and intimate corners. The smells clinging to all of its fabrics: smoke, and incense, and the flavours of cooking food.

It was just as I was preparing to leave, around the time of the day's third bells, with the sun growing rosy over the city, that a rapid series of knocks sounded at my gate. Strange, I thought. I wasn't expecting any visitors. I opened it to find a royal messenger standing in the street, with two of the king's heavy bodyguards standing on either side.

'Master Asanka, the King wants to see you,' he said, and I felt the blood turn cold in my veins. I looked from the messenger to the steely expression of the guards, and their tall, glittering halberds.

'The King?' I said. 'I saw him the day before yesterday. What does he want?'

'It's a matter of some urgency,' the messenger said, with a sympathetic smile, and one of the soldiers put the butt of his weapon between the gate and the post, so I couldn't close it. 'Please come with us, Master Asanka.'

My heart was pounding. I could feel sweat breaking out on my forehead.

'Right away,' I said. 'I'll just gather my—'

'No, you're to come immediately,' the man said, and the guard turned his weapon so the gate levered open. Their faces were set.

I nodded, and walked with them to the palace, a sense of foreboding growing inside me. They said nothing the whole way, and the guards walked in unison, the loud tramping of their steps and the rustle of their armour plates the only sounds that I could hear. There was a flock of birds circling over the high palace roof, the sun gold on the tiles. When we got to the top of the steps, and the messenger knocked on the door, there was no answer. He knocked again, and then pushed upon the door. It was almost completely dark inside – the shutters of the windows were drawn, the only light from an oily lamp on Magha's desk. The King's voice came from within the murk:

'Come in, Asanka.'

One of the guards pressed the butt of his halberd gently into the small of my back, and I stepped inside, out of the sunlight. I was trembling. I knew that I was in trouble, and thought immediately that Magha had discovered the true reason for my visit to Pushpakumara, that the ink-maker had given up my secret under torture or out of hatred for me. That Magha would demand to see the vulgar texts I'd been left. As I stepped into the darkness and my eyes became more accustomed to the gloom, I began to concoct lies: the rebels made me do it; my treacherous wife had written them; I was going mad.

Inside the room, Magha was standing aside from the door. The difference from the way he had behaved in the baths couldn't have been more pronounced. He looked extremely tired, even in the dark.

'The shutters have to be closed at all times,' he told me in a quiet, sharp tone. 'Any determined assassin could scale the walls of this palace. They could get in here with any manner of weapon.'

'Of course, Raja,' I said. 'It's always wise to be careful.'

He grunted, and I noticed that he was wearing his armour again. There were no guards in the room. He said nothing.

'You're not at your desk, Maharaja?' I asked, just to break the silence. He didn't answer, but glanced over at the floor table where I usually found him sitting, poring over maps. I wondered if he suspected assassins of tampering with his cushions, filling them with poisoned needles or cobras, or some such thing.

'They hate me, Asanka,' he said. 'The common people. The peasants. Even the people of the city. Even the lords. They all hate me.'

There was a strange high-pitched quality to his voice. He turned, so that he had his back to me: in the gloom, I could see the curled hairs on the back of his neck, and what might have been a few beads of sweat glistening among them. His armour must have been like a clay oven in the heat. He began to pace the room, scuffing his feet on the wood. Then he sighed and fixed me with a direct and penetrating stare.

'You don't hate me, do you, Asanka?'

I kept my voice very still. 'It is not the place of a servant to hate his master, my lord.'

Magha sat down at his cushion, and cast his hand around the map on the desk, now nearly obscured by charcoal scribblings.

'Before raising my army,' he said, 'I sailed half the world. It's a whole empire my father rules from Kalinga – a million lives, all its distant lands linked only by our trade routes. Ten thousand ships: Arabian barques and dhows, split-log catamarans from the shores of great Africa, the huge sharp-sailed ships from China. There is such inexhaustible wealth in the lands that lock this sea. You can't even imagine the things I've seen, Asanka. I've passed over the undersea palaces of Hanuman, their roofs glittering in a thousand colours; I've seen the giant white shadow of Varuna beneath my ship, riding his sacred crocodile. I've touched the farthest reaches of our dominion, sailed to its very edge, and looked out over those endless vastnesses. Even then, the ocean goes on – can you imagine it? I've seen flocks of birds so large they seem like clouds of smoke, and birds the size of men that never touch the earth, sailing for ever on the winds. I have seen the great fish – the great fish, Asanka. A survivor from the time when all life was huge and noble, when men walked a hundred cubits tall upon the earth. This island,' he said, and smeared his hand across the map so that all the charcoal smudged, 'this tiny island is nothing but a pearl in that ocean, do you realise that? For all its trade routes and fine cities and rich temples, it is just a tiny pendant that India wears on its ear. Do you realise how small you look to me?'

I was silent for a moment.

'All men are small before giants, Maharaja.'

'Giants,' he said wistfully, and his shoulder sagged. 'Do you know, Asanka, that I am a bastard? Me – the great Magha of Kalinga. A bastard.'

He glared at me, daring me to laugh, or smile – or give any kind of reaction.

'I was born the fifth son of our great father,' he said. 'A splinter on the family tree. An embarrassment. Nothing to inherit, nothing to my name. Not even the love of my father. He—' Magha's lips pulled back from his teeth like a dog's. 'He detested me. He threw me this island like a scrap – I see that now. While my brothers inherited kingdoms, he sent me to wage a war he didn't think I could win. But look at me now: a king, just like him, surrounded by more jewels than all my brothers put together. And still—'

He took a long, deep breath, and then rose to his full height. I remember how I felt in those endless moments. I felt as if I was going to die. Magha stepped towards me.

'I understand,' he said, and his smooth voice was shaking a little, 'that your mistress, the one we spoke about – I understand that she is a servant in this palace. You kept this hidden from me.'

My stomach became a nest of scorpions. My voice was tiny. 'No, Maharaja, I—'

'I knew something was wrong. The way you schemed and skulked and called me your friend. I remembered all those months ago, when I cut out that idiot's eyes and you asked me to save a girl from my soldiers.'

'Maharaja—'

'And then when I realised that, everything else began to make sense. The way you asked for your apprentices to be protected, and told me that their names were on a list. It dawned on me all at once, as I was reading your latest instalment, how words can mean two things at once and I thought to myself, "I bet if I go and look in the palace records, I'll find a girl's name on your list of apprentices. I bet I'll find Asanka the poet's mistress."'

'My lord, please let me—'

'Might I remind you,' he said softly, 'that the women of this palace are the property of the King?'

I looked at the floor. Whereas death threats might be hissed and battle-cries screamed, I think that the worst news of a man's life is often delivered like this, as if commenting on the heat of the day.

'I don't think that has ever been the case, Maha—'

'It is the case if I say it is the case!' he roared, swinging around and striking a pillar with the flat of his hand so that reverberations hummed into the rafters. Every muscle in my body was rigid. But Magha relaxed and sighed. He ran a hand through his hair, which was slick with sweat and oil.

'I'm sorry, Asanka. It's not right for me to lose my temper so easily. We're still friends, aren't we? You're one of my only true friends, I think. One of my only—'

Magha's voice wavered a little. In the darkness I couldn't see the whites of his eyes, so they showed like bulbs of black stone.

'It's my way,' he said, 'in the course of my time as ruler, to test the loyalty of my servants. I told you that once, didn't I? We're lucky, actually, to have this opportunity. You, in fact, are lucky, that I will be able to test you.'

'Test me, Maharaja?'

His voice was calm, but he was speaking slowly, measuring each word.

'That's right. Since your Queen betrayed me, I've been left a bachelor. A king without a queen. It's right and proper for a king to have a queen, isn't it?'

He watched me carefully.

'Right and proper, my lord.'

'And I have chosen my queen. This servant girl will be my new wife. They will call her Saraswati, the peasant Queen of Lanka. She will make the peasants love me. And if you are lucky then you, Asanka, will write the vows for our wedding.'

I've read descriptions of rage in poetry. In the hearts of heroes, rage is always a fire burning in the chest or a trampling elephant. To me, it felt as though salty ocean water was flooding down my throat, filling my lungs, bursting out through my skin. It was this – this use of your full name – that broke something in me. Without thinking, I knelt and reached down to Magha's desk. I took his golden inkwell in my hand, felt the heft of it, and leapt at him. I struck the King with all my strength on his forehead and he reeled, spun down on to the floor. He let out a whimper, and I advanced on him, watching as though in a dream as he put a hand to one eyebrow and blood seeped through his fingers.

I lifted the inkwell over my head, squinting against the tears that popped in my eyes, prepared to bring it down on him like Bhima's mace on Dushasana's chest. I would spill his blood as he had spilled King Parakrama's and the Queen's. I was shaking with rage. I felt drunk, my eyes bulging from my head. I was Rama casting Ravana into flame and shadow; I was Arjuna, sending Bhishma to the afterlife with a thousand arrows; I was Krishna, cutting down Shishupal in a flash of light.

Magha looked up at me, and caught my eyes in his. He waited as I quivered there, holding me in his gaze with a look of seething contempt.

'Guards!' he called, not in panic but a measured order. The door to the throne room burst open – a band of large men stepped in and, seeing the King sprawled on the floor, rushed towards me.

I could have killed him – I knew that – but in that instant I also knew how Queen Dayani had felt as she crouched over him in the darkness. As the guards seized my arms and legs, and struck me hard across my mouth, I dropped the inkwell. It clattered across the wood with the sound of '*sakarana narakasa*', and I surrendered to their grasp, to their blows that fell again and again, to the inky tendrils of sleep.

In the blackness I was struggling through the briars of Lanka's dark forests. I swam in the depths of the lotus pool, and then it was a pool of ink, then a river, drenching my robes, filling my lungs, my eyes, with its haunting smell. Then I was the statue of Buddha – I swear it – unmoving, stone to the core, cold and silent for a century, watching the world fall into ruin around me.

When I awoke, I knew immediately where I was. My pillow was sand. I had no cover. I sat up in a panic, and because I had become well accustomed to the Kalinga's cruelty over the last six months, I knew that on one wall of my cell I would see 'O man of hill country . . .' right where I had chalked it for the condemned Queen. Despite knowing this before I turned around, I still wailed aloud to see it. I ran to the rough stone wall and smeared it with both my hands, wiping the sweet thunders from the hills. I sat and wept, shaking with rage.

The days blurred together. The anger came and went in waves, that saltwater feeling, leaving the blackest despair behind when it left. I found ways to pass the time: I paced my cell endlessly, counting as I went; I composed furious poetry, sometimes writing it into the sand with my fingers, speaking it to the hissing beetles that crawled from the wall's crevices; I spent hours dreaming about Magha's violent death, what decorations could be made from his entrails. I slept too, at first – I dreamt of the outside world – but after a week or so, my dreams caught up with reality, and I was imprisoned in each one. Sometimes I dreamt I was buried alive. Things began to live in my hair.

When food was pushed through the bars of the cell, it was very fine at first: rich curries of river fish and tender jak, soft rice and roti. I refused to accept Magha's insult, but that didn't last long. Every day I would eat as slowly as possible, to take up the maximum amount of time. The fine gravies. Sweet curd, sometimes, with honey or sugar crystals. After a few days, Magha must have got tired of this joke. I ate dry roti and daal like all the other prisoners.

I made endless, endless lists: lists of round things, sorrowful things, lists of things that can only happen in dreams. I seethed and rocked with anger, biting down on my hands when I felt it would overpower me. I read books, too, in my calm moments, though I didn't have them with me. I reconstructed them in my head, line by line, sometimes taking hours to recall what line came next, but always digging it up in the end. In this manner, I reconstructed the first three sections of *Kuruntokai*, and most of *Akananuru*. It kept me occupied for much of my time, and I knew that I had to keep myself busy so that I didn't think of you, what was happening to you in the world outside, what the Kalinga had done with you. I thought I might be kept there for ever, locked in a room alone with my demons. I would have gone mad in the darkness. The heat. Sometimes I broke out in wailing and ran around the cell, slapped my face, anything to surprise myself, to make one hour different from the next.

During my imprisonment, I received two visitors. The first was as welcome as the first signs of leprosy.

'This is most unfortunate,' came Magha's smooth voice from outside, without introduction. At first I thought that I was dreaming, for he was often the voice of my nightmares. I looked up at the door, and saw his eyes narrowed through the bars.

'Don't look at me with such hatred, Asanka,' he said. 'You've fallen for the poet's curse. Look at Kalidasa. Unrequited love. Suicidal. Murdered by a courtesan. All you poets are slaves to your desires, but fearful of action. You think, but don't act; you observe, but don't experience.'

He thought for a moment, and then said triumphantly and with much emphasis, 'You write things that are worth reading, but you never do anything worth writing about!'

I didn't react, but continued to stare with an iron hatred through the bars. He looked back at me the way a tiger might look at a prawn. One of his thick eyebrows was deformed by an angry cleft where I had struck him. There was a clank, and the door swung open. The King stepped into the cell with a bearded guard beside him. What he carried in his arms made my heart shrink even further: the black leather of the *Shishupala Vadha*, a handful of blank pages, stylus and ink. I shook my head, and when I spoke, my voice was hoarse from lack of use.

'I won't write one word for you,' I said, and scuffed the poems I'd written in the sand with my foot.

'You will,' Magha said simply. 'Just one more instalment, Asanka, and the poem will be finished. Just one more.' Then, to the guard, he said, 'Go fetch some of our tools to show the poet.'

The man left and returned with a box. He opened it for me, and revealed what was inside. Rows of sharp points glinted in the dull light like the broken teeth of a *rakshasa*: I saw a hammer, a pair of pliers and pincers, tongs, a selection of knives. The man took them out of their box and showed them to me, one by one, handling them gently like fruit in a marketplace. I felt myself go white, felt a violent shaking take over my body. I know that some men can withstand pain – for their ideals, for their duties, for love – but I'm not one of those men. I found myself wishing for death.

'Let the poet think about it overnight,' Magha said with a smile. 'I will leave the paper and ink with you, Asanka, in case you change your mind.' Then, to the guard, 'If he hasn't started to write by morning, start with something painful. Make him shriek like a little monkey. But don't damage his hands or eyes.'

Then he turned, knelt and drew his face very close to mine, so I could smell the oysters and wine on his breath.

'Even the great Sri Magha died in rags,' he said.

The door of the cell shut behind the King like a monsoon's first roll of thunder. Alone again, I heard myself whimper as the image of the guard's toolbox failed to fade from my mind, and I felt tears run down my cheeks. I didn't even consider not beginning to write. This, perhaps, was how I had always imagined finishing the *Shishupala Vadha*.

When the guard returned in the morning, I hadn't slept, and had already written several pages, moving every hour or so to follow the narrow shaft of moonlight that slanted from the window. I must admit that after nearly a week of sand and stone, of endless lonely hours, I relished the task. The poetry was so bright, I wept and marvelled at it. Through the night I dizzied in the bloody, sickening whirlpool of the story's end, as Shishupal is beheaded not in the cool hall of Indraprastha, as in the *Mahabharata*, but on the battlefield. In the darkness of the cell, Magha's verses spun around me as the forces of Krishna and Shishupal did battle, as the complex formations of the two armies were mirrored in the poet's intricate verse forms. A circle, a spiral. I felt myself draining away, like some liquid from the bottom of a cracked jug. When I finally slept, I used the book as a pillow, and its words mixed with my dreams. I dreamt of rivers for the first time. And hair. Drowning.

In the morning, the guard came to see me. I showed him my work, and he grunted, squinting at it for a little while. I could tell he couldn't read, but he shrugged, and turned away from the door. His footsteps rattled as he went, and I realised with a quail that he had brought his tools with him.

My second visitor was you. When you arrived at the door, I felt my heart explode in my chest. You stood there, wearing a green-and-gold sari, with bangles and earrings, a rich bindi a point of light on your brow, ringed in yellow. You looked so beautiful, so grand. Like a queen.

I felt ridiculous: translating cross-legged in the sand, unshaven, probably crawling with lice and surely smelling awful, the sarong that I was wearing when captured now grey with dirt. I remember the first time you heard about my writing for the King, how disappointed you had been. *What must she think of me now?* I kept thinking. Your eyes were red with tears.

'Asanka!' you said, voice small. 'Asanka, I'm sorry. They won't let me open the door.'

I stood up, with some difficulty, and came over to touch your hand through the grate. I could hardly speak, and only croaked your name back.

'Sarasi,' I said, and grated my forehead against the bars. 'Sarasi.'

You leant forward and kissed my forehead, spoke quickly and in a high-pitched voice. You told me about how the Kalinga had proposed to you.

'Asanka, he said he would kill you if I said no. He said he'd pull out your tongue.'

Tears were making riverbeds on your cheeks.

'And Asanka,' you murmured, 'he told me that he knew my village, that he knew General Sankha's men had been harboured there. He said he'd burn it to the ground. Impale everyone. All the children, too.'

I remembered the men with swords that I had seen at the village, and felt my stomach drop. You spoke for some time, and punctuated each sentence with kisses on my forehead, my eyelids, my lips. I remember thinking that perhaps Magha had never really intended to marry you, not really, when he announced it in the throne room. Perhaps it had all been just a test, and this was the price of failure.

I couldn't look you in the eyes. I felt my lips moving around a thousand sounds, but an intolerable dryness crackled each one like a dry leaf before it reached my tongue. I looked up at you then, hoping to find words in your wet, golden eyes.

'I'm scared,' I said. 'I've always been scared, Sarasi. I thought it would make you hate me.'

You cradled my head in your arms through the bars.

'I'm so scared, Sarasi,' I kept whispering. 'I'm so scared.'

The guard came soon after that, and you left me with a kiss that lingered and broke softly, like the damp petals of flowers stuck together in the rains. I stayed by the door for some time, and watched the lamplight of the guard disappear down the hallway, gloom drawing back over me like a curtain. Then I returned to my work.

Before long, I had nearly finished the *Vadha*, and because all else in that cell was maddening boredom, I found myself prolonging the task. I ran Sanskrit words through the curl of my tongue as I translated them, conjugating the Tamil verb forms, the declension of its complex nouns.

I heard footsteps, then, as I sometimes did in the gloom of the dungeon, but on this occasion they stopped outside my cell door, and I froze like a grey monkey startled in the treetops. I heard the rattling of bolts, and a man in the sarong of a palace servant entered the room, flanked by the bearded guard. In his hands were some papers. He bowed, without a word, and placed them down before me, in the sand. I saw the soft binding, the sinew cords, and knew immediately what it was. My voice was like a cane of bamboo in which bees have burrowed holes, whistling in the breeze.

'Who gave this to you?' I wheezed. The servant's eyes didn't leave mine, but he said nothing. 'Who gave this to you?' I tried to shout, but collapsed into a fit of coughing as the man backed out of the cell and the door shut behind him. I shouted after him until my cries became wordless, until the voices of the other prisoners echoed down the corridor.

'Keep quiet,' they shouted. 'We're busy rotting in hell.'

I backed away from the door, closed the *Shishupala Vadha* and my translation, and opened the new manuscript. That same smell. Rain, and maybe a hint of tears. Dry stone. The air before a lightning storm. Perhaps now, I thought, perhaps after all that had happened, the truth would be revealed.

For the remainder of my imprisonment, when not working on the translation, I made it my task to memorise, word for word, the exact text of these pages. This isn't as difficult a task as it appears to the uneducated. In the temple college we would work to memorise hundreds of scriptures and poems, using a variety of mental techniques and simple tricks. I would start with the first line. I would say it forwards, then I would say it backwards, then I would say it in a tessellating order: first word, third word, second word; second word, fourth word, third word; third word, fifth word, fourth word.

'I am Shishupal.'

'Shishupal am I.'

'I Shishupal am.'

I am Shishupal

Do you want to know what it feels like to die? I would describe it, but I am afraid no earthly language has the words. It felt like fainting, you could say, but at the same time, not at all. I was aware of the mortal wound, but it was the memory of a dream – the fading world of a newly blind man.

I was no longer inside my body, but suspended in the air like a cloud of smoke. I remember struggling against forces that tossed me like a leaf in a strong current, and I watched from above as a circle of people closed around my corpse. The thought that dominated my mind was: I had no idea my body contained so much blood! I could smell its copper tang, and at the same time, I could smell the scent that rises off dusty flagstones when they are struck by raindrops, and, indeed, it was beginning to rain.

I felt surrounded by light. Untethered. On the other side of the hall, where Krishna stood only moments before, was a being of the most pure intensity. A billion arms. Seven billion faces. Radiating light brighter than the sun. I wanted to weep. He was so beautiful. So immense. I felt the suction of powerful forces, dragging me towards him, and when I entered his orbit, he put out his hand and threw me up, up above the rooftops of the city, where a breeze caught me and I continued to rise.

I floated above Indraprastha, where I saw the markets and workshops with men busy at work, the women carrying water from the wells. I was flying higher than any bird, and I could see everything beneath me in immaculate detail. Here was a cross-legged potter, spinning his wheel with a stick, the oozing waves of clay tanning his fingers. Here was a naked hunter crouched in the treetops with a bow, his pupils narrowing at a deer. Soon I was higher than the clouds, and their immense expanse stretched out into the distance, right to the edge of the world, broken only by the snowy mountains far to the north. At once, I was enthralled and excited that all my beliefs were true – I was surely re-entering the circle of rebirth; I would soon be greeted by the gods.

This did not happen, though. I do not mean to disillusion you, pious reader, but the gods did not greet me with welcoming arms, and nor did I see the endless rivers of milk and wine and honey that the Persians speak of. I saw a library – enormous – with shelves stretching in every direction as tall as sheer cliffs. I smelt dry leaves, the smell of paper. The sounds of running water. There was a river there, running through the great library, crashing between the shelves as if down the sides of a towering hill. Its water dark as the deepest night. I have been here ever since, dreaming of my Princess Rukmini.

I will not pretend that there is dust in my eye this time. Let me weep, and pray that in the next life, I will at least have forgotten the slow closing of Rukmini's eyelids, and the gentle pinkening of her lips. If not, I think another life on this earth would be intolerable.

Chapter Sixteen

When I cut the final symbol of the *Shishupala Vadha*, I knew that soon I would die. I didn't care – that's the truth. It meant nothing to me. The translation of the *Vadha* had been the last ounce of purpose left in my life, and it wasn't with a feeling of relief or achievement that I finished it, but one of deep and all-pervading sorrow.

In this body of mine, with its thin arms and weak stomach, its hundred bones and sinews that ache in the rain, there is something that has never found peace with itself. That's what I realised in those final days. It's this thing inside me that made me begin writing poetry, so I owe it my position, my wealth, my whole life – but it means I've always wavered between doubts of one kind, or fears of another. Many times, after poetry became my profession, I sank into the depths of dejection. In these times I wanted to give it all up, to throw out all my styluses and never touch palm leaf again. Other times I became so puffed up with pride in my own achievement that I celebrated only false victories, and forgot what was real. The fact is that this thing inside knows nothing else other than the writing of poetry – even in the dark cell where

I would end my life, it clung to that pursuit blindly, and I felt lost the moment my task was over.

I allowed the ink to dry without blowing on it, and closed the book slowly. The previous day, I'd spent hours piling all the sand on the floor of my cell into one corner with cupped hands, and now I slumped back against it and stared at the ceiling. Then, in a fit of courage, I went to the door of my cell and beat it with my fist.

'I've finished!' I cried out of the barred window. 'Come and get it! I've finished!'

There was a new guard on duty, with a curling beard like a thousand pepper tendrils. He wandered lazily to the door of my cell, and struck the bars with his baton to make me get away from the door. I showed him the book, and he didn't seem to care, just shrugged at me and left without a word. He must have spoken to someone, though: later that day, Magha's creamy voice sounded from outside my cell.

'So finally it's finished,' he said, and I felt that familiar cold creep across me. The bolts in the door slid open, and Magha walked into the cell, without a guard.

'It's been quite an epic journey, hasn't it, Asanka?' he said. 'Quite an adventure. We've had our differences, of course, but we're still friends, aren't we? Nothing can change that.'

He watched me for some time, but I said nothing. Only stared up at him, feeling that seawater sensation again, my hands shaking. The King took the book from the floor with a smile, showing all his shining teeth, and I noticed, in comparison to him, how thin I had become.

'Asanka,' he said, 'I don't want you to waste away in here. In two days' time, at Divali, I'm holding a grand festival for the reading of the last instalment. There'll be a ceremony, and a parade: food, and dancing, water for everyone, music and hundreds of elephants. All the people of the city will be there – I've even ordered for one of Kalinga's finest scholars and singers to be brought across the sea to read the poem. I won't have you rotting in this cell while our great work is unveiled, Asanka.'

I seethed, and he came over to where I sat, knelt down to my level and narrowed his eyes. His face was very close to mine, the cleft on his eyebrow still shiny like the underside of a petal.

He said, 'I'm not your enemy, Asanka. I know that I've been harsh when you've strayed from your *dharma*, but I understand anger. I know how it feels. You weren't in your right mind, I'm sure, but you've had time to think about it now. You've realised that there are other women all over the world. That this one isn't worth dying for.'

In my mind, I rushed at him – leapt up from the ground like a monkey and wrapped my hands around his throat, crushing his windpipe. But my body was wasted and tired, and I didn't even twitch.

'Asanka, I want you to see it,' he breathed. 'To see the poem. I want you to be there when the crowd chants my name. You'll see, Asanka, when their faces light up, what an impact I've had on this island: what a change I've brought about in its people. Even the villagers have started to obey me,' he said, with an unhinged gleam in his eyes. 'Their rebellions have died down, the temples to the Buddha are empty, and now half the country is back under my control. It's because of the poem, I think. Its civilising effect has begun to eat away at their barbaric natures. You will come to see it, won't you Asanka? Come and see the poem?'

I looked up into his face, and saw that he was completely serious. My eyes wandered across his unshaven cheeks, his eyebrows grown even bushier than before, and the angry veins lancing across the whites of his eyes. The thought of seeing sunlight again made my breath come quickly, and I felt a yearning in my bones to see the great lake again before I died. I was stung by the humiliation of my helplessness and found myself thinking for the millionth time: *I could have killed him.*

'Yes,' I croaked. 'I'll see it.'

He patted me on the shoulder, and then leant forward and placed a kiss on my forehead, right between my eyes. Then he took the final scribbled pages of the *Vadha* from the floor, stood up and went to the door.

Before he left, he said, as though trying to make conversation, 'Look outside: the moon is nearly black. Divali, I'm told, is considered a good time for marriage. Or Deepavali – what is it you call it? Your people have such strange customs.'

He left, and let the door slam shut behind him. The guards rushed forwards to bolt it, and I sat with my head in my hands.

Magha was true to his word. His soldiers came to me on the morning of the first day of Deepavali, bursting into my cell and shouting at me to get up off the floor. I could already hear the faint sounds of faraway musicians, out in the city, and the footfalls of elephants had been thudding through the earth for some time. The noise of crowds. The noise made me feel nervous, the way I imagine people feel when they take their first journey on the ocean, or speak in front of a large crowd, the way I felt on my first pilgrimage to the holy mountain.

The soldiers were six men of the usual build and thick mainland accent. They were armed with hooked poles, knives slung in their sashes. They tied my hands with flax rope, and I noticed that when they touched me, there were looks of disgust on their faces. My clothes smelt like sweat and urine, my beard was long and tangled, and I hadn't chewed fennel seeds for weeks. My mouth smelt the way stagnant water does after days of pooling beside a road.

The men pushed me gently towards the door, and I stepped out into the narrow passage that lined the cells. Even that dark, choking corridor felt like a new world. I was afraid, and I thought that this must be how it feels to die: terrifying, but at the same time wondrous. We left the dungeon through a series of doors that had to be unlocked, and the light seared my eyes when we stepped outside. The smells of cooking food, animal dung and burnt sesame seeds rushed at me, and the sun tickled my skin. When the scorching earth touched the soft soles of my feet for the first time, I stifled a sharp intake of breath.

It still hadn't rained, all through my imprisonment: the ground cracked like a gourd; dust hung in the air like smoke, making ghosts of everyone. All the people I saw, from the naked children to the white-bearded ascetics with painted faces, coughed and spat the dust from their mouths. There were seeds of corn, trampled onion skins, flowers and okra fingers littering the ground everywhere, while fresh flowers hung on every surface, and flags and streamers on every corner.

The guards led me through the streets in a band, with spears and knives glittering in the sun. Festivals in that season are always loud, since the heat means palm wine is sold cheaper than water, and people were laughing everywhere, falling into each other, drunk and happy. A small part of me wished for the peace of the dungeon.

Nearer the city centre, jugglers and fire-breathers entertained applauding crowds; pained sitars sent dancers and acrobats whirling, and mountainous elephants rose above the streets, bright in their caparisons, with men sitting on their backs on thrones. The beasts passed right by me – heavy footfalls, breath reeking from their mouths – and my whole body was seized by trembling. My guards led me past the parade, and I tried to catch sight of you on top of one of the elephants. Soldiers were everywhere, leaning on weapons, chewing betel.

My escort brought me to the crowded Vatadage quadrangle, where charred paper still stained the cracks between the stones. Hundreds of people were there, sitting on the steps of buildings, on their roofs and in trees, gathered in the shade of awnings and buildings. They cheered, whooped, threw lotus petals and rice – and all for Magha. I didn't understand how they could shout and cheer for him.

Stands had been constructed for the crowds between the temples, steep stairs of split planks for the people to sit on, and all the acacia trees were strung with pennants. At the quadrangle's centre, in the shade of the great bo tree, there was a wooden stage lashed together with sinew, like the one where the Queen died.

The guards hauled me up on to one of the stands, striking spectators on their backs with the butts of their weapons so that people were jumping out of their way in every direction. People began to crane their necks to get a better look at me, the fearsome criminal who needed six men to guard him.

The soldiers sat me down among the gathering crowd just as Magha stepped on to the stage with deep, hollow footsteps. He was surrounded by half a dozen soldiers, just like me, and he was still wearing his armour. I wondered if he slept in it these days. Then my heart stopped as I saw you beside him. You looked so beautiful, radiant in gold and finery, with diamonds glittering in your red sari like broken glass, and a jewel in the centre of your forehead flashing in the sun. You looked like Sita or Rukmini. I felt faint, nauseous and about to burst into tears, all at once.

The spot that the guards had chosen was close to the Vatadage temple, and the carved frieze of Bharata Natyam dancers that runs along its edge. Crowds filled the square, a sea of heads perforated by the banners, streamers and palm fans being sold at the entrances. The white umbrellas of the wealthy sailed above the crowd of dusty bodies, the litters of the nobles spilling their silk-dressed riders in the shadows of the buildings. The noise was terrific. Magha took one step outside of his circle of soldiers, and raised his hands. One by one, the people fell silent.

'My subjects!' he began, his voice echoing from that cluster of old temples. 'Today, on the first day of Divali, I shall be married to my queen!' and he gestured at you. 'A common girl of Lanka, like any among you.'

My mouth flooded with saliva as I struggled not to vomit. Your head hung low so that your hair covered your eyes, and I couldn't see your expression. The shade of one of the trees lapped at your shawl. There were some cheers.

'Divali,' Magha went on, raising one hand theatrically, 'is held to celebrate Rama's return to Ayodhya, when rows of glimmering candles guided him home after his victory against the Demon King of Lanka. In this festival of lights, we celebrate not only these lights, but also the lights that guide our souls, and all the demons that together, and only together, we have conquered.'

He paused for this to settle on the heads of the crowd.

'Today, my crowning glory will be complete,' he said. 'We will read the final instalment of the *Shishupala Vadha*, the greatest epic of the mainland, and all bask together in its beautiful words and fine phrases. I brought this wonder to Lanka so that it could act as a light to this kingdom, guiding it home through the darkness of superstition and false belief.'

People cheered, and not the same begrudging, scattered cheers as usual, but a hearty cheer from the very belly of the crowd. I felt numb. Were these actually Lankans? Had Magha paid them with water, or threatened them with flogging, for them to stand there and cheer him like that? The King stepped aside with his entourage, and took a seat on the edge of the stage in a makeshift wooden throne.

I looked around at the cheering people, and they weren't foreigners – they were the same thin, sun-leathered brothers and sisters I'd always known – Sinhala, Tamil, all of them appearing to genuinely enjoy themselves. Those outside the quadrangle, who couldn't get in through the throngs of people, were laughing, drinking, queuing noisily and impatiently for mango and betel stalls, eating rice out of coned banana leaves. I wondered what had happened to my country while I was imprisoned.

As the King sat down, a high-foreheaded man in stately robes climbed on to the stage holding a book. He bowed to Magha, who nodded at him in approval, and I realised that this must be the singer from the mainland. He had sleek, oiled hair and a moustache curled at either end. He turned to the crowd and held out his hands, motioning for them to be silent: they hushed gradually, the noise dying in a pattern like the fall of raindrops.

'This great poem is a gift to the people of Lanka from King Magha the conqueror of the world,' the man said in a thick mainland accent. 'The lord of the three Sinhala lands wishes that his people might learn and better themselves with its beautiful words. Praise Vishnu the preserver!'

More cheers. Birds scattered, the air alive with noise, and once the calm had returned, the singer took a deep chest full of air, and began to read the poem.

I had to close my eyes. My heart swam. His Tamil was beautiful, rich and calm, his singing voice melodious and tinged with a strong mainland accent. He laid the poem over a regal, soaring *raga* that I'd never heard before. It was so beautiful. I felt every wasted muscle in my body relax. My lips moved with the words. I closed my eyes and, through a cloud of tears, allowed his tonal voice to wash over me with the poem that I had translated in the darkness of my cell. The words of the poet sent shivers through my body.

The crowd, too, although numbering many hundreds, remained completely silent, all watching. Even those outside the square had fallen still and quiet; even the vendors at their stalls. I couldn't open my eyes had I tried; a single cold bead drew a line down my cheek, and then another. This was why Magha had insisted that I attend, I realised: he wanted me to see what my poetry had made happen, how I had brought my people to him in chains. Everyone was rapt, hanging on the singer's every word.

Then, a minute or so into the poem, the scribe read one of my additions.

'Shishupal's eyebrows leapt upward like bounding dancers,' he said, and there was uproar. Cheers and cries rose up out of the crowd, and a shiver bloomed down my spine. Laughter, whoops and jeers sailed overhead, feet stamped the ground and hands clapped, and I realised that these people hadn't come to see the King married. They had come from all the villages and towns of Lanka – from the hills and the plains, the lagoons and the swamps, to hear the final instalment of my poem – not to honour the King, but to mock him.

On stage, the scribe faltered, and had to wait for the noise to cease before continuing. When the crowd finally settled down, he went on, but it wasn't long before he struck another rock: 'Shishupal dragged his insults behind him the way he dragged King Babhru's queen, a woman of such bravery and strength that she would fight the most fearful king with even the smallest knife.'

The cries this time were darker, angrier, and the scribe had to stop for considerably longer. In the trees that ringed the courtyard, a troop of monkeys began to screech over the noise of the crowd, obviously enjoying the clamour. I saw the shadow of a frown begin to creep over the scribe's face, and a mad, suicidal glee filled my entire body like fire. I couldn't help a smile from splitting my face. I realised that this scholar from the mainland must have once read the original Sanskrit text of the *Vadha*. It was coming, the moment when Magha would find out. Soon the King would know what I'd done to him with the poem he loved so much.

On the throne beside the stage, I could see Magha's features darkening. He was leaning to whisper to one of his generals: what was going on? Why were these peasants shouting at the most inappropriate points in the story? How dare they disturb the reading? A high-ranking soldier stepped forward to the edge of the stage, and tried to quell the people like a teacher quieting a class of students.

Once the noise of the crowd died down to a manageable level, the scribe began once more, almost shouting over the bubbling multilingual chatter. I could see sweat glistening on his brow. My smile spread wider as I remembered what was coming. I leant back, lifted my chin to the sky, breathed in the hot air and watched the red dust curling overhead. For several passages, I allowed Sri Magha to speak unsullied, for he does a marvellous job. The crowd kept jeering, and that was beautiful too, in its way.

Here we were: the final scene. As Shishupal's insults fell on Krishna like hammer blows, the crowd hissing and laughing as each one landed, I closed my eyes. I imagined that I was a member of the court at Indraprastha, watching the fateful exchange. Stuttering over some of my baser comments, the scribe looked increasingly flustered, and turned to the King as though to excuse himself. The crowd whistled and clucked when I included some dialectical curses that you once taught me. I watched Magha's brow furrow deeper as he registered the unfamiliar words, and beneath your hanging fringe I thought I saw your lips curl into a smile.

Then the hundredth insult fell, and Krishna spun the Sudarshana Chakra at Shishupal's neck. A flash of light. An enraged scream, and Shishupal lay spilling his blood out on to the palace floor. The Polonnaruwa crowd fell silent as that verse came, and the scribe paused, breathing heavily. He took a moment to continue, and I realised that I was holding my breath. This was it. In Indraprastha, Krishna began to speak, and his voice sounded from the scribe's mouth, echoed against the walls of the courtyard as though the god himself were speaking from heaven. Rhyme and metre fell away, Sri Magha the poet's voice became mine.

'Today,' he said, 'we have witnessed the death of a tyrant!' and the scribe looked tired as the crowd burst once more into rapturous applause. He struggled on: 'This King Shishupal has outraged justice with his rule: with his flogging of children; his mutilation and murder of good women and men; his burning of villages and men and books. This despot has claimed a land for himself by force of arms – a land whose people have seen too many wars, too many cruel rulers, too many kings who have owned the land but never loved it; whose people refuse to bow to him and his gods. Let all men see what has happened here today, and know that this is the only end for men like Shishupal! Let each man who sees injustice in his land be not afraid of pain or death, for let him know that he is one among thousands! Let him know that if he dies in the fight against evil, he will be reborn into a world of justice that he helped to create! Let all the downtrodden people of the earth rise up now, and strangle their rulers with their chains!'

The first mango landed with a thud feet away from where Magha was sitting. I saw him turn pale even from that distance. He leapt to his feet, and screamed, 'Guards! Find who threw that and cut out his eyes!'

Soldiers rushed to surround the King – from all around the square they surged into the crowd, knocking people aside with their spears, but already more mangoes were following the first. They came like the first drops of tentative rain, but soon gave way to a torrent, bouncing off the stage with squelches and thuds. Soon stones joined the mangoes, and Magha shielded his head with his hands. The King's bodyguards closed like the petals of a flower around him, and clangs like metalworkers' hammers sounded off their armour as the stones hit their backs and shields. In the barrage, some of the guards spun and fell; I could see men in the crowd prising up cobblestones to use as missiles, whooping and shouting: 'Death to Magha the Tyrant! Death to Shishupal!'

The guards surrounding me stood and drew their knives as the crowd rounded on them, but already stones were hurtling in our direction. As they tried to cover their faces, they were set upon by men with sticks and tools – everywhere, makeshift weapons were appearing from the folds in men's cloths. I curled into a ball with stones and fruit falling all around me, scared and heartbroken, but with a feeling of dark triumph coursing through me that I can scarcely describe. I felt strong hands grab my arms, and at first thought that I was being hauled back to the tomb of my cell, back into the darkness. I looked up into the face of a young farmer dragging me to my feet, sawing at my ropes with his sickle.

'Come on, brother!' he shouted, and I didn't think that any stranger had ever called me 'brother' before. I found myself suddenly adrift in the chaos, borne away on a tide of people surging towards the stage, stones and fruit still falling like a monsoon. The touch of flesh pressed against me. The cry went up all around: 'Death to Shishupal! Death to Magha the Tyrant!' and I felt my heart swell. A thought floated into my mind that this could have been a battle in one of the great epics, like Kurukshetra, or Rama's battle for Lanka. I remember thinking that this was why Sri Magha thrilled so much in their chaos.

I pushed my way forward as best I could, desperate to find you. Here was our chance! While the soldiers were occupied, we could escape together, disappear into the forest the way we'd planned! We would have our Deepavali wedding that very night.

The ground was slippery with trampled fruit, and I was weak from my time rotting in prison, but somehow I fought my way to the edge of the stage, where people were already setting upon the guards surrounding the King. Through the wall of their armour I saw Magha's face like a thundercloud ready to burst, bleeding from a head wound. I caught a flash of colour from your sari, but already a new contingent of guards were beating their way up on to the stage with their shields, and darted between the King and the crowd. I saw Magha wrap his arm around your neck, and then I saw a tall Tamil man sliced almost in half by one of the swordsmen with one swipe of his blade. An unholy spurt of blood went up in a cloud like waterfall mist, and people began to slip on the gore and mango pulp coating the stage. Spears bristled around the king, jabbing out into the attacking crowd, and before I could even get close, the whole band of guards was ushering Magha and you down the steps from the platform and back in the direction of the palace.

Waving their swords like talismans against demons, and slicing down anyone who stepped too close, Magha's bodyguards cut a swathe through the crowd, moving quickly and urgently. They were well trained, and moved like the multifarious limbs of an avenging god. They fought their way to the citadel gate with you and Magha among them, shielding themselves from a fresh volley of cobblestones. On the walls, archers began to send arrows darting into the crowd, and more soldiers spilled out of the open gate. I saw you kicking Magha, stabbing at him with your elbow as he dragged you under the shadow of the gatehouse. The diamonds from your clothes were scattering into the dust.

'Sarasi!' I was screaming, 'Sarasi, don't let him take you! Sarasi, I love you!'

The gates screeched on their pins as I was shouting, and their chains rattled on hidden spindles – they began to close around you and Magha, slowly but inexorably. You were kicking out at Magha's legs now, and screeching all manner of horrific curses. I saw you sink your teeth into his hand and he let go momentarily. I thought I saw your eyes catch mine, even from that distance, and your outstretched hand implored me to rescue you as a guard caught you by the sari and they dragged you inside. The gates closed over you with a thud, and I dropped to my knees and screamed and screamed and screamed.

From all corners of the square, fresh reinforcements were joining Magha's guards, pushing the crowds back through the streets. The tide washed me away, this limp piece of drift. All the hundreds of men fleeing through the streets carried me, pushed me, dragged me, through all the alleys and rookeries, and out through one of the gates. I was a leaf caught in the canal, on its way out to sea.

Outside the gate, I saw Polonnaruwa spilling men the way a broken hourglass spills sand, and as we all ran, the dry heat of the day withdrew from the air. I could taste metal on the breeze. I looked up: the sky had turned purple, clouds plastering it with their wet mortar, dark like a ripening aubergine.

And then it began to rain. The smell of it rose up from the earth, and as the drops fell thicker and faster its taste filled my mouth. Raindrops came down like judgement, bathing my eyes and my hair, washing the filth and the pallor of the dungeon from my skin. I felt the drops like fingers through my hair, felt the water running down behind my ears, through my beard, and I shivered with the pleasure of it. Everywhere running men were raising their hands to the sky.

Chapter Seventeen

Rain blurred all boundaries. It washed the dust from the leaves of the trees, darkened the earth, turned roads to rivers and steps to waterfalls. Puddles grew in potholes, glazing the cartwheel furrows, the half-moon hoofprints of water buffalo. The people fleeing Polonnaruwa soon disappeared like deer into the forest, back to their villages and homes, leaving me alone. I walked north alongside the tank, away from Polonnaruwa, with tears and raindrops running down my cheeks. My hair clung like weed to my scalp; my filthy cloth was heavy as a suit of armour. Mist was rising from the lake as the rain made chaos of the water. The dry banks darkened, began to run in copper-red rivulets. The stalls beside the road were empty, water frothing in the gutters, chickens panicking and running for shelter.

I walked on until I reached a canal bridge, where I fell to my knees, clutching on to one of its upright struts, wailing, holding myself. I was one man beside the vast lake, the city, the misty peaks in the distance. I felt incredibly small. I thought of my books in the sunken temple, thought of them ruined in the rain after surviving so much. I knew I had to go to them. Someone had to save them. I stood up and began to walk. I would rest when I got there, I told myself; I would lie clutching my books in the mud, half-submerged in the water, until sleep overcame me. I would feel cool, right before I died; a rush of beautiful, peaceful cool.

On my way, I kicked at puddles like a child, skirting up curtains of water. I jumped from the path and waded through the field tracts, enjoying the cold of their rapidly filling canals. The kurakkan grass reached as high as my shoulders. Everywhere, the sound of pattering on earth, of rain and water and leaves. As I passed the reclining Buddha at the Gal Vihara, with his stone eyes closed to the world, I didn't even look his way.

By the time I reached the trampled elephant path, where the huge footprints were filled with water, I felt delirious. I was close. Soon I could be with my books. Then I rounded a corner, and came face to face with one of the largest beasts I have ever seen. It was standing right in front of me. An enormous bull elephant, with long, jagged tusks, one cracked, staring at me with its eyes like polished pebbles. My greatest fear in all the world, less than ten paces from where I was standing. It was swinging its heavy trunk. My whole body became like stone, my arms and legs like beams. The animal huffed out a breath of stinking air and stepped towards me. A large branch cracked beneath one of its feet, and water oozed up out of the mud where it stepped. Its sides were streaked black with rain like a boulder. So this was it, I thought. The perfect way to die, without even my books to comfort me. My whole life, my half year of suffering in Polonnaruwa, had all been leading up to this.

The elephant stretched out its trunk towards me. I closed my eyes and waited for the blow to strike, to be lifted into the air and thrown into the earth like a dart. I could smell the foulness of its breath, hear the rain spattering on its hide. And then it touched me with the tip of its trunk. Just once, gently, and right in the centre of my forehead. I felt the wet, slightly bristly tip of it press against my skull, and I opened my eyes to see the beast turning away from me to continue on its way, walking past me as though I didn't exist. It let out a low croon as it went, and the grumbling sounds of its digestion sounded somewhere deep in its gigantic belly.

Those were some of the strangest moments of my life, and to this day I can hardly convince myself that it actually happened. Since then, though – since the moment the elephant touched me with its trunk – I have never been afraid of them. They are quite beautiful animals, in a way, though I still can't suffer their stench.

As the elephant's footsteps faded into the distance behind me, I walked on to be with my books, stumbling and slipping in the mud. It wasn't much further. When I reached the sunken lake, I heard voices coming from among the stones of the ruined temple. *Demons*, I thought at first, feeling delirium washing over me. I kept low and crept closer, through the scrub, and peered down into the ruin. There were no demons. Instead, nine or ten soldiers were stepping among the stones, searching for something in the mud and mire. Magha had sent out soldiers for me already, I thought. He knew somehow where I would go – perhaps you had already told him about the books. These soldiers were here to take me back to prison, to waste away there and take my eyes, to leave me tortured in a darkness deeper than the darkest night.

I ran fingers through my wet hair in horror as I saw them bend and straighten with bags slung over their arms – leather bags, like the one I had left there, canvas sacks like the one I had found that desperate midnight when I had come here to read. I watched as each of them slipped and stumbled through the rain-churned mud, gathering an armful of these bags like farmers harvesting some strange crop, then climbing to pack them on to a cart that waited at the lip of the crater on the other side. I knew without looking inside the bags that they would be full of books. They would be taken back to the city, back to Magha, back to the fire. The cart drew away as another arrived, and the soldiers continued collecting the books, fishing through the mud with their hands, elbow-deep. I was transfixed for some time as they worked, piling the bags into heaps: there must have been hundreds of books piled up there, sodden and muddied. When the next cart was full, one soldier slapped one of the horses' haunches.

'The rain's tearing up the paths,' he called to the driver in Tamil. 'Take these up to Gangadoni before the cart gets any heavier!'

Gangadoni. The name sent a shiver running through me. The hill of the river daughter. I remembered the lights I had seen in the sky, Ravana's chariot. I remembered the name that I had seen on Magha's map, the name on everyone's lips: General Sankha. I looked harder at these men, and saw that most of them were barely more than boys, carrying bamboo spears. I thought that I was dreaming. I stood up to see more clearly through the scrub, and one of the men caught sight of me.

'*Aiyo!* You! Who are you? What are you doing?'

They all drew their knives and lowered their spears in a panic, and swung around to face me. I raised my hands to show that I was unarmed. Soaked and shaking and bearded, caked with mud and with my hair clinging to my scalp, eyes red from weeping, I must have made quite a fearful sight.

'I am Asanka!' I shouted, in a voice I didn't recognise. 'Court poet to King Parakrama Pandya!'

The men said nothing, but looked at each other.

'Isn't Asanka dead?' one of them asked.

'Parakrama Pandya is dead!' another shouted up to me.

Another, a young-looking soldier whose armour didn't fit him, said, 'If you are Asanka, then you will know the first lines of *Kuruntokai*!'

It seemed my curse: to hold discussions about poetry only at those times when I least wanted them. I didn't even have to expend the energy to explain that many poets in Lanka knew the first lines of *Kuruntokai*, just as many woodcutters knew the three most basic types of cut. I recognised the boy's voice.

'Kitsiri?' I said. 'From Aliyagama?' and the young scholar tipped his helmet away from his eyes.

'Master Asanka?'

The boy looked gaunt and tired, but a smile broke out on his face. He turned and nodded at the others. 'It's him,' he said.

They all climbed the side of the crater to meet me. Kitsiri looked older, more worn than when I last saw him. He still had his leopard-tooth necklace, though.

'When the Kalinga took Sarasi, the men in the village took up arms and left for Gangadoni,' he told me. 'We thought you were dead.'

His companions each bowed and grinned as they told me what a pleasure it was to meet me. They kept using those words: 'brave'; 'defy'.

I was tired in a way that I'd never been before; I felt drained of flavour, like a boiled plantain, and I could do nothing but murmur thanks to these soldiers. Some of their voices hadn't yet dropped from the reedish voices of boys.

'Sarasi told us about this place,' Kitsiri went on excitedly, fingering his leopard-tooth necklace. 'That you hid your books here. Word spread fast: people from *yojanas* around

Polonnaruwa came to hide their own collections. They knew we'd find them and keep them safe on the hill.'

'You have to come with us,' another of the child soldiers announced. 'Back to Gangadoni. Everyone will want to meet you!'

The idea of more people trying to shake my hand and calling me brave made me feel faint.

'No,' I mumbled. I remembered my vision of dying in the beautiful cool of the temple. The world was fast dissolving into blackness. 'No, I don't want to go. Leave me here.'

I was aware of collapsing, of the earth rushing up to meet me, of the cold slap of mud as it hit my cheek, the breath knocked from my chest. Then strong hands lifting me up, laying me out on a bed. Something was digging into my spine. I felt that I was aboard a ship on a rough sea, rocking and keeling side to side as I sailed to some unknown and unreachable shore. I opened my eyes, and saw the sky. The rain had lessened. I was in the cart, lying on my back on a heap of books.

'Wait!' I slurred, like a man delirious with sweating sickness. The smell of rain filled the air, set my nerves on edge. 'A bag,' I said. 'Leather. Hidden by the large fallen statue without a head. Covered with ferns.'

Without questioning, one of the men left back down the trail to fetch it, and some minutes later returned with my bag. He placed it beside me. I put out a hand, felt the firm weight of the books inside, and as if this were all the confirmation I needed, I fell back into unconsciousness. If I dreamt at all, I dreamt that I was dead.

When I awoke, the first sensation that came to me was that of a cloudy, gold-coloured comfort. I hadn't felt anything like this for some time. Above me, a thatched roof pattered with raindrops as soft as falling grains of rice. I sat up and looked around the room: walls of uncut stone and bamboo beams, a carpet of reeds. Heated stones in the corner, warming the room. I lay back and listened to the sound of the rain.

Sometime later, there was a knock on the door, and when I called enter, a man I'd never seen before stepped into the room. He was tall and young. He had dark eyes, and held his chin at a sharp angle. He bowed to me.

'Welcome to Gangadoni,' he said in a voice that I liked. 'Allow me to introduce myself: I am Vijayabahu the Third, Prince of Lanka, long-lost descendant of King Sirisamghabodhi! I am the leader of this fortress.'

I sat up in bed, feeling every muscle in my body ache, and looked this man up and down. If you've been reading the chronicles, you'll know that King Sirisamghabodhi was King of Lanka nearly a thousand years ago, and so his claim to the title 'Prince of Lanka' didn't much impress me. Still, I could see he didn't have a carob of cruelty about him.

'It's a pleasure,' I replied, bleary and feeling a little foolish: beneath the covers, I was completely undressed. 'But I thought – the people are saying that a general called Sankha was the man who held Gangadoni.'

The Prince laughed. 'I'm afraid there's no such man,' he said. 'Or at least, he's nowhere near this place. When I built this fortress, I knew Magha would never risk open attack. He could send all his armies up the narrow paths to fight us here, and all his armies would go marching back down defeated. I knew he'd send assassins and poisoners, so I decided to create the ghost of a rebel general that would have them chasing shadows through the forests. But at the same time, I needed him to be someone that our people would follow, a name to rally around. When I read your poem,' he said, and tapped a book on the desk that I realised was a copy of my Tamil

Shishupala Vadha, 'I knew what name I would use. Asanka. Sankha. It changed in the mouths of the locals, but it's your name. I always hoped you would come here.'

I looked into the eyes of this prince, not knowing what to say.

'Then it was you,' I said finally.

'I'm sorry?'

'It was you – you sent me those edicts from the *Mahabharata*, the Tamil texts – the characters of the story speaking right out of the pages. It was you!'

He smiled politely, but his eyebrows furrowed. 'I'm afraid I don't know what you're talking about. Master Asanka, you're very tired. Perhaps you should rest a little longer.'

'I don't need to rest,' I said, which was a lie. I felt a great hopelessness, as if every muscle in my body was made of water. Some part of me began to believe that the dead themselves had written those letters, that Shishupal, Rukmini, Krishna and all the others had sent them to me, through the ages, from Yama's land. Vijaya laughed.

'You had the whole of Polonnaruwa rioting in the streets yesterday,' he said. 'It took hours for Magha's men to reclaim some areas, and hundreds of those who fled have made it up here, to join our fight. Magha will be furious, now that he knows what you did. I've heard that the scribe from Kalinga has been looking through the whole of the poem, making a catalogue of all the changes you made. You're lucky to be alive at all, to have escaped that place.'

'I don't feel lucky,' I replied, but knew immediately that this wasn't true. I was in agony at having lost you, but I was free of the dungeon. I could hear rain outside, and my stomach yawned at the smell of fresh curry that wafted in from outside. I remembered the prison guard's toolbox, and I fought the urge to weep with relief that the pincers and knives hadn't torn my flesh. I felt guilt at this joy, but I couldn't help it.

'You saw how the people followed your example in hiding their books,' Vijayabahu said softly. 'You're a hero to them. I want you to live here, Asanka, to be safe inside Gangadoni's walls and enjoy our hospitality. Here, we pay as little attention to the rule of Magha as we would to a blade of grass. Here, you can write poetry that will help tear that hateful Kalinga down from Lanka's throne!'

'I don't feel like writing poetry,' I said.

The Prince paused.

'Get dressed!' he said. 'Allow me to show you my fortress.'

He left, closing the door behind him and leaving me alone with the cacophony of my thoughts.

After a little while, I got out of bed, and dressed in a gleaming white cloth that was waiting for me. I stepped outside to meet the Prince. Gangadoni was beautiful: the fortress town perched high up on the stony elephant-dark hilltop. There were many levels, with bridges and gantries strung between them: the faces of the rock crumpled like the pages of a book, trees and grasses clinging to any hold. A single white spire on its pinnacle showed where the old temple still stood.

Vijayabahu showed me to his garden, on the east side of the rock, which he told me he had based on Polonnaruwa's own Nandana. We passed workshops where men were beating iron, or using the battering winds to heat crucibles of steel. There were livestock pens, mostly filled with goats and chickens, and a training ground for militia and archers. And the garden itself, when we reached it, was filled with many flowers and trees – white champaka, saffron-coloured naga, beautiful mallika. It was perched on the edge of the highest outcrop of the hill, so that you could sit among the flowers and look out over the whole of our land. From there, I could see the whole wide, glittering expanse of Parakrama Samudra in the distance, with its ragged coast, and beside it Polonnaruwa's walls curving like a dropped silver thread, the sloping roofs of the palace rising above. All of it just a thumb-smudge in the distance.

The sky blushed many different shades of purple and dark blue, a dish of old plums, and I could see where sheets of rain were falling across the land. Already the first drops of a new storm were beginning to fall. Vijayabahu knelt down in the grass of his garden and pressed a tiny flower between his index and middle finger.

'Do you know what this is?' he asked me, and I took a sharp intake of breath.

'Is that a kurinji flower?'

'Yes. Very rare in this part of the country. It's a delicate specimen. It only flowers once every twelve years – did you know that? Come, let's go inside,' Vijayabahu said, smiling. 'I believe it's beginning to rain again.'

I am Krishna

On the day I returned King Shishupal's crown to his parents, even the soldiers at the border crossing into Chedi knew why I had come. Their faces were stone as they nodded me through the river passes, the dirt paths that led through the hills to the capital. It was lonely on that road. Forsaken of all life. Soon the city of Suktimati oppressed the horizon, that palatial fortress that people call 'the Oyster' after the shape of its rounded walls. I worked my way up the steep slopes of the Kolahala Mountain, where titanic locks irrigate the city and the lands beneath it, and goats cling to the outcrops of the high passes.

My whole way up that mountain, I asked myself the question: why did I kill King Shishupal? All I could think about as an answer was something that happened to me when I was a little child. When I was growing up in the village of Nandgaon, my mother once found me eating mud beneath a mango tree. Horrified, scolding me, she parted my teeth to scrape it out – but what she saw inside transfixed her. Inside my mouth, she saw the entire world. She saw the great disc spinning on the axle of Mount Meru, garlanded with cloud. She saw the four continents, ringed by the glittering, boundless sea, the forests and even our little village, with her standing in it. She saw in an instant all the kings who had ever ruled, and all the cities that had ever crumbled; all the lovers ever parted and reunited; the endless length of the chain of human stories.

My mother saw the world in me, but I see myself in the world. I killed King Shishupal because I am its reflection. The world has become rotten, and filled with spreading fire. The great families will destroy each other – I have known this for a long time – but I also know that when the world dies its sad, humble death, so shall I. A hunter named Jara will mistake me for a deer as I meditate under a tree. He will shoot me in the ankle, and I will die alone, far from my home.

When I brought Shishupal's crown back to King Damaghosha and Queen Srutadeva, the old woman knew immediately why I was there. She had known ever since that day long ago, when Shishupal's extra arms and third eye disappeared at my touch, that one day I would come to her like this, holding her son's crown. She is my father's sister, and her sorrow cut me deeply. She reacted as you can imagine a mother would: she ran forward and wailed, seizing his crown from me and clutching it to her lips, kissing it and weeping for the child that Brahma himself had saved from the waters of the Betwa, but not from me. The King stood back from all this, looking directly at me with his grey eyes, as if to say 'Time marches on. Some mistakes we can never take back.'

The Queen's grief turned quickly to anger, and my aunt stood up and beat her palms against my chest, wailing all the time that I had killed her son, that I was a murderer. I looked down at this woman and remembered how, many years ago, she had come to my chambers to beg for her Shishupal's life. How her tears had fallen on my feet as I lay in darkness and tried to sleep. What a tragedy, I thought, to have the same woman's tears twice wet one's feet.

When the Queen once more collapsed under the weight of grief, I approached the old King, who suddenly looked much older.

'Thank you for returning his crown to us,' he said to me, and never took his eyes from mine.

As I rode away from the Chedi palace that day, I wished that I had told Arjuna something different on the battlefield of Kurukshetra. I wish I could have told him to act on his first impulse, to turn away from the battlefield and refuse to slay his brothers. Perhaps if he and the millions of other men who rode to war that day had done the same, the world would not look so grim today. Perhaps if I had led by example, if I had walked out in front of Indraprastha's court and embraced Shishupal even as he hurled insults at me, then my dearest friends, the best and wisest among us, may have survived. Perhaps then the sun would not have set on our golden age. Perhaps then it would not rise every morning over the marsh-sunken ruins of Indraprastha; perhaps the earth would not have been dyed black with the blood of those who fell.

We men are butterflies trembling at the coming rain. Look to the east – see how the sky is stained! Every morning it blushes scarlet with my anguish. Every evening it is tinctured by regret.

Is this what you have come to hear?

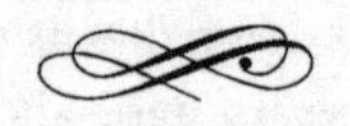

Chapter Eighteen

Fifteen dark monsoons have come and gone since the day I left Polonnaruwa. I've seen the kurinji flower bloom, and wither, and bloom again. Even now, I wake up some nights convinced that I'm locked in the hot dark of Magha's dungeon, others that I'm still writing the *Shishupala Vadha* in the shadow of that cruel king, that the years since then have been a dream.

At first, I tried to learn everything that happened to you. I interrogated merchants and soldiers who passed through Gangadoni, refugees from Polonnaruwa and travelling ascetics, monks and medicine men. They brought me many rumours, some of which were obviously false – but after a few months, Magha took another wife, and then another, and soon any news of you was lost. The King's wives, people said, were all dark, beautiful and sad, and they didn't know which one I wanted news of. There were stories, though. I heard one day that one of the queens in Polonnaruwa wrote poetry, which the peasants loved. I remember my heart racing when I heard it.

Some weeks later, I heard a wood-charrer singing one of her poems while he worked beside the steep path up to

Gangadoni. A poem about waiting, and loss. When the words came to me, I dropped the bag of writing materials I was carrying, and sat down on the ground near the workman, the curls of charcoal smoke circling my head. I knew those rhythms of speech that were so unmistakeably yours: the ups and downs, the forced silences. My eyes filled with tears, and the man apologised.

'Begging your pardon, my lord. The smoke can sting your eyes if you come too close.'

I began to dream of Shishupal and Rukmini again, and your face gradually took the place of the Queen's. When Vijaya sent spies into the capital, I gave them messages for you. I sent spies myself, sometimes, and though the messages never found you, the men brought back other rumours. They told me that many of the prisoners in the dungeons had been released as a wedding gift requested by the new queen. They told me that the puppeteers of the city, previously some of Polonnaruwa's poorest citizens, had been taken from their rags and given fine robes and enough money to tour all the villages of the region, giving shows. One rumour in particular filled me with curiosity: people said that one room in the servant quarter had been set aside by one of the King's wives. The King had agreed, people said, that the room would never be touched, or changed. That it would remain as it was on the day of their marriage, so the Queen could always remember her humble beginnings. People whispered that the woman who asked such things of Magha must be braver than Rama.

It was these stories that kept me going, when all my messages failed to reach you; even when a wine-tapper's boy was strung up outside the walls for smuggling one of the poems I wrote for you into the city. Some days were dark; others, I hardly even thought of Polonnaruwa, or Magha, or you. Time passed. I watched Kitsiri grow up, a young soldier with a face more serious every day. I kept growing the beard left from my time in prison, and it, in turn, grew grey. I wrote poetry in Sanskrit and Sinhala that Prince Vijaya enjoyed tremendously, and which he told me would help spur the rebels on in their cause – although I think few outside of Gangadoni ever read it, and though I worked hard at it, I took little pleasure in its production. The irony of my situation was never lost on me: that the one work of mine that everyone remembers is the *Shishupala Vadha*, the hated labour that set me free.

For more than a year, Magha made it his mission to hunt down and burn every last copy of my *Vadha*. I thought he would do it, too, but years later that cursed poem was still circulating with the speed and persistence of plague. Singers memorised it and taught it to others by heart. The paper copies themselves became highly sought after, tripling in price over that first year. Men with knowledge of writing copied parts of it down in secret workshops, and distributed their copies in alleyways and bathhouses. I'm sure that everyone who touched it made their own additions: when I hear the poem being sung these days, beside the mountain path up to Gangadoni, or in the free villages around Polonnaruwa, I no longer recognise most of it. On some holy days, Prince Vijaya organised readings, sometimes with hundreds of people coming to listen to me read the poem again. He would laugh and hoot as I read out the parts mocking Magha, an infectious laugh that spread easily around the crowd. After a while, I let someone else do the readings.

I read Tamil poetry in the evenings, and imagined it spoken in your voice. I spent much of my time sitting in the gardens of the mountain fortress, surrounded by its orchids and temple flowers, writing poems and letters that I would give you if we ever met again, or else reading through the mad poet's messages that had survived, and reconstructing from memory the ones that hadn't.

I showed the mysterious pages to every scribe I had met at Gangadoni, every man who knew anything about paper and ink, and every religious man, too. They either told me nothing, or expressed their disgust at such blasphemy – against the gods and poetry itself. Some knowledgeable men identified the ink, too: ground bone and shellac resin, they said. Very fine.

I felt for years as though I were living in an unfinished story. I began to wonder whether the stories that play through life are ever finished. Whether the neat, happy endings of Kalidasa, for instance, are as much of a fantasy as a bridge built by monkey men, linking Lanka to the mainland, or Krishna beheading his enemy in a flash of light. I watched monsoon after monsoon wash away the red dust of the dry seasons.

Prince Vijayabahu grew in popularity all over Lanka, and soon he began travelling the country. He sealed alliances with other rebel chiefs: Lord Senapati with his fort on the height of Mount Subha, and Buvanekabahu on the summit of Govindahala. He built a court in Dambadeniya, a fortified hill town washed every day by cool winds. He went from town to town and gathered support from the common people – from the fortresses cut into the hill country rock, the villages of the Sinhala chieftains, the Tamil enclaves on the coast. Men flocked into Gangadoni as the garrison grew every day, and each wore the pallid mask that meant Magha had touched their lives. One day, when Vijaya had won the trust of the remnants of the Sangha, and Magha's area of control had shrunk to little more than the area surrounding Polonnaruwa and some key fortresses, Vijaya announced that the Buddha's tooth relic would be returned to the people. He paraded it through all the towns he'd liberated, and crowds flocked from all over the country to see it pass by. When it came past Gangadoni, I went to see it. I admit I wept to see its gold-covered casing, and the joy of all the people who saw it go. The tooth never returned to Polonnaruwa, though. Vijaya built a temple for it in Dambadeniya, in the hills, where it would forever be safe.

It took many years before Vijaya left for the heat of Vanni in the north, and massed his army – reinforcing himself with a large force of Tamil mercenaries from the far shore – and marched on the great city. Faced with this viable threat, and his forces as ever overstretched, Magha fled Polonnaruwa and retreated north, to skulk among the dense jungle of the peninsula and await his father's reinforcements. If you were still alive on that day, then he took you with him.

As Magha retreated north, he burnt villages, sunk bridges, blocked the canals. He used the last of the gold that he stole from Polonnaruwa's temples to buy his own hordes of Tamil mercenaries – men whose families he himself had ground into poverty, whose land he had dried to dust. His final act when he left the city was to set the palace aflame.

On the night that Polonnaruwa burnt, I watched from the garden of Gangadoni. The distant fires glimmered in the night like gold coins at the bottom of a deep well, the plumes of smoke huge and underlit in tangerine. As I watched, I knew what I most wanted. I summoned a servant.

'Take me to the city,' I told him, and he bowed and ran off in search of some riders.

The roads were massed with our soldiers, their eyes wide and fearful in the torchlight, their spears moving over their heads like the blades of a field of grass. The sounds of battle sounded through the trees. Siege engines pulled by elephants rolled like great beasts through the crowds.

In the months that followed, Sinhala people would flee south, away from the Kalinga army camped on the peninsula: every day, there were hordes of them on the road – families with bundled belongings and sad eyes, carrying children. I saw the first of them fleeing in their thousands as I rode back to the city, their frightened faces cut out in torchlight. Another journey; another sudden unsettlement. In the weeks that followed, I would see Tamils fleeing in the other direction, as Sinhala mobs in the south began to exact their tragic and impotent revenge.

My heart beat faster and faster as I followed the column of soldiers up the long south road, with children and families hiding in the trees and watching us pass. As we got closer to the city wall, I saw that one gate tower was ablaze, its paintings and sculptures blackened by soot. The gate was smashed in. There were ladders on the walls, with men pouring over them like swarms of ants.

And so there I was: I returned to Polonnaruwa fifteen years after I'd left, to find the city I'd known engulfed in flames. The blood of Magha's garrison was welling up between the cobbles; there was the stench of charcoaled buildings and mass pyres everywhere. I left my horse with a steward, and wandered through the city on foot. The darting shapes of frightened citizens filled the alleys; the hopeless wails of men left to die. I made my way to the garden through the noise of battle and the heat of the fires, past the canal where a squirrel could have crossed the water, jumping from body to body. The citadel gate was burst open – Vijaya's soldiers had swept through here already, on their way to the palace. I wandered through the garden at night, empty and lit up in orange.

I sat in the pavilion then and watched the palace burn. The reflection of the flames scattered in the lotus pool. Even from that distance, I could hear sealed pots bursting inside like seed pods, the whine and pop of lacquered wood as the pillars split open and the rafters sagged. Around midnight, a wall yawned open on the third floor, and the roof caved in, coughing sparks into the sky. The heat surged with new fuel, and soon the copper from the lanterns, the statues and everything else was flowing down the front steps. When the wind picked up, the flames blew on to the south-east wall tower, then spread from there to the guardhouse and the stables. Horses screamed and kicked at their stalls, but no one went to release them. When I put my palm against the ground, it felt hot as the side of an oven. My face felt raw by the time I left, as if I'd spent hours lying in the sun. There was soot in my hair, in my eyelashes, between my teeth. I felt more alive than I'd felt for fifteen years.

Then I walked down into the city. I made my way, for the second time in my life, through the chaos of Polonnaruwa changing hands, as Vijaya's men crossed from house to house, searching for any remaining soldiers. They kicked in doors, ripped down curtains, dragged people from their homes, and when I passed they bowed to me and called me 'Master Asanka'.

I headed to the servant quarter, walking through it all as though through a dream, with running footsteps echoing through the halls, flashes of memories surfacing. A hospital somewhere near the canal was burning, and a falling eave sent up showers of sparks as I walked past. By then, the wind was coming in off the tank and blowing the flames to the east, so I didn't need to hurry.

The servant quarter was quiet, and empty when I got there. Almost unchanged. That's the way with buildings:

how many men and women, how many mornings, have died beneath these walls? I wondered if you would even remember me now, if you saw me, or whether I would recognise you, if we passed in a crowded market. I walked with only the thought of your room, left just as it was, after all these years. If I saw it again, I thought I might remember some last detail about you. I might remember your face.

Soon I reached the courtyard with the shade trees where, nearly sixteen years before, we sat and watched a Muslim man selling his lamps, and the mynah birds in their flock. There was your room, behind the lattice. I climbed the steps and pulled aside the curtain. The furniture was exactly as I remembered it, all the eaves and beams, the neat mats and pillows. I half expected to see you sitting there, combing your hair on the end of your bed or practising Tamil, asking me how a particular letter ended its curl. The room was empty, though: only the imprint remained.

I found some tinder and lit a lamp, and even the smell of coconut oil brought back memories of you, and your black, flowing hair. I wandered around and looked idly through the chests and alcoves, white with dust. I sorted through the abandoned clutter of another life, and then sat down on one of the mats. It was still slightly worn in the centre, where an indent of your shape had once pressed into the reeds. Then, on a whim, I walked along the wall to where your bed used to be, and traced the cracks between the bricks. Your old hiding place. I applied pressure, and felt the stone shift. Dust peppered my hand. I pulled at the bricks, edging them out of their cavities.

Your treasures were still there, and a sob rose in my throat as I saw them. I removed them each as though they were made of cobweb silk. Here was a necklace I had bought you from Dedigama, back in the time of King Parakrama Pandya, here a faded spinning top, and the tiny slips of palm-leaf poetry that we had passed each other in the banquet hall, all those years ago. A peacock feather. Your red-brown servants' sari was folded in there, too, and I imagined I could breathe in a hint of the scent that once hung on the cloth.

There was one other item, right at the back. A clay jar, maybe a seer or two in volume, stamped with a mainland merchant's stamp in faded red. It fitted into my hand almost perfectly. It was heavy, but I felt the shifting weightiness of liquid inside, and I believe I knew instantly what it was. I cannot tell you truly how I felt, for some moments are too large, too sudden and brilliant for introspection, but my hands must have been shaking as I uncorked the bottle and breathed in the aroma that rose from its neck.

Rain. The first drops of rain falling on dusty earth. Sweet, and full of hints of stone. As I crouched there, the years peeled back, and I saw time open to me like a day lotus at the sun's touch. I didn't see the full truth in that moment, nor as I sat down on the mat in that corner of the burning city, and held my head in my hands, but it came to me in bits and pieces as the days beyond that wore by.

The seer of ink had been a gift from your parents, maybe, or the only thing they left you. Perhaps you stole it from the priests at Tanjavur before you escaped, or from some merchant in your days as an urchin. You kept it all those years, unable to sell it due to its worth; not wanting to sell it, because one day you always wanted to write stories, like your parents. You learnt the ancient legends from them, those poor puppeteers, and you hated me at first, for being Magha's puppet.

You set out to teach me a lesson – that's what I realised as the days went by and the ashes of Polonnaruwa cooled. You wanted to leave me a message that I couldn't ignore.

You must have taken care to hide all elements of your style from the writing, for I'd never detected a hint of your voice, or the distinct curls you often left on the ends of your letters. I considered whether you might have employed Kitsiri's help with the writing, but he denies all knowledge of it to this day, and I don't think him so callous as to deny an old man desperate for memories. You would have been too afraid of implicating him, too. And, of course, too proud.

I began to imagine that, like myself, you had begun your transgressions on a whim, and had found in them a new language. You began to enjoy your blasphemy, your small rebellion. With them, you had encouraged my madness, pushed me along, planted ideas in my head. And after all of that, I had lost you.

I burst into tears as the voices of the gods and demons, the beautiful princesses and jealous lovers came back to me from the texts, memorised after all these years. I coughed, wiped the tears from my cheeks, and found in the dust of the wall cavity the final treasure you had hidden. It was a tiny slip of palm-leaf paper, much newer than the crumbling notes we had passed in the banquet hall – so new it could only have been written in the last month. It was a poem, carved and blacked in that same shining, rain-smelling ink:

Torrents rush down from the mountains,
sweeping along with them
the flowers that lie upon the cool fragrant pools,
left by the previous rains.
Yet he has not come, my friend.
He may have forgotten us,
but how can we forget him,
he who gave us his word, before he left,

that he would return
before the dark clouds of the rainy season,
gathering in the evening,
brought thunder's welcome roll?

Kuruntokai. I walked out into the soft orange light of fires, brushed the tears from my eyes and smiled like a man who has seen the true face of a god, if only for a moment. The seer was in my hand, its heft reassuring. I went back to the garden, because I didn't know where else to go. I sat beneath the flame tree, which was taller, and back in flower. I dipped my hands in the cold water of the lotus pond, washed the dust from my skin, from between my fingers, thinking on the cruelty of the world.

As I sat in the garden, I imagined what the city would become with time: the blackened walls of the palace crumbling, its statues and carvings sinking into the earth. I imagined vines and creepers bursting from the cracks between the bricks, roots reaching out to clamp the stones together, the walls softened by rain. I imagined the palace crumbling and empty, the monkeys returning to reclaim their kingdom from the men who had curated it so poorly, leaping among the stones, climbing the staircase of broken bricks that would wind for centuries into the sky.

I circled the little seer, felt the liquid sloshing inside. There was still a lot of ink, I thought, more than a man would ever need to write his story. And right then I decided that I would do it. I would write my story down for you. Perhaps now it will spread from person to person, just like the *Vadha* did, down all the tributaries and deltas of human thought. Somewhere, in some far-off village or roadside, you might hear it being told, and you might return to me. Yes, I would relive it all, through my own eyes, before the weight of it drove me mad. I would write it down in one unbroken stream, like a river of ink making its way to the sea.

Look – hold this page to your nose, and breathe.

In the days that followed, Prince Vijaya became King Vijaya III, and set about restoring the temples and libraries that Magha had sacked. He was as good a king as I could have hoped. Kalinga Magha met his end in the swamplands of Jaffna, cornered by Vijaya's armies and a variety of Tamil chieftains that had joined his cause in the north. His father's armies never arrived to save him. I imagine him kneeling the way King Parakrama Pandya did, trembling in the mud and awaiting his end. I hope, strangely, that when he died, he thought of me. When I heard the news, I wept, and lit a lamp.

By some absurd chance, I heard news of my wife the other day. She's back in the city, and married again to a merchant who did well out of the inflated price of kurakkan. I've heard she's heavy with her fifth child, something that made me sit and think for a while. I heard that she's happy.

Another three years have passed in Polonnaruwa while I've been writing this. I wish very much to leave. The city is dead now, and Vijaya is spending more and more time with his court in the mountains, where he says it's safer, and cooler. Kitsiri has gone with him, and I hear he was gifted a small plot of land in the hills for his service to the new king. He tells me it's beautiful in the rain – that there's a bo tree at one end of the field and a well at the other. I see him sometimes, and we talk about old times, about the half year of our torment under Magha, and about you. About what you're doing, and where you are. He tells me that he rarely reads poetry these days, as he's starting a family and has work to do in his fields. Elsewhere life goes on, but in Polonnaruwa the ruins are growing. They spread from the centre outwards. The canals are rank and full of mosquitoes. Monkeys have made their home in the burnt-out palace, and the temples have fallen into disrepair. Only the monks still walk the streets, bright in their tangerine robes, lighting their lamps and singing their hymns.

I wish so deeply to sail to Gujarat and walk its vaulted libraries, or see the Snowy Mountains turn gold and blue at dawn. I want to cross the mountains to Persia and see the Sultan's minarets glistening in the light of sunrise. But I know that if I ever leave the city, I'll spend the rest of my life wondering if you're still alive, if you escaped whatever captivity you live in, if you ever returned to Polonnaruwa to find me.

Writing this to you, I can almost imagine you sitting next to me, murmuring the sounds to yourself as you read. For now, I spend my days sitting in the gardens, like the lovers in *Kuruntokai*. I eat rice, I bathe. I dream of the day you'll return, when longing has reached its peak, the day I'll look up from my book and see you looking down at me, your eyes wet with tears.

Ah, look outside: the kurinji flower is blooming again.

Acknowledgements

I would like to thank the countless people without whom this book would not have been possible, all those who shared their friendship, their expertise and their honesty throughout the time of its writing. Special thanks are owed to: Premasiri Herath and his family for sharing their home and their life with me during my time in Polonnaruwa; St Thomas' College in Gurutalawa and the Al Aksha Muslim Vidyalaya in Diwulana for inviting me to teach at their institutions; and all my friends at the Polonnaruwa Library. I am further indebted to Janaka Sampath and Nadeesha Yurangi for extending me their friendship, hospitality and assistance in Sri Lanka, and helping with Sinhala translations that eluded me. Also Nuwan Lakmal Rathnayaka for his friendship and guidance, Sanjeevika Karunaratne for being the most excellent friend and Sinhala teacher, and Dhruvni Shah for her early interest and help with research. To Professor Lakshmi Holmström, Peter Blegvad, Maureen Freely, Sian Evans, Upamanyu Pablo Mukherjee, Sarah Morreau, Ambalavaner Sivanandan, Rebecca Stott, George Ttoouli, Annabella Massey, David Devanney, Tim Leach, Trezza Azzopardi and

Amit Chaudhuri, I offer apologies and gratitude in equal measure for their enduring the early stages of the manuscript and offering their kind encouragement. Further thanks go to Prof. Michael Hulse, who gave up his time on many occasions to help me translate my German edition of Magha's *Shishupala Vadha*. I am also infinitely grateful to my family, David, Margaret, Catrin and Duncan, for their unwavering belief and support, and my wonderful agents Eve White and Jack Ramm. My editors at Bloomsbury, Helen Garnons-Williams, Elizabeth Woabank, Himanjali Sankar and Rachel Mannheimer have also bowled me over with their enthusiasm and dedication to my work. My gratitude further extends to Eugen Schultz and Hippolyte Fauche, without whose turn-of-the-century German and French translations of Magha's *Shishupala Vadha* I would have had to drastically improve my Sanskrit, and to William Geiger for translating the *Chulavamsa* into German, and Mabel Haynes Bode for translating his work into English. Honourable mentions also go to Dr M. Shanmugam Pillai and David E. Ludden for their unparalleled translation of the *Kuruntokai*, the lady known as Sei Shōnagon and her translator Meredith McKinney for inspiring Asanka's lists and providing some items, and of course W. H. Auden for supplying me with Asanka's erstwhile motto. Finally this book goes out to all the translators, artists and writers around the world who continue to create beauty and freedom from beneath the heel of oppression. Today you are more necessary and powerful than you could possibly imagine.

A Note on the Type

The text of this book is set Adobe Garamond. It is one of several versions of Garamond based on the designs of Claude Garamond. It is thought that Garamond based his font on Bembo, cut in 1495 by Francesco Griffo in collaboration with the Italian printer Aldus Manutius. Garamond types were first used in books printed in Paris around 1532. Many of the present-day versions of this type are based on the *Typi Academiae* of Jean Jannon cut in Sedan in 1615.

Claude Garamond was born in Paris in 1480. He learned how to cut type from his father and by the age of fifteen he was able to fashion steel punches the size of a pica with great precision. At the age of sixty he was commissioned by King Francis I to design a Greek alphabet, and for this he was given the honourable title of royal type founder. He died in 1561.